To Harris and Nancy Hulburt:
The stories began with you.

And to my readers
David, Bill, Olivia, and Grace,
who helped me be better than I am,
and to Jason and Julia,
who cheered me on.

And to the countless artists I have known
whose art and stories
are the stuffing and stitching
in this crazy quilt called *The Liberty Guild*.
Though all the characters in the novel
are completely imaginary,
You, my friends, have given the quilt its "hand."

Preface

I fell off the edge of the earth when, for love, I—a product of Yankee parents and a mid-Atlantic suburban childhood—moved south and moved rural after college. The language, the culture, the weather, the music, the religion, even the color of the earth were all new to me. But the thrill and romance of living as a farmwife in the middle of nowhere lasted about two weeks.

Folks did their best to be kind to me, this awkward interloper in their midst, but being a stranger in a strange land branded me with a scar unsightly and painful. Believe me, I tried. I joined every class and club there was: Jimmy's Basket-Makers, Women's Club, the Busy Fingers Quilt Guild, the Grassroots Arts Committee, Fort Valley Tailoring, Southern Living Cooking School, Friends of the Library, the local artists' guild, Suzy's Suck-it-up Buttercup Exercise Class, and inevitably the Presbyterians and the PTA. I volunteered for everything. But career opportunities were scarce and involved leaving my comfort zone, which was, unfortunately, a very tiny zone indeed. I taught school. I sewed drapes and flower girl dresses. I took deposits at the drive-in window. I schemed to pursue higher education. Through it all, an air of the alien persisted.

For a long while parenthood redirected my energy. Babies came, grew, and left for greater things, leaving me here with a sensation of moving backwards as the trains beside me pulled forward out the station of my life. Now I shake my head in disbelief: All my adult years have been spent as a sojourner in one particular two-stoplight southern town in a county with more than its fair share of dead-end dirt roads.

Wisdom has not come as surely or as steadily or as solidly as I would have thought. But what I have undeniably learned in half a century is this: Many disappointments or detours in life end up being blessings beyond anything we could have designed for ourselves, and we often overlook them because we lack flexibility of vision. So suddenly, after five decades of squinting through the same old telescope, the thought strikes me: I am marooned here, true. A Robinson Crusoe on this little island in the Georgia heartland. But what if that's been a blessing and not a misfortune? And in fact I see now that it has been an incomparable blessing. I may have skidded off the map all those years ago, but here I have been privy to life—love, loss, subterfuge, betrayal, birth, oddity, generosity, misery, triumph, loneliness, joy—in this super-microcosm of humanity. The sap of human experience is distilled here to a fine syrup, all for me to savor. Time to do a little cooking.

In my year of Jubilee, I decided to give myself a present in the shape of a task: Write the novel that's been percolating in your brain for the past fifty years. The topic was never in question. I have been drawing and painting all my life and have known, met, and/or observed all manner of artists along the way. Their creative processes have never failed to fascinate me. In them, I see the reflection of our Maker. So I chose to write the tales of a group of fictional artists working towards the Midsummer show of a recent summer. What do they have in common? Not a lot, only a compulsion to make things, a longing for beauty, and a search for personal freedom.

What people make says a lot about who they are, and I decided to let the characters' artwork do a lot of the work of characterization. I found "making" art through fiction incredibly rewarding: It takes a lot less time, effort, and capital to invent a sculpture, oil painting, or quilt in words than in fact, but the "rush" is the same.

As the novel came into its own, a mosquito of a thought harried me: Make the art. Really make it. Previously a proud disparager of technology, I unaccountably conceived the idea of creating the characters' art for a website and sharing it along with sections of the novel. And so the characters take flight off the page. They are truly free to make what they make (limited only by the capabilities of their author) and to continue exploring each other beyond plot and page.

I look over my shoulder at the last three decades: That dead-end dirt road I thought I travelled has become a scenic highway to the artistic Liberty of a lifetime. I am deeply grateful to my travel companions for their kindness and truth and encouragement, and particularly to my husband, David, for his love and support and forbearance.

Linda Hulburt Aldridge
October 1, 2016
libertyguildunbound.wordpress.com

THE

LIBERTY

GUILD

READY to RELEASE
the INNER CREATOR
in YOURSELF?

Join the **Liberty Artists Guild**
The first Thursday of each month
Corbie County Library, 7:30 P.M.

*Program this month: Show and Tell
led by special guest Vera Crabtree*

AND ANNOUNCING:
The First Annual
**Liberty Artists Guild/
Corbie County Historical Society
Midsummer Art Show
& Gala Celebration**

Coming to Reaves Hall on June 23, 2012

* * *

Corbie County Chronicle advertisement,
March 29, 2012

The April Meeting

T he last time Lucy Bloom fishtailed, it hadn't ended so well— upside down in a ditch suspended by her seatbelt, glass grit from the "shatterproof" windshield drifting down like grains of sand into her nose and eyes and gasping mouth, sifting through her swaying black hair like diamonds. "STEER IN THE DIRECTION OF THE SKID," words of authority she'd picked up somewhere, had led her to a serious blunder—overcorrection.

She'd replayed the accident in her mind countless times since that wet afternoon six years back, rehearsing the best way to avoid disaster, all the more important now that she was a mother three times over. So this time when the car slung itself from side to side, zippering down the slick road after she swerved to miss a fallen limb, Lucy tuned out that old commanding voice in her head and listened to a softer one that steadied her with its cool wisdom, echoing words she had heard often when she was first learning to drive ten years ago: "Easy does it, Lucy, easy does it." And this time she knew what to do: With small adjustments to the wheel and her eyes locked on the target, the road twenty yards ahead where she willed the car to go, she wrestled the old wagon into submission.

As Lucy pulled into the library parking lot a few minutes later, the skid seemed unreal. She would have dismissed it completely, but her foot quivered on the brake and her fingers tingled as they released their death-grip on the wheel. Maybe the incident was a sign that she should have stayed home. She glanced into the back seat and saw that the plastic bag with her paintings inside had slid to the floor. She had respectable excuses to miss the meeting—the close call with the car, the young children back home. But no, she was not going to let excuses win out, for once; she had already made her choice for tonight. She grabbed the bag, locked the car behind her, and hurried toward the library entrance.

The bigger choice remained for Lucy, though she did not recognize it yet. A passion for painting was unfurling in her, as jolting and beautiful as a parachute slipping from its pack, catching a sudden updraft. She would be powerless to gather it back into its pack anytime soon. Or to measure its cost.

She was not alone in her impulse. The evening roads, shiny, strewn with slain-leaf litter, and slick at the tail end of an early April thunderstorm, discouraged not one of the Guild. They converged at Corbie County Library in historic downtown Liberty, Georgia, population 3,261, with their monthly offerings bundled against the damp, cradled in their arms.

Lucy was a newcomer this evening. At first glance, the members of the Guild seemed remarkably normal, as artists go. She followed the trickle of people through the main doors and down the corridor into the harsh buzzing light of the conference room. She set down her paintings alongside the others propped against the wall, still plastic-bagged, rag-wrapped, and cardboard-cartoned, lined up like shy children waiting their turns to be called on. The packaging might conceal masterpieces or complete disasters. Like with the artists, all clothed as differently as could be, the wrappings gave nothing away, or perhaps in some cases gave everything away: It was too soon to say which. Lucy took a seat among the lines of chairs and twisted around to search the room half-filled with strangers for one familiar person, the woman who had invited her.

She spotted her now, entering the room, moving here and there, greeting various members with a murmured sentence or two. The woman stood her own parcels against the wall and made her way to the podium at front of the room. From there she caught Lucy's eye and waved, then rested her hands upon the lectern. She stood smiling faintly at the gathering of twenty or so as she waited for their talk to dwindle and for them to take their seats.

"Welcome, everyone, this stormy evening," she said. "I hereby call to order the April meeting of the Liberty Artists Guild. For those of you who are new, I'm Eleanor Wood, this year's president. As usual, we have a little business to conduct before we move on to our program for the evening."

As Eleanor called for the officers' reports, and the dry elements of the meeting were duly served up, Lucy studied the president of the Guild. She noticed Eleanor's middle-aged grace and the soft grey-brown waves framing her intelligent face. Her movements and speech were slow and thoughtful, calm and steady. Lucy coveted the older woman's equanimity. Her mind drifted back to the flower show she had happened upon here at the library when she'd come with her children to borrow books a few weeks ago.

She had smelled the flowers immediately as she opened the main doors and herded the children inside. Looking around for the source of the smell, her eyes were drawn to color and movement in the small glass tower room off to one side of the library proper. The transparent walls of the little room were covered in tiny droplets like the ones her sons' breath left on the kitchen window on a cold, cold day when the boys were trapped inside gazing out, just waiting full of rich, warm breath for something to happen. In places the droplets had joined others and still others until they slid heavily in teardrops down the hard, clear walls of the tower room.

3

What a beautiful thing, she had thought then, *to have a flower show in February*. She marveled at the care the gardeners must have—what love, really—to nurture beauty indoors all winter when outside the elements were cold and hostile. The urge to plant herself in the center of that smell and those colors struck her. It trailed her as she helped her five-year-old find his allotted seven books, check them out, and settle them in his backpack. It tugged at her as she restored the pile of audio-books that her three-year-old had industriously stripped from their stand. It dogged her until at last she settled the baby on her left hip more comfortably, adjusted the diaper bag over her shoulder, and stepped through the glass doors into the atrium.

Lucy stopped short and breathed in, holding the perfumed air in her lungs. She looked around at the abundant blooms filling the small glassed space with color, shape, and scent. She prayed, without much hope, that her boys wouldn't crash into anything and spoil this delicate loveliness. They seemed to feel compelled to hurl their bodies about at the most unpredictable and inopportune moments, shouting with glee as they tested the dimensions of the world and of each other. But, for now, the boys were subdued by the novelty of the little Eden and stayed close to her.

They came first to an arch formed by staggered pots of ferns, and as they passed through together, they brushed against the curtains of draping fronds. Before long a woman in a denim apron greeted them and introduced herself as Eleanor.

"Oh, hello. I'm Lucy, and these are my boys, Jack and Ian, and the baby here is Evie."

"It's so nice to meet you all," said Eleanor. "Boys, would you like to come over to the children's bench and work on a special project?" She soon had Jack and Ian industriously decorating small clay pots.

Lucy took a breath, moved forward, and immersed herself in

the luxury of spring in this oasis within the glass tower amid the stronghold of books surrounded by the black tarmac of the parking lot with the color-less, still winter-dead world settled all around for miles in every direction. From inside the glass room, the outer library looked grey, misted, wavy, and unreal.

Lucy moved amongst the sculpture-like orchids, bonsai, amaryllis, and lilies, the innocent paperwhites and the tiny hummocks of daffodil and hyacinth and miniature roses. Trailing blue lobelia nestled in wire baskets that bulged with moss and peat, permeating the damp, glassed-in air with earthiness. There was a pot of pale pink peonies, whose heavy blossoms with all their layers spiraled inward to a secret knot of beauty. She studied curve and shadow and hue, storing them up to paint later, while she drifted around the densely-flowered space, barely conscious of the baby still clutched on her hip, weightless.

The woman, Eleanor, stepped into Lucy's circle of musing and said, "Lucy? Would you like me to hold the baby for you while you look around? I miss holding a little one. My children are all grown and off living their own lives now." Lucy smiled and passed the baby over with instant trust. She could feel The Mother in the other woman.

Now that her hands were free, she remembered her camera in the diaper bag, where it had been banging against her hip since Christmas. She fumbled through the clutter and found the camera at the bottom. She began to frame future paintings in her mind's eye and the camera's viewer.

Some time later, voices began to penetrate her reverie. She looked over to where Eleanor stood with the baby propped on her left hip and her head bent over the two tousle-headed little boys, who were busy and chatty, their fingers now grubby with potting soil.

"Can I put cu-number seeds in mine, Miss Lady?" Ian was

saying over and over, pulling on Eleanor's sleeve.

And Jack was saying, "Sunflower seeds are the best 'cause they grow the tallest." She could hear Eleanor's pleasant, unruffled murmur weaving between their sharp boy-voices.

Lucy walked over to collect the children. As the baby reached for her, Eleanor smiled and said, "What a treasure she is! So sweet! And those eyelashes..."

"Thank you," Lucy said. She kissed the top of the baby's head and settled her back on her own hip.

"And your boys are just darling. Very bright, very creative." Eleanor turned to Jack and Ian and said, "Here boys, don't forget to take your pots with you."

"If by bright and creative you mean a handful, then you are so right."

"One seems to go with the other." Eleanor laid her hand for just a moment on Ian's mop of hair.

"Are you, by any chance, an artist, Lucy?"

"Well, yes... I guess I am. How could you tell?"

"I saw how you were with the flowers. I'm an artist myself, so I'm tuned in to that sort of thing. There's a guild that meets here at the library the first Thursday of each month. Seven o'clock. I hope you'll come." She looked into Lucy's eyes and cocked her head. "You might enjoy the company of some other artists. It's stimulating and inspiring. It cracks open your own little world and lets some daylight in."

How did she know that Lucy needed light? Lucy didn't know it herself until the woman spoke it.

"I'm not sure I could get away, but I'll keep it in mind. Thank you so much, Mrs....?"

"Oh, it's just Eleanor. Call me Eleanor. Please."

Lucy was startled by the kindness of this woman. *What a rare thing to meet a person who really looks at you,* she thought.

"Eleanor, then. I'll try to make it." Jack and Ian were pulling her now toward the door, and she and Eleanor laughed at the same moment.

Lucy and the children passed through the glass door together into the manila-smelling library with its millions of dry, crisp pages and right angles and human constructions of story and fact. They passed through the library exit into the flat grey winter world. Only when they reached the old station wagon and began to load up did Lucy happen to glance at the baby's face. Evie's deep blue eyes were shining and large and round like deep twin crater lakes reflecting a clear sky. Lucy suddenly registered the three gasps she'd heard in her ear as they had first entered the glass tower room. She realized that Evie had not stirred in her arms while she'd carried her amongst the flowers. It was almost as if the baby were holding her breath. What did it mean? Was Evie as spellbound by the flowers as she herself had been? Surely a child so young couldn't react that strongly to beauty, a child who couldn't even talk? But that had been Lucy's first thought, remembering those gasps and the child's stillness.

She pulled Evie's coat and white fur-edged hood closer about her so that her pale round face appeared like a small shining moon with a white halo around it. Evie reached her little fist toward her mother. It was then that Lucy saw the white swelling with the red dot at the center of it. There must have been some stinging insect, hidden, waiting, in the trailing fern fronds. But the baby had made no sound, no cry. Lucy pressed her lips to the baby's hand, rubbed it gently with her thumb, and laid her own cheek against the smooth, warm, creamy blossom of the child's still-shining face.

Lucy's daydreaming ended abruptly when Eleanor the guild president cleared her voice at the lectern.

"I see two new faces here tonight—I want to recognize our newcomers, Lucy Bloom and... and... I'm afraid I didn't catch your

7

name when we spoke earlier?" Eleanor was looking toward the very back of the room.

"James. James Caldwell," a voice answered.

Lucy glanced back and saw a young man, several years younger than herself, half-standing with his hand raised. *Good, I'm not the only new one here tonight*, she thought.

"Welcome, Lucy and James, we're glad to have you," said Eleanor. "We look forward to seeing your artwork tonight."

Eleanor cleared her throat again. "And now we come to our program. Ms. Vera Crabtree of the Linden Art Center in Athens has agreed to be with us this evening to lead a critique of artists' work. Of course, this is voluntary, just for those of us who would appreciate a fresh, unbiased, informed response to our art as we work toward the big show in June. We'll all want to put our best effort forward since some large purchase awards and several cash prizes will be given at the show. So, let's welcome Ms. Vera Crabtree."

The assembly clapped dutifully as a tall, slender woman in her thirties took Eleanor's place at the front, lugging an easel from the side of the room with her. She surveyed the crowd a moment and then began.

"I'm honored to be here this evening. I'll try to give constructive criticism which I feel might lead you to consider aspects of your work that, alone in the studio, you might overlook. My comments are intended to help, not to hurt. In other words, this is for your own good!"

There was some snickering at this, though all in all the members of the Guild seemed excited about sharing their work.

"But seriously," she continued, "as long as you keep your remarks constructive, you're all welcome to comment on whichever work is under view.

"Now let's begin with the pieces closest to the front here and continue in turn around the room."

Lucy was glad her paintings were close to the exit so she could focus on the other members and their work one at a time. If she judged her own efforts unworthy, she could slip out with her pictures still under wraps before her turn came.

A tall, gaunt, well-dressed man of sixty-five or seventy strode up to the front, accompanied by a portable oxygen tank and a platinum-haired sixty-ish woman with a designer purse dangling from the crook of her arm. The woman wrestled a large canvas, still draped, in an awkward dance from the edge of the room to the easel. As she wobbled, struggling for balance, Vera lunged forward and grasped one side of the canvas to help.

Meanwhile, the greying Abe Lincoln took command of the podium and announced, a little too loudly, "For those who have not yet met me, I am Vincent DiAngelo." He indicated the plump, well-coifed blonde now handing out papers to Vera and the audience and said, "My lovely wife, Lorraine." He adjusted the plastic tubes about his nose. A faint hissing sound escaped.

"Pardon my reliance upon this burdensome device—a nuisance I must tolerate upon occasion since the incident with the plane. But I will not bore you at present with the details of that event." Vincent DiAngelo cleared his throat and went on.

"Now, if you will, turn your attention to the handout. Here you have copies of my planning sketches, the sequence indicated for you by Roman numerals." On the page were four rectangles, each meticulously gridded, containing various perspectives of a shadowy charcoaled figure, in seated position on the ground. The legs were both angled, with an arm crooked around to hold one bent knee upright while the other flopped down. The other arm, straight and stiff and untenably long, stuck out to the side propping up the figure's stiff torso. Lorraine remained beside the easel, gazing at her husband. Vera stood by politely, her hands clasped, as the man went on.

"Now. You will note the development of these constructions into the final phase, the *demoiselle* as represented on the canvas." He nodded to Lorraine, who swept the drape from the canvas with a suspiciously practiced motion. She folded the drape neatly and settled into a chair in the front row. For a moment Vincent paused, looking out triumphantly at the group. As he glided to the seat beside Lorraine with his canister in tow, the silence in the room was broken only by sporadic hisses of oxygen and a squeaking wheel.

The audience gaped at the large figure propped on the easel. Larger than life, the vague sepia-toned figure appeared cramped upon the linen rectangle, like a mime, a nightmare mute, a magician's assistant trying to escape from a box, or perhaps like a woman buried alive, desperate to find a way out. She somehow appeared veiled and extremely naked at the same time.

"Yes, now, Mr. DiAngelo," Vera began, as she stepped back to the podium. She positioned herself so that she could see both painting and artist. Her eyes stole for a moment to Lorraine, who sat, placid, her elegant hands displayed across the large, supple purse in her lap. Lucy, Eleanor, and a few others slid their eyes toward the wife and back to the canvas in question.

"Now, let's see. You have made quite effective use of the entire canvas, and you have used a fairly broad spectrum of tone— except, perhaps, you might consider judicious use of some lighter tones to relieve the somewhat murky effect. Also a little more detail might enhance the viewer's understanding of the subject and help to establish a connection between us and your, uh, *demoiselle*." Vera smiled earnestly in Vincent's direction. The artist leaned forward in his chair, his jaw line suddenly tense.

"Clearly," he said, enunciating with care, "I have merely established form and light and dark with the umber underwash. As

I was largely pleased with the effect, I decided to share the process with the group so that the *demoiselle's* ultimate manifestation might be appreciated when viewed at the Midsummer Show."

"Oh, certainly, Mr. DiAngelo," Vera said with a few too many nods. "You have done a fine job with composition and shading. I only meant to say that detail and clarity can be keys to emotional connection for the viewer. Certainly this lady has something to say to us. But she is, as yet, a woman of mystery."

Vincent shifted in his seat and pressed his grim lips together. Lorraine sat studying her admirable manicure.

"She looks perfectly clear to me," he said.

"Umm... ah... yes, artistic license and all that," Vera said. "Well, thank you so much, Mr. DiAngelo, for sharing this ambitious portrait with us, as well as a glimpse into the intricate planning process behind it. I'm sure we all look forward to seeing the finished painting." The pitch of Vera's voice was rising.

"Would anyone else care to comment on this piece?"

Silence.

"No? All right, then, let us move on."

Lorraine said, "Oh!" and jumped up. She removed the painting from the easel with the help of Eleanor and Vera and set it, draped once more, against the wall. As she returned to her seat, Lorraine glanced at her husband's face and started. Lucy could see her flinch from several rows back. What could have surprised the woman in the face of her husband? Some flash of pain, some watery depth she had not seen in his eyes for a long time? Could they still be a puzzle to each other after what were, surely, many long years of marriage?

Lucy and the Guild members looked around, awaiting the next presenter. A woman with red frizzy hair rose and began to sidle out of her row. Suddenly a florid-faced gentleman with a worn plaid driving cap angled across his shaggy white hair, rose to his feet and interrupted the silence from the middle of the room.

"I have something to say now," he barked. "I came tonight with the purpose of saying it. And say it I will."

The red-haired woman froze. Her eyes along with everyone else's swung toward the eruption.

Eleanor stepped back up to the podium. "Hello, Boone. You're welcome to say your piece, of course."

He nodded. "Eleanor." He puffed his chest out and went on. "I'm going to have my say, and then I'm going to leave, and I will *not* be coming back!" He was gathering steam, growing louder and redder.

"Many of you new people won't know me, but I've been here since the beginning of this organization, that night back in 1989 when a group of us, the founding members—myself and your lady president here, some others, six of us it was—sat around a corner table at the Remus Tavern and started this Guild."

The crowd stared at the interrupter and waited, uncomfortable and utterly attentive. President Eleanor Wood, however, appeared un-disconcerted.

"We agreed upon a course for this venture," the man went on. "We set sail. And somewhere along the way we lost our bearing, our ship *foundered*, and this group now is way afar off from where it was supposed to be. We started up as a group of *professionals* with a bond as such. Now what are we doing? *Workshops!* These little *show-and-tells!* For *Sunday painters!* An art show with the *Historical Snob* Society! People, what are you thinking? Well, I'm not going to be a part of it anymore. Just remove me from your roster. That's all."

Every pair of eyes in the room followed the back of the thick red neck, the thin white hair and the two different plaids, cap and blazer, as the man stomped to the door, leaving silence and a whiff of rank cigar in his wake.

Eleanor sighed, nodded to Vera Crabtree, and took her seat. Vera managed to catch the eye of the frizzy red-haired woman who had sunk nonplussed back into her seat, and beckoned her up to the front.

"Guess I'll try this again," the woman muttered, and jangled her way, heavily braceleted, to where her bundle leaned against the wall. She was dressed loosely and loudly and wore too much stale make-up on her once-striking face; she gave Lucy the impression of a retired belly dancer. She removed several large pieces of heavy grey paper from a plastic trash bag. She propped four pastel paintings side by side, against the wall on the floor, and set another upon the easel. On the paper were a series of architectural fragments floating against a Magritte sky. Some of the fragments had wings.

The woman hesitated beside the easel, then spoke. "Yeah, O.K., so I'm Aylin Borden." Her voice was rough, a little battered. She sounded like she had as much mileage on her as she looked.

"I completed these pastels in my... uh... studio from a number of on-site sketches in Greece at the Temple of Poseidon." Aylin jangled to a chair in the empty front row to await her critique.

Vera took a deep breath and released it slowly, looking relieved. "Quite an impressive series, Ms. Borden. Were you in Greece recently?"

"Not too recently, no. It's been several years. But I hope to go back some day."

Vera shifted her glasses to inspect the corner of the painting on the easel more closely where the date, 1998, and above it the signature, AYLIN, shone in fiery red, looking as fresh as the day they were painted.

"Oh, yes, I see now. Have you been working along this same vein recently?"

"No, not so much," Aylin answered. "But this is representative of where I see myself going as an artist."

"Ah, interesting, Ms. Borden." Turning back to the easel Vera began her comments: "The contrast between the warm tones of the temple details and the cool bold sky behind them is a clever way to bring optical tension into what might otherwise be a..." She went on at length with assorted compliments while Aylin Borden in all her gypsy glory perched on the edge of the folding metal chair, chin in the air at a hopeful tilt. Lucy observed that, in contrast to the artist's thrift-shop aura, her profile was oddly noble.

Vera asked for remarks from the audience.

After a long pause, Aylin herself broke the silence. "As I said before, this type of pastel painting is the direction I'm going in, but I also draw charcoal portraits while-you-wait, just for a little ready cash. I'm kind of new around here, and I could use some suggestions of festivals or public events where people might get into having their portraits done.

Eleanor spoke up. "As a matter of fact, there's a two-day arts and crafts festival early next month at Box Hollow Farm out in the county. It's a brand new festival in our area, and I want to encourage as many of you as possible to participate. We'll be skipping next month's Guild meeting since it would fall during the same week as the festival. Aylin, maybe that would be a good venue for your impromptu portraits."

"Sounds perfect," said Aylin as she gathered her five pastels. She stacked them carefully one upon the other, and slipped them into their trash bag protector.

"Is anyone here interested in carpooling to the festival? I really need to save on gas, if possible."

The crowd looked at random corners of the room.

"I'd be happy to," Lucy heard herself say.

She immediately felt her offer to be a mistake. An arts festival with three small children in tow would likely be disastrous. And this woman was a complete stranger. A *complete* stranger! There was no telling what darkness might reside in her soul. Still, Lucy recognized desperation in the woman's demeanor and could not resist the powerful urge to rescue.

"O.K.!" said the red-head. "I'll get with you at the end and we'll nail down the details."

Lucy nodded back in response. She stewed over her bold offer for a while, working through how she was going to explain it to her husband and how to handle the logistics with the children. She vaguely took in the next few artists.

First there were two older men, Charlie Blue and Solomon Tingle. They looked roughened by hard labor, but clean, and they brought their work up to the front together. They were explaining to Vera how they met at lunch at the plywood mill each day to draw in crayon on scraps of cardboard.

Lucy caught a snatch of Vera saying, "...refreshing examples of Outsider Art." She thought to herself how their colorful scenes resembled her children's drawings, innocent and unpracticed, and then tried to figure out how in the world she would manage to discretely nurse the baby in the crowds and open air of the festival.

After the two crayon artists came a tall, well-built African American man with a reclaimed Ore-Ida French fries box full of eight- by ten-inch landscapes more remarkable for their abundance than for their impact. The man came with a stout shadow, a woman exactly like him in face only. His voice was soft. Lucy's attention veered off again. She wondered what was happening at home. How were they getting by without her? It was almost bedtime. The baby would be getting hungry soon. She shouldn't have left...

After the tall man with the small paintings came Eleanor herself. Lucy snapped out of her mental wanderings and watched her gather her two sturdy cartons from against the wall, in no real hurry, and carry them to the front of the room.

Eleanor pulled out a painting from the larger box, set it on the easel, and stepped back. The painting showed a portrait of a child in an elegantly smocked dress and bare feet sitting on the grass in a garden, her arms around a black Labrador. Her pink cheek was laid against the shoulder of the dog, whose ample tongue gracefully overflowed its lower jaw in an unmistakable grin.

The painting was astonishing. Lucy looked from painting to artist to painting and back to artist. Vera admired the painting aloud, on behalf of the whole room, really, for surely every person there could not help but acknowledge the mastery in that portrait, which was in such contrast to the unassuming nature of the woman who had painted it.

Into the silence that followed, Eleanor said, "I painted this portrait as a commission for the Apple family, of their little daughter Audrey. It's actually one of a pair—I recently painted their college-age daughter, too. Soon this one will be dry enough to be varnished, and then it will take up its new home with the Apples. But they've given me permission to show the portraits at the Midsummer Show, since the Historical Society is one of their favorite charities."

Vera asked, "What do you charge for a portrait like this one?"

"Several thousand, which sounds like a lot, I know. But I spend upwards of three hundred hours on each portrait. I do numerous sittings to get to know the subject, make photographs, do color sketches, and adjust the work in progress in order to capture the subject's posture and coloring, their expression, the play of light on their skin and hair, all of that. And then I spend countless hours just looking, just painting. So I guess it comes out to a little over minimum wage, when all is said and done."

"And how long, Eleanor, have you been painting portraits professionally?"

"Oh, about ten years now. I was busy being a doctor's wife

before that, but then I was... then we... well, it was about ten years ago that I began painting in earnest. Not a lucrative change, I must say, but then lucrative is not always an option." She paused, looking thoughtfully at the girl and the dog. After a few moments, she stirred herself.

"Now I'll show you my favorite painting of the two that I brought with me tonight." She removed the girl's portrait and bent to exchange it for the other. "This one is not a commission. It's an image that has been haunting my mind's eye for a while now, and I finally just had to paint it." She put a smaller painting on the easel.

An arched window was painted meticulously onto a wooden panel. Outside the arch was a rich texture of ancient brick and mortar, of lichen and wild rose, painted so skillfully that it seemed unfathomable that the wall was made only of paint on wood. Within that arch sat a woman, a pale woman with long, gently waving hair and a simple dark red dress. Her hand, resting partly in shadow in her lap, clutched a fistful of paintbrushes, their pointed ends splayed upon the dress, reminding Lucy of arrows seized from a quiver. On second glance, a long-stemmed rose lay tangled among the paintbrushes, and a few drops of blood showed where thorns pressed into the meat of the woman's thumb. Her countenance, however, was radiant and at peace, not fierce and warlike. Around the head of the serene lady of the window arch, in stark contrast to the darkened room which seemed deep within the picture's space, hovered a perfect nimbus in gold leaf.

Now Vera Crabtree, the guest interpreter and expert, was silent, as was everyone else in the room. "Ah, well... hmmm," she said at length, "Ms. Wood, there's nothing I can say to add to our experience of viewing such a painting. It is beyond fabulous." The word hung in the air in all its inadequacy.

Eleanor's voice faltered as she said, "Thank you." She reached the painting down from the easel. Bright red splotches spread across her face and neck. Nothing much seemed to ruffle Eleanor but attention.

"Might I ask if you had any particular inspiration for the smaller painting?" asked Vera.

As Eleanor continued to package the canvas and the wooden panel, she said, "Actually, I've been studying books on Catholic icons." She turned to face the room, regaining her composure.

"Their serenity, their violence, their woodenness fascinate me. In the Southern Baptist Church, where I've belonged most of my life, icons aren't a tradition, of course, so they're new to me, but at the same time they're very old, and I feel myself transported in time when I study them. And then again, they're painted on broad wooden panels: They're painted on a slice of a once long-lived thing, a once real, growing organism. It makes me think the icon itself might at some moment suddenly take root and begin to grow."

The crowd was quiet now, looking clueless as to what Eleanor was talking about. Her face still glowed as she made her way back to her seat, now perhaps more from passion than from embarrassment.

That'll be a hard act to follow, Lucy thought.

The next artist to move forward was a small man who snatched up a painting wrapped in grimy newspaper from the side of the room. He moved on short, over-quick legs; his upper body seemed to glide motionlessly to the front. He tore the newspaper away with long thick yellow fingernails and set the canvas on the easel, then quickly backed up to the wall where he could watch at a safe distance. The man was slight, between forty and sixty, with unwashed hair and oversized glasses missing a temple. His mouth moved in a continuous fluid grimace.

Vera stepped forward to examine the self-portrait, oddly colored and angular, with features distorted and proportionless, yet

18

somehow recognizable as belonging to the artist himself. The painting appeared to be done in poster paint on a hard, cheap canvas board, warped and unframed. Vera took a long and quiet three minutes studying the painting.

Lucy found the awkward portrait more comfortable to look at than the painter, which was really saying something. The portrait made disconcerting continuous eye contact, while the artist himself, disconcertingly, made eye contact with no one at all. Lucy decided that the most fascinating thing about viewing this picture was wondering what Vera would find to say about it.

"Well, now, Mr., uh...?" she began. The artist looked into the middle ground and tilted his head, mantis-like. He did not speak.

"Mr., uh... E.G.," said Vera after looking again at the signature, two letters only, scrawled at the base of the picture.

"Now this is quite arresting, Mr. E. G, quite distinctive. An unusual example of expressionist and cubist approaches combined in one portrait. This piece gives us pause to consider what is *inside*."

And in fact there now was a pause while the audience did just that, stealing furtive looks at the man who was previously invisible and who seemed himself to look at nothing at all through the thick lenses and dark, heavy frames. With his arms straight down at his sides, he pressed his palms against the wall on either side of himself, flattened there like a hapless bat pinned by sunlight against a bright wall.

"Any other comments for Mr. E. G.?" Vera asked.

The room was silent but for the buzzing of fluorescent lights.

"All right, then. Thank you so much for sharing this portrait with us, Mr. E. G. We hope to see further exploration of this subject from you in the future."

He made no move at first. Then the artist launched himself from the wall toward his painting, grabbed it from the easel, and carried it on silent, quick, small feet out of the bright room into the night. He would be quickly forgotten, leaving no words or even a proper name behind in the memory of the room.

But Lucy shuddered; the shadow of E. G. lingered. She considered the peculiar man: Toward what lonely place was he headed? Did he eat alone every meal of his life? Was there no mother anywhere, nor ever any friend or lover for such a man, to praise the things he created, whether strange or not? She closed her eyes and shook her head to fling thoughts of the odd little man out of her mind.

The next few artists presented less of a challenge for Vera. First an assistant school superintendent showed four hyper-realistic acrylic paintings of sweeping golf course scenes. Next a short, barrel-shaped woman, who introduced herself as Chamber of Commerce Social Liaison Magdaline Dismukes, showed three more-or-less delicate still-lives in watercolor of antique china and embroidered linens. After that, a cabinet maker from Redbud, which was just a cluster of homes around a railroad crossing out in the county, showed a crate-ful of wooden bowls he had turned. As one of the bowls was passed around, Lucy stroked it and marveled at the smooth warmth of the curved maple, strong and firm outside like a young man's shoulder, welcoming and protective inside, open to whatever treasures its owner saw fit to keep within.

Lucy felt stillness returning to the room now that the bowl maker had taken his seat, and she realized that her paintings were next, the last in line for the evening. She found it surprising that she had never once, after her initial doubts, considered leaving. As if from above, she saw herself moving sideways along her row of chairs and up the side aisle, gathering her trash-bagged paintings as she walked to the front. Her knees trembled—whether from nerves or excitement or the lingering effect of her near-disaster with the car earlier, she couldn't be sure. She loosened the plastic drawstring, reached in to pull the paintings out, and set the sheaf of stiff watercolor paper on the easel. Then she sat, waiting, in the empty front row. In the silence of the room she felt that her booming heartbeat could be heard by everyone.

Vera surveyed the painting on top of the sheaf and smiled at Lucy. "And you are...?" she asked.

"Oh! I'm sorry! I'm Lucy Bloom." Lucy's face was hot.

"Well, now, Ms. Bloom, what a lovely portrait of a flower you have here. I call it a portrait, and not a still life, because we can feel that we know this blossom intimately from the care you have put into painting it. The flower jumps forward as if to greet us eagerly, posed before the dark green background with its mysterious fernlike texture. In its largeness, filling the page as it does, and in its isolation as the only subject depicted, you invite the viewer to examine in detail a single radiant specimen of nature that would be easily overlooked in the many bold strokes of a garden."

"Umm... thanks?"

"How long have you been painting, Lucy?"

"Oh, just a couple of years, since my second child was born. I have very little time to paint. I have three young children now, and that keeps my hands busy. But I love to do it; I love to paint." Lucy felt that she had babbled idiotically.

One by one, Vera removed the pieces of heavy paper to reveal another flower, each painted in fluid delicacy, in intense subtlety, with a personality of its own. In the supple curves rested colors which Lucy had perceived, not seen, and this in itself is what gave the flowers life on the paper.

Vera removed her glasses and looked intently at Lucy. "Ms. Bloom, Lucy, my advice to you is this: Hire a babysitter! Keep painting! Do whatever you have to do to make that happen!"

"Thank you," said Lucy, startled, unsure of what else to say, and slightly disappointed at the lack of constructive criticism.

Eleanor came forward to change places with Vera at the

podium. She flashed a smile down at Lucy in front of her, and said quietly, "I knew your paintings would be beautiful." Then she gathered her breath and focused on the crowd.

"What a wonderful way to end the evening! I'm sorry to say we have to wrap this up now, since we're running over our allotted hour. Thank you to everyone who brought pictures for the critique. And thank you especially to our guest, Ms. Vera Crabtree." The audience clapped politely as Eleanor turned to the woman.

"We hope that you'll come again to share your insight with us?" Vera nodded vigorously.

Eleanor addressed the room. "I want to remind you all once more of the Box Hollow Arts and Crafts Festival. Call me if you want to exhibit there, and I'll give you the details. We'll skip the meeting in May, so our next meeting will be the first Thursday in June. And, of course, don't forget the Historical Society Midsummer Show on the twenty-third of that month." She closed the meeting, and voices rose and mingled as the artists began packing up their belongings.

Eleanor gathered some papers from the lectern and said to Lucy, just getting to her feet before her, "I'm so happy you could come tonight. I'm just astonished by your flowers—how anything so simple can be so intriguing. I do hope you'll enter them in the Midsummer Show. They are just stunning and such a contrast to the other Guild work."

Lucy was carefully settling her watercolors back into the trash bag. "Thank you so much. I'll try. I really haven't spent much time around other artists before like this; actually, I never have at all, and it *is* inspiring, like you said." After a pause she added, "And your pictures—they're so amazing! I didn't realize you were a professional artist."

"Yes, well, in fact it was a necessity. When I found myself a single mother with four teenagers, I had to think of some way to get them through school and out into their own futures. Painting was my only skill."

"I guess I've never thought of painting as a skill, more as a luxury."

"To paint what you love is a luxury. To love what you paint is essential for painting well. So I find painting for pay does broaden my scope," said Eleanor.

They made their way to the door with the crush of other artists, laden with their bundles. Lucy bumped into a young man she recognized as the other newcomer, carrying a sketchbook under his arm. He was slightly shorter than she was and wiry, lightly bearded. He somehow managed to pull off blue jeans and a bow tie at the same time.

"Oh, hey," he said. "Lucy, right? I'm James..." He turned to the older woman. "Hello, Mrs. Wood."

"James." Eleanor smiled and took his hand for a moment. "I'm so glad you could come. I look forward to seeing some of your artwork next time."

She looked at James and Lucy, her smile fading. "Listen, I just want to say to you both—I hope you won't let Boone Carmichael discourage you from coming back. He shows up every so often to give that same speech—I guess he forgets he's said it all before. He's a retired commercial artist from New York City, and he's come back to his old hometown to paint and, as you can see, to grumble. But Boone is an artist of great ability, and we've learned to take him with a grain of salt. He's seen and made more art than all of us put together."

"Oh, no, ma'am. I am definitely hooked. I'll be back. That old guy didn't scare me off." James looked at Lucy. "How about you?"

"Oh, no. He didn't scare me off either," Lucy said with a laugh.

"Well that's good to hear," Eleanor said. "I'll look for you both the first Thursday of June. And don't forget: Be working on something to enter in the Midsummer Show." She smiled and turned aside to talk to another artist just inside the doorway. Lucy and James headed out into the hallway amid the current of departing people.

"Hey, Lucy," he said, as if he had known her forever, "your paintings are beautiful! Much better than I could do. I decided after seeing everybody's pictures that I would just keep these to myself." He lifted his arm a bit with the sketchbook under it.

"Thanks. But I can't pretend it's serious art when I make it at the kitchen table. You should have shown us your pictures." She pointed to his sketchbook. "Maybe you could show me a couple of them now?"

As soon as Lucy said it, she realized the risk in asking to see a stranger's drawings. She might look directly into his mind. That could be uncomfortable—ugly, or creepy, or alarming, or even boring, and there she would be, one-on-one, confronting the soul of this other unknown person. And maybe he would take her interest the wrong way. *But no*, she thought, *you ought to quit second-guessing yourself. Trust your instincts... this guy is fine. He looks like he could be your little brother.*

"Oh, they're just pencil sketches, stuff around the farm that kind of makes me want to draw. I just play around with it, not much time to draw anyway. But O.K., maybe one." He moved to the side of the hallway out of the way.

"Here's my favorite."

Lucy leaned over a bit to look at the first sketch in the book, a drawing with vigorous parallel pencil strokes shading a mule hitched to a plow.

"Oh, a mule! Do you actually use it on the farm?"

"I sure do. I'm an organic farmer. I like to do things the good old-fashioned way, which, according to the agriculture department at the university, is now the new-fashioned way, again. I just finished school up there last year, bought the old farm—lots to learn. So, yeah. It's a challenge. And *she's* a real challenge!" he said, pointing at the mule.

"Well, I think you should share next time. Don't keep your drawings to yourself. I'll see you at the next meeting?"

"Definitely," said James the Organic Farmer. They followed the others out to the parking lot still wet from the earlier storms and glistening under the scudding ghostly remnants of the storm clouds, the emerging stars, and the moon. She said goodbye to James and headed to her car.

But Lucy's encounters this evening had not yet ended. As she reached the old brown station wagon and looked down, fumbling for her keys, she felt a hand on her arm and, startled, looked up to see the frizzy-red-haired woman standing close in the moonlight.

"Oh... hello," said Lucy.

"Hi there. About that carpooling..."

"Carpooling?"

"To Box Hollow. Do you want to meet here in the parking lot that Saturday morning about seven?"

"Uh... I guess so. Yes," answered Lucy, "that'll work out okay." Although really it wouldn't. How was she going to get three children up and dressed and fed and out by 7:00 in the morning? But she'd have to take them if she was going. Her husband would be working.

"Actually, uh... I will have my kids with me, but I'll try to make it by seven."

"Oh. I see." Aylin looked taken aback. "Well, that's fine," she recovered. "I keep my daughter's kid for her sometimes, so I'm used to children." Somehow, Lucy doubted this.

"But I do need to get there early. Eleanor tells me exhibitors are supposed to be set up by eight."

"I'll do my best. I may not be able to stay the entire day to give you a ride back, though."

Aylin waved her hand, bracelets clinking. "Oh, I'll work that out somehow. You want to drive and I'll just give you some gas money? Or maybe you'd like to trade gas for sketches of your kids? I've done thousands of pictures of kids. I'm really good at them, actually."

"Oh, I'm sure you are," Lucy said quickly. "Your artwork tonight was lovely. But that's all right. I have drawings of the children I've done myself. Too many, in fact. And you don't need to give me gas money, really. It'll just be nice to have company."

Now Lucy felt serious doubt about this last statement, but she was yet hopeful that it would prove to be true. She wondered what she had gotten herself into as the woman sauntered off, jangling and humming into the night.

Aylin's Day

Aylin greeted the first truly warm day of spring, a week or so after the April Guild meeting, with a long pull of deep red wine from the bottle beside her cot. She reached down for her glass, half-forgotten on the floor, splashed wine into it, and set the bottle down in its place. Wedges of early-morning sunlight crept over her through the naked windows of the lean-to as she curled around her wine, wrapped in a faded quilt flattened by age and misuse. Sunwarmth butted through the grime on the old glass panes that time and neglect had sullied, and prodded Aylin until at last she shed the quilt and dragged herself out of bed.

She set the glass down on a nearby crate, pulled on a blouse and a skirt, tugged a brush through her red tumbleweed hair, and made use of the commode in the corner. She touched up the worst of her make-up before the tiny silvering mirror over the sink. Rust and mineral from decades of dripping water had blemished the white porcelain beneath the faucets with two bruised teardrops, larger than life. *You can't fake that color—can't just mix it up on your palette*, she thought. *That color only comes from life.* She grabbed a tapestry bag, stuffed clothes from a heap on the floor into it, and moved over to the main room of the cottage where she dropped the bag onto an old captain's chair.

Aylin found a can of tuna in a jumble of bottles and cans piled at one end of a tattered sofa. She opened the can, grabbed a fork and her wineglass, and carried them just outside to a bench on the stone-paved ground beneath the roof overhang. She sat there, idly forking bits of pink tuna from can to painted mouth, looking out through the spindly screen of oak and poplar saplings to thicker, taller, older trees through which a few glints showed of the sparkling cove down the hillside. A trace of wind lifted her hair from her shoulder.

A pale grey cat she'd seen loitering around the cabin a few times appeared just then, tuna-bidden. Aylin lowered the can to the stones at her feet and watched as the cat pushed its smoky face in and around the tiny can. She marveled at the length of its tongue and wondered how it was that a cat never seemed to be hurt by the pried-open circle of tin that could, with one careless movement, slice its flesh wide open.

Aylin left the can to the cat and carried her glass some yards down the lake path to a clearing. In the clearing—just a small comma in the woods—stood a stack of river stones higher than Aylin's head beside an old fire circle. At first glance, the stones looked similar, but closer inspection revealed how unique each was. All the stones were of earth and lake in tone and make, but they were quite varied in their patterns, shades, shape, wear, and especially in their raiments of moss or mold or lichen or fungus or clay, parasitic accumulations of years and happenstance and habit that could be beautiful or repulsive but were all undeniably matchless.

The utter loveliness of the totem, however, lay in the way in which the stones were arranged, stacked, balanced in seemingly random ways, and in how each stone touched another, or several, but not all, and yet all were connected through the weight and tenuous posture of the whole. The wonder of it lay in the balance, in the precarious form that the gathered stones created there in the clearing together. Aylin stepped up to the altar, held her glass high, and poured the dregs of her wine before it, leaving a dark stain on the sandy, leaf-strewn earth.

She knew by the angle of the filtering sunlight that she must be leaving for work. She swept back up the trail to the cottage, her ex-father-in-law's fishing cabin which she knew he had not used in years and which he would, in fact, never use again. Apparently his accountant still payed the taxes and the minimal utility bill. Lucky break, for her at least.

Inside, she left her glass on the edge of a large, round, scarred oak table heaped with heavy paper and pastel sticks in bowls of dry rice. She picked up three sheets of the paper she had stacked together with care the night before, along with an envelope and a scrap of newspaper with a phone number on it. She grabbed her tapestry bag and keys and followed the uphill path to where her once-red Toyota Corolla crouched at the edge of the woods near a forgotten corner of the back nine of the golf course. This morning the car started right up without her having to roll it down the hill first.

The drive through twisted retirement lanes to Mrs. Law's house took ten minutes. Aylin parked the car along the road, facing downhill, and crossed the manicured yard with its over-green grass and chiseled boxwoods to a red brick ranch with slick white trim. She had begun by covering the night shift with Mrs. Law, but she had advanced by sheer endurance to four day-times a week and half a day on Saturdays. She followed a path around the side of the house and walked down a flight of cement steps to the basement door where she met the nighttime sitter, a thin, wordless young man in scrubs with an impressive array of facial piercings, anxious to be relieved.

Aylin bundled her bag through the cellar door and dropped it in the laundry area. She moved through the sitting room raking up food wrappers left by the previous sitter. She tidied up the kitchenette, then went into the stale-smelling bedroom where Mrs. Law, the world's tiniest woman, lay rigid and angry upon the pink painted bed, chenille bedspread pulled up over her chest, her arms straight out and fists clenched at her sides.

"Mrs. Law, are you ready to get up today?" Aylin said in her loud sitter voice.

"Been ready!" snapped Mrs. Law. "You're late!" She worked her jaw in a circular motion. "Who are you anyways? Never seen you before! What are you doing in my house? You just get out, now! Go on with you! Clear out!"

Aylin moved about the room, opening shades, straightening furniture. "Mrs. Law, I'm Aylin. I stay with you. I'm here to help you get up and start your day."

"You just clear out, now, you hear!"

"No, Mrs. Law, I'm here to help you. Time to get up and get your shower."

And so the morning continued. Aylin worked her way down a long list of readying Mrs. Law, the Cellar-Dweller. But readying for what? Daytime television was the only goal beyond all the bathing, dressing, medications, breakfast, and general chores. Game shows. Sit coms. That was it. That and her crazy knitting.

"Let's get you settled in your easy chair, Mrs. Law," said Aylin as she steered the woman, fragile but tight as a coiled spring, to the plastic-covered La-Z-Boy in front of the box T.V. She turned on the television to "Let's Make a Deal" and adjusted the volume as high as she herself could tolerate. Mrs. Law glared at her, pulled her pink flowered cane from beside her chair, and began striking Aylin over the back and shoulders with it.

"That's not it! That's not the one, you stupid, stupid girl! I watch 'Petticoat Junction,' and you know it!" Aylin wrestled the cane away from Mrs. Law, amazed at the strength left in the shriveled body that could hardly walk or even stand.

"No, Mrs. Law. That show hasn't been on for forty years. This is the show you always watch first thing."

Mrs. Law worked her jaw around and around, popping her dentures. "Stupid girl!" she muttered. "Don't know what show to put on! What's she doing here anyway? Don't need nobody messing with my *tee*-vee!"

Aylin watched from a few steps away as Mrs. Law relaxed with the familiar theme music and the clapping and the cheering and seemed to settle into her morning haze. Then Aylin moved into the laundry area and began filling the washer with clothes from her own tapestry bag. A few minutes later, she closed the lid on the churning and thrashing, and peered from her shadowed corner at Mrs. Law. The old woman's head was flopped forward facing her lap. Aylin stole across the room, through the bedroom and into the bathroom, and began removing her clothes. She showered, straining her ears to hear any commotion from beyond the door. She toweled off, only half acknowledging the soreness between her shoulder blades. The steamy ghost image in the mirror showed her hair a mass of chaos with a half inch of white now close against her scalp. Time for another red rinse. She twisted around to get a look at the welt raising up on her back. *That's nothing—I've lived through a lot worse.* She grimaced, remembering.

She dressed again and smoothed her wrinkled clothing as it relaxed in the steam. She liberally reapplied her make-up, then left the bathroom and crossed the main room in a wide arc around the T.V.-anesthetized Mrs. Law. Aylin sat at the table in a cracked-vinyl-and-chrome dinette chair to read the newspaper, the want ads in particular. Although she had lived in the area nearly a year, she had not yet managed to find a job that fit her skill and interest, and she was experiencing cash flow difficulties, to say the least. She found nothing of promise in yesterday's paper.

She saw by the wall clock that 10:00 had come and gone. Aylin pulled a scrap of paper from her pocket, dialed the phone number penciled there, and cleared her throat. A man's voice answered.

"Yes?"

She cleared her throat again. "Mr. Brinton?"

"Speaking."

"Mr. Brinton, this is Aylin Borden. I'm calling to let you know that the portrait you commissioned is ready. I'm happy to deliver it if you'll just give me the address."

A long pause grew into uncomfortable silence before an answer came. "Yes... uhh... I have a busy day planned..."

"Mr. Brinton, I realize you are quite busy, but I'm willing to meet you anyplace that's convenient for you. The charge, as I said before, is three hundred and fifty dollars. I'll bring the portrait to you anywhere you say."

"Uh... All right, Ms...."

"Borden."

She heard rustling and muffled speech on the other end of the line. "Say... one o'clock, at the Marathon Gas Station on Four Forty-One on the south side of Athens."

Aylin momentarily thought it strange to meet at a gas station, but she didn't care much, even if it was an odd location, even if she had to use a quarter tank of gas to get there, if she could only pass the portrait over and get paid for it. It was a haul, but she could just make it there in time after work.

"That'll be fine, Mr. Brinton. I'll see you there." She heard the click on the other end before she finished speaking. Aylin felt relieved, a bit. She hung up the receiver of Mrs. Law's pink rotary phone and looked over at her charge, who was cackling at the greedy mayhem on the television screen. The tail of the cat clock in the kitchenette swished back and forth mocking time as Aylin sat at the table with her chin propped up on her hands, staring at the peach cinderblock wall where her mind projected scenes of the coming encounter.

She roused herself at the sound of the washer signal and moved over to the laundry area to heave the wet twisted bundle into the dryer.

"What's all that buzzing and banging about over there?" shouted Mrs. Law. "Can't hear my show!"

Aylin wordlessly went on with her task.

"Hey! Who is that over there? Why are you in my house? You just clear out of here!"

Aylin stepped into her line of sight and shouted over the sound of the blaring T.V. "I'm Aylin, Mrs. Law, your sitter. I help you out here. You know me, Mrs. Law. I come here just about every day."

"Don't need no stinkin' help!" Mrs. Law looked about her chair with darting black diamond eyes. "Where's my stick? I'll show *you* to come into people's houses unwanted!" Aylin slid her eyes over to the edge of the doorjamb where she had propped Mrs. Law's cane just out of reach. She changed tactics.

"Mrs. Law, look what I brought you today." She rummaged around in her tapestry bag and pulled out a Wal-Mart sack.

"Look, Mrs. Law, I got you some more yarn so you can work on your hats." Mrs. Law grabbed the bulky skein of grey yarn out of the sack and fingered it intently, turning the skein over and over in her lap. Her tiny hand pinched and plucked at the yarn like the merciless beak of a yard fowl striking at scurrying insects.

As she handled the soft yarn, her body relaxed visibly. Aylin judged it safe now to bring out the knitting needles. From under a tray table she pulled out a pink plastic laundry basket stuffed with ragged balls and knotted wads of yarn, various sizes of knitting needles, and dozens of knitted sock monkey hats. The hats were of all sizes, some shaped more reasonably for a human head than others, some trailing stray yarn lengths, some with random gaps in the pattern, but all resembling to some degree an old sock monkey of mottled grey and white and black with outrageous jeering red lips.

Mrs. Law snatched up the needles and began casting on stitches. Her cramped face softened as her hands found the old familiar rhythm. Aylin's clenched muscles eased in response, but she remained wary as long as the needles were in play.

And they were in play for quite some time, while Aylin swept, finished the newspaper, folded her laundry, packed it back in her bag, and tried to tame her humidity-stricken hair. She freshened her make-up, with special attention to eyes and mouth, which had always been her best features. She added an extra flourish with the eyeliner—artsy effect for the benefit of the client she would soon be meeting. She dug a curled-up receipt book out of her bag and in deliberate calligraphy wrote, *"Mr. Brinton, 1 portrait, 18"x24", pastel, $350.00."* Then she marked the same on the booklet's stub.

She grew a little taller as the morning trudged on toward noon. She prepared an early lunch for her charge on a tray and for herself at the table. She tidied up once more and secured the now forgotten knitting needles and yarns in the basket under the tray table. Then she prepared Mrs. Law for her afternoon nap in the pink painted bed in the pale peach painted block bedroom with the tiny high window and the buzzing fluorescents, underground beneath the red brick house in which the old woman had once made her life. Now the son had taken up residence above, though there was no sound from upstairs, no sign of anyone around.

Aylin paused in the bedroom doorway after tucking the bedspread around the grim and rigid Mrs. Law and thought how the old woman's stare looked familiar. It reminded her of the cellblock stare she had seen before, a long time ago, the stare of boredom, impotence, anger, and loss. She hefted her belongings over her shoulder, locked the stairwell door behind her, and climbed up into the precociously hot, aggressively green April world.

Mrs. Law's family was to care for her the rest of the weekend, or such was the arrangement. Aylin never saw the family, just assumed that filial duty did, in fact, take over where she left off. They placed her pay, cash money, in a sealed envelope on the kitchen table every two weeks, and that's all she needed to know about them.

As Aylin followed the path around to the front of the house, she could even now hear Mrs. Law shouting, "Don't need no stinkin' help! Just leave me alone! Go on, get out of my house! Just clear out!" She quickened her step. She breathed in green, breathed out cinderblock dungeon pink. She inhaled April, exhaled crazy hat factory.

The car cranked with some downhill encouragement, and Aylin was off to her appointment at the Marathon Gas Station. Her head pounded from lingering echoes of the blaring television and the angry, shouting invalid. But she was oddly hopeful with the fresh laundry bundle, the familiar engine tattoo, and the receipt already filled out in her most elegant calligraphy.

The faded red Toyota pulled in to the Marathon at 12:59, according to the bank sign across the road. The station was sprawling, flat, and heavily cemented, with twenty-four pumping stations which were, on a Saturday at mid-day, teeming with vehicles of every description. Belatedly, the thought struck Aylin that she had no way to recognize the client, having only spoken with him on the phone. She would have to trust that he would somehow spot her and recognize her for an artist. Fortunately, she had dressed the part.

She maneuvered the car around the spasmodic commerce of the gas station and backed it into a parking space at the side of the

Marathon Kwikstop Shop. She cut her engine. She checked her face in the mirror and stepped out into the dazing cement-reflected light. She folded the driver's seat forward and bent into the back seat to pull out the portrait she had laid there, carefully sandwiched between two blank sheets of paper, before Mrs. Law's this morning in hopes of reaching her client on a Saturday. She had not been able to get him on the phone all week.

Aylin might have checked the portrait again, but she did not. She knew it was fine. She had plenty of experience with portraits, and they did not give her much trouble anymore, especially if she took her time with them, as she definitely had with this one. Still, deliveries of commissions always set her eyelid to twitching, always made her crave a drink.

Aylin scrutinized the ever-changing cementscape around her, searching out the one car, the one driver, she had come to meet. Her face grew moist, then fiery, beneath the mid-day sun. The voluminous folds of her skirt seemed to weigh her down. Her ankles felt elephant-like, stocky, stiff and heavy.

At 1:28 Aylin eased her rear down upon the hot black vinyl driver's seat, her legs stretched straight out before her with her heels on the griddle-hot ground. The bank across the way flashed ninety-eight degrees on its sign. How was that even possible, in April? She cradled the portrait in her lap. Her hair hovered about her head and neck and shoulders like a tornadic cloud. She thought of going inside the Kwikstop Shop for a bottle of water, but she feared missing her client, so she remained in the heat trap of her old faithful, if not perfectly robust, car. As she leaned back, she could see a slice of alarming red face in the rearview mirror, her careful preparations in Mrs. Law's cool bathroom now undone by the relentless sun.

Aylin would not allow herself to wonder at his tardiness, would not allow herself to consider if he might simply not come. She focused on each new car as it entered the Marathon Kwikstop and dismissed every one in turn as the driver emerged to pump gas or enter the store.

At 1:53 Aylin observed a shiny black convertible pull in. A young-ish man wearing Ray-Bans, a pink golf shirt, and khaki shorts jumped out and began pumping gas. He leaned back against the car and waited, his legs leisurely stretched, his arms crossed in front of him. Finally, he removed the nozzle, hopped back in the car and swung it around towards the shop. Aylin rose stiffly, thinking that at last this might be her client. The car pulled past her and out of her sight beyond the front corner of the store. The driver had seemed to look in her direction and then away.

Aylin felt her hopes begin to falter for the first time. She slumped against her car and resigned herself to studying anew the incoming cars and drivers, trying to focus, though everywhere she looked black spots darted, the shadow spawn of chrome-magnified sun glints.

All of a sudden the man in sunglasses came around the corner of the building and walked directly toward her. Aylin straightened abruptly. She squinted at the tan, well-built young man with short, dense, dark hair, at a loss as to what to say. She just stood there, rooted to the pavement, red-haired, red-faced, and framed by the faded red car, as he neared her.

"All right, let's get this over with," he said. "Show me this thing you've got for me."

Aylin searched for her voice. "Uh, Mr. Brinton?"

He nodded.

"Oh. Well, first... first I want to give you this." She handed him a well-worn envelope. "These are the reference photographs you sent me a few weeks ago. Your invoice is in there, too."

The man took it and shrugged. "I have no need for the pictures anymore," he said as he wadded up the envelope—receipt, photographs and all—and tossed it on the ground.

Aylin's lungs would not fill completely. Her chest was sluggish; the air was viscous. She wrenched her eyes away from the discarded envelope.

"And here..." Aylin said, uncovering the portrait with care and placing the extra paper back on the car seat behind her, "...here is your portrait." She held up the pastel painting by two corners so that he could see it. She felt the heavy grey paper between her fingers, the best she could buy, the richest thing she owned. The man seemed to study it for four seconds, maybe less. The painting that had taken thirty-five hours of her time and best efforts and a lifetime of honing her skill had taken only a sliver of a minute of his to judge.

He rocked forward on his feet, his face not far from hers, and said, "It doesn't look like her at all."

Aylin blinked. "Excuse me?"

"It doesn't look like her *at all*," he repeated.

The heat was making her a bit dizzy.

"I don't understand, Mr. Brinton. Clearly this portrait is of the woman in the photographs you sent me?"

"No, *clearly* you *don't* understand. Let me be candid. The portrait does not look like her, and I don't want it. You have wasted my time bringing me out here to look at... this." He flicked the painting with the back of his fingertips.

Aylin backed against the car for support, the painting still held before her like a shield, or perhaps more like a plea. She could not tell where the man was looking. At her face? At the portrait? Over her shoulder? Or anywhere at all? The sleek dark glasses were flat, impenetrable. His lips were straight and emotionless, forbidding. She looked down at the portrait which she still held in front of her, and looked up again at the client.

"And, moreover," he said in unmistakable lawyerese, "you have no business selling art to me or anyone else. You are *sadly* lacking in talent. Frankly, you're misrepresenting yourself as an artist. The whole affair verges on fraud."

"But the bill there, Mr. Brinton. I... I need to be paid for my time," Aylin said.

"I don't think so. This," he jabbed a finger at the pastel face between them, "is a joke."

He strode off, leaving Aylin crumpled and sweating, still gripping the portrait. She felt stabbing pain in her neck and shoulder. She looked down once more at the painting that she had sincerely tried her best with, the painting she had pondered night and day and poured all her experience and skill into. She turned it around to look at it full-on, and with a jolt realized that she suddenly *loved* it, that what was intended for a mere transaction had become in its moment of rejection incomprehensibly dear.

She looked up automatically at the roar of the black convertible tearing from the Marathon lot, her lips still parted in shock, her eyes, once squinting against the light, now open wide in disbelief. Aylin carefully covered the portrait again and placed it gently on the back seat. She sank into the driver's seat and pulled her legs in after her. She gazed for a minute at the now-ridiculous sales stub marked with the studied slant of her own script, thinking, *It looks like a ticket, a front-row ticket to my own public humiliation. I've just been pilloried, tarred and feathered, burned at the stake.* She began to laugh at the thought. It was a joke, after all. But she laughed grimly, without joy.

She felt unsettled, off balance. A teetering stone atop a tower's crumbling parapet. She felt the need for a drink, a long drink. She turned the key in the ignition with no faith whatsoever, sure that the old engine would not turn over this time. All the car gave up was an empty click. She threw the shift into neutral and dragged herself back out onto the hot pavement. Door open, she pushed the car off with all her remaining strength on the level gasoline plaza. The car rolled into some slight invisible declivity, and she scrambled in, threw the shift in second, and popped the clutch. This time the motor caught. It coughed and sputtered, and Aylin grappled with the wheel, dodging as best she could the unsympathetic frenzy of the Marathon Kwikstop Gas Plaza on a Saturday afternoon.

From above, from up in the innocent April sky, the station resembled a colorful hive, full of meaningless impersonal coming and going and filling, but not without some unarticulated master plan. Not one other insect in the hive had given heed to the small faded red beetle-like Corolla or its occupant. And no other visitor to the hive had observed the stealth and the sting and the quick retreat of the shiny black wasp.

Eventually, Aylin did cool off. The open car windows allowed air to bluster in and around and to suck some of her damp hair out to dance in the blazing afternoon. Some other day Aylin would have fancied the wind was a lover playing with her tresses, and she would have let herself imagine being young and beautiful and desired. But today the way home was a long grey tunnel of darker thoughts. She drove automatically without seeing the blooming riot along the roadsides. At one end of the tunnel was the blistering gas plaza. At the other end was the wine bottle at her bedside, and she drove from one to the other unerringly.

Back at the cabin, Aylin dragged her load inside and dropped it. She uncovered the portrait and propped it on a window ledge. She picked up her morning wineglass from the table, hobbled into the tiny lean-to, and set the glass beside the bottle on the crate by her cot. She sank down on the quilt. She untied and shook off her worn espadrilles, and rubbed the marks the laces had left on her swollen ankles. She splashed wine into the glass full up to the rim and gratefully drank long and hard until the glass was nearly empty. She felt her joints loosen. A tolerable humming began to replace her throbbing and pain. She put the glass down and fingered the contents of her pocket. She pulled out a few damp, crumpled bills, a penciled phone number, a tangle of grey yarn, and the wadded-up stub from the receipt book which she had torn out before she started for home. She rose and placed them, one by one, on the broad, rough windowsill in front of the portrait.

She moved away to study the picture from across the room for the three hundredth time. She tilted her head. Again, a flood of tenderness overcame her. The young woman, an auburn-haired, amber-eyed girl, was no subdued Mona Lisa: She barely contained her liveliness and laughter. She was not yet trodden and tired, had not yet learned to hide. Some time ago, when Aylin had first pulled the photographs of her face from the envelope, the young woman had been a stranger to her. But now she knew the girl as she knew herself; she knew the girl *as* herself, only not yet shattered.

Aylin snatched up the portrait and the objects from the windowsill. She grabbed the wineglass and headed out the door. As her bare feet padded over the path toward the clearing, senseless to the prods and pricks of the forest detritus, a small green chameleon darted across the leaf litter. Birds scolded and scuffled about in the saplings. Muffled voices and the grating whine of engines on the lake to one side and the golf course on the other seemed far away from the clearing and inconsequential to its solitude.

Aylin paused, peering at the play of light and verdure around the old stone altar. She laid the portrait on the ground inside the fire ring and arranged the objects from her pocket upon it. Then she walked over to a low, ragged stump, set down her glass, lifted an upside-down rusted coffee can and found there a half-spent box of matches. She moved back to the stone circle, and began striking a match. She hesitated. She crouched down, looking around her on the ground. She picked up a twig and tore loose a long dandelion stem. She broke the stick and crossed the two pieces, one long and one short, securing them with several twists of the slender stem, binding them tight. Then she placed her new creation upon the portrait as well. She lit the match and touched it to the corner of the heavy grey paper, which browned hungrily and twisted and smoked and flashed up into a tall flame. The yarn caught and blackened, then writhed briefly. Brinton's phone number flared with a spark and vanished. The stub and the bills burned more slowly, damp as they were with her sweat. But finally all was consumed leaving behind only hot, brittle black flakes and the unburnt twist of dandelion stem.

Aylin replaced the matches and retrieved her wineglass. She carried it back to the fire circle, held the glass high, and poured out its remains before the altar. The wine dregs clotted and stained the ground. The mark would linger at least until the next heavy rain, maybe longer, as black and sure as spilled blood.

She headed back up the path to the cabin and into its dark interior, shedding her clothes as she went, until she stood naked before the mirror over the weeping basin. She saw her hair, like a mushroom cloud born of sweat and wind. She saw her lipstick melting into the creases about her mouth like tiny frayed red threads. She saw glistening trails running from her eyes over her high cheekbones and down the hollows to her jaw. She saw a strange purplish mark at the base of her neck between her left ear and her shoulder, a sharp bruise inside a welt with redness radiating angrily from it. She ran water and splashed it on her face and hair and all about herself, or the parts that she could manage to bathe over the sink. She removed the fallout from her make-up. Her hair dripped into the basin and formed ringlets as she studied in the mirror a face unfamiliar and old.

Aylin drank deeply once more from the newly-filled wineglass and moved slowly about the cabin, shifting things here and there. She breathed in fully, her lungs sated at last; it was easier to breathe now that she was weightless. She reveled in the air upon her skin, all of her skin. The oxygen came in through her pores, no longer just through the raveling hole of her mouth. Finally, she felt free. She picked up a charcoal stick, thought for a moment, and began to draw.

The Eighteenth Hole

T he three gentlemen in the golf carts motored into the shade at every opportunity. This particular Saturday, when they met for their weekly round of golf at Whitetail Cove, the weather was unexpectedly hot, especially for mid-April. As the afternoon progressed, the sun seemed closer, bigger, and more malicious than usual, without any sign of its sometime companion, the breeze, to temper it.

Assistant Corbie County School Superintendent Bob Short sadly felt the need to avoid sunlight as much as possible since his recent skin cancer scare. Vincent DiAngelo routinely avoided heat himself, as it raised his blood pressure and made his breathing more labored. And Chesley Fox Chiswell affably accommodated their preference. Sun did not intimidate him in the least. In fact, even well into his fifties, his skin continued to color to a manly cowboy shade, and his flowing hair, moustache, and goatee continued to bleach attractively so that he looked like a cross between a legendary rock star and one of Rembrandt's Dutch Masters. Chesley was quite content with that combination, especially as the ladies seemed to find it appealing.

Bob, Vincent and Chesley had first met at a Liberty Artists Guild members' show some years ago. Standing around Bob's acrylic landscape at the reception, Vincent recognized the course and complimented the painting's accuracy and realism. Chesley admired the sculptural qualities of the ninth hole and compared Bob's style to Grant Wood. From that moment on, the three had an unspoken bond, not forged by their creative milieu of paint and canvas and stone, but rather of the Fraternal Order of Golf. Any time two or three of them were present in a room they gravitated toward each other and talked of handicaps and eagles and bogies and the latest in golf footwear and the pretty new girl working in the pro shop at Whitetail Cove. Eventually, casual meetings did not sufficiently feed their need to share; they began meeting once a week to play out their common dream to beat The Course and their unspoken dream to beat each other. Their mutual passion dwarfed their differences in occupation and persona— professional educator, retired oil company executive, and celebrated sculptor—and overshadowed their common avocation, that of promoting themselves through their artwork.

Despite the heat, on this particular Saturday, Vincent was breathing a little freer than usual, and his game had reflected that. Still, he felt troubled, remembering all the years when he could walk all eighteen holes, back when he was vigorous and long-strided, back before The Incident. Today was the first time he had been able to continue playing through to the last hole in two years. But now he felt fatigue creeping up on him. He sat in his own cart parked in the shade at the edge of the fairway while Chesley and Bob finished out the round. He sat very still; his thoughts were turbulent. Darker scenes and darker days not forgotten, never forgotten, flashed before his inner eye.

Suddenly, a movement in the sunshine just to his right stirred Vincent back to the present: a mockingbird poking at the ground. He began to be aware first of the green and the little peninsula of fairway surrounding it down in this far reach of the course. The other two men were just making their final putts. Vincent shifted his notice to the woods beyond, over to his right again. He had always disregarded the woods; they merely served to frame the picture that was The Course. They formed a sort of containment wall to the meandering sea of undulating manicured grass. He had never tried to look deeper, beyond the groomed facade. He saw now that there were individual trees, quite a depth of overlapping trees, and as his eyes adjusted, he perceived the movement of creatures or undergrowth or both, of actual living organisms there in the enticing shade.

At the edge of the woods, not far from where he rested, sat a light grey cat, narrowing its eyes to the sunlight and bobbing its head backward with its nose lifted to catch—what?—a trace of something in the air. Then Vincent too caught a scent, and he looked down the hill into the near-impenetrable gloom of the woods that sloped down to the lake. He could see glints of the water here and there through sparser areas. And above the treetops, down toward the water, he saw a wisp, a writhing eel-like shape of grey, rising up through the air. It seemed that someone had a cooking fire going down that way. Vincent knew as a board member of the country club that there was no beach on this cove of the lake and that there should be no habitation there either. This was all country club property or green space, as far as he knew. His brow wrinkled. He would have to mention this up at the clubhouse office later on. He himself was certainly in no shape to go investigate. Though, he had to admit, the shade, the cool, the peacefulness of the woods were inviting...

Just then, Bob and Chesley called to him as they walked toward their cart, and Vincent drove up to meet them. The two carts rode in tandem back up the fairway, skirting the woods, pursuing the shade, in no hurry to end the triumph of this day when they had all magically, inexplicably shot a seventy-eight.

They parked their carts at the pro shop. Bob and Vincent

scraped their golf shoes on the boot scraper, and sat down on a bench to wait for Chesley, who had gone into the shop for a bag of peanuts. They knew for a fact that he had really gone in to make time with the new girl. Twenty minutes later Chesley emerged, and the three walked thirty or so yards up a gentle manicured slope to the broad flagstone patio of the clubhouse, where Lorraine DiAngelo sat playing bridge with three other ladies under a large umbrella. The men stopped at the edge of the patio near the coy pond with its granite fountain, reliving aloud each hole they had just played. Vincent sat abruptly on the stone wall, winded. The gurgling and splashing of the water all but drowned out his labored breathing and the sound of the women's gossipy tones.

Chesley placed one foot on the low stone wall by the water with both hands picturesquely resting upon his raised thigh. While he chatted with his golf partners, his eye roved to the stone maiden of the fountain, spilling water endlessly from her Grecian urn. The girl's robes clung to her as if she had none on, in such a way that all the detailed nuances of her form were visible. He felt that it was one of his best works.

Eventually, as the conversation meandered along, Vincent followed the sculptor's gaze. When the fountain had first been installed, he had admired it. Now, however, he could see that the girl's head was a bit too large for her body, the neck a bit too long, the back twisted in a way not consistent with human anatomy. He prided himself in being an advanced student of the human figure. *I guess with stone,* he thought, *you can't just paint over something to fix a mistake. Well, no matter. It's nice, anyhow. Gives the place a little class to have a statue. Dresses things up a bit.*

Soon, raised voices and laughter from the bridge table punctuated the ladies' girl-talk. The slap of the cards ceased, and Lorraine tapped each trick before her with a perfectly-shaped scarlet nail. "Made it!" she said, beaming at her partner as she tidied her expert tricks into a pile, tucking in the stray cards with her lacquered nail tips. She glanced briefly over at the three men and then turned back to her companions.

"Well, girls," she said, "I see my Vincent is back, and we've got to be running along now. See you next week!" She rose and gathered her large, supple white leather bag from a chair under another nearby umbrella. From the bag a small flat face peered out, its huge eyes glistening in the dark cave.

"Time to go, Muffy," Lorraine chirped to the anxious little creature.

She turned to the men and smiled coyly. "Hello, Bob... Chesley." Bob nodded and said hello. Chesley closed his eyes, took her hand, and bowed slightly.

"Ah, the lovely Lorraine," he said. Lorraine dimpled and turned to Vincent.

"Hello, hun," she said to her husband. "Good round today?"

"Better than usual," admitted Vincent. He shook hands with the two men and said goodbye till next Saturday.

He and his wife made their way through the clubhouse, its interior dusky after their time in the sun. Vincent had a lingering feeling that he was forgetting something. He paused as they passed the club's office, straining to capture the wraithlike thought. In a moment, though, he shrugged and moved on. He realized that on the good days, the days when he was able to be free of the oxygen tank, the shiny silver cylinder's absence left him with this haunting sensation. His not-quite-grasped memories hovered about him like the ghostly images on film negatives that he used to develop during the war—underexposed, over- or double-exposed, thanks to the madness and inferno of battle—they were not there, and yet they were. It was just that he was missing the oxygen tank; that was all.

The Box Hollow Festival

The early May sky was so clear that it lifted Aylin's scalp toward it. Her pores breathed in the new air, sharp with the change in barometric pressure since last week's heat and storms. Her French sketchbox easel, two canvas stools, and the big tapestry bag fit snugly amid the stroller, diaper bag, and piles of kid stuff. Lucy slammed the hatch and pulled her sweater closer around her in the unexpected early morning chill. Aylin needed no wrap; she was always hot these days, and her bare arms relished the cool air. They climbed into the low-slung station wagon. Lucy cranked the car, and they eased out of the empty Corbie County Library parking lot, heading toward Box Hollow.

Aylin turned briefly and glanced at the three cookie cutter faces lined up in the back seat all staring at her with large inquisitive eyes. She found their silent observance odd and unsettling, like the gaze of miniature jurors in a jury box, motionless and probing. They appeared to be doing a lot of thinking, for children.

Three high-pitched chimes emitted from the dashboard as the station wagon rattled and squeaked through town. Aylin took no notice of it; she was accustomed to noisy cars.

"Is it far, out to Box Hollow?" she asked the young woman at the wheel, whose regret about coming, unbeknownst to Aylin, was deepening mile by mile.

"About thirty-five minutes," said Lucy, already thinking that it would feel twice that long. She prayed that the baby would not tune up because she sensed that the noise would irritate her passenger. The woman beside her seemed to be someone in touch with the adult world only. Still, she *had* mentioned a daughter and a grandchild...

The three chimes sounded again, and then again, precisely every sixty seconds, into the silence of the car, like a persistent, unanswered S.O.S. signal.

After some miles Lucy finally said, "I'm sorry, but it's going to keep doing that all the way if you don't fasten your seatbelt." Aylin tilted her head back, rolled her eyes, and released an audible breath through her nose. She began yanking the shoulder strap across her once, then twice again, jabbing the seatbelt clip unsuccessfully at the hard-to-reach latch. Eventually, the buckle clicked home, and the chiming ceased.

"It's a beautiful drive out this way," said Lucy.

"So you've been before?" asked Aylin, readjusting her black tank top and tugging her skirt into place beneath the seatbelt. As she shifted in her seat, an alien scent filled the car, something spicy and Eastern, Indian maybe, mixed with a more familiar odor— what *was* it? A fruity alcoholic twang, mixed with a hint of sweat. And smoke. Definitely smoke.

"I've been down this road, but I haven't been to Box Hollow itself," Lucy said. "The area used to be private farmland, all just one or two big farms, but it was bought a couple of years ago by a developer. Or that's what I gather from the newspaper, anyway. I think the festival is a way to draw people in to see the upscale houses in the model neighborhood they're building on the old pasture land. I guess they think it's a good opportunity for publicity. There's still some open field left, I hear, so we'd better enjoy it while we can." Lucy glanced down at her camera tucked between the front seats and hoped her hands would be free enough at some point to use it.

She could not think of a thing to say to fill the next long silence.

"Quiet kids, aren't they?" said Aylin eventually, jabbing her thumb over her shoulder.

"Uh, no, not usually." Lucy stole a quick glance in the rear-view mirror, wondering for the first time why they weren't squabbling or swinging their feet into the backs of the front seats or asking endless questions. There they were, strapped immobile into their boosters, like three peas in the peapod of the sage green back seat. *Sweet peas, often, but not often in the car,* she thought.

"I think you mentioned having a daughter?" Lucy asked.

"Yes. I have a daughter. She has a daughter herself. Sometimes I keep her for my daughter," said Aylin. Lucy noticed that the woman had an odd way of expressing herself now and then, as if her speech was translated, even. But that was crazy—she had no accent at all.

"So they live close by, then?"

"Sometimes." Aylin looked straight ahead and paused. "I like to give my daughter a break. Everybody needs a break now and then."

"Oh, yes. I guess that's true," Lucy said, calculating how long it had been for herself.

"So the lady doing the critique at the Guild meeting—she said you should get a babysitter. Do you have grandparents or anybody around to help with that?"

"No, no grandparents." Lucy was quiet a minute, thinking how life turned a different color when there was no longer anyone to watch over you. It had happened to her in an instant, when she was still young, losing both her parents, and her path had never seemed very clear after that.

"Sometimes I leave the children behind with my husband, but he works two jobs, and I hate to go off and leave him on child duty too often. I know how tired he is."

"Men can't deal with babies, anyway," said Aylin.

Lucy made no response. She navigated the grey strip of two-lane highway with the red clover growing high on the shoulders at the cautious rate of fifty miles per hour.

Aylin continued, "She was right, that woman at the library. You should definitely keep painting. Those flowers are leading you somewhere, and you need to follow them."

Lucy wasn't sure if this was a compliment. She wasn't sure at all what Aylin meant. She only knew the irresistible pull that those flowers at the garden show had had for her, how they attracted her, swallowed her whole, how they pulled her out of her space and time and consciousness until she felt herself one of them, a sister. It was a captivating thing, not easily denied, a thing glorious and guilty at the same time. Certainly not easily explained.

"Do you work?" Aylin asked.

"Well, no," said Lucy, never quite comfortable with that answer. "But these guys keep me busy every minute," she gestured to the back seat. "Never a dull moment, but never a quiet one either. I just steal moments here and there, and, eventually, a painting gets done, but it takes a while. I'm not very prolific.

"Kids and men." Aylin grunted. "You have a husband, you say?"

"Yes, his name is Jackson."

"You're so young—what, twenty-three? Twenty-four?"

"Twenty-six, and I don't feel so young."

Aylin snorted. "What do you want a husband for anyway? Husbands only hold you back."

"He keeps me tethered... rooted, somehow?"

"Yeah, I bet."

"No, no, not like that. He's the most solid person I've ever known. And I'm so... not solid." Why was she going on like this about Jackson, trying to defend herself? It felt weak. It was too personal, but she couldn't stop.

"We knew each other in high school. He was uncomplicated and kind, not like anyone else. I'd never had a rock like him. My parents were kind of flighty, always moving, and then they were gone from me so early, in an accident when I was eighteen. And Jackson, he's just this anchor that keeps me from drifting." *And he really knows how to love*, Lucy thought, but she didn't say that to Aylin. She felt Aylin wouldn't understand what she meant. And after all, the woman was a stranger.

Shocking bright green frisked about on the highway verge, bounded over fields, festooned trees, spring flaunting itself everywhere. Lucy refocused her eyes on the grey road. As the car grew silent again, she glanced at the car clock, still on winter time. A quick look in the rear-view mirror showed her the baby in the middle with her eyes closed, Ian stuffing Cheerios into his mouth from a baggie, and Jack staring, fascinated, at the uncontained red hair of the stranger directly in front of him. None of them were looking out the window. How was it possible that they could *not* look out the window and see all *this*? It was remarkable what a person, even a little person, did or did not see, making choices every moment with their darting glances. Or maybe it was merely the twitching of the tiny extra-ocular muscles that made the choices for them. Where the eyes go, the soul follows.

She abruptly tore her mind from its rabbit trail; she needed her wits intact for driving.

At 7:52 they pulled into the parking lot near the Box Hollow Farm Pavilion and Model Estate Properties. The entrance was unmistakable, marked by three very bright, very tall inflatable human-form tubes dancing with wind machines at their base. The boys clamored at the sight of them.

"Mama, can I have a balloon?" Ian asked from the back seat.

"No, Sweetie, that wouldn't fit in the car," Lucy told her son as she followed the signs marked "Exhibitor Parking," past the giant contorting figures, past the white gingerbread pavilion (no doubt made of PVC) by the storybook pond, past the ornate, richly-landscaped gate to the model neighborhood and on into the parking lot. She found a space reserved for exhibitors and cut the engine.

She climbed out and lifted Ian out of his carseat. "Balloon, balloon, balloon, balloon...," he sang softly. She set his little legs down on the ground and took his hand with one of hers while with the other she helped his older brother on with his backpack. In it were things without which Jack would not leave home, important things: a shark's tooth and the prized matchbox car of the day, certain rocks and an arrowhead and a ragged cardboard version of the periodic table of elements. His mother had months ago given up reasoning with him about carrying these things.

"Now Jack, I want you to take your brother's hand and don't let go. Parking lots are dangerous. We've got to keep an eye out for cars, and we can't let Ian wander off," Lucy said. Then she and Aylin unloaded all their baggage from the back of the station wagon and looked around the parking lot, already partially filled with seventy or eighty or more cars with trailers behind, trucks with campers on the back, vans, and other assorted vehicles. At the back and to one side of the lot was a wide gate marked by a string of fluorescent plastic triangles, neon yellow tape, and a sign which read: "Guest Parking / Guest Shuttles." Men in orange vests were motioning to a few early visitors' cars to drive on through while more men in orange vests directed them to parking spaces in a stubbled meadow, neatly gridded with spray paint. A series of golf carts crawled up to the gate and huddled there like one shiny overgrown caterpillar.

"Where in the world are the booths set up?" asked Lucy. "I

don't see any sign of them."

"Eleanor said that the festival is in the middle of all the property and that people are going to be bused in to it," Aylin replied.

"Oh, I see," said Lucy, uneasy, wondering what that transport would entail. "I guess that explains the golf carts? But I still don't understand how the other artists, the ones who have a lot more to set up than you do, are supposed to get all their stuff over there, wherever 'over there' is." Aylin just shrugged.

Lucy gathered the baby up from her infant seat, settled her on her hip, and locked the car. Stowing the two folding stools and some bags in the stroller, Aylin and Lucy managed to schlep their belongings over to the gate and load them onto the back of one of the longer golf carts. A young man with strawberry blonde hair and eyelashes and perfect white teeth strapped their belongings down with bungee cords and hopped behind the wheel. Aylin sat beside him, leaving the rear seat to Lucy and the three children. At least there she wouldn't have to put up with any more prying questions from Aylin. Lucy herded the boys onto the slippery vinyl and sat beside them, still holding the baby. The driver, taut beneath his golf shirt and khakis, looked over his shoulder inquiringly.

"We're ready," said Lucy, and the cart lumbered off silently across the spiky turf. They gathered speed quickly, but after several minutes there was still no festival in sight.

"So, where is this thing?" Aylin asked the driver, leaning close and squeezing his arm. The stacked bracelets on both her forearms jangled continuously with the jouncing of the cart.

"Oh, it's just over these few hills here, ma'am," he said, looking straight ahead. The cart continued to pick up speed, a remarkable amount of speed. Lucy did not know that a golf cart could go so fast. It lurched over the uneven pasture, and she felt them all set free, airborne from the seat, over every bump. She clutched the baby in her lap with one arm. She alternately tried to hold on to the cart and the two bouncing boys next to her with the other. Evie began to hold out a long note just to hear the judder in it, which made her brothers hoot. Ian slapped his knees in exaggerated imitation of his older brother.

Lucy snapped, "Boys, hold on to the cart!" as visions of their small ejected bodies flying through the air passed before her eyes. The swaying of the cart flashed her back to her fishtailing car just a few weeks ago on the way to the Guild meeting, only this time she had no steering wheel to grip.

"Ha, ha, ha, Mom! You can hold on to me if you want to, but *I'm* not holding on to *anything!*" shouted Jack. His face gleamed with fierce joy. Lucy was quite dismayed. She could not hold on tightly to all three children and keep her own self grounded in the seat. She couldn't have made her voice heard to the clueless driver in front of her over the clatter and creak of the cart and all its load if she'd tried. She clung to the baby and fussed at the boys again to hold on.

The driver kept up the reckless pace over pasture hill and vale, his legs casually slung apart, his body at ease, totally one with the cart like a bareback rider on his horse. Aylin gripped his arm over one or two of the larger bumps and drawled away, clearly enjoying her proximity to the college boy with the cosmetic muscles and the cosmetic smile. The boy never turned his face to her, not once. Lucy stole a look over her shoulder and saw that their belongings were still there, strapped to the back, rattling and shifting, but still there.

Finally, as they flew over yet another hill, she saw the festival beneath them. There was an oddly medieval look to the scene: the little tent village in the shorn field surrounded by hills with a not-too-distant tree line, peopled with bustling artists and artisans setting out their wares, banners and flags flying here and there. The temporary shops were set up in rows, shoulder to shoulder, with a few extra clusters of tents on the outskirts of it all. What was most remarkable was what was missing: power lines, buildings, roads, parking lots, neon signs, cars.

As the cart careened down the long final hillside, Lucy feared that it might keel over onto its side at any moment. Jack threw his arms straight up into the air and shouted, "Wooo-oo-ooo!" This was probably the very best day of his life, but Lucy regretted dragging the children out here to the middle of nowhere. They could have been maimed or killed on this crazy ride.

But as the cart slowed and drew up to the tent village, curiosity about the fertile field before her overcame her remorse. The crop here was not vegetable, exactly. It was all manner of bounty reformed by human hand, not just grown from the earth, but a harvest captured, shaped, molded, and beautified. From where the cart stopped, she could see ironwork, woodcarvings, paintings, pottery, sculpted and painted gourds, and stained glass. She climbed out after the boys, her legs quivering after her futile attempt to brace herself in the bounding cart.

The driver helped them unload their things and jumped back behind the wheel, thinking, no doubt, about Saturday evening, the real stuff of the day after this work was behind him. Lucy settled the baby in her stroller with a sunhat and a cookie and rounded up the boys. Aylin was giving the driver one last appreciative glance while she hefted her tapestry bag onto her shoulder.

She turned to Lucy and asked, "Okay if I stow my stools beneath the stroller?"

"Sure, I'll help you get your stuff to your spot," Lucy replied, and they wedged the folding stools on the little shelf beneath the baby. "Any idea where it is?"

"According to the information they sent me, I'm in booth space one twenty-nine," said Aylin, looking at a scrap of paper from the pocket of her skirt. She grabbed the handle of the folded sketchbox easel and headed off, weaving between the tents, looking at spray-painted numbers on the stubbly squares of ground not yet covered with art displays. Lucy followed. She pushed the stroller with some effort as it twisted and yawed over the uneven turf. The baby did not protest. Jack trailed behind his mother, and Ian trailed behind him. They formed a little meandering parade through the center of the colorful circus-like camp.

"Stick with me, boys. Jack, grab your brother's hand," she called over her shoulder, feeling sure that little Ian would wander off toward some sight or smell that drew his attention and never be seen again.

After some searching, Aylin stopped on top of a scrawled neon 129. She set down the compact easel. She slid the large bag off her shoulder and dropped it heavily on the ground. She turned around just as the others were coming into the clearing.

"O.K., this is it. Thanks for bringing the stools this far," she said to Lucy. "I'll just pull them out, and you and the kids can go do your thing."

"Do you need any help setting up? It looks like everyone else is pretty much open for business."

"Nope. You can take off. I've got this thing down to a science, I've done it so much. I'll be up and running in five minutes." She already had the stools set up, and was beginning to stretch out the legs of her compact apparatus and unfold and extend its parts so that quickly the box was transforming into an easel. Jack had followed his mother into the paint-marked square of turf and now stared in fascination at the conversion of the box.

"Mom, we *need* a box like that!" he said. At that moment Ian, who was still looking back over his shoulder in spite of all his forward momentum, careened into the back of his brother. The two boys began scuffling in the stubble.

"Boys! Jack! Ian! Get up off the ground!" Lucy said. The fight was over as fast as it started.

"Hey," Jack said to Aylin, "what comes out of that box?"

She gave him an annoyed look and said, "Art."

"Oh," he said. He looked a bit crestfallen, like he was hoping for pirate treasure.

"Okay, boys, let's go walk around and see what there is to see," Lucy said, brushing the dirt off the seat of Ian's pants. "It's time to leave Miss Aylin here to her business."

Aylin did not look up from her work setting up the easel and arranging the tools of her trade. Her hands were quick and sure below the bare arms ringed in many, many circles of glinting silver.

* * *

Cordelia Wise was unpacking her small wooden creatures from a worn egg crate when she first spied the young mother some ways off. The carver paused with a tiny fawn in her hand, watching the woman with the baby on her hip push a stroller along, one-handed, from booth to booth. Two little boys clamored around her, darting this way and that in the dazzling sunshine of the stunningly clear day.

Cordelia's tent was situated near the top of a little rise, exposed somewhat, with the sides of the tent rolled and tied back, and from where she sat in her wheelchair, she could feel that the wind had risen a bit along with the sun. She had a splendid view of the newly cut field that quivered as the breeze scampered across in endless patterns, oblivious to the human activity in its midst.

The wind tossed the young woman's long smooth dark hair, sometimes to one side, sometimes to the other. The baby laughed and laughed as she tried to catch the silky dancing hair in her little fist. She might as well have been trying to grasp flowing water. The baby seemed to think this game was designed for her own personal delight, and her delight was the delight of Cordelia's own heart in that instant. The corners of her mouth did not lift in a smile. She had long since lost that ability, but she had not lost her capacity for joy, which had grown, strangely, along with her growing inability to show it.

She turned her eyes again to her task. She smoothed down the fruit-patterned vinyl tablecloth where it lifted in the wind and anchored it with some larger carvings she excavated from the crate. The two card tables weren't large enough to hold all of her creatures, so she turned the crate on end, covered it with a square of muslin, and arranged more carvings on top—a tiny open boat with even tinier animals in it and around it. Printed sideways on the make-shift pedestal were the words: 30 Dozen—Fragile—EGGS—Keep Refrigerated.

Off to one side of the card table menagerie, Cordelia set a basket, shaped like a shallow open bowl, intricately woven of smooth, sienna-colored pine needles. The basket was empty but for a small card lettered with archaic capitals: GIFTS. Beside the basket Cordelia placed several piles of pamphlets. She laid a polished twist of wood on top to keep the fitful breeze from blowing them. She wheeled herself backward a bit to focus better and survey all that she had arranged. She nodded curtly.

Then she reached deep into the pocket of the apron tied around her middle and pulled out into her lap an X-Acto knife and several small gnarled chunks of wood. She picked up the wood piece by piece, turning each one round and round, fingering it gingerly, thoughtfully. She finally settled on one. She snapped the blade out into position. She gripped the piece in one hand while she sliced and gouged and smoothed with the X-Acto knife held in the other. And all this shaping of the throwaway scrap, the wooden piece that looked like nothing promising in any way, Cordelia did with large, sure, strong hands, stopping to finger the wood time and time

60

again. She rarely looked down at the work in her lap but saw it keenly in her mind's eye. Her touch was sensitive and knowing, and the razor-sharp blade of the knife did not cut into her skin.

Cordelia sat in her chair carving under the luminous, gently-flapping white tent top. She was completely still except for her tireless hands and her eyes roving continuously over the dozens of industrious, hopeful artists, both near and a ways off, each in his or her individual cells as if they were honeybees in a teeming honeycomb. She watched the first visitors trickle in.

"Cordelia, do you have everything set the way you want it?" asked a young man striding up to her booth. "Can I help you do anything else before the hordes arrive?"

"You've done enough, Eli, just getting me here, setting up the tent and all," Cordelia answered. "I don't need another thing. Now you go on and sell your pictures. Look, there are some folks now, looking at your paintings."

"Sure? You don't need coffee or anything?"

"No, Eli. Got my water here. I'm fine." She held up an oversized clear plastic drinking bottle with "St. Mary's Hospital" printed on the side.

"O.K. Just flag me down if you need anything," the young man said as he waved once and re-crossed the grassy aisle to his own booth. Cordelia watched as Eli walked up to a woman with sunglasses on top of her head and a fancy pocketbook who was studying his paintings. They talked for a while, and eventually he took a check from the woman and reached down two paintings which she in turn handed to her male companion to carry. Cordelia watched Eli hang two more canvases expertly on the portable walls he had constructed a few years ago when he had outgrown the little white tent she sat under now, back when he had started the art show circuit in earnest. Inwardly she smiled. Eli was a hardworking, generous soul with a good eye. And given time, he would learn to *see*; she was sure of it. He was an old soul, in spite of his twenty-nine years. She set the new figure she had fashioned on the card table and began anew, fingering another piece of castaway wood, feeling for some direction the shape should go.

A series of carts moved intermittently over the hilltop towards the festival. The carts deposited visitors in two's and three's near Cordelia's corner of the show and in turn retreated in the direction from which they had come, like a line of foraging ants. Little by little the visitors came by Cordelia's tent. Most glanced her way and walked on by.

The first group to stop was a well-dressed couple, each one absorbed in a palm-sized electronic device, trailing a boy of perhaps nine. Cordelia did not pay much attention to technology—she really had no use for it—but she knew enough about it to peg these people as strangers to the area. They had not yet figured out that cell phone reception here in this county that was largely covered in farmland, national forest, and long-abandoned cotton fields was hopeless. None of the natives bothered with the things. And then, too, there were their citified clothes.

"Hey," said the boy.

"Hello, young man. I am Cordelia. And who might you be?"

"Tristan. I'm Tristan. What are you doing?"

"I'm carving. Want to see?" He came a bit closer, eyeing her wheelchair.

"Yeah, so, what's all this stuff?" he asked, looking around him.

"These are things I carve from roots and branches and bits of wood. I just make whatever my mind takes a fancy to make."

"So, what do they cost? I don't see prices anywhere."

"They *don't* cost. If you see something you like, you may have it, and take one of these pamphlets too."

"Sweet," the boy said as he pocketed a handful of the creatures and turned to go.

"Oh, wait, young man," said Cordelia. "Don't forget the pamphlet. And take one for each of your parents, too."

"O.K., sure." The boy jammed some of the paper booklets in his back pocket and wandered off toward a nearby booth. The woman and the man sauntered after him, still engrossed in their palms, sensing that the boy had moved on. Cordelia watched after them a moment.

Some yards off, the man glanced up from his phone. "Hey, what's that you got in your pocket, Bud?" he asked.

"Just some papers the old lady made me take," the boy said, shrugging. "Got a pile of rocks on the front of it."

"Rocks, huh? And what else do you have in there?" persisted the father.

"Oh, yeah, this wooden stuff she made."

"Really? How much did it cost?"

"I don't know. Nothing. She said it was free."

"That's a crock. Nothing's free. People don't just..."

They wandered out of earshot.

Cordelia noticed quite a little crowd gathering in Eli's fine tent across the way, although generally speaking attendance at the festival was rather sparse so far. She watched as several more visitors left his booth with paintings under their arms. All the while that she surveyed the scene, her hands were busy in her lap.

Quite some time went by, and the water from the St. Mary's jug took its effect on Cordelia. She wheeled herself slowly, deliberately, far over to the other side of the display area, all of which was slightly downhill from where her tent huddled off to one side and a little way apart from the rest. She found a row of porta-potties squatting there labeled "Jiffy John," testaments to human haste and waste. She rolled her chair up close to one end of the row and waited for a vacancy.

She watched two little boys digging with sticks in the dirt near her, and presently the door to one of the units opened. The young dark-haired mother she had seen earlier stepped out holding the sleepy baby cradled over her ribs with one arm, adjusting her bra strap under the shoulder of her shirt with the other. Cordelia thought how tricky it would be to nurse a baby in that tiny space, sitting over a putrid hole with the urinal mounted on the side wall, perilously close to the baby's head or the mother's elbow. She thought how hot and still the air would be with the scratched skylight overhead distorting and magnifying the pure May sunshine. She thought how sad it was that the beautiful giving act of the mother should be relegated to the privacy of this abysmal water closet.

In fact, the mother looked red-faced and sweaty. But the baby, with the firm, pink cheeks of the well-sated, seemed content. Her mother laid her in the stroller parked nearby and pulled the shade further over the top. Then she drew out a water bottle from the bag hanging on the back of the stroller and began trying to wash her hands with it. She was rubbing vigorously but losing water too fast to do much good.

Cordelia spoke. "Dear, there's a row of outdoor faucets at the other end."

The young woman started, not having noticed someone close by with all her intent focus on her hands.

"Little portable sinks," Cordelia went on. "You may find that easier for washing hands, and you can fill your water bottle to your heart's content." The young woman's face reddened still more, but she looked relieved.

"Oh, thank you so much! That's just what we need," she said as she herded the little boys and the stroller over to the other side.

"Mom, why did she call you a deer?" the older of the two boys asked his mother as they strolled away, his face turned up to hers. The smaller boy was following behind watching over his shoulder the lengthening mark of the stick he was dragging behind him in the hard red clay where the grass had been worn away.

Cordelia waited again; someone more mobile had quickly occupied the unit. At last, she pushed herself up out of the wheelchair with considerable effort and claimed the Jiffy John for herself, dragging her right leg as she walked the few steps to the threshold, leaving a mark of her own in the red clay.

* * *

Jack was quick and agile; he flitted and hovered, never quite alighting, like a young dragonfly in endless pursuit of its infinitesimal prey. He darted in and out of the booths while his mother tried her best to keep him in sight, hampered by the unruly stroller. Evie was sitting up in it at the moment with her tiny legs sticking straight out in front of her. She lurched and reeled with the jolting, but she held on to the padded front bar with unlikely strength, her sun hat slipping down toward her nose while she babbled secrets to the cropped blades of grass below her toes. She had had to remove her socks simply because of their sheer removability, and she had cast them overboard on random occasions over the warming course of the morning.

Eventually, their mother wearied of trying to keep track of the quick boy out front and the dawdling one in the rear, so she scooped up Ian and wedged him in the stroller behind his sister. He wailed with the removal of his stick.

"Look, Ian, I'm putting your stick right here under the seat, and you can have it back later," said Lucy. Ian sniffled a bit but seemed resigned. He popped a thumb in his mouth and threw himself backward flat on the stroller bed to gaze straight upward. His large round grey eyes reflected three tiny white clouds scudding far above in the otherwise pristine sky.

Lucy followed Jack as he wended his way through three or four rows of open walkways between booths that were arranged in a long chain on either side, most with tents or canopies, some without. She could see clear across to the opposite side of the festival space from the porta-potties they had just left, over to where a tent sat apart, just a bit higher at the knee of the hill over which continued the trickle of golf carts bringing a few more visitors. She realized just then that the festival seemed fairly unpopulated, and this at nearly noon. The thin crowd was better, safer, for her sake with the children, but she thought that it was a shame for the artists. At that moment she passed by a deluxe-looking booth with a well-dressed older couple sitting in director's chairs, and she heard the man say, "We should not have made the effort to come, Lorraine. I'm all out of breath today, and there is no audience to speak of for my work."

Lucy slowed and let her gaze linger as the woman replied, "Yes, hun, but now we're here, we might as well stay a bit longer. Maybe the big spenders will come on out after lunch." She tapped his hand with long, expensive fingertips. The manicure appealed to Lucy's memory. The exquisite nails and then the large murky oil paintings behind the couple which Lucy had at first overlooked brought to her mind a certain awkward moment at the Liberty Artists Guild meeting last month. The pair were oblivious to her passing by, and she had no thought as to what to say to them about the artwork, or about herself for that matter, nor could she even remember their name. Was it something Italian?

She did not speak and continued on past, pushing her load firmly. She had discovered that keeping the stroller moving, however slowly, over this rough old pasture was easier than stopping and fighting inertia to get it started rolling again.

And there was Jack, on up ahead at the end of the row of booths, jumping around, grinning, and waving wildly at her.

"Mom, Mom! Look at this stuff! You just gotta see this, Mom!" he hollered. She pushed past intricately designed dyed eggs, home-spun wool shawls, and hand-thrown pottery, all of which she longed to investigate, until finally she reached the end of the grassy aisle. She stopped short. The hand-painted board sign over the booth Jack had found read "Corbie-Well Organic," and there stood another familiar person from the artists guild, off to the side, brushing down a brown mule tethered there.

"Mom, this is great! It's a real live mule, Mom! He says her name is Sadie!" said Jack, hopping on one foot and then the other.

Lucy laughed. "Hello there, James the Organic Farmer. I never imagined I'd see you here," she said to the young man who had shown her his sketchbook full of mules and plows at the meeting the month before.

"Yeah, I know. Truth is, I just need some publicity for the farm. I'm going to need people to come out and buy some of the produce that'll come rolling in in another couple of months. Folks that run this show, they're all Green, said they'd give me a free booth if I wanted, and, well, sure, free is good, right? So here I am." He grinned at Lucy.

By this time, Ian had clambered out of the stroller and sidled up to his brother, near the mule. Suddenly Sadie stretched her sturdy neck over and lowered her muzzle to the top of Ian's head, chomping gently, experimentally on the boy's thick hay-colored hair. Ian rolled his eyes upward to see but did not move.

"No, no! Sadie! Here's your hay!" said James, thrusting a handful of the real stuff under her muzzle.

"Sorry, Buddy. You okay?" he said to the boy.

Lucy picked up Ian, whose face was beginning to cloud over, and smoothed down his hair. "No harm done," she murmured.

"Hey, did you bring any of your artwork?" she asked James over Ian's head. She looked around the booth at the antique tools displayed there, the tiny brown envelopes of heirloom seeds, and the collection of home-canned jellies from last summer.

"Oh, no. I wouldn't put them up at something like this. Not with all these real artists," he answered with a grin.

"You should, you know. It's another dimension to your farm, another thing you do with your hands. It's organic too. It grows out of you and out of the work you do."

A merciless tugging on her sleeve brought her eyes down to Jack's beaming face. "Mom, can I ride her? Please?"

"Uh, well..." began Lucy.

"Tell you what, Buddy," said James, "she's an ornery old girl, and doesn't take too kindly to somebody on her back, so we better not try it today." Lucy was very grateful. Jack's face fell, then brightened again.

"Look at this thing, Mom! He says it's a real live plow, a real old one, with real leather straps and everything!" Sure enough, there next to the booth was an ancient-looking iron plow.

"And he says he uses it to plow up his dirt! Can you believe it? Can we get one of these?"

Lucy laughed some more. "No, we don't have farmland to plow up the way he does, Jack." She looked over at the lightly bearded young man and smiled. Jack shook off his disappointment and dashed off to the next spot of interest.

James smiled back at Lucy and said, "That's a great kid you got there. Lots of curiosity!"

"Oh, yes, he's got that!" Lucy replied as she leaned her weight against the stroller to get it started again. "I'll see you at the next meeting then?"

"Yeah, I'll be there."

"Keep drawing," she called over her shoulder as she followed Jack around the corner. James busied himself again with brushing down the spoiled four-legged girl who stood swishing her tail, stamping, and twitching her long ears jealously.

As Lucy rounded the corner into the next aisle, she could see that Jack was standing silent before a worn tent-top, gazing at something she could not yet see. When she neared the booth with Ian and the baby now tangled together drowsily in the stroller, she looked back and forth from the five-year-old to the occupants of the tent. A brown-skinned man with shoulder-length curls dressed in a crisp white shirt and jeans sat in a folding chair with a board across his lap, painting. Surrounding him on several long folding tables were dozens of eight-by-ten canvases covered with every conceivable Georgia landscape in every conceivable mood and color. They were the same, and yet they were not. Red hand-painted letters on a piece of cardboard read: "Art by Orvelle—25 Dollars." In the shadow, at the rear of the booth space behind the man in the blazing white shirt, sat a bulky woman, bent over bits of brightly colored shapes in her lap, arranging and rearranging. Jack was mesmerized by the man and his board and his attention to the half-painted canvas. The finished pictures held no appeal for him, nor did the woman and her shapes almost lost in the background.

After watching for a few minutes in silence, Jack moved over next to his mother's side and they moved on together. He was unusually quiet. He reached in the stroller and patted the baby.

"Mom, when are we going to eat?" he asked with a note of desperation. Lucy realized that the shadows had shrunk to neat squares beneath the tents and that it must now indeed be noon. She could rely on Jack's stomach to be an accurate timepiece for the day, any day.

"Okay, Jack, we'll work our way out to the hillside over there. That looks like a good place for a picnic, doesn't it?" she asked. He nodded soberly, and they continued on down the last row of booths. They passed painters of all kinds, the cabinet maker she recognized from the April meeting with his wooden bowls, potters, a basket maker. At the end of the row stood a large tent with tall display panels draped in raw linen and a beautifully painted carved sign that read: "Eli Cooper: Fine Art."

"Let's just step in here a minute, Jack, and then we'll go have our lunch," said Lucy, now in the lead. Seeing that the cumbersome stroller could not navigate the narrow zig-zag path through the booth's display, she parked the two sleepy children under the corner overhang of the tent in gentle shadow. She took her older boy's hand. They wandered into the portable gallery and through the maze of draped panels, looking in turn at each large canvas hung there. The walls and the paintings and the tent supports barely moved in the little wind gusts, so solid and well-anchored was the whole display. The paintings were abstract meditations of color and texture, layer upon layer of acrylic color thickened, tamed, and scraped away in places like lovely scars.

As Jack reached his hand toward one of the paintings, Lucy said, "No, Jack! We can't touch the artwork!" The boy pulled his hand back. Lucy had only just resisted the temptation to feel of the complex surface herself.

"Sure he can touch it," said a voice just then. Lucy looked away from the painting to see a young man coming near them, and her face pinkened.

"This picture isn't just another pretty face," he said, his glance lingering on Lucy. "It has depth. I'm glad he sees that."

Then he turned to Jack and said, "I'm Eli. And you are Jack? Pleased to meet you." He stuck out his hand toward the boy, and they shook, Jack wide-eyed with his eyebrows up and his mouth open a bit. Eli looked to be in his late twenties or early thirties, with long-ish unruly brown curls and smooth olive skin.

Jack reached his hand back to the canvas, his pointer finger held out straight to feel the painted surface. He pulled it back and looked quickly at Eli.

"What makes it so rough?" he asked.

"Very astute question. The acrylic paint I use is like plastic. It's smooth and slick. I add a powder to some of the layers called pumice and mix it in real good, and when the paint dries, which is pretty fast, it's bumpy like this. I can scrape it and sand it and get all kinds of colors to show through from underneath."

He looked at Lucy then. "Paint, dry, scrape, paint, dry, scrape: I'm my own force of nature shaping up the image." In fact, the textures of the paintings did remind her of a weathered mountain outcropping or a creek bed or the bark of a tree. But he was smiling wryly, not taking himself too seriously.

His eyes were green with curly dark lashes. One eyelid was lower, slightly, perpetually, but whatever the cause of the peculiarity, it did not seem to affect his vision. His gaze was a bit unsettling. And he seemed so familiar, somehow, but Lucy was sure she had not met him before.

"Your paintings are incredible," she said. "I don't think I would ever get tired of looking at them. There's so much there that you don't see at first."

"Oh, thanks. Are you an artist yourself?"

"Oh, yes, I guess so. Well, I don't have much time to spend on it because of my... Oh! Let me go check on my two little... Um, they're parked just outside here." And Lucy dashed a few steps around the panels to see that the baby and Ian were still content. They seemed to be asleep. She returned to Jack and the painter, Eli, and said, "They're fine... Everything's fine... And, uh, yes, I just do a little watercolor painting." Eli nodded.

"And I've done a few murals as well," she added.

"Do you exhibit anywhere, any shows or galleries?" asked Eli.

"No, not really, not yet, but I am working on some watercolors for the show the Liberty Artists Guild is having at the Historical

Society headquarters in June."

"Oh, really? I've heard of the Guild, but I didn't realize they were doing a show. I'd like to see what some of the other artists in the area are doing."

"I'm sure you'd be welcome to come to the meetings and all, the first Thursday of the month at the library. I just started going myself."

"I'm not much for meetings. But would they allow outsiders to exhibit in that show, do you think?"

"I guess if you paid the Guild dues—which aren't much, thirty dollars—they'd be happy to have you join in the show. Your paintings are just so good and so different from everything else the people in the Guild are doing." He nodded thoughtfully. They talked a few minutes about painting. Jack began to clamor for food again, and Lucy sighed and started to move toward the entrance.

"Oh, may I have one of your cards?" she asked as she noticed a pile of them on the small antique table set up in the booth. "I like to collect cards from the artists I meet, to help me remember, later on. And for inspiration."

"Oh, sure. Please. Take one," said Eli, handing her a granite-grey card. "And do you have a card?"

"Me? Uh, yes. Yes, I do, actually," she said, reaching into two or three pockets before coming up with one. It had been softened by a couple of trips through the laundry. As she handed it to him, an errant puff of wind blew several of his cards off the desk onto the stubbled ground. Lucy bent down to help Eli gather them up, and her eyes fell upon his shoes. They were old-fashioned heavy black brogans, well-worn, maybe even ancient, but still completely intact, wrinkled up and curved at the bending place of the foot, molded to the wearer after no telling how many years of use. They certainly seemed older than Eli himself. The wiry black laces looked kinked and brittle, like they had not been untied in a very long time, like they perhaps could not even be untied anymore. But the most striking thing about the shoes was that their blackness was showered with a galaxy of tiny paint spatters.

Lucy looked up, straightened, and smiled. "I guess we'd better go now. I'm really glad we got to see your work."

"I'm glad you came by. It was nice to meet you...," he looked at the card, "Lucy Bloom. I hope I get to see *your* work sometime."

Lucy colored again, unaccountably. She nodded, not knowing what else to say.

"Oh, and um, you might like to go by the white tent set up on the slope across the way—the woman over there makes little animals. And she loves children. Just be prepared, though—you might get stuck there a while if she gets going with one of her stories."

"O.K., thanks, I'll keep it in mind. Bye."

Eli the Painter just smiled and lifted his hand.

Jack had bounded on out to the stroller, and when she caught up, he was making monkey faces for his brother and sister. Ian was still lying back, rubbing his eyes, but the baby was sitting up laughing at Jack from her belly with no sign of sleep about her. She had been faking it. Lucy removed the lock from the stroller wheels and leaned into the handle. Looking around, she saw a lone white tent top across the way and began pushing her load over to the gentle slope beside it.

Lucy maneuvered the buggy to a stop sideways, a little way up the incline, secured the brake lever, and pulled out an old Indian blanket from under the stroller. She spread it on the ground and smoothed it down, feeling for the thousandth time in her life the familiar old knotty surface. Its fuzz had long ago been lost to the inevitable pilling of beloved blankets; it was perfect for Evie. She lay on her belly, propped up on her arms, scratching with a persistent little inchworm of a finger at one tiny ball of pilled blanket after another. Evie entertained herself in this way while Lucy set out their sandwiches, cookies, and water in paper cups.

When Ian saw his mother unpack the food, he began to wail, feeling pangs and suddenly knowing them for what they were. She sat down cross-legged on the blanket, and the boys did the same. She handed them a sandwich half, and they charged into their food with gusto, like they had not eaten in days. She ate a little herself, while Evie became more and more quarrelsome with the blanket, carrying on an argument that only she understood. When she began to cry outright, her mother picked her up and sat her in her lap.

Lucy looked around. There were very few visitors on this side of the festival ground, and those who were seemed to be absorbed in the artists' booths. The porta-potties were doing steady business, but they were on the opposite side of the field. In the white tent a little way beyond where she had laid the blanket, she could see a woman working on something in her lap, completely engrossed in her handwork. So Lucy decided to do what she never did in the open: She cradled the baby, who was already tossing her head back, pulled her shirt out of the top of her jeans, and tucked the baby under it. She was sure that anyone who did look her way would not realize what she was doing. Mostly sure.

She leaned forward a bit and the curtain of her hair fell forward, sheltering the nursing baby a little more. She closed her eyes, and for that moment, she and the baby were alone in a perfect sphere of contentment, the distant sounds of the make-shift village, of visitors, of artists going about their business, of a few animals, of whispering electric vehicles, of a plane far overhead, and even of the two little boys closer by, dedicated to their chewing, murmuring softly in their satisfaction, all blended in a hum outside and far beyond that momentary bubble of mother and infant.

Fifteen or twenty minutes passed. The baby was satisfied and drowsy, in earnest this time, and the boys had eaten up all the food Lucy had packed. She rolled the baby onto the blanket and covered her with a well-worn flannel diaper, as white and thin as a gentle dusting of snow, then shifted her own position so that the baby lay in her shade. She looked around her at the splendid day and thought how safe it felt here, cupped in this hollow, almost like... a basin, yes a basin of holy water, set apart from the complex world, placidly reflecting the sky, awaiting the bestirring of the priest's hand for baptism.

She wondered again what on earth had gotten into her to decide to come, but it had worked out all right, for the most part. The kinship she felt with these people, these artists, all making things, all using their hands, had taken her by surprise. The itch to paint was growing stronger. She thought of her camera, settled by gravity and the stroller's jostling to the bottom of the diaper bag, unused. Some days her hands were too occupied by life to take even a few photographs. But she would commit the beauty of the day to heart.

Lucy shook off her musings as the two boys scampered over to the unassuming nearby booth. She sat a while longer, watching, and presently Ian and Jack ran back to her with something in their hands.

"Look, Mom!" "Look, look, Mama!" "Look what the old lady over there gave us!" clamored the boys. They stood side-by-side, each cupping their palms together, their round eyes proclaiming disbelief at their good fortune of the treasures bestowed upon them: little wooden figures, creatures carved and rough, but with character and full of innocence.

"Come see what all she has, Mom!" Jack said.

"Come see, come see!" shouted Ian.

Lucy picked up the baby, diaper cloth and all, and nestled her against her chest, her sleep-limp body collapsed into a floppy little peanut shape with her face against Lucy's neck. Lucy stood a little unsteadily, found her balance, and then followed the galloping boys over to the tent.

Like a sharp nudge she recognized the woman from over near the porta-potties, seated there in her wheelchair, and was vaguely ashamed that the recognition had come from the woman's disability, not from her face.

"Oh, hello!" Lucy said. "I didn't realize you were over here in this tent! It's a nice spot for a picnic, with this view that you have."

"Yes, my dear, hello. I was wondering when you would come to see me," said the woman in the wheelchair, as if they were old friends.

Lucy was perplexed. "Have we met before? I don't believe I know your name."

"No, not really, only way over there near the latrines a little while ago. But sitting here where I am, I can look out over everybody, especially the children, and I've seen you from time to time walking about, enjoying the festival." She paused. Lucy felt the woman smiling somehow, although the corners of her mouth remained unmoved.

"I am Cordelia Wise," said the woman. Although she looked like a pauper, she measured out each word like a solemn queen.

"Lucy. Lucy Bloom. It's nice to meet you."

"Look what she makes, Mom! Just look at it all!" shouted Jack.

"All right, now, Jack. I'm looking. You just need to turn your volume down," said Lucy.

"Look, look!" shouted Ian.

"O.K., Sweetie, I'm looking." Lucy patted his shoulder for just a moment before he wriggled away. "It's wonderful."

Cordelia had turned her attention to the children. "Now, boys, have you seen these animals over here? They are the smallest, but they're my favorites. And see the little boat they have to sail in? My animals are all friends. They don't squabble or eat each other!"

Jack picked up the boat and rubbed the smooth side with his palm. "How do you decide what to make next?" he asked.

"Well, you see, I study the pieces of wood with my fingers, and try to feel what they want to be, and then I imagine what that would look like and I just start smoothing off the extra pieces with my knife here until that creature is set free."

"How come you don't get cut? My mother says not to touch knives because they can hurt you."

"Yes, your mother is right. But I have used my knife for so long now that we know each other well, and my fingers know just the time to stop before they touch the sharp part of the blade."

Ian held up an odd wooden figure to Cordelia and asked, "What's this?"

"Oh, my dear, that is a special creature I made up. It's not any animal on the face of the earth, but it is what that piece of wood wanted to be, and I love it all the more because people don't have a name for it."

"And how about these?" joined in Lucy. "These larger twisted woodcarvings here?"

Cordelia turned her gaze upon Lucy. Her eyes were huge behind large plastic-frame glasses of a few decades ago. The lenses were filmy with the tiny scratches of thousands of rubbings-away of dust and debris. But the eyes behind them were soft and bright, their color shifting with her thoughts, like opals in firelight. Her hair seemed to be of considerable length, rolled back out of the way and pinned there, not yet fully grey.

"These sculptures are the same," said Cordelia. "I just study their shape and imagine what's inside them. They come from the roots of a particular tree in a particular swamp, or what used to be a swamp, way up in Virginia. Not the great big one that everyone knows. No, this was a smaller swamp tucked away in the midst of the forest, not too far from the Great Dismal."

Lucy sensed a story coming on, something out of this world, a fairy tale, maybe, of Cordelia's own spinning.

"A long time ago, it was a beautiful place with branches hanging down low over the water lilies, and cattails and foxtails and yellow-eyed grass crowding the banks of the little waterways, much more beautiful than you would ever think a swamp could be. Dappled light filtered down through the high whispering leaves, through the trailing jasmine and wisteria and Spanish moss, and here and there the sky shone down from the heavens and up from the water at the same time. Frogs and birds and insects all made the loveliest music.

"Sweethearts would sometimes glide canoes through it, though they had to travel far to find it, and sometimes they couldn't *even* find it, because it wasn't near the city. It was tucked away in one of the back places. But my tough, sun-browned feet knew all the higher pine-needle-covered trails. I was born and raised in those parts, you see. Never had a need for store-bought playthings; little turtles and salamanders and weavings of pine needles and vines and wildflowers were my playthings. The birds got used to seeing me. They seemed to think I was just one of them, and often they would come quite close and peer at me with their wise little black-bead eyes.

"After a time, the swamp water all drained away and dried up—nobody knew why—and a fire came and burned through the undergrowth and trees that used to be homes for all kinds of little animals and birds and such. Then the mud was dried and cracked and scorched from the fire. The animals were gone: squirrel, possum, raccoon, white-tail, black bear—all gone. Fish were gone, and salamanders and little water snakes, all gone. Nobody ever went there anymore. There was nothing left. But I would still go, now and then, and sit in the midst of the dead old swamp, to listen and to watch, like I had when it was alive. It was absolutely silent, and that made me sad.

"But after many, many visits, I began to hear a humming sound, like something was alive thereabouts, like insects or something, but I could see nothing living in all that place. I felt the earth vibrate, trembling up through my feet, like the low music from the largest pipes of an organ that you feel more than hear. I went home and asked my sister, 'Did we have an earthquake?' 'No, no earthquake' was the answer. I went back. Again and again.

"Finally I began to see what *was* there: These roots were there. They were everywhere around me, protruding from the shrunken mud. And I began to really look at them, not as burned-up trash, but as things that might have captured some of the beauty that used to be there in that swamp. I thought to myself, 'Of course all that beauty couldn't just disappear without a trace, could it?' All that energy and life must be trapped somehow, somewhere. Maybe I could see a way to set those things free. And that is the very day I began carving, and these little carved things you see here are the things that were trapped in that swamp—it wasn't dead at all! It was just waiting for someone to come along and wake it up, like Sleeping Beauty and her prince."

Lucy and the two boys were speechless.

Cordelia went on. "You see these roots here, how the faces are carved into them? They are just the old, old spirit of the swamp peering out." She held one of the twisting roots out to them, and Ian and Jack each traced the kind, wizened visage with a finger. "The Good Lord of Heaven and Earth has put more life into the natural things around us than we could ever know. We see them as dumb or dead or separate from us, but that's because we're not really paying attention. What God has made—be it rock or tree or bird or person—can never die, only change.

"Listen, now, boys," said Cordelia. "I want you to take the little boat with you and all these little creatures that go with it, and I want you to play with them, but also take good care of them, because I think your little sister here will need for you to tell her this story one day. She is too little to hear it now for herself, but you can be the guardians of the story."

Jack nodded, looking thoughtful. "What happens when you run out of sticks?" he asked.

"Oh, I'll never run out of these roots. I can't go out to the swamp anymore myself, as you can see, but my sister can arrange to get me some. Eli sometimes goes to Virginia to visit her—she is his mother, you see—and she always thinks to send him out to the swamp to dig me up a few. I will never run out! Bless Eli's heart."

Lucy looked across the grass at Eli's booth. The relationship between the two artists surprised her considerably; one so young and vigorous, the other so old and frail; one's art so sophisticated, the other's so simple. They seemed nothing alike, not in any way, except that they were both makers.

Lucy looked back at the woman in the wheelchair. She noticed then the translucence of Cordelia Wise: Her skin was like onion paper, only softer—like delicate, undyed silk that swathed her fragile frame with the drapiness of age, the ropy veins running beneath undisguised, branching haphazardly like the trees that once lived in the faraway swamp. While gazing at the children, her unsmiling face looked nevertheless radiant, pale and smooth, luminous from some inner light, as if she were beginning to transfigure.

"Now, boys, gather your little boat and the little animals together," said the rootcarver, "and here—here is a little canvas bag you can tote them in. This is from me to you."

"That is such a wonderful gift, Miss Cordelia," Lucy said. "Boys, you need to say thank you."

"Thank you," Jack said.

80

"Thank you," said Ian. "Mama, how do you say the lady's name?"

"Can you say, 'Cordelia'?"

"Goodie?"

"No, Kuh-deal-ya." Lucy parceled the name out with the old southern pronunciation the woman herself had used.

"Goodie. And what's her other name?"

"Her other name is Wise. Miss Cordelia Wise."

"What does wise mean, Mama?"

"It's just her name, Sweetie."

"O.K.," Ian said. "Thank you Miss Goodie Wiselady," he said, patting her leg.

Lucy sighed. Cordelia's eyes laughed.

"Your carvings are so beautiful," Lucy said. "I'd like to give you something in return, but all I have with me is a ten-dollar bill," and she placed it in the bowl-shaped basket with the card that said "GIFTS." Alexander Hamilton looked mighty lonely in the basket.

"I wish I had more to give."

"Thank you, that is most kind, my dear." The old woman cocked her head to one side.

"But I wonder... I know it is bold to ask, but might I hold your little one just a moment? It's been so very long since I held a baby."

"Oh, certainly," said Lucy, and she lifted Evie off her shoulder, smoothed her damp dress, and placed the sleepy child in Cordelia's arms. Startled from her sleep, the baby shuddered a bit, twisted and stretched. Lucy was afraid she would cry and disconcert the old woman. But Evie opened wide her deep blue eyes and gazed up into the old woman's soft face. Then the baby came all aglow with a sudden smile that showed her four tiny teeth. She reached up her hand to Cordelia's cheek.

It seemed to Lucy that the two had some kind of communication going on that she was not privy to, and she wandered a few steps away to look again around the small booth. A stronger gust of wind shuddered and swayed the spindly tent-poles and rifled a stack of papers. The movement drew Lucy's attention to a large stack of folded pamphlets on top of one of the card tables with a long polished root laid across to hold them down, something she had missed before. She pulled a paper from out of the pile. On the front was a crude charcoal sketch of a spring, or a stone fountain of some kind, with water flowing from it. Around the fountain was a suggestion of tree branches, moss, cattails, wildflowers, and flying insects. She opened the pamphlet and saw handwritten in careful archaic lettering with serifs long since forsaken:

Let him that is Athirst Come.
And Whosoever Will,
Let him Take of the Water of Life Freely.

And on the facing page, more writing, a story of some kind.

A tract, then. Lucy folded it up. Her hand moved automatically to put the pamphlet back in the pile, then paused in mid-air and tucked it in her back pocket instead. She sent a covert glance at Cordelia, thinking that the woman was sweet but must have unrealistic hopes for her audience here at the festival if she thought she could disseminate even a fraction of this number of tracts. Still, Lucy thought she might look at the pamphlet again at home, show the picture to the boys and ask them what they thought of the story their new acquaintance had told them today.

Evie was sitting up now and getting restless, though the old woman held her securely. All the vitality left in Cordelia's body seemed to reside in her large muscular hands, toughened, thickened, and strengthened by the constant carving. The boys, too, were scampering around a little too much. Lucy walked up to the wheelchair and squatted down.

"We'll be going home soon," she said as she gathered the baby back up, "but I'm so glad we met you today."

"Oh, the pleasure was mine, dear," said Cordelia. She paused a moment. Her huge eyes behind the thick magnifying glasses studied Lucy's face. "You are a *rich woman!*" she said.

Lucy was taken aback. Of all the adjectives she would've used to describe herself, that would not have been one. She shifted the baby on her hip, tongue-tied for a moment. She felt her face flush.

"Well, I, um, never thought about it... about my life that way before." Then she shook her head to dismiss her confusion and smiled.

"Thank you again for the wonderful gifts to the children. We will treasure them. Maybe there's something I can get you before we leave?"

"No, my dear. I have everything I need. And besides, Eli looks in on me from time to time."

"Oh, yes. Eli," Lucy murmured as she glanced back across the grass toward the linen-wrapped booth. She felt an impulse to take Cordelia's hand and warm it in her own, but the woman's hands were already busy again in her lap, so she merely said goodbye and called to the boys. She noticed as they moved out of the tent that in the pine-needle bowl on the card table was her ten-dollar bill— and Jack's very best matchbox car.

"Jack, you left your car behind."

"I know, Mom. I put it there. It's for the lady," he said matter-of-factly.

"That was a very generous thing to do, Jack Bloom." He shrugged and dashed away. She pondered this, how her son never ceased to surprise her, as she packed up their belongings at the picnic spot.

She heard Cordelia Wise calling faintly, "Goodbye Jack,

goodbye Ian, goodbye Little Evie," from the unsmiling mouth in the unmoving face. Lucy looked back to the solitary figure under the white tent on the slope and raised her hand in farewell.

She felt the benevolent, unwavering gaze follow after them. She sensed that Cordelia could see them all the better the farther away they went, and she was oddly comforted. It wasn't till much later that Lucy wondered when she had ever said Evie's name for the woman to know it.

"O.K., guys, it's time to go home," Lucy told the boys, who were now re-energized and frisking about, "but first let's check on Miss Aylin one last time." She leaned into the handles of the loaded stroller. Jack dashed ahead, toward where he knew Aylin to be, in a gleeful zigzag path like a young deer. Ian had pulled his precious stick out from beneath the stroller and was trotting along behind his brother, looking over his shoulder at the little rut the stick plowed up between the tufts of the cropped grasses of the once-open field.

* * *

Along about ten o'clock Aylin began to see the writing on the wall. She had yet to do a single portrait. Rather than write the day off entirely, she pulled out a piece of grey, heavy sanded paper and clamped it to her drawing board on the easel. She uncovered an old margarine tub full of stubby pastel sticks nestled in dry rice. She studied every part of the clear sky overhead, not finding what she was looking for. Aylin was feeling a bit stormy, and without the inspiration of some longed-for turbulence, she projected the storm in her mind onto the maddeningly blank sky. She began drawing dramatic clouds and amongst them a pedestal with a winged and draped woman standing tall upon it. She sketched in the figure darkly along with the shapes in the sky, allowing for the middle and lighter tones to come later. Her hand moved quickly from woman to sky and back again, filling the entire surface with short, blocky, practiced strokes of deep, raw pigment. A passerby might have thought the picture outré, but Aylin did not notice the eeriness of it; she knew the finished result would be a balance of dark and light. This transitory darkness did not daunt her, or even register as such.

Time fled as she worked. The sun rose close to its apex. Aylin felt it blazing away upon her unshaded head. She knew that the sun was reddening her shoulders and back as fast as it was fading the red from her hair. Tucked between two booths with canvas sides, she was blocked off from what would have been a welcome cross-breeze. She could hear intermittent puffs playing against the flaps of the other tents, jostling the framed pictures against their supports, but here, across from the latrine station, walled in with no air movement, booth space number 129 must be absolutely the worst spot in the whole place. She could see up across the rows of booths to where a lone white tent sat a little way up the hill near where she had come by cart earlier this morning, and she longed, briefly, to be in that place instead. But here she sat, on her stool, sweating. Her clothing felt oppressive.

Aylin stood up. The gauze of her skirt clung to the backs of her thighs in dense, moist, random wrinkles like a chameleon skin ready to be shed. She left the company of the partially-drawn winged woman and set off to look for the girl she had come with; she might ride home early with her. She sorely regretted taking this Saturday off from work, exchanging a sure half-day of minimum wages for the heat and disappointing non-income of the festival. She weaved her way through the booths, looking for the young woman with the long dark hair and the kids with the probing eyes. Surely they had not left already.

In fact, Aylin had seen very few children here at the festival, which was a shame because children's faces were her best sellers. Children and Pekingese, but she had seen none at all of those. Not so pleasant to draw, either one, but popular, and she did have a knack for them. She passed a tent occupied by the rich couple from the Guild who had a booth full of those appalling nudes. Aylin had nothing against nudes, had painted many such paintings herself, not to mention had posed for more than a few, but the murky oil of these, the misguided, disjointed anatomy, was sad. The woman—Lori? Lorene?—looked like a Pekingese owner, maybe even like a Pekingese herself, but there was no dog in sight. She knew it was futile to interrupt the querulous conversation the couple was having with a solicitation for a portrait.

She passed a young man with farm tools and a mule who looked vaguely familiar. He was small, but he definitely had possibilities... What a mule had to do with art, now *that* she could not imagine. There were always a few oddities at these festivals, a few booths that did not belong.

Moving on, she passed two more Guild people, black folks, always together, those two. And what were they to each other? Husband and wife? Brother and sister? Lovers? Whatever, they were always together. She glanced at the dozens of miniature paintings, so small for such a big man. Who knew if he could *really* paint? All these tiny inconsequential landscapes—always landscapes. There were empty spots where some were missing. That meant he had sold some of them. *Well, good for him,* she thought. *I'd like to see him try to sell a* portrait *in this market, though.* The man sat busily painting, contentment plain in the ease of his gestures. The woman was occupied with something in her lap. She looked up sharply, straight at Aylin, eyes piercing into her, then looked down again at her handwork.

Aylin gave a start. She walked on, still casting about for Lucy and her entourage. She squinted and blinked against the stinging sweat that trickled into her eye. The top of her head was so hot she felt like flaming tongues were shooting out of it.

She worked her way up to the opposite corner from hers, and there she saw a very professional-looking display with large, colorful paintings. The booth appeared to be doing a brisk business, one of the few in which visitors were even willing to make eye contact with the artist. She made a mental note to add more bright colors to her paintings. The buying public seemed to go for that. She saw the artist—Eli Cooper, according to the sign— shepherding a small blonde with an oversize designer purse and sunglasses on her head, bejeweled sandals and extravagant nails on her feet, through his collection. Aylin did a double-take at the artist. He was worth looking at, not conventionally attractive, perhaps, but there was undeniably *something*. He was occupied, unfortunately, so she made no attempt to talk him up. Yet.

Still no sign of her ride. She backtracked, peering up and down rows for Lucy. Finally, she gave up and made her way back to her booth. At least she felt a little more comfortable now. Her skirt had dried a little, anyway. She sat back on her stool and cast her eyes on the winged woman, tilted her head a minute, and began to paint again with some intensity.

The image emerged quickly, but then Aylin never labored over any of these architectural paintings; her vision for them was strong. She never labored over the instant charcoal portraits either. People are so much simpler if you only consider their shades and not their colors. For some, all that is left is shade. She thought briefly of Mrs. Law. Nothing but shade there, surrounded by all that hideous pink. The commissions were the only real challenge for her. They were the trick. She labored and labored over them, trying to distinguish those face colors, those face shadows, those face shapes, from her own, which tried to surface again and again in the finished paintings of other people's faces. But in the end, the pastel portraits came out equally well; all that was required was time. At least, that is what she used to believe.

While she painted and mused, she grew aware of eyes watching her. She looked over her shoulder and saw there a boy of nine or ten with sleek blonde hair, longish, and piercing blue eyes.

"I see that angel you're painting," he said.

"Angel? Ha. That's no angel," said Aylin.

She pointed her sign out to him: "Aylin Borden: Portraits While You Wait."

"Want your picture done? It takes twenty-five minutes. Only costs twenty dollars. Great present for your mom. Moms love them." The boy was a seemly subject, the kind that would not be hard to flatter.

"Yeah, sweet. Let me go ask."

The boy came back and said, "She says yeah, go ahead. She'll be here in a few minutes with the money." He was crumpling up some paper he had pulled out of his back pocket. He threw the trash over his shoulder. It rolled under the wall of the next tent.

"So what do I do, sit on this stool or something?"

"Yes, you sit right there. Let me just put up a new sheet of paper and get my charcoals out." She rummaged in her tapestry bag and pulled out her box of charcoals, different shapes, different sizes, vines, twigs, broader sticks and stubs.

The boy was seated on the stool, twisting this way and that, experimenting with his feet propped on the rung. Aylin lifted the newly-started pastel painting away from the easel and placed it out of the way, flat on the ground, supported on the cropped points of many sturdy blades of grass—*like a yogi lying on a bed of nails*, Aylin thought, *lost in his meditations and with the nails drawing the pain and tension out of his body, yes, but with his soft belly exposed and vulnerable*. But surely nothing would jeopardize her work-in-progress laid safely in that sheltered corner. She clamped new white paper up in place of the winged woman, and gazed intently at the boy's face. He stared back, unabashed, the blue eyes a little too pale, a little too bold.

"So, what are you, some kind of gypsy lady?" he asked.

"Uh, something like that," said Aylin. "Now, just put your left leg up on that rung, and turn a little bit this way. Yes, that's right, a little more toward me. O.K., that's great," she said. "Now, hold it right there. Pick out something far off to look at, and keep your eyes glued to it. That will help you keep from moving, and we'll get a better picture."

"Yeah, O.K.," said the boy. "I can do that."

Aylin looked hard at him for two or three minutes before beginning, calculating his proportions, burning his image into her mind's eye. She picked up the most delicate vine charcoal and began to sketch rapidly, her eyes darting back and forth between his actual face and the growing facsimile of it on the paper. The boy flicked his head back to flip the hair from his eyes, then reset himself perfectly, looking off at the spot he had chosen in the distance.

Before long, a man sauntered into the booth, followed several minutes later by a woman talking on her phone and looking down. "Can you hear me now?" she was saying. "How about now? Hello? Can you hear me now?" So annoying. Didn't the woman know it was hopeless?

The man stood watching Aylin. She sketched all the shadows she saw; they were certain, well-defined, and a little troubling. An artist sees things in a face that lovers and casual acquaintances of that face miss; right or wrong, the artist does see things. But the boy *was* good looking, and his image developed the same way with ease.

The man broke the silence. "So, the name there, Aylin Borden. That is you, I presume?"

"Yes," she said, shading in the lids of the startling pale eyes.

"So," he paused for witty effect, "is that Borden as in 'Lizzie' or Borden as in milk-cows?"

"My name," she looked at the man directly now, "is Aylin, as in 'Halo around the Moon.' The other one means nothing."

The man was silent. His smirk faded. He shifted his stance and looked away. He began to fumble with his wallet, ready now for the session to be done. The woman still barked into her phone; she had not yet accepted defeat in her quest for reception. The boy sat remarkably still, his focus unwavering, with just the occasional hair flick to interrupt the artist's progress.

Aylin finished the portrait, sprayed it with fixative, waved it in the air a minute to dry, and handed it to the boy.

"Wow, sweet!" he said.

The man handed over the twenty for the portrait and said a perfunctory "nice." The father and the son, if that's what they were, moved away, looking at the picture together. The woman never looked up, never ended her one-sided conversation, but she seemed to know that the man and the boy had left and meandered off after them.

Aylin felt that the portrait had gone quite well. She was satisfied. She chafed at the Borden comment and was glad to be out of their presence, but with renewed hope she decided now that she would stay till the end of the day and see what other luck she might have. And she might just head back over to that deluxe booth after a while...

In the meantime, she thought that she would try to draw a picture of the children from the car this morning from memory. Actively drawing might attract more business. She clamped a new white sheet up on the easel and closed her eyes a minute, remembering.

The sketch came quickly. The three were not difficult to recall, with their grey-blue eyes wide open—three faces, it seemed to her, just the same but for a few minor differences shaped by age and gender, maybe personality, too. She drew them all three in a row, like she had seen them—only closer together—watching the viewer from the surface of the paper, following her steadily with disquieting, thinking eyes.

Aylin felt less agitated now, though once more thoroughly hot and sticky. She closed her eyes again and again, picturing the small faces, perfecting the sketch. Unbelievably, when she opened them for the last time and glanced around, those faces, in the flesh, were making their way with their mother toward her along the row of vendors, moving slower than the last time she had seen them. Maybe they were feeling flogged by the sun as she herself was.

With a shock, Aylin realized that she had captured the children very well. She did not know herself capable of such a feat. *As it turns out, I don't really need to* see *faces to draw them. Maybe I could have been some kind of police artist*, she thought, and laughed low at her private joke.

Lucy maneuvered the stroller into Aylin's booth and stopped short.

"You've really captured them! That's amazing! And not even looking at them? Or even at a photograph? I don't know how you can do that." The charcoal drawing was simple: three faces, sober and innocent. They were unmistakably her three children.

"Aylin, I wish I had money to buy it from you, but the truth is, I don't."

Aylin shrugged. "Doesn't matter. This is clearly not my day to make money. Anyway, I want you to have this sketch. For bringing me out here. Consider it 'gas money.'" Aylin winced at her own generosity. It was a trait she couldn't much afford.

"Well, thank you. It's really amazing." Lucy rolled the portrait carefully and nestled it under the stroller. "We just came by to see if you might want to change your mind and ride home with us.

We've had about all the art and sun we can take for one day."

"Thanks, but I'm going to take my chances and stick around. Who knows, maybe the crowd is just about to show up."

"Maybe so. But how will you get home?"

"I'm not worried about that. I have a few leads I'm working on." She brushed charcoal dust off her fingers and raked them through her hair.

"All right, then. Good luck with the portraits and the crowd," Lucy said. "And the ride."

Just as she was turning to go, a commotion sounded from the far side of the festival: wind-snapped canvas, shouts, a strange frantic rustling, all growing louder and building in intensity. The paper on Aylin's easel began to peel back, and nearby tent flaps slapped the neighboring poles fitfully.

"Look, Mom! Look at that!" Jack shouted, pointing.

Lucy and Aylin looked in the direction of his finger, across the tent tops. The sky was a brilliant blue, with no clouds anywhere in sight. But some unseen force was sending debris swirling heavenward, about fifty yards away. The two women backed up, trying to get a better view of the disturbance. Other people, artists and visitors, were doing the same. Their voices rose together like a rush of wind as a white tent on the opposite side went sailing up into the air and tumbled across the hillside, bouncing crazily, before it slammed down again, three poles driven akimbo into the ground, a fourth shooting horizontally like a javelin.

Above where the tent had been, a spiral of small objects, indefinable at this distance, but certainly some paper, much paper, flashing in the early afternoon sun, was being sucked skyward. Some of the darker objects seemed to be flung outward when they reached a certain height from the ground—fifty feet, a hundred feet, two hundred. But the flashing white paper danced and spiraled ever higher, up into the clouds, except that there were no clouds, no agent to be seen to account for this astonishing sight beneath the clear, clear, almost too-clear sky. The column sidled off and up over the brink of the hill, lifting the paper higher and higher like a flock of kites escaping into the stratosphere. As debris rained down here and there, voices called out in alarm—thuds and shouts punctuating the collective human murmur. Aylin stared after the whirlwind, until all she could see was a few tiny specks of white still soaring upward, nothing but sparkles now against the vibrant sky.

"What in the world was that?" Lucy murmured, following the path of the spiral with her eyes.

"Dust devil," Aylin said. *Haven't seen one of those since my Arizona days*, she told herself. Her stomach knotted. She thought of the spinning *chindi* of the Navajos, and how trouble seemed to dog her like an evil spirit, even here.

Out of the blue something smacked onto the roof of the tent beside them and slid to the ground in Aylin's lot. Jack and Ian rushed to pick it up. The two women walked toward them to see what they had found. It was a small wooden carving.

Lucy gasped. "I've got to go check on something. Come on, boys. We need to go *now!*" She wheeled the stroller around and began moving back the way she had come. "Good luck, Aylin. And thanks, I love the picture," she called over her shoulder.

"Yeah. Thanks yourself," said Aylin as she turned back to her booth, already losing interest in the strange weather phenomenon that had not, after all, affected her.

It was only then that Aylin's eyes alit on the empty corner of her booth. The unfinished pastel painting of the winged figure and the storm clouds was missing from the grass where she had carefully laid it.

* * *

Lucy hurried through the booths, through the minor disarray caused by the blowing and falling debris. She grappled with the stroller, bumping and rocking the baby and her craft perilously across the uneven turf while the two boys scurried on their short legs in her wake. When they reached the opposite hillside where the lone white tent top had been, they saw nothing but grass. In places the grass was swirled and matted and twisted in little depressions, as if a herd of deer had lain there for the night. Not far off, the scanty parade of golf carts continued unfazed, down into the hollow and then back up, appearing and disappearing with no particular rhythm over the top of the rise.

They stopped before the deserted spot, staring at the neon number 11A spray-painted on the turf and four ragged holes in the red clay. Gone was the crate with the carvings. Gone was the fruity vinyl tablecloth. Gone was Cordelia. Off to the right some twenty-five yards, where the white tent was jammed into the ground at an awkward angle, strangers were righting card tables and gathering up objects strewn around on the ground.

"Where did Miss Goodie Wiselady go?" asked Ian.

Lucy shook her head, speechless. She felt strangely bereft. Soon voices behind her began to register, and she thought to turn around. There at the entrance to Eli Cooper's booth the artist knelt before the familiar old wheelchair, leaning in and holding a rag to his aunt's brow. Her glasses were aslant across her face. Red splatters showed stark against her white blouse and faded blue apron.

She was reassuring him in a low voice, "Eli, what a fuss. You know I'm all right now. It's just a little blood, nothing that time won't heal. I'm just fine."

"I think you might need stitches, Cordelia. Maybe an x-ray."

"Oh, nonsense. It's just a cut. Stop hovering like a mother hen!"

"Is your vision all right, Aunt? You know that whack might have given you a concussion."

"Just as right as it ever is," she said. "No concussion here. Once this bleeding stops, I'll be good as new." But she looked paler than ever. She pushed Eli's hand away, taking the makeshift bandage in her own.

Lucy did not wish to intrude, but her concern would not let her turn away. She managed to catch Eli's eye, and he came over to where they were standing.

"What happened to her? Is she all right?" Lucy asked.

"Oh, she'll be all right, I guess. She sure hates being fussed over. She doesn't want any attention, ever. She would be mad I'm even telling you this." He paused.

"It was the strangest thing," he said with a trace of shakiness in his voice. "That cloud... that wind, I guess... whatever it was came right down on top of her tent and sucked it straight up into the air. Tables, boxes, all the other stuff under the tent just seemed to explode up into the air, swirling around and taking off, up and out in every direction, wood flying through the air all around. Then the tent came slamming down over there. Luckily nobody was standing or sitting or walking by at the moment, or they would have impaled by those poles." He shook his head slowly. "I've never seen anything like it. And through the whole thing she just sat there in her wheelchair, not moving at all, mayhem all around her. Didn't call for help, didn't yell, nothing. Just sat there, quiet. I think one of the tent-poles grazed her head when it blew past her."

"I guess it was just a lightweight tent?"

"Yes, it was, but I anchored the poles in all around when I put it up for her. I thought it would be safe no matter what came along. And it should have been. They had given her that booth space there to be close to mine, you know, since she's in a wheelchair and all. I thought I could help her, whatever came up."

"Well, I don't want to keep you from her. You're sure we can't do anything?" Lucy asked.

He attempted a half-smile. "No, it'll be fine. Thanks." He tossed this last over his shoulder and, looking a shade grim, went back to his aunt.

Just then, a man walked up and handed him a cardboard box. Eli crouched down to show the contents to the old woman. Lucy could just hear their voices.

"Cordelia," Eli said, "here are a few of your things people have picked up. I'm afraid most of it's gone, though, blown away who knows where... your carvings, your pamphlets... I don't think we'll ever see them again."

Cordelia held the rag to her own forehead. "Now, Eli, it's all right. Whoever picked these things up, tell them thank you. And whatever is gone, it doesn't matter a bit. And wherever it went, well, it probably just needed to go there anyway. If it's all swept away, it makes no difference. Nothing, no one, is ever *really* gone. And the roots are still there, back over yonder, way back in Virginia. The roots will always be there. Don't you know that, son?"

Lucy wanted to speak to the old woman, but she thought of what Eli had said, that Cordelia hated being fussed over, hated attention, and she reluctantly turned the stroller away, toward the golf cart shuttles. She made her way over to the short shiny caterpillar line. Ian, poking along behind, suddenly stopped and darted back to where Cordelia sat with her back to them in the wheelchair. He ran around to the front and picked up her spare hand resting in her lap and pressed something into it. Then he closed her fingers around it with his little chubby hands and darted off again. Not a word was spoken between the child with the stray grass caught in his hair and the old woman who could see everything with her strong, knowing hand.

Hours later and miles from the Hollow, scraps of rough wood and polished root dropped down at random. They called little attention to themselves—just plunked down, unobserved, into newly-plowed earth, or rattled, solitary, onto ragged country roadways or settled, unseen, into the rich rustling decay of woodland floors. The papers sailed upward yet, weightless, proclaiming aloft to the skies in their ancient script:

It is Time for Jesus Christ—Accept Him!

Cordelia's Tale

T he next day, before dawn, Cordelia sat alone in her room in the old wooden frame farmhouse with the shades pulled down to close out the coming day. The gash in her head had stopped seeping. Cordelia had slept only in brief snatches, and when the windows began to materialize as pale rectangles in the gloom, she realized that the flashing lights that were with her all through the night hours were there to stay. Sometimes flashing, sometimes flickering, always there. If her eyes tried to follow the fleeting, teasing, darting lights, she felt sudden sharp pain so she tried to keep her eyes still, closed or staring straight ahead. Once, though, she turned her head toward the door and felt an electric shock sensation in her neck. She knew it had nothing to do with the tent pole's blow to her head. She had felt this way before from time to time. There was nothing to do but sit quietly and wait.

The room and its murkiness recollected to Cordelia the swamp thickets of her youth, and rather than feeling fear in the darkness with the odd lights and electricity, she felt comfort, familiarity, sanctuary. The basic shapes of her room and its sparse furnishings emerged from the lessening night: the iron bed, the arms of the old brown rocker she sat in, the little painted dresser, the stool with the lamp, and beside it a plain weathered old book—just one book, a book without the author's name on it, the only book she needed.

Cordelia released her desire to rise, to move, to carve. She rested back in the motionless rocker and listened, prepared to receive whatever her Lord would bring to her this day. And the vision arose in the darkened room. Whether it *was* a vision or a legend or just a muddle of memories, she could not say. Fog had crept into her world, and often these days she could not be sure even of what century she belonged to. Her hands rested gently on the arms of the rocker as the other place, the faraway place, came close.

* * *

Two children, their faces round as little moons and just alike, huddled together in the back of a two-wheel mule cart, covered by an old blanket that smelled of leather, mule, smoke, and mouse urine. They clenched their teeth to keep from biting their tongues as the rough cart jounced over the gumroad where felled sweetgum trunks had been wedged down into the peat to make a firm enough passage for mule hooves and wooden wheels. They knew the driver was taking them into the swamp, deep into the swamp where they had never been before, and they were afraid. They were afraid, but they were even more terrified of what lay behind, and they knew that they must not make a sound. Rielle, the girl, jammed the knuckle of her first finger hard against the base of her nose. Maybe sneezing would alert their pursuers. Maybe sneezing would mean their capture and their death. With her other hand she clutched her brother, Oliver, and he clung to her with both of his.

They had faith in the driver, Hark. They had seen him on the plantation sometimes, when he had snuck up to the kitchen door around in back of the big house, to tease his sweetheart Bessie. He was fearsome to behold, tall and broad as the old stone ice house, with scars across his face. The children had run to hide behind the pie safe whenever they saw him come striding up the path from the barn. Sometimes they had not seen him come, and he would suddenly appear in the open doorway and block out all the daylight. He was fearsome to behold, but Bessie laughed and smiled to see him, so they were confused. How could a man look so bad, but still be good for Bessie?

Earlier that horrible night, when a large band of murderous runaways, as Bessie called them, ran through the farm killing all the white people they could find, and some black ones too, Bessie had scooped Oliver and Rielle together from her bed just off the kitchen in the little borning room, where they would sometimes creep for consolation from bad dreams and bad storms, and had deposited them in the arms of Hark. They could hear shouts and screams and roaring flames and were too afraid to speak, to even ask. Bessie had told them, "Be good, chilren. Hark gon' take you in de swamp. He know people dere. You gon' be safe. Member always, Bessie love you." So they had faith in Hark because they had to, because Bessie told them to, but not because of the way he looked.

But now, they could not see Hark's fearsome face; they could only feel the jostling of the cart and hear its creaking and rattling over the gumroad. They sat facing backwards, facing back towards home, towards where they had come from, and even through the heavy blanket a red glow filtered through. Yet they knew that night was just beginning, and why should it be brightening when the night was new? They had heard tell of the Giant Firebird who had nested once in the center of the great swamp near their farm. Maybe this ruddy illumination was the Firebird returning to her nest, and she was angry because she found it filled now with the shallow water of the big lake. Maybe the horrors of this night would never end. Their only comfort was in each other. They could not speak, but they could feel some of the thoughts of the other, and so they were not alone.

As the glow through the blanket increased, so did the speed of the cart, so that now it hammered along the gumroad and jolted the children violently. At length the glow faded, and the blanket was black. The cart slowed and finally drew to a stop. They felt the mule cart lurch as Hark jumped down from the driver's seat. He pulled the blanket off them, and they could just barely see his form before them in the darkness.

"Come, chilren, be quiet, be quick. We gots more journeyin' 'fore dis night be over." He lifted them down from the cart like they weighed nothing, even though they were pretty big now, five years old. They stumbled along behind the huge dark form in the dark, dark night. Their bones hummed with the vibrations of the cart that seemed to still be with them. But the sounds of the swamp at night were so deafening that gradually they drowned out even the bone-hum.

They had only heard these sounds before from afar. They remembered Bessie many a night chuckling as they ran spooked to her bed. "Oh, chilren, you hear dem ol' bull-frogs down in de crick an' down in de swamp a-ga-runkin' fo' dey lady friends? Long as you hear de ol' bullfrog a-carryin' on you knows de Lor' is in his temple, an' everything gon' be right wid de worl'."

But now the night, the frogs, the insects, the unknown and unseen noisemakers, were thick around them and the sound was overwhelming. It vibrated through them as surely as the jolting of the cart had done. They could see nothing but a faint glow far behind them and, roughly discernible only because of the questionable light of that distant glow, the shape of Hark moving about, covering the cart with branches, tethering the mule in the undergrowth, and finally dragging something low and heavy from the darkest dark of the underbrush. They heard the sound of water close by.

Hark crouched down before them and whispered, "All right,

chilren, we gots to get in de boat here—can you see it?—climb on in, an' I's gon' pole you outta here, way from dis road, to a safe place I knows 'bout way back in de swamp, an' you ain't gotta worry no mo' bout dem ruffians a-comin' fo' you. Dey don't come back here, white folks neither, only swampers. You's gon' be safe an' live in dis' place till Bessie and Hark come back fo' you."

The children obeyed, for there was nothing else for them to do, and they found it easier to trust Hark in the darkness where they could only hear his kind voice, where they could not see his terrible scars.

Hark helped the two children into the boat and wrapped the blanket around them, though the night was not cold. He stepped in himself, pushing the boat away from the raised gumroad. The boat was low to the water with all three in it. The gunwales barely rose above the unruffled surface. Hark stood tall, balanced himself, and poled the boat silently through the water, but even *he* seemed tiny in the night that was full of the enormous sound of life. Hark laid his pole down across the boat for a minute while he lit a lantern and hung it at the bow on an iron rod with a hook. The lantern had a shade that directed all its light forward, but still they could see his form, a little. He took up his pole again, and they glided their way through the maze of the swamp. Finally, as it seemed safe now to speak, with the lantern and all, Oliver could contain himself no more.

"Where are we going? Will you stay with us? Will we be alone there?" His voice barely sounded amongst the millions of swamp voices.

Hark looked back at the two children huddled together in the bottom of the boat. They could see his eyes gleaming, two gentle twin flames reflecting the lantern's light.

"I can't stay here wid you. Too dangerous. I be missed. And I gots to go see 'bout my Bessie. Couldn't bring her in de cart; it be too heavy fo' the mule to go so fast, and they would of catched us. But don't you chilren be worryin' none. I knows a woman, had thirteen chilren herself, knows dis ol' swamp, lives de maroon life, and she gon' be yo' granny fo' a while, jus' till Bessie can figure dis thing out, how to get you back, when it be safe."

Oliver felt no better. He reached down and took Rielle's plump hand in his. "It will be an adventure, sister, like that story 'bout Robinson Crusoe that Papa was teachin' us to read. You'll see." Then they both thought about Mama and Papa and Celia and Robert and Josie and Baby Girl. They asked Hark no more questions because they were afraid of the answers.

The motion of the boat gliding through the water with the rhythmic gentle tugs of the poling soothed and lulled the children, and soon Oliver and Rielle fell fast asleep leaning against each other in the bottom of the little boat.

They awoke with a start when the boat hit solid ground and they felt it being dragged up onto land. They stirred and stretched, and could see the sky just barely lightening directly overhead, but the forest around them was reluctant to give up the night. *Maybe it never does*, thought Rielle. She shuddered. *Such a scary place.*

Suddenly an ancient woman, shriveled and dark, stood before them in the lantern light. Hark bent down and gathered her in a hug. They passed some strange-sounding words between them that the children could not understand, and then Hark said, "Granny, I brought you dese two to stay a while. Dey Bessie's precious ones and de insurrectors done come and wiped everybody out, all de family. Dey gots to stay wid you till we can figure something out."

"Yes, son, it be all right. I knows what to do wid de young'ns. You knows I do," croaked the woman.

"I knows it, Granny."

The two moonfaced children wondered at just the same time if the woman was an old swamp witch; she certainly looked like one and sounded like one, too. And maybe what she did with young'ns was to fatten them up and then eat them. But even with a five-year-old's immature logic they knew deep down that Hark would not have gone to so much trouble and danger on his own account to bring them way out here just to be eaten. And besides, Granny had not paid him any gold for them.

"Good-bye, chilren," said Hark then. "I be prayin' to the Good Lord a' Heaven and Earth fo' you every day and every night."

Oliver and Rielle watched as their savior shoved off and climbed back in the boat in one fluid motion and immediately and completely disappeared into the riotous night. Granny took them into her hut with the blanket still wrapped around them. She gave them each a piece of fish, a hunk of cornbread, and a drink of cool water, though they were almost too weary to swallow.

As they ate, she said, "Granny see you chil'ren coming from away afar off. You be jus' fine in dis place, jus' fine with Granny. You safe now."

But they still did not trust this shriveled old stranger. They still did not feel safe. "How, when it's so dark, did she see us coming?" whispered Oliver to Rielle. His sister just shook her head.

Granny cackled.

She must have good ears, and good eyes, both, the two children thought at once.

The old woman made them a pallet on the floor, and they curled together as they had since they grew in their mother's womb, with the blanket tucked around them, in spite of the warmth of the early morning dark.

After daylight, none too early, the two little moon faces came awake at the same moment. Granny was moving about the dim hut, straightening what little there was to straighten. Rielle sat up first, rubbing her eyes. Even before her first yawn she asked, "Granny, will Hark come back for us today?"

"Not today, chile," said Granny, busy with something in the corner.

"Tomorrow, then?" she asked.

"Not tomorrow," said Granny. "Now, let Granny show you how to roll yo' pallet up and stow yo' blanket. Not much space here. Gotta get it all neat and tidy, 'fore breakfast." They busied themselves about the task for a minute or two.

"Come eat, chilren," said the ancient woman, and they could see rich yellow scrambled eggs on two wooden shingles, set on a stump in the center of the dirt floor. Their eyes opened wide.

"Granny, how do you have eggs in such a place?" asked Oliver.

She cackled. "You have much to learn, young Moonface."

And so their tutelage began, for Hark did not return any day that week, or any day the week after. Granny taught them about living in the swamp: how to gather eggs from the chickens in the little pen, how to noodle for catfish, how to harvest vegetables from her garden plot in a little clearing on higher ground, how to tell the pizeness snakes from the harmless ones, how to rub beautyberry on their skin to keep the insects away and witch hazel to sooth their bites, how to tell north from south by the moss on the trees. She taught them to know her trails, to make their way to the enormous shallow lake, to swim in it and to pole her little boat around on it, and to recognize from the lake the cove where her footpath began.

Granny was wrinkled and fairly toothless and bent over—no telling how old she was—but Oliver and Rielle came to see how very strong and how very smart the tiny woman was, and how very well she could survive in this place that everyone from Before feared. She did not eat them. Instead, they grew lean and brown. Still, in the early morning, before the forest began to lighten, before the brightness of the lake came fingering through the trees and thickets, before Granny stirred them for the day, the children woke

105

and strained their ears in vain for the sound of the rhythmic gentle pole splashes of a swamp dinghy.

Summer turned to fall with flaming color reflected in the still lake. The primeval night sounds lessened as the crickets began to sing from late afternoon to early morning. Hark did not come. Then the leaves began to fall until they covered whole lagoons and all the edges of the lake where the flat water slid into the undergrowth without pausing at the shore. Hark did not come. The leaves settled into the forest floor to add to its cushion and into the lake bed to melt into the peat and left behind only the dark green of the juniper and pine to color the forest. Still Hark did not come.

The cold came instead, and Granny taught them to make fires in the small stone hearth of her hut. Owls hooted and bobcats screamed, but the insects had hushed for their winter rest. And the cold stayed for a very long time, but they had the blanket that Hark had wrapped them in that horrible night, and they had the fire and the hut and hot sizzling bullhead catfish to warm their bellies. Hark did not come. Their shoes pained them by spring and they took them off and hung them from the rafters in the little hut because no single thing of possible use could be discarded and because each thing from Before was precious. And still, their savior did not come. When they thought of him now, the children no longer remembered the scars on Hark's face. Neither could they recall the shape of Bessie's, try as they might, only her sweetness, her warmth, the feel of her arms around them.

One day, they were weaving baskets from pine needles, a knack Granny had learned as a little girl from an old Nansemond woman. Rielle sat cross-legged on the ground engrossed in her basket, whistling a little tune Bessie used to sing as she worked. Oliver puckered his own lips: nothing but puffs of air. Try as he might, he never could get any music to come out.

Granny was squatting beside Rielle, fashioning her own basket, and she said, "Chile, the knack be in you, I see. That jus' yo' first try and it look good as mine, almos'. Life be struggle, it be powerful hard sometime; we bes' make it more beautiful any way we can." Rielle just worked away, twisting and smoothing the needles and whistling softly to them.

"Granny," she asked at length, "if I settle this basket in the crook of a tree, will some little bird come nest in it? Would the wood thrush come live close by and sing for us that sweet song you taught us to hear?"

"Dat bird have to find her own spot, chile. She know zackly what she need, where her special place be. She sing for finding her one true love, and she sing for joy of warming her little ones, and she sing because it in her nature to make the forest beautiful, a little bit of heaven. She not singin' jus' for you, but for all God's good creation."

Then Oliver, growing tired of bird talk, remembered something. "Granny, why don't your children live with you anymore? Hark said you had thirteen children of your own."

Granny leaned back on her haunches and cocked her head. Her black eyes reminded him of a crow's. "Young Moonface," she began, "my chilren all grew up here in de swamp, dey learnt 'bout noodlin' and growin' things and makin' clothes and catchin' game same as you, but dey got tired of livin' in de back places. Dey all learnt soon enough dey jus' traded dere prison of briars and copper moccasins for iron shackles and such out in de real worl', but den it too late. Hark, he my youngest grandson, his mama borned him out here, left him back here to learn de ways, left him so he be 'way from de plantation. Now he work as a bondsman. He earn his way to be free by cuttin' shingles in de swamp. He earn his way to get his Bessie free, too, some day. She de light of his life." Granny shook her head slowly. "It de way of de worl'. Any man give up free to have love."

"But why doesn't he come for us, Granny?" asked Rielle.

"I don't know, chile, what be keepin' him." A dark shadow passed over her face; she pursed her lips and said no more.

Oliver grew to be very skilled with making things, building things, inventing things. When he was eleven, and Oliver could see that he and Rielle were now taller than Granny, he added a little room onto the hut so that they might have more space. He built Granny a roof over her cooking fire circle twenty yards from the house. He built a little trolley from the spring to bear the weight of the water buckets to the house. He built Granny a new canoe. Then he tried his hand at building his own flat-bottomed pole boat.

Another year passed, and Oliver grew restless. He felt that he was now a man, and that as a man, he needed to seek out his family, or what might remain of them. He felt he was old enough, wise enough now in the ways of the swamp, to navigate in and out of it. So he told Rielle and Granny of his plan, to make his way back to the farm, not far past the edge of the swamp to the north, as he recalled. He would see if any family or farm were left. He would return in a year or sooner.

Rielle could not speak. She was bereft at parting from the companion of all of her twelve years, longer even. She wept and embraced her brother. Granny approved the trip, however.

"Yes, Moonface, it de noble thing, an' you know de way now. Jus' keep de moss on de right side of de tree an' you be fine." Her sharp black eyes peered out of her dark face with its mass of wrinkles like a gnarled old cypress knee, and she said quietly, "Jus' know dis, son, dat if you ask questions, you get answers, an' sometime dey not be what you want, dey be hard for de heart to take, but ever-what happen, you come on back for dis sister who love you. You be 'memberin' her every day, and you be fine." She walked with him down the footpath to the lake where the little boat he had just finished lay pulled up onto the spongy ground. "Chile, if you 'member nothin' else I tol' you, 'member dis: do not follow de lights in de marsh. Follow de moon, follow yo' own light, but do not follow de lights in de swamp, no matter who carry dem, no matter how beautiful."

"Yes, Granny. You have told me before. I will not forget." She pressed something into his hand. He looked down and saw two stiff, tattered little leather shoes tied together with the laces. "You keep dese safe. You gon' need dem." What could he possibly need with shabby old shoes that had not fit in years? Oliver did not know. Granny seemed confused sometimes, but he had learned long ago not to argue. She watched as he tucked the shoes into a feed sack holding his few belongings. Her tiny black crow eyes fastened on him without tears, with something that could have been pride.

"All right, that jus' fine, then," said Granny, and Oliver was off, eagerly it seemed, shoving the boat and hopping in all at once. He reached for the long pole and stood again with easy balance. He skimmed away across the water, glassy today and reflecting the dozens of cloud puffs in the blue sky of April. When he looked back, some yards out from the little footpath, Granny had vanished. She had no time and no use for sentiment, he knew, nor did he need it himself. The lake opened wide before him, and there was sky above and sky below. It was as if Oliver stood on a perfect flat plane that cut between two worlds.

He crossed the large expanse of lake to the north and passed into the shade of the far forest edge. Here, as he looked down into water now shielded from the sky's reflection, he could see the bottom of the shallow lake, only two feet deep. The sand was red-brown with charcoal grey lines tracing rivulets in the lake bed, like a child's pencil maze his father had shown him in the Richmond newspaper once, only this maze had no end and no solution, constantly changing at the whim of the playful lake ripples. "The swamp is like that," said Oliver to no one in particular, or perhaps he said it to Rielle, forgetting she was not beside him. He paused a moment to tear strips off an old pokeweed-dyed rag in the bottom of the boat. He tied one to a gum sapling here at the edge of the water, directly north from Granny's footpath. He tied a few more now and then as he progressed.

When the sun was high overhead, he laid down his pole and sat in the boat in the shade of a cypress stand. He unfolded a rag and drew out a hunk of cornbread. He dipped tea-colored water from the lake with a gourd dipper and drank. Insects had begun their early spring congregations, buzzing lazily, without all the intensity of their summer riots to come. He began to feel drowsy, and his shoulders were aching; he lay down in the boat for just a small rest, barely rocking on the glassy lake.

Oliver sat up with a jolt as an animal screamed close at hand. He had drifted up against a cypress trunk and the sun had nearly gone down. He could not understand how he had slept so long and so hard. He must be about his journey quickly now. It was far more difficult to navigate in the swamp after dark. Soon he located a little natural landing where the boat could be pulled up and hidden in the underbrush close to the gumroad. He secured the boat and the long pole, slung the drawstring sack over his shoulder, and headed off north up the gumroad, relieved to have his legs stretch out in long strides across the solid gum tree trunks instead of bracing, stiff, in the boat.

The gum road passed through dense forest, though in April it was less dense than it would be a month from now. Very little of the remaining daylight filtered through to the swamp now that the open lake was falling further and further behind. The narrow, crooked road crossed rickety bridges and skirted lagoons. It was flooded with water in places, but Oliver was light and sure-footed as a whitetail yearling.

As he came around a bend in the road, the forest opened to his right into a meandering lagoon. He saw far ahead—whether over the water or in the trees, he could not tell—a blue flame, a light, much larger than a firefly, about the size of a lantern light, but cold, too cold certainly for a torch or a campfire. And he saw the light move. And then he heard amongst the familiar sounds of the swamp night a sound he had never heard there, a sound he had longed to hear, a high-pitched thin, "Oliver-Rielle... Oliver-Rielle..." It repeated over and over. He had to be sure he was not fooling himself. Again he heard it, "Oliver-Rielle..."

Bessie! It was Bessie, with her lamp, searching for them! He could just make out her pale dress, her arm raised holding the lantern high. He had known she would come! He had never stopped believing she would come!

Just then the light went out. He strained his eyes in the gloom, the near darkness, and on further ahead. He held his breath. Soon he saw the flame again, this time reflecting in the water. He called out, "Bessie! Bessie, here I am!" But there was no answer. He listened.

Farther away he heard the faint call, "Oliver-Rielle... Oliver-Rielle..." with the same odd intonation as before.

Oliver remembered Granny's warning. It took all of his will to remain on the road and not wade out into the water to look for Bessie. He called to her again and again, but she did not answer. Three more times he caught sight of the flame off deeper into the undergrowth to the right. "I'm here, Bessie, right here on the road!" he called. There was no answer. He would stay on the path and hope to meet her where the road left the swamp up on higher ground. Oliver trudged along in total darkness.

At last he realized that the road beneath his feet was solid earth. He had left the swamp and was in higher, dryer forest now, and he knew that a two-hour's walk should bring him to the track that led to the edge of their farm. All he had to do was keep to the road, deserted now at this hour. There was no sign of Bessie. There was no sound or sign of anyone.

He began to contemplate his approach. He was glad that he had bathed in the lake, at least, early that morning, and that he had on what might pass for plantation clothes. Where Granny had come up with them, he did not know, but he was grateful for them, suddenly conscious of his wildness. He drew his long curly hair back and bound it with a strip of rag as he walked, hoping he would look fairly civilized, trusting that he would be recognized, welcomed.

Finally, he approached the farm and came first to the old quarters. He hallooed so as not to spring upon the place and frighten folks in the night. He could smell tobacco as he drew nearer, and soon saw the glow of a pipe on the little porch of a shanty. He neared the shack and called out, "Hark? Hark, that you?"

"Mmmm... Hark ain't been seen fo' some long time... dese seven years. Who dat call out de name of Hark?" said an old man's voice.

"Zeke? Is it Zeke, then?" said Oliver eagerly as he hurried toward the shanty.

"Zeke I be," the man answered slowly, cautiously.

Oliver heard the caution and slowed his steps. He stood before the porch at a respectful distance.

"Old Zeke, it's me, it's Oliver Thompson."

"Oh, dat right," said Zeke, unconvinced. "How I know it be you, now, not some upstart?"

"Ask Hark. He'll know me. He's the one that took me and my sister into the swamp and hid us away from the insurrectors. Ask Bessie. She'll know me any time, anyhow."

The old man struck a light in the lantern close at hand.

"Now I guess you do favor dat boy chile dat Bessie use to take on over." He puffed on the pipe a couple of times. "Now what you come back here fo'? What you want from Ol' Zeke?"

"Please, where are Bessie and Hark? I want to see them. Hark told us they would come back for us in the swamp, but they never did. I figure I'm a man now, I'm old enough to come home and see what happened, see if there are any kinfolk I need to look after, anything left of the old place."

"Sweet Jesus in Heaven," sang Zeke softly. He was silent a moment. Then to the boy he said, "Well, now, I ain't a one to be givin' bad news, but all yo' people, dey be gone now, Master Oliver. Dey be gone ever since dat terrible night. Hark disappeared in all dat confusion, he jus' gone, and den he show back up jus' as de white-masked vigilantes comes through, lookin' to punish dose murderous insurrectors dat did all de evil deeds to yo' people. Den dey see Hark jus' comin' up in de mule cart, and dey get all 'spicious. Dey say, 'Where you been, young fellow?' and dey see de scars on his face and think he be a trouble-maker, and he say, 'I been takin' de young master and missie to a safe place, way from all dis murderin' an' burnin',' and dey say, 'You done kit-napped dem two! What you done wid 'em? We don't see dere bodies round here!' And Hark, he say, 'Dey safe, I tells you, can take you to dem sho' 'nough.' But dey say, 'Ain't goin' nowheres wid the likes of you,' and dey done strung him up, right over in de pecan grove, dey done strung up Hark till he dead, and he ain't never been nothin' but a true soul. And den dey ride off. Dey don't care nothin' bout you young folks. Dey jus' cares 'bout killin' and gettin' even." He stopped abruptly and puffed in earnest on his pipe.

Oliver felt as if he'd been punched in the stomach. He staggered back and retched, but his belly was hollow.

"Hark is gone? Dead? All this time?" He shook his head, trying to shake himself loose from the truth of it.

"But what about my folks? None of them are left? Not Mama, not Papa, not even Baby Sister? Not one of them? Maybe they got away. Maybe they went to hide somewhere."

"Like I say, I ain't fond of givin' bad news. But it seem right fo' you to know. Dey all gone." The pipe glowed brighter, an evil eye in the night, as Zeke sucked in. "And by gone, I mean, kilt dead."

The ground lurched, tried to shake Oliver from his feet.

"Well, w-w-what about B-B-Bessie? Where is she? I thought I heard her calling me in the swamp as I was finding my way out?"

"Oh, Sweet Jesus. Preserve us in dis hour of darkness. Keep us from de evil one," the old man sang softly. He puffed furiously on the pipe. Then he looked down off the porch at Oliver and said, "Bessie, she done broke. Times bad here. Jus' three of us lef'. We try an' pick up de pieces. Don't know where to go, what we s'posed to do wid out de family. Bessie, she like a empty gourd wid'out her Hark, wid'out you young'ns. All she say is, 'Gots to go find my chilren'. Lor', Lor', gots to see if dey all right.' Night and day, she say it, night and day. She look like a ol' woman overnight, all bent over, caved in, now Hark gone."

He puffed some more. Oliver kept silent, trying to keep his knees from buckling.

"But den de war come. We gots no food, gots to scrounge what we can and hide it too, livin' off de land on what-all de soldiers don't take. Got no mule fo' to drive on some fool mission into de swamp anyways. Bessie keep say she goin' but she don't. I tells her, 'Bessie, you don't know de way. You get lost in dat swamp or worse. Dey ruffians, scoundrels in dat swamp. Dey snakes too.

"Den after all dose years when we keeps from starvin' somehow, de war over—yes young master, a whole war be fought while you be squirrelt away in dat swamp, as you say—'bout dat time, 'long come dis new family, say dey de heirs, dis dey farm now.

114

Say dey cud'ns of yo folks. Talk real funny, dese folks. And dey comes sweepin' in and starts carryin' on like befo', only 'lot wuss. Treatin' us like slaves, but we not be slaves no mo', Mr. Lincoln say. Dey build dis big fancy house over yonder. Dey grab Bessie fo' de house maid, de nuss'ry, but Bessie, she say she can't nuss no mo' little'uns, she gots to see her lost lambs. So Bessie run off into de swamp, jus' a few pieces of biscuit tied up in her apron. She tell me goodbye, she say she be back in a week. But Bessie never did come back.

"Some runaways passin' through, while after dat—dey been hidin' in de swamp runnin' from de bloodhounds and all—dey say dey sees a Indian lady in de swamp, in de dark curly lagoons, and dis lady paddle a white canoe, gots a blue fire in her lantern. Dey hears from de swampers, 'Don't you follow de lady in de white canoe, de lady wid de blue lantern light, don't you even look at her, dat Indian devil lady!' But dey look, dey can't help it. She so beautiful. Dey see her once, twice. Den dey see her third time, and lo, she gots another lady in de boat wid her! She dark, all dey see is de pale dress, and she trailin' her hand back in de water, and ever-where her fingers ruffle de water a little it be glowin'. So dey decides it time to get on out of de swamp, soon as de war be over.

"Bessie, she never come back. It be a year, no, two year now."

Oliver was speechless. He shifted his feet.

"Which way did you say the new house is? I guess I'll go on up and offer my acquaintance to the cousins."

"Sho', sho' now. You go on up de path past de well house and follow it around and jus' keep on going till you see dat big tall white house standin' dere. Sun near to comin' up," he pointed out. "You be seein' it clear as day. Can't miss it, since dey logged all dose old oak trees."

And so Oliver followed the well house path. The old farm seemed quieter, tamer, more open than he recalled. He approached the veranda of a grand house, the likes of which he had never seen. He was greeted by a brown-faced stranger in fancy dress at the door who bade him wait in the parlor. The gleaming brass and mahogany mantel clock measured out eleven long minutes before an unfamiliar man, pale of face and hair, strode into the room.

"Charles Joseph Hunter Thompson. How may I be of service to you?" he said courteously.

"More likely, I of you," said Oliver, remembering his courtly manners. "I am Oliver Thompson. My sister Rielle and I are your cousins, or so I am told. Our family lived here until the massacre seven years ago."

"Is that so?" said Charles Thompson, looking skeptical.

"It is, sir."

"If that be so, young fellow, how come you to be here now?"

"Two of our people saved us from the murderers and hid us away in the swamp. I am told they died before they were able to bring us back. But having reached twelve years, sir, and being now of an age to make the trip from the swamp independently, I desired to see if any of my family had survived and if I might be of service to them now." The smell of bacon made his mouth water. He could hear a stampede of quick little footsteps overhead.

"I congratulate you on your survival," said Ronald Thompson, his face turning red, "but I cannot be sure that you are who you say. It seems most unlikely." His accent was not familiar. Oliver felt his roughened condition to be under the scrutiny of the cousin.

"I wonder, have you any papers to produce to prove your identity?" said the young gentleman in lace and spotless breeches.

"No papers, no. Our nurse fled with us in the night. No doubt the fire destroyed all the papers there were."

"Well, without papers..."

"I do have these," said Oliver, remembering the shoes that were in the feed sack slung almost forgotten over his shoulder. He drew out the once-fine little leather shoes, still connected in a chain by their laces. "My sister has kept hers as well." He held them out in his hand for Charles Thompson to see. The gentleman threw back his head and laughed. The corners of his lips turned downward, suppressing further mirth, as he addressed Oliver for the last time.

"Ragged old shoes prove nothing, young sir. I suggest you take your confidence game to some other man who is less canny than I! Go, be off with you! Do not return without papers! Papers are the thing these days!" He laughed again, without restraint. Oliver heard in that laughter the thin sound of the coyote's revel, sharp and high and choking on its own bloodthirst.

And so Oliver left the tall white house in shame, for he was ashamed to be connected to such a person with far more style than honor. He clutched his shoes, his treasure, to his chest, and fled down the path the way he had come, past the well house. He swerved down an overgrown trail where he now remembered the old house had been. The sun sifted through the high poplars and oaks and the smaller gum trees, the feathery green in their tops swaying against the brightening sky.

Soon he emerged into a clearing whose shape he recalled. The circular drive was still discernible where the grass was yet reluctant to grow, but the home he recalled was replaced by charred posts, blackened clapboards, crumbling chimneys, and slabs of fallen roof. He went around behind, picking his way through privet and scrub that had grown up in the once swept yard, to where the kitchen had been. There was nothing left of it but the hearth and the old stone stoop out back. A large old cracked black kettle lay on its side behind the house.

Scenes of horror, sounds of violence flashed upon him, and Oliver began to run. And he ran and ran and ran, past what was left of the quarters, clear off the farm, back to the track that led to the road that led to the swamp that led to the watery trail to the only home he had left in this whole wicked world.

Oliver knew well how to survive in the swamp. And he did, some long time, all the long spring and the longer summer. He found himself a back place to squat in, an abandoned shelter, a little shack that kept rain off his head. He fashioned himself a canoe and told himself each day that today he would return to his true family, to Rielle, and to the old woman who had taken them in. But he could not bring himself to go. He could not form the words to tell what he had found. He remembered what Granny had said to him at the last, her warning about asking questions. It would have been better not to go at all, not to ever leave the little shanty in the far-back place with the two women, young and old. There was no place for the brother and sister in the now-alien world outside the swamp. There was nothing left for them there. But he would feel such disgrace in telling them, such desolation in saying the words, "All the ones we loved are dead and gone." And so he lingered.

At last, as the nights grew cooler and the fireflies petered out and the insects lessened their cacophony, Oliver began to think of the hardships of the coming season, and that thought superseded all his grief and shame. He must return and help Rielle and Granny prepare for winter. He would spare them the details and dishonor.

The journey home through the swamp was not difficult. Oliver only lost his way once or twice, but the moss on the trees helped him orient himself. At last he found one of the stained rag strips at the landing where he had hidden his flat-bottomed boat. There, sure enough, in the underbrush still huddled his boat and the long pole, too. He exchanged the rough canoe for it, and from then on he followed the trail of rags and then his own reckoning back home.

As he walked up the old familiar footpath at twilight, infinitely older than when he had set out six months before, he smelled fish frying and heard whistling. His heart leapt at the sound. Rielle! The sister and brother embraced and wept. They clung to each other as they had in the mule cart on that horrible night seven years earlier. Then Oliver stepped back to look at her. She was taller, her hair darker and longer, her face thinner, her cheekbones stronger.

"There is nothing left, sister, nothing for us out in the world," he said. And then he pulled her over to sit on the bench outside the hut, and he told her every detail in spite of himself, for Rielle was the other side of his coin; she was a part of him as surely as the back of his hand, as his left arm or his right leg. She was his eternal friend who knew all his pain and joy as he knew hers. And the shame to which he could not even put a name miraculously ebbed away.

"Brother, that is just fine, then. Let them keep the old farm. It would only remind us of the people we've lost. And anyway, I'm not ready to leave this place yet. It's where we came to know Granny, where our second life began."

"Where is Granny then?" he asked.

Her face clouded, and she looked very sober. "She is gone, Oliver. She took the little canoe you made her last winter. She could hardly paddle, and I asked to go with her, but she said, 'You stay, daughter. I will see you soon enough.' So I did not think anything more of it, but then she did not come back. I called for her. I took the old pole boat out and looked in all the usual places, where we fish, and such. I even did the swamp holler, like she taught us to do if we were lost. I stood straight up in the boat, put my fingers in my ears, and hollered as loud and long as I could. But there was no sign of her."

"I should go look now!" he said, jumping up.

"No, Oliver, it was months ago now, not long after you left. I think she knew she was going to die and wanted to spare me the sadness—she somehow knew what all we had lost—she knew you would come back, and so she just flew away.

"But I waited for you—let's have a little service for her now. Come and see the cross I made for her," and she pulled him by the hand to the clearing near the old stone spring where she had transplanted a few wildflowers and had set a cross made from the root of a cypress tree, tied in the center with a strip of pokeberry rag. And on the cross Rielle had faintly carved the words, "Let him that is athirst come. And whosoever will, let him take of the water of life freely."

She turned to her brother and said, "She gave us everything without price, Oliver—drink, food, knowledge, care. I don't know why she did it. I don't know why Hark did what he did, and even got killed for it. I don't know why Bessie loved us so, and lost what she loved most for us, and even died for us, too. Why did they do all that, Oliver? Was it because of the Good Lord of Heaven and Earth that Hark and Granny talked about?"

Oliver shook his head slowly. "All I know, sister, is that this is the way that those who loved us lived, and this is the way we will live too."

And so they sang a song for Granny, and they sang a song for Bessie, and they sang a song for Hark, and they sang for Mama, and Papa, and Celia and Robert and Josie and Baby Girl. And they sang a song for their old farm, for the warm old kitchen and the big old farmhouse and the sweet smelling tea olive by the well house and the cats in the barn, and all the things they had loved and remembered together from Before. And then they sang a song of thanks for the humble little cabin and the lake and the fish and the sky and the sheltering swamp. And all the while a little crow sat upon the uppermost stone of the spring. It cocked its head at them, and peered down at times into the sparkles of splashing water catching glints of the last sunlight of the day. Its tiny bright black eyes looked for all the world like Granny's canny gaze.

As the woods fell into gloom, Oliver and Rielle returned to the hut and ate their supper of fried catfish and cornbread. Then they wandered together out to the pole boat and pushed off into the water, but they did not cross the lake. Instead, they poled slowly along the lake edge, where the water slid away under the tangle of vines and shrubs. For some time they aimlessly, silently nudged the boat along the lacy meandering shore. Then, in an inky lagoon to their right, just as the indigo night saw its last punctuation of firefly for the year, they spied a blue flame hovering not far off, a blue light that wavered and danced and drifted across the surface of the black water. Its twin danced and drifted below it.

Rielle drew in her breath. "Oliver, what is it?" she whispered.

"A blue flame and its reflection, nothing more than that," said Oliver in a low voice. And he braced his legs and turned the boat with the long pole and slid the two of them away from the beckoning flame, back toward home. Rielle trailed her fingers in the water, leaving a little phosphorescent trail and a softly whistled tune like a sweet birdcall drifting behind.

* * *

Cordelia's darting lights had lessened. The season for those particular meteors was almost at an end. The pain in her head and neck was all but gone. But she felt wrung out somehow, like an old faded damp rag. She was not sure what to make of the vision. She felt closed in now, like the room had grown smaller, danker, and airless. She rose with great effort, pushing up on the arms of the rocker, and paused for a moment to balance. Then she walked slowly, dragging her right leg—it was so heavy!—behind her. She kept her hand flat on the wall beside her as she walked. She made her way to the kitchen for a glass of water, and then through the screen door to the front porch. She sat down in her old wheelchair, still there on the porch with the brake on. She gazed out into the yard and listened to the spring peepers just cranking up in the twilight. She was disoriented; was it sunrise or sunset? It seemed impossible that she could have spent the entire day in her room. How had so much time passed?

As she peered into the yard, she saw fireflies darting here and there, or were those the teasing lights in her eye? Her hands felt empty. She felt in her apron pocket and discovered there the carving the little boy had pressed into her hand the day before. She rubbed the shape of it all over, a small form of a worn, old-fashioned child's shoe, cut from wood, not from leather. She smiled inwardly and set the shoe on her knee.

Her thoughts went to the children of her vision and gentled there for some time before they meandered to Eli, and then to the young mother she had met at the festival. Cordelia sat rooted to the weary wheelchair on the peeling front porch, but her mind took flight and soared above the earth. Her inner sight, unconstrained by time or by the confines of the flesh, gazed at the souls navigating the maze of life below. She could see that, like the swamp children, Eli and Lucy were two sides of the same coin. They were shepherds of the vulnerable, both of them. And something more: They were drawn to the wonder of the natural world and felt compelled to reflect it back. These high callings would require sacrifice. Sacrifice, yes, and perhaps loneliness as well. Eli and Lucy would sometime go adrift. They would need a word here or there to guide them.

She fished in her apron and pulled out a hunk of Virginia swamp root and her X-Acto knife and began to smooth away extraneous bits of wood from what she knew to be inside, the crow with its bright round eyes, calling to be freed.

Orvelle's Call

Orvelle Armstrong settled himself in his brown vinyl easy chair in front of the television just as "The Price Is Right" was beginning. He lifted the three-foot length of two-by-twelve from off the floor beside him and arranged it across his lap. Late-afternoon sunlight and a late-May breeze played together in the old muslin curtain at the open window to his left.

"Oh-rilla, fetch me that box of canvas over there, please," he called to the woman at the kitchen stove. Orilla finished situating six floured chicken parts in the hot grease and wiped her hands on her apron. She shuffled a few steps over to the stack of boxes in the corner, rummaged through the cardboard jumble, and pulled out a carton marked, "8 X 10, 12 pieces, Made in China."

"Umh," escaped her bulk as she straightened, then made her way to the easy chair with the canvases. The air was heavy with the rich smell of the chicken popping in the crusty skillet. Greens sent pillars of tangy steam up to the ceiling from their bubbling pot.

Orvelle took the box from her and set it on the floor. He pulled out a virgin canvas and held it before him at arms' length for fifteen or twenty seconds, nodded, then set it on his lap board. From the floor beside his chair he eased forward a milk crate with a jar of battered brushes, another jar of turpentine, misshapen tubes of oil paint, and a clipboard covered with heavy white freezer paper. He

123

arranged dollops of color around the edges of this make-shift pallet, every now and then stopping to hold the canvas out before him and gaze at it a few seconds more. He mixed the paint into a dozen puddles of varied hues, and then began quickly smoothing strokes onto the canvas, forming shapes that emerged, grew, and evolved into the landscapes of his mind.

Behind him, the frying pan popped and spat. Before him, contestants edged their way toward fame and riches. The studio audience cheered as Orvelle, across the room on his vinyl throne, slapped out another eight by ten. He had already replaced the pictures he had sold at the Box Hollow Festival two weeks ago, and then some. But he liked to have a good supply of them; they were his best money-maker. And besides, painting them just felt good.

Orilla parted the clutter on the oak pedestal table. Like the table, she was short, round, and sturdy. She placed a chipped teacup in the center with three purple pansies in it, their faces nodding downward as if to read today's mail. She moved around the weary linoleum on sure-footed slippers, setting two places, serving up two ample platefuls of dinner and two Ball jars of tea.

Orvelle sensed that dinnertime had arrived. He set aside the painting board and moved to his place at the table. When Orilla eased down onto her chair, they bowed their heads, and he began to speak. "Oh, Lord, we your children are grateful for this bounty. You brung us manna sure as you brung it to the children of Israel in the dry, dry desert. Oh, Father in Heaven, look kindly on us. Bless our efforts, we pray. Amen."

Orvelle shook water from a small bottle of jalapeños over his greens. He broke a large biscuit apart. He sopped up juice from the greens with a large hunk and thrust it in his mouth. "Oh-rilla, it don't matter how many times I eat your biscuit, it still taste like a little piece a' heaven to me," he said.

Orilla's cheeks dimpled. She was extremely proud of her biscuits. "Well, that just fine, then," she said. "You lucky them biscuits doesn't settle in to stay 'round your belt the way they does mine." In fact, Orvelle was a fine figure of a man, tall, muscular, not too thin either, with an even face, not too light, not too dark, and longish black ringlets. He never missed a day of work at the plywood plant and never seemed even a bit tired when he drove the old Chevrolet truck into the yard every evening. Orilla was about as proud of him as she was of her biscuits, possibly more so.

"Oh-rilla, you a fine looking woman yourself, and that a fact." Orvelle finished off the chicken thigh, placed the bone on the side of the plate, and picked up a second piece.

"Now. You tell me 'bout your day." He bit into the chicken and chewed as he looked over at the plump woman with a bit of silver in her hair seated across from him.

"Oh, same old, Orvelle. Well, that is, all 'cept I did take a phone call today, after I got home from my spell with the McAdams children. It was them Farrow folks callin' again. Want you to go tonight and take some pictures. Said it gon' be tonight for sure."

Orvelle nodded, set the stripped chicken leg down neatly next to the first, wiped his mouth with his napkin, and took a long pull of tea before answering. "I guess I'll drive on over to the Glades after dinner, then. You want to ride with me?"

"That fine, then," said Orilla. The two of them carried out this eternal ritual of asking and agreeing although there was really never a question of whether or not Orilla would go along. Anywhere, anytime.

The meal-sharers lingered over their plates in companionable silence, cleaning up the last of the drippings with swipes of remaining biscuit, which they then ate, so that there was little left to wash off in the dishpan set in the old porcelain sink. Orvelle reached for his Pentax 35-millimeter camera with the automatic

125

flash and slung its strap over his shoulder. With the Ball jars and plates left in the drainer, Orilla secured her big black vinyl pocketbook under her arm. They went out through the screen door and settled themselves onto the front bench seat of the Chevrolet for the ride over to the Glades.

Orilla hummed an old church tune while Orvelle guided the truck down Highway 16. "Orvelle," she said after a few verses, "how we gon' celebrate our birthday comin' up?"

"What? Our birthday comin' up? Again? Seem like our birthday always comin' up."

"Um-Hmmm. They does not stop. But we goin' on forty-five. Seem like we ought to celebrate. Halfway to ninety, after all."

"I knows *that* right. Well, how 'bout biscuits? Nothin' better anytime. Little sorghum syrup to sop that biscuit in. That be some *kind* of celebration—all the celebration I need."

"Orvelle, you gots to branch out. Live a little. You stuck on biscuits. How 'bout pound cake?"

"Yes, ma'am, I can live with that."

"All right. That just fine, then. Nine eggs, three sticks butter. All that crusty goodness on top with the smile sinkin' in where it still a little gooey. Pound cake—nothin' better than *that*."

Orvelle had to agree.

"Biscuit, my foot," Orilla muttered to herself. "Birthday food? I don't *think* so." She resumed humming.

Orvelle crossed over onto Glades Road and ten minutes later turned up a gravel drive to their destination, a rambling two-story house. The sagging, crooked building before them crouching in the twilight with wings and additions of all ages and descriptions had long been an actual home to generations of Millers. Now it was home to the aggrieved and mourning of all the African folk in the Glades and half of Corbie County. Orvelle and Orilla left the truck parked in the swept yard and passed through clusters of people dressed in Sunday best all about them, laughing, crying, gossiping, calling out to one another. Children dashed about like birds startled up from the edge of the road at dusk. The newcomers nodded, spoke a word here and there, but kept on toward the front porch, warmly lit in the yard's deepening twilight.

Stepping into the glow of the porch bulbs, Orvelle was suddenly seized by a woman in a voluminous hat. He knew her to be Overseer Crutchfield, caretaker of the flock at Freedonia Holiness Faith and The Body of Christ Church.

"Brother Orvelle, God bless you for coming. God bless you for using your magnificent talents in His service this day. Lord Jesus, help these grievin' folk in their dark hour of sorrow. Come this way, Brother Orvelle. I'll take you to the Sacred Spot of the Blessed Dear Departed." As Overseer Crutchfield engineered a path through the crush of mourners all talking at once, several shrieks rose above the din. The newcomers followed the hat through the front door into a large crowded parlor and on through a labyrinth of hallways lit by dim bulbs in dusty, tilting sconces. They came to a windowless room deep inside the house illuminated only by two fringed lamps on tiny tables. Between them on a chrome stand stood a shiny silver casket, and therein lay what remained of Lester Farrow.

Just at the moment Orvelle peered into the coffin, a short, round woman in full black wig flung her arms around his waist and raised up her tear-stained face.

"Oh, Mr. Orvelle! I heard you done the most beautimous pictures of folks! I never had no pictures of my Lester here. Serious man. Had no use for takin' pictures. But he a godly man, Mr. Orvelle. Yes, he follow The Law all the days of his life. He a godly man and a good provider for me all these sixty-two years and the children too, and now he gone, Mr. Orvelle! Gone!" At this point she flung her hands upward, and Orvelle knew her to be the source of the shrieking he had heard before. After some moments of piteous sobs and heaving chest, Mrs. Farrow held her handkerchief to her nose and blew. As quickly as the storm brewed it dissipated, and the tiny widow was calm, at least for the time being.

Orvelle bent his softened face down to her and said, "I'm sorry for your loss, Miz Farrow. How can I be of help?"

The widow blew her nose several times again. She gathered herself and spoke, "Well, Mr. Orvelle, it like this. I got no likeness of my husband here 'cause, like I say, he a *serious* man. Got no use for pictures and such. All his life, a hardworkin' man. *Serious.* But I done got use to havin' him by me after all those sixty-two years. Sixty-two years! I gots to at least have his likeness when I can't have him with me no more, 'specially at dinnertime. It be like somebody to talk to, you know. Lester, he did love his sweet potato pie. Ohhh!" She wailed again for some minutes.

"But now he gone. No pie gon' bring him back." She wagged her head slowly back and forth. "I jus' needs some little piece of him to keep me comp'ny. At dinnertime, 'specially."

Orvelle nodded, gently patted her shaking shoulder with his large hand, and looked down into her puffy fading eyes. "Yes, ma'am, Miz Farrow, I knows what you mean about dinnertime." He glanced over his shoulder at Orilla who stood quietly, leaning slightly forward, surveying the scene, her shiny purse clutched at her middle with both hands.

Orvelle glanced again at the figure in the gleaming coffin. The still, dark form of The Departed seemed almost to hover, weightless, above the pearly lining—a thin, small, angular man, straight as a weathered fencepost, dressed in a pewter suit with a sheen to it, the likes of which Lester Farrow had never, not for one day, worn in his entire life, a large-collared white shirt, and a wide leprechaun-green polyester tie.

Mrs. Farrow sniffed, trembling, her brow pinched from some

private perplexity. She brightened, then, and said, "Mr. Orvelle, I wants you to paint me a picture, a picture of my dear departed Lester. I jus' gots to have a piece of him with me for old time sake. I knows you will make him look like hisself again, not stiff and shut down, like here, though he do look good, don't he? Bless his soul! Lester, he a *serious* man. But maybe you could jus' give him a hint of a smile, Mr. Orvelle, jus' right here at the corner of his mouth?" She pointed a gnarled finger to the long, straight line on Lester's face, the mouth sealed forever against all the secrets inside.

As Orvelle looked into the smooth silver capsule, he saw from the set of the jaw, the thin straight pursed lips, and the number eleven carved deeply between two straight brows that, indeed, Mr. Farrow had been a very serious man. Orvelle studied him intently, searching for some clue of kindness or warmth, some trace of color in that ashen visage, but none did he find. Orvelle paused, closing his eyes, one moment only. Then he turned back to Mrs. Farrow and enveloped her small knobby hand with both of his. He murmured, "Miz Farrow, I can paint this picture for you."

Mrs. Farrow's chest heaved once or twice as tears spilled down her soft crumpled cheeks. "Oh, thank you, Mr. Orvelle! I gots a little money set aside from selling my pies. I can pay whatever you say. I jus' got to have a little piece of my Lester. Now you jus' take his picture with your camera. You brung your camera? Oh good. You jus' take all the pictures you needs to make your painting from. You go on now."

"Yes, ma'am, Miz Farrow." Now Orvelle ducked his head as he pulled the strap from around his neck and held the camera to his chest a moment. He glanced around at the tiny dim lamp-lit parlor and hoped for the best from the automatic flash. Orvelle circled the coffin, composing mentally, then settled on a position close to the foot and to one side. He focused, froze, then depressed the shutter button. He leaned closer for a detailed shot. The flash bounced off the sheen of the coat, the luster of the oyster satin, the silver rim of the vessel, but shed no light on the face itself. That face seemed to absorb all the light in the room and not give any of it back.

"I knows you make him look good, Mr. Orvelle! Thank you so much! I jus' knows he gon' look real good!" said Mrs. Farrow. She smiled for the first time.

Orvelle nodded. He knew that, in fact, he *would* make Lester Farrow look good. His paintings just *came out* somehow, with the help of the Good Lord of Heaven and Earth. There was no doubt in Orvelle, no doubt at all.

Mrs. Farrow was bent over the casket now, smoothing Lester's suit front with her knobby little hand, shaking her head slowly over the man-shadow cradled in satin that had been her partner for all her womanly years.

Orvelle looped the strap over his head and tucked the camera back under his arm, satisfied that all that there was left in this world to see of Lester Farrow was captured on the twelve-exposure film coiled tightly in the belly of that camera. He breathed a deep breath and turned toward Orilla, who was standing behind him, her bright eyes taking in the scene. He took her by the arm and moved toward the door, through the tangle of passages and out into the warm, weak light of the porch. If anything, there were even more people gathered, jostling, and more voices, raucous and mournful at once, on the porch, and the two visitors waded through more islands of mourners in the nearly-dark yard.

As Orvelle and Orilla moved toward where they remembered the truck to be, a startling blue-white light assaulted their eyes. Suspended beneath a low branch of a huge old oak tree, the specter swayed and shimmered in the spring evening and glinted off the side-view mirror of Orvelle's truck. Before Orvelle's mind settled on its function, a sudden electric jolt betrayed the light's true purpose, not to warn or beckon or portend, but to reduce the mosquito population thereabouts.

Orvelle and Orilla climbed back up onto the truck seat, he with graceful ease, she with more effort, and sat in silence for half a minute before Orilla, her purse cradled in the shapeless folds of her lap, said softly, looking straight ahead, "He beat her, you know."

"Oh-rilla, how *can* you know that?" Orvelle said. "You don't know those people!"

"I just knows some things, Orvelle, and this thing do I know— I saw it hundred-watt clear, standin' in that musty parlor room, Orvelle—he done beat that woman. *Um*-hmmm. And what she do? She bake him sweet potato *pie*."

Orvelle put the truck in gear and the Chevrolet ambled across the yard back out to the road. In the rear-view mirror the blue light hovered and twisted and shrank and vanished, a wraith in the dusk.

They rode home in silence. Orvelle felt sadness like a lead jacket pressing him down into the cracked vinyl. Orilla's bright eyes smoldered in the darkness.

Back home once more, Orilla slipped her loafers off and slid her feet back into her slippers. She set to work putting away the dishes, sweeping, straightening up a bit. Then she scuffled over to the sofa and sank down onto it with an "umh." She looked to Orvelle like another of the oversize earth-tone roses that scrolled across the cream-colored sofa where she sat; so round, bright and pretty was she.

Orilla reached down beside the sofa for a brown paper grocery sack and set it next to her. She pulled out shapes of bold fabric and resumed piecing them together in an unspoken pattern that she translated into life as it unfolded in her mind. After a while she spread the squares she had already sewn one by one in her lap, smoothed their wrinkles slowly, deliberately, and said, "That just fine, then."

Orvelle settled himself back into his armchair and positioned the painting board across his lap. He turned the television on, down low. He arranged his supplies around him once more. Soon he would begin something larger, something for the Liberty Guild art show next month. Now, though, he held up a blank eight-by-ten canvas at arm's length before him, thinking to begin another of his landscapes, as was his custom in the evening. But all that his eyes projected onto the pure white rectangle was a pulsing black star the shape of the wraith-light under the mourning oak tree in the Glades.

The June Meeting

On a Saturday morning, just as fickle May turned in earnest to warm, constant June, the phone rang at the Bloom house. Lucy answered, tucking the cordless receiver between her shoulder and ear while she pulled hot bed sheets from the dryer. The baby scooted, salamander-like, across the kitchen floor after her, whimpering. A raspy voice spoke on the other end of the line.

"Hey. Lucy. You know the Guild meeting is next week?"

"Hey, Aylin. I guess I remembered that was coming up," said Lucy, reaching her arms into the hot metal drum and trying not to drop the phone.

"Yeah, well, the fact is, I'm having some car trouble and I could use a ride over there." Random crackles jumped across the phone line, and Lucy could hear cheering and applause in the background—stale, unmistakable sounds of some game show on an aging television set. Lucy scooped up the whimpering baby and nestled her among the warm sheets in the laundry basket.

"Actually, I wasn't too sure that I would go. There's so much going on around here, and it's hard to get away at the children's bedtime," said Lucy.

"Listen, girl, you've got to go. You owe it to yourself," urged Aylin.

Lucy hefted the laundry basket onto her hip, baby and all. She

133

picked her way through the obstacle course of the den where toys were strewn everywhere. Ian was sprawled on his belly crashing a tiny police car into a pile of blocks over and over. Jack was sitting in a child-size lawn chair snipping slivers of paper from old catalogs. He had just caught on to using scissors and was fanatically slicing everything from the recycling bin into a blizzard of white, grey and colored slips.

"I haven't had a chance to do any new artwork in weeks," Lucy told Aylin. "I've had my hands full with, well, with other things. I know the show is coming up, and I should be getting my paintings to a framer in the next week or two, but I can't seem to get anything done."

"Listen, Lucy, I'm willing to come babysit for you. I have done lots of babysitting, well not a lot of *baby*sitting, exactly. More like old-person-sitting, mostly, but it's got to be about the same, right? And then of course there's my daughter's girl too. Just say the day."

"Uh, thanks. I'll keep that in mind. Thanks for offering." Aylin seemed all right, but then again... When Lucy pictured her husband meeting Aylin as the babysitter, she decided to put off anything definite. On the other hand, this woman was the only person who had ever offered to help with the children, and she had to feel grateful for that. Didn't that generosity in and of itself make Aylin a good person?

"Hey, give yourself a deadline," said Aylin. "Say, 'I'm going to get a new painting done by Thursday night.' Then bring it to the meeting for show-and-tell. That will help motivate you."

"O.K., that's a good idea. I'll try," said Lucy, bouncing the baby along the hallway in the basket. Evie chortled deep in her throat.

"So, Aylin, tell me how the rest of the festival went after I left, after the wind thing," she said.

"Awful. No one came. It was deserted all afternoon and hot as blazes. All the artists started packing up early, even though we had signed this contract saying that we would stay set up for the entire two-day duration. What a waste. Nobody sold anything, except that guy with the fancy booth. He *said* business was off, but he sold five paintings. That sounds like success to me." Aylin was talking louder now and faster.

"Hey, you know what I'm going to do? I'm going to contact the organizer. I'm going to get my money back, the money for the booth fee. It was all a racket! I mean, *really*; they had to know people weren't going to go way out to that old hayfield in the middle of nowhere to buy art. Taking our money was plain, outright *fraud*."

"Maybe. But it was worth a try, wasn't it? You won't ever sell much just sitting in your own kitchen," said Lucy, spreading the clean sheets on the bed. She shifted the phone to the other shoulder to relieve her neck.

A shrill voice was screaming in the background on the receiver: "Just clear out! Just clear out, I say!" There were some other words that were unintelligible, and then, "Where's my stick! My *stick*, I said!"

"Is everything all right there, Aylin?" Lucy asked, wondering who the screaming voice belonged to, wondering what was going on at Aylin's house, wondering for the first time what her house *was* like.

"Yeah, fine. Same as usual," said Aylin flatly.

"Look, I'll try to make it Thursday. I'll call you that afternoon to let you know for sure."

"Not necessary. I know you'll make it."

Lucy found Aylin's certainty annoying. "Well, where do you live?" she asked.

"I live out at the lake. That shouldn't be too far for you," said Aylin.

"No, it's just a few miles." Actually it was thirteen. That would

135

add half an hour to her trip both before and after the meeting. That was an extra hour out of the house, an hour she really couldn't afford. "How do I find your house?"

"Tell you what, I'll just meet you at the entrance to the golf course, where the big gates are. My place is a little hard to find."

"All right," agreed Lucy. "I think I know where the gates are."

She was intentionally silent then, hoping the conversation was over. She heard more crackling and television noise and the loud voice still ranting in the background. Aylin did not break the silence.

Finally, Lucy said, "All right then, Thursday. See you in a few days."

"Yeah, Thursday. And don't forget: Bring your new painting." The phone clicked.

Lucy held the receiver out in front of her, looking at it for a moment. She stuck it in her back pocket and smoothed the haphazard bedclothes. Thursday was only five days away. How would she get something new done by then? She corralled the roving baby and carried her off to find a clean diaper.

Lucy went about her chores for an hour or two, and always, it seemed, just beyond her peripheral vision, were the large seductive blooms of the magnolia next door calling her out. She had seen them there, showy and voluptuous, on her way back from the grocery store. Midday plodded closer, and she tried to focus on the children and the work, but hovering nearby were the blossoms. She was already painting a new watercolor in her mind.

Somewhere within her divided consciousness she noted that the boys had been unusually peaceful today. She had not had to break up a single scuffle. She wondered if someone was running a fever.

At that moment the door opened and shut, and she heard her husband's footsteps in the kitchen. She hurried toward them with the baby creeping behind, whimpering again.

"Hey, Jackson Honey," she said to his damp, grimy, tired back. He had already sunk onto a kitchen chair and was bent forward taking his work boots off.

"Hey there, Lucy Girl." He smelled like rich, black earth and crushed leaves.

"Daddy, Daddy, Daddy, Daddy!" shouted Ian, scrambling up onto his father's lap.

"Hey, there, little buddy." Jackson smiled a bit and rubbed the little boy's head.

"You're home early," Lucy said. He glanced up at her.

"Yeah, well, it's raining. It's hard to do landscape work when it's this wet."

"Oh, I hadn't noticed the rain," she said. She was glad to have him home, but the flip side of that was a smaller paycheck, and she knew he was thinking about it.

"I'll get you something to eat. I bet you're hungry anyway."

"That'd be great." He sighed. "I'm just going to go get cleaned up first." He rose, set his boots by the kitchen door, and picked his way through the chaos of the den. Clearly, now, Lucy saw through Jackson's weary eyes the cluttered kitchen table, the laundry piled high, the floor covered in kid stuff, and she felt a wave of guilt. She had worked all morning trying to make inroads, but there was little visible evidence.

"Come on, boys, let's get some of this mess put away now so your daddy can walk through here better." She handed Ian a plastic pail, and with glee he began dumping his cars into it as fast as he could go. Lucy hurriedly shuffled things—mail, toys, books, crayon drawings, odds and ends—on the table, making room for plates and bowls and cups. She set a pot of soup on the stove to heat up. She stepped back into the den.

"Come on, Jack, let's pick up this mess. *Now*," she said to her older son still sitting in the little folding chair. He did not answer.

"Jack?" she said, and moved over beside him, near the window, to look closer at what he was doing. Jack sat in the middle of an avalanche of paper clippings, of long slender shapes with sharp or blunt ends. Across the arms of the lawn chair rested a wooden board. Lucy wondered where the board had come from, then recognized it as a loose board from the old coffee table on the back porch where the boys liked to picnic when the weather was nice. On the board were spread dozens, no *hundreds* of slips of paper. They formed an elaborate maze of shapes, a floor plan of rectangles, ells, bays, towers, rooms and anterooms, porches and walkways. Jack was adding a small rectangular shape off to one side.

"This is a window flower box for the kitchen of the castle," he said.

Lucy did not know what to make of the design. How could a little boy, a five-year-old, imagine how a building would look from above? Maybe she was mistaken about what he had done. "Jack, tell me what you're making there."

His voice was small and quiet, as if he were speaking from another room or from across the yard, or perhaps as if he were explaining something very simple to a smaller child. "I'm making a castle. I can see it from the air." He continued arranging the strips without looking up.

"What do you mean, you can see it from the air?" Lucy asked.

"I can see this place from my dream. I'm in a helicopter, you know, the kind that goes to heaven. Or maybe I'm on a cloud, I don't know, and I can see this place down through the air, and it has rooms, lots of rooms, and I just want to make it real because people can be happy here. But they need this box by the kitchen for flowers because flowers make people happy."

He looked up, straight at his mother, and said, "Flowers make *you* happy." Jack looked down again and went on carefully placing the paper slivers.

"Is this a place you have seen in a picture? In a book, maybe?" she asked.

"No, Mom," he shook his head soberly, "not in a *book*. I *dreamed* it. And I saw right down through the roof at all the people moving around. And I saw straight into my room, right here." He pointed to an inner rectangle. "And I saw myself sleeping in the bed. See where I put the bed?"

"Oh, yes, I see it. I like what you made here, Jack."

"And you know the best part, Mom? I can move these walls around on the board any way I need to, because the rooms in the castle I saw move around. The people can go through doors into one room and then that room moves and they can walk into another room, and they can see each other and play or talk. Well, the grownups talk because that's what grownups do, you know. They talk and talk and talk."

"Can you tell what this place looks like on the outside?"

"Mom," he said with great patience, "it looks like paper. All paper. And paper is falling down from the sky all around like snow. But some people don't know the castle is there because the paper hides it. See?" Jack swirled his two hands around in the piles of tiny paper snippets around him on the floor and grabbed some up and then let them drift little by little down upon the shapes on the board.

It's funny, thought Lucy, *how you can raise and nurture and feed and be with a child all the days of his life and not know a fraction of what goes on in his mind.* A flash of foresight hit Lucy, a knowledge that the growth of a child is accompanied by a tearing away, a separation sure and steady from his parent all of his moments until he stands alone, free, unencumbered, and entirely unwrapped. Then it is for the parent to just stand back and look and look and look.

"Well, Jack," she said. "It's time for lunch."

Hunger made sense to him. He rose slowly, like a little old man, and turned to set the board back down across the arms of the lawn chair with utmost care, glaring at his little brother in preemptive warning.

Four chairs and a high chair barely fit around the small, round kitchen table. The family slid into place, a living Chinese puzzle. They breathed each other's air. They fed together like one organism, like a starfish. Lucy had heard once that sometimes one arm of a starfish would start marching away; it would march away and break itself loose, and just keep walking. And no one knew why this was so. She shuddered.

Even with all the lights on, the room was dim, especially for noontime in the spring. The rain had thickened to a downpour that brought a false twilight. Lucy heaved up the reluctant sashes to the two windows in the corner where the table sat to let in some of the freshly laundered air. Throughout their lunch of soup and crackers and cheese, she could smell the rain-exaggerated fragrance of flowering jasmine insinuating itself into the pleasant aroma of warm food, newly-showered husband, and busy-bodied children.

After the lunch was eaten and the dishes were cleared away and washed and the laundry was shifted and the baby was nursed and changed and the library books were read quietly while the baseball game played on the T.V. across the room—after all these things, Ian asked to bring out the little wooden animals that Cordelia Wise had given them at the festival. Lucy pulled the cloth bag from the top shelf of her closet and removed everything from the kitchen table, with a momentary pang of regret that she could not now spread her paper and her paints out on it. Instead, she gently spilled out the contents of the bag on the table, the little open boat and the creatures both familiar and strange. She set Ian up on his knees on top of the old dictionary laid on his chair seat. She set the baby in her high chair beside him. Jack scrambled up on the other side.

Lucy stepped back and watched for a moment. Without hesitation, the two boys began setting up the animals using the Grand Logic of Children, that mysterious gift lost to most people past the age of ten or so that whispers how to arrange, to move, to interplay objects, that lets wood or plastic or paper come alive. Both boys took for granted this Grand Logic; without speaking they knew what the rules were.

When they were ready, Ian reached out a grubby hand toward the baby to get her attention and said in a sing-song voice, "Once upon a time there was a swamp. It was very pretty. It was where Miss Goodie Wiselady lived." And together the boys, taking turns, one picking up where the other left off, like the meandering, irresistible flow of a river, told to the wide-eyed baby the story that the old woman had told to them, with only a few added convolutions.

Unseen, inconsequential for the moment to her children, Lucy looked at the three glowing faces. She breathed in the lingering odor of the soup, the seductive jasmine. She listened to the slow sighs of the resting man and the soft percussion of the rain. She picked up a small wooden fawn with a tiny white tail and rubbed its smooth side where Cordelia's hands had whittled away the rough edges, had cut away the snare holding the struggling creature inside the old root. And Lucy could not choose any of her loves to deny.

* * *

Sadie was disgruntled on Thursday, more disgruntled than the spoiled old girl had any right to be. She refused the harness for the plow, kept shaking it off with every attempt James made to settle it on her. She stood with her head down twitching her ears compulsively, looking at James out the corner of her eye with suspicion. It took an hour longer than usual to get going that morning, and James was thinking that at this rate he might not have things wrapped up in time to get to the Artists Guild meeting tonight. He could not say why he was set on going. Except, maybe, spending his days with mules and pigs and manure and chickens and red clay was not as completely satisfying as he had first thought it to be. And he did like to draw.

Once Sadie shook her mood, however, around mid-morning, she stepped up and pulled like a pro, and the plowing went smoothly the rest of the day. As the sunlight began to slant low across the field and throw shadow stripes from the barn across the paddock, James figured he would chuck it in for the day, grab a shower and a sandwich, and head on over to the library. He brushed down the mule and gave her a bucket of corn, securing her in her stall in the old barn. At last he crossed the thirty or so yards to the house.

He had only minimal plumbing in the cabin, just one ancient cast iron basin for a sink and a tiny round commode in what had once been a pantry, a gun cabinet, or a broom closet—it was hard to tell which. An earlier occupant had rigged up a cold water shower outdoors, just outside the door in the ell formed when the bedroom was added on fifty years ago, joined to the side of the original one-room house. A couple of sheets of lattice screened the shower from the road, and a few planks underfoot allowed the water and dirt to run through. James was certain the mail lady came early in the day, and nobody else came by much; he was confident as usual that his evening shower would not be interrupted or even noticed.

This particular day, he planned to allow himself the luxury of a bit of shampoo and a little more energetic scrubbing than usual. The temperature was perfect. James took off his boots and socks and reached around the lattice to stash them there to keep dry. He stripped off his sweaty, grimy field clothes and hung them on a nail over the boots. He turned the old daisy-shaped spigot, and water spluttered and spurted out of the faucet in an unreliable stream. James ducked his head under the stream and gasped.

"Hoooo-eee!" he yelled. The water was dependable as far as temperature: always water-table cold from the deep, deep well. He blew as he faced into it and scrubbed through his beard vigorously. Then he gave in to the sweet old song that had been running through his head the whole afternoon. *"When the blackbird in the Spring, on the willow tree, sat and rocked, I heard him sing, singing Aura Lea."*

With his eyes closed, he felt around on a shelf for the handmade soap and rubbed it all over himself. It worked pretty well to get the grime off, but he did have to admit he missed lather. *"Aura Lea, Aura Lea, maid with golden hair..."* He cleared his throat. *"Maid with long black hair..."* He spent extra time on each foot, lifting and crossing one leg at a time in front of the opposite knee so that he could reach.

"Sunshine came along with thee, and swallows in the air."

Now, all done except for the hair. He grabbed the travel size shampoo bottle from the shelf with one hand. He leaned back to let the water run from his forehead down over his neck and back and looked up. The rectangle above was clear and warm and pale yellow as a smile, framed all around by the weathered wood.

He crooned toward the sky: *"Sunshine came along with thee, and swallows in the air."* He dabbed a bit of shampoo into his hand and began to work it into his hair, luxuriating in the aroma and the lather with his eyes tightly closed against the sting. It was not organic; it was Herbal Essence. *We all have to indulge our vices from time to time,* James reasoned.

At that moment, he began to sense a disturbance in the natural unfolding of his solitary evening shower time. He sensed, rather than heard, footsteps, slow and stealthy. Fully lathered, he leaned forward out of the water stream and said, "Hello?" There was no answer. Now he heard a scuffling sound. He opened his eyes and saw a dark shape beyond the latticework. James looked around him, suds streaming down his face and chest and shoulders, for something he could use as a weapon, if need be. Anyone this stealthy had to be up to no good.

He reached into the corner by the door and grabbed his kayak paddle, still propped there from the previous weekend when he had gone kayaking on the river up north with his university buddies. James crouched there on the wet planks fully alert, tensed, and ready to spring into action with the paddle, his hair full of aromatic white foam, bubbles coasting down his skin, his eyes squinting back the sting. He was not a big guy, true, but he was wiry, and he was sure he could take an intruder on his own turf any day.

As he crouched there waiting, tightly-coiled, around the end of the lattice edged a grey-white half-moon shape, with black chin whiskers and an enormous gaping nostril. Soon a long chestnut head followed with huge black eyes and long, lady lashes until the entire head and neck were thrust around the lattice and into the shower stall, the huge dark velvet ears splayed out from the pointy head like arms on a windmill. James eased upward from his crouch, gaping at the mule in disbelief. Sadie threw back her head and let out a loud, "Whiiiiiiheeeeeeehawheeeeeehaw-heeee," with a snort for punctuation.

"Oh, you! Sadie! What do you think you're doing? I'm gonna get you, girl!" He stamped his foot, brandished the paddle, and lunged at her. "Get on out! Get out of here!" He started to chase the unfazed mule with the paddle but realized five yards outside the opening to the lattice shower stall that he was naked as naked could be. Sadie just stood there, barely out of reach, not falling for

144

his feints, taunting him with her bristly lips pulled back from her teeth. He did not want to see himself chase the mule all the way back to her stall wearing nothing but a kayak paddle and some lingering suds. There was nothing for him to do but rinse the shampoo out and finish his shower.

The soft water from the well was maddeningly slow at rinsing the soap away. He opened one eye as often as he could to make sure Sadie kept her distance. She stood there in the opening again, staring and grinning away. Never had he felt so naked in all his life. He toweled off and slipped on his clean jeans. Then, finally, he picked up the paddle and prodded the unrepentant mule into a gallop. He ran after her, cursing the sharp Bermuda grass stubble beneath his bare feet. She threw back her head and cackled gleefully, moving just fast enough to keep out of the paddle's reach. He chased her all the way back to the stall where she knew she belonged, where he had left her half an hour before safely secured.

It wasn't until James stomped back up across the yard and around the house and reached the lattice entryway that he realized his boots were missing. He stopped short, shaking his head, sputtering some inventive words, and looked down at his feet, which hadn't stayed clean for long. He would not have thought Sadie capable of theft and subterfuge, but then, she was more human than mule, it seemed. The boots would turn up, sooner or later; she couldn't have carried them far. He threw on the rest of his clothes and a pair of tennis shoes, grabbed his sketch pad, cranked up the old truck, and ate a sandwich on his way to town.

The Guild meeting was already well underway by the time James arrived at the library. He sidled into the back row with his sketch pad under his arm and sat near the woman with the long, smooth black hair. Lucy, her name was. He had only spoken to her twice, first at the previous meeting, and second at the Box Hollow thing, but it seemed as if... He waved to her over the heads of the two little boys who sat between them, swinging their sneakers against the chair legs. Lucy smiled in return, and as she swept back her silky hair, he noticed the baby sitting in her lap bent forward fingering her own tiny bare toes delicately. *Beautiful*, James thought.

He shifted his attention to the meeting room. Surveying the crowd, he noted that the same number of people were in attendance tonight as were at the previous meeting, nearly all the same folks too, and they were sitting almost to a person in the same seats they had occupied before, as if a teacher had assigned their seating. He could not remember their names, except for Lucy's, but he could remember the details of their faces, their artwork, their clothing, every visual thing about them. James did not find his observational skills remarkable; he had always perceived the world this way. He was simply an observer, a recorder, not a wonderer, not a philosopher. His perception of visible details and his memory for them stood him in good stead as an amateur sketch artist, if not as a mule-handler.

The president, the lady with the greying hair who looked remarkably like his mother—Eleanor was her name, he remembered then, a queenly name—was speaking, something about elections for next year, not at all interesting, so he began again to observe.

In his first minute James noted and recorded the following: The red-haired hippie woman had a badly-peeling sunburn and wore the same clothes she had worn last time. She had a purple smudge like a dark crescent moon on her left temple. A young girl, a teenager, sat in the front row with unlikely yellow hair waving down her straight back. She was new. The African American pair sat together unspeaking and perfectly still except for the woman's hands moving restlessly in her lap, occupied with something he could not see. The wealthy couple sat together also, also unspeaking. The wife's hair dye shade, her unnatural nail color, and her huge matching red handbag on the chair beside her were different tonight. The bag was moving and appeared to have some sort of small living thing stowed in it. A lapdog? The grey cast to the man's face and his tether to the oxygen tank were unchanged from last time.

Eleanor's voice interrupted his survey by announcing, "Well, folks, that's most of our business for tonight. Time to begin our show-and-tell." Everyone looked around to see who was making a move to the front. No one rose from his seat.

"All right, then," Eleanor said. "Why don't we let our newest member, Morgan Satterwhite, show us her work first. Morgan is a sophomore at Liberty High School and a neighbor of mine. She is quite a talented young artist. So, Morgan, why don't you share with us what you've brought?"

The girl with the yellow hair looked left and right and then stood up slowly. She carried a cardboard box to the front with her and set it on the lectern. She proceeded to pull out one small canvas after another, all identical in subject and size, about a foot square. She held them up for the crowd to see, held them before her face for several seconds each before putting them back in the box. Every square showed a bright assemblage of shapes and pattern; every single painting was composed of sharp color and torn paper plastered even around the deep sides of the canvas, varnished together, paint and paper, into images that were undeniably houses, even if unconventional ones. If he had been a wonderer, James would have wondered why a teenage girl would paint house after house after house. That seemed like more of an occupation for a little girl, maybe a kindergartener. But he did not wonder; he merely observed.

After the girl, other artists moved forward one at a time to share what they had brought with them. There were more misguided botanical still lifes, more oily nudes, more turned wooden bowls made from fallen trees with surprisingly beautiful and apparently desirable insect damage, another slick acrylic golf course in unnatural green, and one truly noteworthy giant bug painted menacingly in poster paint on cardboard. This last was from the strange non-speaking man whose quick, sporadic movements were reminiscent of an insect's, and who, again, made zero eye contact. This was all great stuff. James had not seen anything nearly this entertaining since before he had given up his T.V. set.

Out of the corner of his eye, he caught Lucy making motions, and he looked over at her. "James! It's your turn," she was whispering. "Now get on up there! Go!" Suddenly, he realized that his feet were obeying her against his will, carrying him up to the front of the room.

Once there he said, "Uh, right, so here I am. I'm James Caldwell, organic farmer of Corbie-Well Organic fame. And by the way, we will be open for business selling our organic produce soon, by July first, so come on out." James felt all his careful ablutions undone in an instant by the sweat beginning to pearlize on his skin. He had been far more comfortable in the back row. "Three miles out Apt-to-Miss Road off of Eighty-three, daylight to dusk."

He pulled his sketch book out from under his arm and thumbed through it. "Well, O.K., people, I'm not really an artist like all of you. I just like to draw. But I thought I'd show you a few sketches anyway. Give you a feel for the farm life, if nothing else." He shared several drawings in number-two pencil all built with slow and careful shadow layers of exceedingly parallel lines. For another of James's talents was straight lines, and that talent stood him in good stead when building or plowing or just generally keeping himself on the straight and narrow.

Finally, he held up a drawing that prompted some laughter. He himself was still quite sore at the subject and not yet inclined to laugh at her. But here was a pencil portrait of a long dark face, with darker shining eyes, and unbelievably long, fringed ears splayed out like windmill arms. A long black tassel of hair fell casually over to one side of the pointed head. The brows over the dark knowing eyes bulged with a professorly intelligence. The muzzle was ghost grey with cavernous nostrils, and the bit of mouth that showed wore an unmistakable smirk.

"This is my girl, Sadie. Well, she thinks she is, anyway. My girl, that is. We have a love-hate relationship. But she pulls my plow, and she's good to draw." He closed the drawing pad.

"That's it, that's all I got," he said, and he stepped away from the podium and headed back to his seat.

"Hey, that was good. I love that mule!" said Lucy in a low tone across the squirming boys, one of whom was now worming his way beneath the row of seats.

"Oh, yeah? Well, she's one of a kind." James took a mental snapshot of Lucy's steady grey eyes. Worth remembering.

Eleanor was reminding them all now of the upcoming Big Show, just two weeks away, of the purchase awards and cash prizes, of the swanky reception that the Historical Society was planning, "so we must all dress accordingly," of the set-up date the Friday before the event. She asked for a show of hands from those who could help hang the show. A few went slowly up. Eleanor frowned a bit.

"Oh, well, I guess that will have to do. Everyone must have his or her work suitably framed and to the Historical Society headquarters—Reaves Hall on Main Street—by ten o'clock that Friday morning. Those who can stay to set up, please do. Unfortunately, I won't be able to be there that day; I have an appointment in Atlanta that I can't miss. But if those of you who aren't working can help for an hour or two, I'm sure it will all get set up in time." The audience was politely attentive. Eleanor asked each member to call out how many works he or she was planning to enter, and she jotted down the numbers.

She was intent on figuring for a few moments, and then she went on. "The Historical Society will have its own pictures removed and stored, so we can hang two-dimensional work right on the wall. I've done a rough estimate of how much work we'll have altogether, and there should be plenty of wall space. Also there are a few surfaces available to serve as pedestals for sculptures. I know that Chesley Fox Chiswell will have at least two of his stonework pieces there, although, of course, he couldn't bring them to the library for the critique or the show-and-tell due to their weight."

Really? James thought. *Did I just hear that name right? Chesley Fox Chiswell? That has to be a made-up name. And for a sculptor? Too ludicrous.* James could not wait to meet him.

The meeting was winding down, and just in time, considering the state of the three children in the back row. The smaller boy had collected a handful of plugs from the edges of the meeting room chairs. The baby with her fist in her mouth had a contentious argument going with herself. And the oldest stood glowering at James for some unknown infraction or other.

"Hey, when can I come ride your old mule?" the boy demanded.

"Oh, you remember her, do you? From the festival? Well, she's not much of one for giving rides. She's just used to pulling the old plow and pretty much doing whatever she feels like," James said. "But maybe your mom can bring you out to the farm sometime and see her in action."

Lucy was stuffing a cotton blanket, baby toys, and a half-eaten cracker into a bulging quilted bag. She stood up with the baby on her hip, her hair falling like rain over her shoulders. "Now, Ian," she was saying to the smaller boy, "stick those plugs back in where they belong. You can't take them home."

She turned her gaze to James. "So, will you be bringing

something for the Midsummer Show?"

"Sure, I wouldn't miss it. How about you?"

"Oh, yes. That is, I'll have to see if—"

At that moment the hippie lady walked up, eyeing the boys who were now tussling on the floor and the baby fretting in Lucy's arms. "The kids are getting restless, I see," interrupted the woman.

"You could say that," said Lucy. She turned to James. "It's late to have them out, but Jackson, my husband, had to work till eight tonight, so I had to either bring them or miss the meeting."

Aylin grunted.

"Oh, yeah? What does he do?" asked James.

"He's a mechanic, and he does some landscaping too."

"Cool," said James. Traditional tools were more his line, but he could respect the skills of any man who worked with his hands.

"We're about ready to go," Lucy went on. The baby was squirming and jabbering. "How about you, Aylin? Are you ready?"

"Oh, I thought I'd let you off the hook and find another ride home." She wheeled around toward James. "You're off Eighty-three, right? You're going my direction anyway. Can I grab a ride with you?"

"Well... I... yeah, I guess so," James stammered as he slid his eyes over toward Lucy, who looked surprised and relieved all at once. He couldn't tell how these two women were connected, but there was something...

"I've got to warn you, though; my means of transportation is a little rustic."

"Oh, no problem. Whatever it is, it beats walking."

James nodded. He couldn't argue with her logic. But this woman—she seemed so... enthusiastic.

"Let's get going," said Aylin. "The night's not getting any younger."

"Might as well," he said. "I guess." They turned to go.

151

James looked back at Lucy and waved. "See you at the show."

"Yes. Goodbye, James the Organic Farmer. See you at Midsummer." She pulled a Kleenex from her jeans pocket, wiped the baby's nose, and tucked the Kleenex back in her pocket, all in one fluid movement.

"Oh, and hey, Lucy," Aylin called over her shoulder as she was moving off with James, "don't forget about the babysitting."

"O.K., thanks, I'll keep it in mind," said Lucy, helping the boys gather up their belongings.

James was painfully aware of the jangling and swishing the red-haired woman generated and of looks being cast their way as they moved through the room out into the corridor. He wondered what he was getting himself into. He led the way to the old Ford parked beneath a flaming red evening sky outside the library. He yanked the passenger side door open. It screeched on ancient hinges.

"Oh, a gentleman. Thanks," said Aylin.

James stared at her a moment. She was on his own eye level. Her make-up, thick and moist as mayonnaise in places, was wearing thin over her left temple where a dark smudge—no, he could see now up close, it was a bruise—shone through.

"Let me get this stuff out of the way," he said. "I don't have passengers much." Not ever, really. He grabbed up an old *Mother Earth News*, an axe head, three old cardboard egg flats, a paperback copy of *Silent Spring*, and a length of chain with a hook, and dumped them over back. "There you go," he said. He bowed slightly, then walked around the truck to the driver's side feeling foolish as Aylin climbed up onto the high bench seat. James hoped to get this over with as quickly as possible. He slid in behind the steering wheel, cranked the engine, and threw the stick in reverse. The woman beside him breathed in loudly through her nose, inhaling Old Truck Smell, that mysterious blend of motor oil, rusted metal, clay road dust, and sweat, with a hint of tobacco and stale coffee mixed in.

"Quite the retro vehicle you've got here."

"Yes, well, it came with the farm. Gas mileage is terrible, but it gets me around. Hauls stuff. Sorry, it's rough, I know."

"Oh, it's no skin off my teeth." She reached over and patted him on the leg. "I don't care what a car looks like as long as it gets me from Point A to Point B. And back again."

A painful silence ensued. James had little experience talking with people of her generation, other than his parents.

"If I net enough off this year's harvest, I'm going to look into buying a Prius."

"Ah. A yuppie car," murmured Aylin. More silence. Or rather, a lack of conversation. The truck, long devoid of any capacity for shock absorption, jostled the occupants of the cab without mercy. The jangle of the woman's bracelets joined in with the complaints of old truck joints and the rattle of unsecured cargo over the rough highway. He tried not to imagine her arms in the dark cab—that loose skin older women have there on the back of the upper arm— jiggling with the vibrations.

"So, whereabouts, exactly, do you live?" asked James.

"Out at the Lake. Whitetail Cove."

"I haven't been out that way before. It's a golf course community, right?"

"Yes—golf, recreation, lake-front."

"Did you retire there?" A long pause followed. The truck hit a pot hole and rattled all its bones violently.

"Uh, no, not quite. I'm staying in a friend's cottage till I find my own place. It's just transitional for me."

To break the silence that settled again he ventured, "So do you play golf much?" His only experience with the game was an all-night round of glow-in-the-dark with his increasingly drunk buddies, which had completely soured the game for him.

"No, no golf." Another pause.

"So you enjoy other amenities?"

"I paint," she said.

After an excruciating time, far longer than James had expected, the truck neared the main entrance to the Cove, with its lushly landscaped entryway. On a large wooden sign, the white outline of a huge etched deer glowed in the twilight, signaling the impending end of James's trial. Thankfully. The tail of the deer, held high and larger than life, gleamed like a lantern in the deepening dusk. An alien scent—what was it, incense?—had infiltrated the Old Truck Smell, and the air in the cab felt close and hot. As the truck slowed, James cranked down his window a few inches.

Aylin directed him through the winding lanes of the development, past houses that looked forty or fifty or even sixty years old, interspersed with woodsy lots, till they approached the gates to the golf course itself. He pictured the environs of each turn in photographic detail. He knew as long as the light held out he could find his way back out of this maze.

"All right. Now just follow this little access road here around to the right," Aylin said.

James guided the creaking Ford onto a narrow drive that presumably skirted the golf course, snaking around behind it through dense woods. No houses were visible, and no driveways led from this rutted narrow lane, barely a road at all at this point. The truck labored up a rise to where the lane ended in a rough gravel circle beside what looked to be a little-used maintenance shed. The shadowy open veldt of the golf course, abandoned now to the twilight and the sharp sparks of a few early lightning bugs, stretched out beyond the shed. Inky woods huddled opposite. There was no sign of a dwelling. However, parked off to one side of the gravel, facing downhill, squatted a battered old compact car of the 1970's, empty and derelict.

James shoved the stick into neutral and looked over at the woman beside him. She was turned toward him with one knee casually slung up on the seat.

"And your place is where?" he asked, the back of his neck beginning to prickle.

"Oh, it's just down that trail there." He looked where she pointed and could see no sign of a path, let alone a driveway.

"Carry my bag in for me?" she asked, cocking her head to one side girlishly.

"Well, uh, I don't think I—"

"Look," the passenger cut in, "I really appreciate you driving me home." She reached over and put her hand on his leg. "Frankly, I have no money to give you for gas, but I do want to show my appreciation..."

James stared at her, struggling to comprehend but resisting the conclusions he was beginning to draw.

"So, if you don't have anything else planned..." She smiled, her hand still on his leg.

"I've got to f-f-feed the mule," James said lamely.

"Uh huh. Surely it can wait till breakfast," said Aylin.

"She's temperamental."

The woman sighed. She turned to face the front, leaned back, and sighed again. She hauled her large tapestry bag from the floorboards and looped the straps over her shoulder. She turned up the handle of the door and pushed. It did not move. She shoved harder, and the door swung open with a plaintive screech.

"You can't say I didn't offer," she said in an ironic tone. "See you later. And thanks again."

"Bye," he squeaked. She heaved the door closed again, and he realized the least he could have done was to get out and help her with the ornery truck door. He watched the back of her swaying gypsy skirt disappear into the gloom of the woods down what he still could not distinguish as a path.

He really felt like he might be running a fever, and he felt slightly nauseous. He rolled the window down the rest of the way and heard for the first time the sound of thousands of amorous frogs. He realized that he must be near the water. He saw a dim yellow light appear some ways down into the woods. He backed the cumbersome truck around with several forward and backward attempts, trying to avoid the deserted Toyota, and rattled back down the darkening lane the way they had come.

There was just enough light to see the landmarks. The splayed, dim headlights of the old Ford swept along the winding lanes, capturing the occasional varmint that scurried across the road, in pursuit of some guilty delight, perhaps. James shuddered. As the tires ground their way out onto the highway again, he felt a little better, a little freer. The air in the cab was cooling down and returning to its normal stale smell, with a hint of jasmine from the open window. He would not long remember the awkwardness of the evening; sentiment did not linger with him as it did with some. What he could not forget, in fact what continued to hover before his mind's eye for days to come, was the precise shape of the purple bruise on the temple of the frizzy red-haired hippie woman.

* * *

Lucy's was the last car to leave the library parking lot after the meeting. Ian and Evie both were more resistant to their car seat restraints than usual this evening. They had crossed the sleep-time threshold and were well into their second wind. When Lucy finally pinned them down with their straps and harnesses, they went rigid, like butterflies in a lepidopterist display. She felt bad, subduing them like this, but she refused to drive even a mile without them strapped in. Jack had kept still in his seat during the entire process, a resigned look on his face. He knew by five years' experience how the battle would end.

Lucy wheeled the station wagon through the streets of Liberty and the county roads of Corbie under a sky streaked with all the colors of a summer peach's pulled-open flesh. Jack was keeping count out loud of the few early lightning bugs along the roadside. He was stumped on twelve, not knowing what number came next, so he started over two or three times before it registered with his mother.

"Thirteen," she said. "Thirteen comes after twelve, Jack."

"Twelve... thirteen... fifteen... nineteen... forty-two..." he said.

Before long Lucy turned the car into the driveway and drove past the huge neighboring magnolia with its blossoms glowing in the dusk like Japanese lanterns. She herded the children and lugged all their baggage into the house. She glanced at the clock on the stove: 8:57, late to begin bathtime and bedtime for three young children. She plunged into the ritual with what energy she had left.

Three quarters of an hour later Lucy tucked the boys in, then sat in the rocker in her darkened bedroom to nurse the baby, listening to the steady slow breathing of her already-sleeping husband. He worked long hours at the garage, and more hours evenings and weekends for the landscaping company, whenever the weather allowed and as long as the daylight held out. And when he wasn't working, he ate and he slept, until Sunday when he enjoyed the fruit of his labors, playing ball with Jack and carrying the baby around the yard, telling her in a gentle low voice all about the flowers, the insects, the birds, and whatever things they saw on their treasure hunt. He mowed the grass, with Ian pushing his little plastic lawnmower three steps behind him all the way. He read parts of the Sunday paper aloud to Lucy as she swept the porch or busied herself in some way around the house. Sometimes he would take the mop out of her hands, and finish the kitchen floor himself.

But six nights a week by eight-thirty or nine o'clock in the evening, Jackson was sound asleep, oblivious for a short while to the inescapable coming of his early morning rise. He made just enough money for them to get by. Maybe one day she could help by selling paintings. But when she had mentioned that to him not long ago, he had said he didn't see how that would make much difference. "What's the point, anyway, with all this painting?" he'd said. "Don't you have enough to keep you busy?" He hadn't meant to be unkind; he just couldn't relate to the urge to make things. But his questions stayed with her because they echoed her own doubts.

Feet padded into the room behind her.

"What is it, Jack?" she asked.

"Mom, Mom! You have to come—now!" he said in a loud whisper.

Lucy sat forward abruptly. "What? What is it? Are you O.K.? Is Ian O.K.?" she whispered back.

"Yeah. He's O.K. But you have to come now!" he said as if the house were burning down. "The sky is vermilion!"

"What?" Lucy said. What did a five-year-old know of vermilion? But he had already disappeared through the bedroom doorway.

Lucy laid the baby in her crib, sated, content, and nearly asleep. She followed Jack's bare feet down the hall and out onto the front porch. The sky was approaching indigo now, but low to the horizon, where the sun had just escaped with the day, a hot swath of feral red swept across the west. Black trees in the middle distance reached their fingers up into the disquieting color as if to claw at it and tear it down. As Lucy and Jack stood hand-in-hand and watched, the vermilion turned tail and vanished from the sky, leaving indigo to rule the night, all uncompromisingly dark. If she had delayed for even a minute, she would have missed it.

"All right, Jack, let's get you to bed. And this time for good." Lucy urged him down the hall to his room with a hand on his back.

She tucked him in again. She paused over the rising and falling shape of Ian with his knees tucked up beneath him and his bottom in the air. She hovered a moment over the baby, who smiled fleetingly in her sleep.

Lucy changed into her nightgown and brushed her teeth, lifted the sheet and the cotton blanket, and slipped in, wrapping herself around the crescent of her sleeping husband. He was so warm, Jackson, like a smooth boulder beautiful with living moss and dappled forest light, where she could sun herself, safe and warm, lifted up in the midst of a shifting stream. He stirred, turned over, and put his arms around her. She could feel but not see the moment he opened his eyes to her in the dark.

Later, when Jackson slept again, Lucy lay awake for some time. She watched stripes of moonlight stretch across the blanket. After midnight, she rose and walked soundlessly down the hall and into the kitchen. She closed the door behind her and turned on the single lamp over the kitchen table. As she cleared all the clutter from the table and piled it on the counter, a purple scrap of paper fluttered to the floor. She picked it up and saw there in her husband's scrawl: "V. Hennessey—mural" and a phone number. "Huh," she said aloud, and then anchored the slip to the refrigerator with an ice cream cone magnet that someone, sometime, had nibbled on the sly.

Lucy shook off her thoughts to turn again to her late-night calling. She slipped a large sheet of heavy paper out of a carton stowed behind the door, pulled out a small dented metal tool-kit holding her paints and brushes from a cabinet over the refrigerator, filled an old jar with water, and began to paint.

* * *

In a two story Victorian house across town that night Eleanor

Wood was wakeful as well. But that was not unusual. She still woke throughout the night, listening for her children who had years ago grown and left this house, one after the other, in relentless succession. The night shadows were a cold violet-grey: Life took on a different color when you had no one left to look after.

This particular night the moon was over-large, and so much light came slanting across her bedroom that she could imagine searchlights accosting her window. But it was just the moon and the surprising luminosity of its second-hand light. She heard the old mantel clock downstairs strike one. Her thoughts raced away like startled horses, and when that happened, there was no reining them in.

Eleanor was thinking about Morgan, the girl who lived across the street, the girl with the hair that she would like to paint. Such hair! In the sun, the girl's long, thick sheaf shone like the simple gold ring that Eleanor still wore. Once a wedding ring, she had long since come to think of it as binding her not to her former husband but to her children, across time and age.

When the thought first occurred to her that Morgan's hair might be the same color, she disbelieved herself, but while she was carrying groceries into the house one bright afternoon, she glanced at the circle on her finger and across the street to where Morgan sat in a sunny spot. Back and forth she looked, several times, and saw that she was right. They were just the same. Beyond the mortal realm of hair it was, but too true to be a dye job either. She would like to try to capture the essence of it on canvas, regal and exuberant all at once. But the girl herself was the opposite, sober and withdrawn. *To think of painting it is selfish,* Eleanor thought. *Morgan's hair is something she would not want to share.* Somehow she was sure about this.

She had first seen the new girl at the Sampsons' one day a few weeks ago, when Eleanor was checking her mailbox. It was not

160

Morgan's looks that first caught Eleanor's attention; it was her actions. She was sitting on the crumbling brick wall at the edge of her yard with her knees drawn up. She appeared to be painting something. Eleanor had hesitated, and then she had gone over to speak to the girl and ask about her painting. Morgan looked wary, but when Eleanor told her that she was an artist too, the girl thawed a little. Since then, Eleanor had seen her there some days, and some days not. She was never working on homework or talking on the phone or reading a magazine or doing her nails, just painting. Or sometimes drawing. They would talk for a few minutes now and then.

Finally, Eleanor had had an idea. The girl's artwork was so original, and she seemed so committed to it. Maybe she could benefit from being around other artists. She might gain confidence and direction, two things she seemed to lack. Eleanor phoned the mother of the house to ask, and she had agreed that if Morgan liked, she was welcome to accompany Eleanor to the next Guild meeting.

And so she had. It was a quiet trip, but not uncomfortable. Eleanor had long ago learned how to put other people at ease, how to coexist in companionable silence, during thousands of hours of portrait sittings. At first Morgan had seemed tightly wound, tense, but after a little conversation about her art class at school, she had begun to relax.

It was on the trip home after the meeting that Eleanor had thought to ask, "Morgan, how many are there now at the Sampsons'?"

"Nine in all right now, at least until they move somebody in or move somebody out."

"Oh, I see," Eleanor had said. "And you're the oldest?"

"Um-hmm," murmured Morgan, and they both had sat thinking then about what it was that Morgan would do when she turned eighteen, not at all far off.

In spite of herself, the reticent girl had said, as much to herself as to Eleanor, "You know, when the time comes, I'm just going. School's not for me anyway. I'm just going to pick someplace and go. It's not like I'll be missed here." She said the words without self-pity, as if they were fact.

"Well, you have a little time yet to figure it all out," Eleanor had said.

And now in the moonlit room Eleanor saw before her eyes a vision of the series of startling, vivid, slightly disorienting paintings all lined up in a row that Morgan had shown tonight. *That explains the houses,* she thought to herself. *She wants to make a world where she belongs, even if it's just on paper.* She studied the violet shadows.

And much later she thought, *I'll wait and see how the biopsy comes out in a couple of weeks before I make any plans. Who knows? It will probably all be fine.*

And the runaway horses gradually slowed to a canter and then to a walk and finally to a stop, bending down to graze for a while, their noses thrust deep and searching in the tall uncropped meadow grass. And Eleanor slept.

Morgan's Last Day

Morgan was weary of school by the last day. In fact she had been weary of school since the second week, and the entire year had seemed interminable. June 8 was a much later date for the end of school than any of her other schools had had, and during the last few hot weeks, time had slunk by maddeningly. Now the seniors were gone; other students were celebrating, signing yearbooks, laughing about summer plans, and finishing up their last few final exams. Morgan just sat, daydreaming about the art she had seen at the Guild meeting last night.

She would have liked to skip today—it was a waste of time—but since she rode the bus with all the other kids from her house, her absence from school would have been reported loudly in six or seven little-kid voices. She had nothing else to do, anyway, nowhere else to go. So she went, same as every day, swept up the steps onto the bus like some silent Gulliver in a sea of jostling, shouting Lilliputians, and the only one left on board when the bus pulled into the high school parking lot.

All her classmates were strangers to her, both at the start and at the end of the year. She sat in her desk with her chin in one hand and her pencil in the other, idly drawing in the margins of her notebook, worksheet, test paper, textbook, even on the desk. She filled all the empty spaces she had time for, everywhere around her.

It made her feel safer not to have blanks. It cushioned her from the sharp looks, the prying looks, the helpful looks, of other kids, of teachers. She drew before, during, and after she did her schoolwork. And she did the schoolwork, more or less, not because she cared about it, but because she could, without much effort. She did it without any satisfaction or pride. She did the least amount she could to get by.

After the first few weeks of school, back in September, the other students had given up trying to provoke her or befriend her; they just navigated around her. She helped this process along by keeping her long hair as subdued as possible, in a plain braid down her back, at least while she was at school. Hair was a big thing for the others, and they had apparently never seen any like hers. There were cornrows and weaves, mullets and Mohawks, flat-ironed hair and tousled hair and bleached hair, spikes and odd coloring jobs, but nowhere was there hair like hers. People stared. People whispered. Three people had asked her if it was real. She ignored them.

Morgan was not too surprised when she saw Mrs. Sampson at the school that day, the Last Day, Friday. It wasn't the first time she had shown up there. But Morgan did feel a shadow pass over her of—What was it? Fear? Hopelessness? Mr. McElheney had called her out of second period, and she knew it could not be good. She had never been called out of class for something good. She slapped her notebooks together on the desk and left the room wordlessly. No one called after her; they were all used to her leaving. She walked slowly down to the counselor's office. *What's happening? What have I done? No one ever gets called down to the office on the last day of school.*

She trudged along down the maze of hallways into the counselor's suite and through Mr. McElheney's open office door. Mrs. Sampson was sitting on a vinyl chair with three-year-old

Precious in her lap. Precious had elastics with brightly colored twin balls fastened on the clusters of tight black curls all over her head. She had her thumb in her mouth. She kicked her tiny Disney princess tennis shoes when she saw Morgan come in and sit down.

The small black man behind the paper-heaped desk looked at Morgan through tidy wire glasses and said, "Yes. Ah... Morgan." He cleared his voice. "I have been having a, ah, *conversation* with your guardian here, Mrs. Sampson, about your, ah, *performance* in tenth grade this year."

Morgan nodded and glanced over at her foster parent. The woman's shoulders were rounded, and dark smudges underscored her eyes. Mrs. Sampson had lines at the sides of her mouth, but she was not smiling now. Morgan felt a pang of regret, of guilt for some unknown trespass.

"Now, Morgan," Mr. McElheney went on, "You are not technically passing all your courses. Let's see..." He turned away for a moment and scrolled down his computer screen. "No, not quite all of them. Spanish, 70... English, 69.5, which will round up to a 70... math, 82... biology, 64... physical education, 29... world history, 70... and art, 100." He looked at her over the top of his glasses and pursed his lips. "Now, ah, Morgan. How does one *even make* a 29 in physical education? All that is required for a 100 is to dress out each day. This shows me a lack of cooperation that is *concerning,* to say the least." He frowned.

"And furthermore, you *do realize* that one must successfully complete two years of physical education in order to receive a high school diploma, do you not?" He looked at her again. Morgan looked back steadily but did not answer beyond a nod.

"Now, hmmm, biology? As I have told your guardian here, Mrs., ah, *Sampson*, this course must be taken again and passed satisfactorily in order for one to advance to the eleventh grade."

Morgan slid her eyes over to her guardian who was trying to

quiet Precious. The little girl was gleefully bumping her bottom up and down and singing, "A-B-C-D-E-F-G; gwate big happy fam-uh-wee," over and over again.

"Your teacher, Ms. Jordan, tells me she has spoken with you *repeatedly* about your average. She tells me furthermore that she has provided you with numerous afterschool opportunities to raise your grade." Morgan again nodded. The counselor pushed forward on his desk a manila folder that barely contained a fat stack of oversized papers. He opened the folder, licked his thumb, and began distributing the papers methodically across the desk.

"Now, Ms. Harrington has provided us with a folder of your work from art class. She tells me that you have exceeded *all* skill sets, *all* expectations for Art Survey, that you have worked every minute in class and even beyond, sometimes neglecting to move on at the end of the period." He cleared his throat again.

"However, Ms. Harrington reports that you do not *fulfill her assignments*. You *will* do whatever pleases you, but in doing so, you show more effort and ability than the other students, and so you have *been given* a 100 in her class." He looked disapproving on this professional account. His voice whined higher.

"Now why is it, ah, Morgan, that a young lady such as yourself, who clearly, from evidence of her standardized test scores, has the ability to excel, why is it that you can prevail in a course like art, and yet in biology, or English, in courses which, let's face it, *really matter*, you make very little effort?"

Morgan shifted her eyes toward a paper clip caught under the leg of the counselor's desk. She could not explain what she knew of herself. Mr. McElheney continued spreading the paintings out now on his desk as if they were evidence against her for some terrible crime. Mrs. Sampson leaned forward, her eyebrows pinched toward one another. She looked up at the counselor and then over at Morgan, who did not meet her look.

"Happy, happy fam-uh-wee..." Precious was singing.

"And what about mathematics, young lady? Just out of curiosity, I'd like to know why you seem to have more interest in math than the other core subjects."

Morgan shrugged.

"Ah, I thought as much. Now. Furthermore. I am going to have to refer you for psychological evaluation, ah, Morgan, based on this interview and upon your pattern of non-communi—"

"It's just that math is about shapes," Morgan broke in, "and shapes are about houses." She regretted speaking immediately. She glanced quickly at Mrs. Sampson, who was shaking her head slowly side to side, studying the paintings and drawings spread out on the desk. They were nearly all of houses, of rooms in houses, of windows in rooms. They were all empty of people.

"I see," said Mr. McElheney. The second hand of the cheap plastic clock on the wall scratched away at the silence of the counselor's office.

Mrs. Sampson spoke finally. "I don't see what a psychological referral will do for Morgan at this point. She has been through extensive testing over her years in foster care, and yet she remains the same. You see there that she is of above-average intelligence. In just under a year she'll be eighteen and will have to be her own guardian. I worry for her, Mr. McElheney, truly, but Morgan will soon have to make her own way in the world, and putting her through more of the same will take up a lot of class time next year. I don't think it will help her in the long run."

"I see your reluctance, Mrs. Sampson, but we have protocols for this sort of thing," said the counselor. He turned to Morgan. Wiry hairs were growing out of his ears.

"Now, young lady, as I have told you before, you may come to us here in the career and counseling center if you have anything personal you would like to discuss. As for now, I will recommend

167

you for promotion to eleventh grade, based on your aptitude, but you must repeat biology and physical education, and you are at grave risk of not being on track to graduate with your classmates." He apparently did not remember that she was already a year behind for having been moved around so much. Mr. McElheney looked as if he had been serious every moment of his life, as if he were born to lecture, born to enforce bureaucracy.

"Let me remind you what failure to obtain a high school diploma can mean to your economic future."

Morgan nodded. She wrestled her desolation down and kept her face flat as she looked over at Mrs. Sampson. No words came to mind.

"Wing awound a wosey," Precious was still singing. "Gwate big happy fam-uh-wee."

"Morgan, you've got to try harder, honey," said the woman. "You're already behind in school. You can't let it happen again just because you don't feel like doing the work. You have it in you to do this, to graduate in a couple of years. It's important."

"Yes," Morgan said. She regretted distressing her foster parent. She was a nice woman who meant well.

Mr. McElheney stood up and rubbed his palms together. "I think this meeting has reached its, ah, conclusion." The others rose.

"We are resolved then, that Morgan will continue on to eleventh grade with a renewed attitude and effort." He looked at her sharply. "And meanwhile she will undergo psychological evaluation to determine strategies for better communication skills and adjustment with her peers."

He reached his hand across the desk where all Morgan's artwork was still spread. "Thank you for coming in, Mrs. Sampson."

"Thank you, sir," she replied and shook the counselor's hand as Precious wove in and out of her legs.

Morgan glanced down at her artwork scattered across the desk and hesitated. She looked back at the counselor who was leaning forward with his arms straight and his hands, now palm-down, planted on the desk, papers and all. Her paintings were pinned there helplessly, brittle and curling, like dead butterflies in a collection. Clearly he had dismissed her.

Morgan turned away as Mrs. Sampson reached down to pick up Precious, who was giggling and squirming to get free. Morgan followed them out the door and lingered a second or two beside the struggling pair.

"I'll see you in a few hours, Morgan," said Mrs. Sampson. Morgan lifted her hand in a half-wave and turned down the hallway to go on to her third period class.

The halls were filled now with teenagers changing classes, jostling one another, buzzing about their summer freedom just around the corner. They instinctively parted and flowed around the girl with the long yellow braid walking slowly down the hall without her paintings.

Eli's Encounter

Eli's place was hidden in plain sight in the attic of the Napa Auto Parts store just off the square in Liberty. He had gotten to know the proprietor through regular visits to the shop foraging for components for one or another of his contrivances, and on one of those visits last summer he had noticed the blank stare of the windows above the shop and thought to ask about the upper floor.

"Sure, there's an upstairs," said Currie Smith, the owner-operator of Napa. "Perfect place for bats and the occasional squirrel. Never go up there myself."

"Would you be willing to show it to me?" asked Eli.

"Don't see why not," replied Currie, "but I don't know what in tarnation you're inner-rested for." He paused. "Listen, I'll give you the key and you go on up yourself. Take a look-see. I hate bats. Got to mind the shop anyway." He rummaged in a drawer in the dark varnished counter near the old manual cash register and looked surprised when he came up immediately with the old-fashioned key. "Well, dang! Here it is!" he said as he held it up. He handed over to Eli the long slender key with one end circular and the other notched. "Haven't been up there in, what, ten, eleb'n years anyway."

"Are the stairs at the back of the shop?" asked Eli.

"Naw. Got its own entrance, door outside in the alley, side of the building," said Currie, and he turned his attention to a customer.

"Afternoon. Help you sir?"

Eli went back outside onto the sidewalk and around to the side alley where there was an old wooden door with crazed dark green paint. Some of the paint had given up on the door and lay in chips and splinters, along with old leaves and a Styrofoam drink cup, at the foot of the shallow entryway. Other colors of gone-by years were visible in places across the weathered door: grey, rust, black, white. Eli mumbled to himself, "The perfect door."

He fit the key into the lock and with a minute or two of persistence managed to work the bolt open. He grabbed the latch and pushed hard. The door opened into a steep stairwell, not so convenient for the transport of large canvases and materials, but Eli went up them anyway, two at a time, scattering the debris of years of neglect. The steps complained at being stirred after a long rest, but they felt solid.

The top of the stairs led to one large open space that was entirely unobstructed but for some load-bearing pillars here and there. It smelled only faintly of bats. Dust motes drifted through feeble sunlight from the west and north windows, which, like the windows in the remaining two sides of the room, were coated in soot and grime. The walls showed their naked brickwork, with hardened mortar oozing in places between mottled bricks of every shade of red clay. As he walked around the space looking out the windows, poking the toe of his shoe at long-forgotten piles of commercial accumulation, Eli's brogans left a trail through the dust and droppings and stuff of decades of human disuse. A deep set-tub stood in the corner with pipes running up to it through the floor.

Eli had seen enough. He trotted back down the steps and out the alley door, locking it behind him. He paused for a moment and thought about the dull brass door bell he had just seen mounted on the inside of the door. Here on the outside of the door at just the same place, waist high in the center, was a small oval of metal scrollwork mounted on a short rod, almost like an oversized key, protruding perpendicularly from a square panel. He fingered it, pulled it, pushed it, and finally turned it; at last a bright *brrrringgg!* sounded on the other side of the wood. "Exceedingly cool," he said to himself. He went back into the shop where the proprietor was unpacking a UPS shipment at the counter.

"Hey, Currie, how much is the rent?" he asked as he approached.

"Dang, boy, what you want that place for?" Currie asked.

"It's perfect for a studio, for painting, and I think I could make it livable. It's just me anyway. I could rough in a toilet and a little kitchen area, if you're O.K. with that."

"Thing is, we're zoned commercial, so I don't know..." He rubbed his greying chin stubble. Currie Smith was an unlikely stickler for following the rules.

Eli went on, "I could do a few improvements up there for you, just give it a good clean-up, keep an eye on the place after hours. I wouldn't have a lot of people coming and going. I'd either be here working or away at shows, not much of anything else."

"Well, yeah... all right," said Currie. He thought for a moment. "Tell you what. How about you do them fix-em-ups for me up there, put in a bathroom, clean it up, get rid of the bats—dang, I *hate* bats!—help out in the shop now and then, pay some on utilities, and we'll call it even."

"It's a deal," said Eli, grinning. He shook his new landlord's hand.

That was almost a year ago now, and Eli had found since that working on the old place dovetailed unexpectedly well with his painting. The surfaces and the patinas and the light that appeared with cleaning it up had inspired his artwork, imposing a realness over the artifice that had always troubled him before. Eli found new correlations in his life: The more he worked, the more energy he seemed to have. The less sleep he got, the less he seemed to need. And the less human contact he had, the less he craved, but he could still talk a good talk at the shows and festivals. Eli had the gift of charisma but lacked the God-complex that often goes along with it.

In short, the Napa attic primed Eli's creative generator. In addition to turning out eight or ten large paintings a week, he had added a small bathroom, humble cooking facilities, and an extensive system of storage and display for his art, all in the past ten months. The one drawback to living in town in his studio was that he had vacated Cordelia's barn to move here, and now he saw her far less often, leaving her alone way out in the country, with his cousin, Angeline, who was less than attentive. Angeline went off for weeks at a time camping, drinking, mud bogging and noodling with all her crew. Who knew if she would come back with all her fingers intact from her exploits with the catfish, or if she would come back at all, considering her skill at flipping over four-wheelers.

Eli checked on Cordelia once a week or so. She always said the same thing: "I like it by myself out here. It gives me a chance to think." But since the accident with the tent and that gash on her head, his aunt had seemed increasingly foggy. He would sit and visit with her, and she would fall silent, just answering when he spoke to her, her large pale hands with the ropy veins like long supple vines listless in her lap, the root and the knife all but forgotten on her apron. Then Eli would lean forward and put his hand over hers, and look into her pale, pale face. The huge brown eyes would brighten and gaze at him through her scratch-misted lenses. "I get by, Eli," she would say. "You go on and live your own life; quit worrying about this old girl!"

Otherwise the new location suited Eli perfectly. The alley door went unnoticed by locals, so he had no undesired interruptions. Not one passerby on the sidewalk in front of Napa looked up at Eli's windows or even could have said for sure whether the old building had a second floor. Certainly not one soul noticed that the five tall, narrow windows above Currie Smith's faded awning were crystal clear for the first time in decades.

Napa customers mostly frequented the store in the early morning when Eli grabbed his few hours of sleep and his music was silent. His nocturnal hours were his most productive creative time. The criminal element had not yet made its way to Liberty, and the city police hardly ever swept the square after the sun went down. No one was around to see what signs of life escaped the forgotten upper floor in the night. Light blazed out through the uncovered glass panes, for Eli felt compelled to make color no matter the hour, and without light, pigment is impotent. Quite a lot of sound emanated too, especially in the summer through the open windows, for Eli could not create his own worlds on canvas with the distractions of the natural world, or the human world for that matter, intruding. Music served as an essential barrier.

Over the weekend, when most people were seeking each other out for company or recreation or whatever passed for a good time in their lives, Eli's single-minded energy would not release him, and he remained cloistered upstairs in the old brick building tirelessly working his canvases—smoothing, spraying, slapping, tossing on the paint and then scraping and gouging, only to repeat the process time and again. The contours of acrylic would ebb and flow, form and erode, until they took on a natural history of their own. Eli's topographies evolved a gravity that held him there, in the large open attic, apart. Alone.

And so it was that on a Friday night in early June, very late at night, Eli was working steadily when he heard through a gap between CD tracks a persistent ringing. He barely recognized the bell on his door at the foot of the stairs. Eli crossed the expanse of canvas drop cloth and wood floor to the open window beside the stairwell. This window had no screen in it so that Eli could ease his large finished paintings out and down the side of the building to the alleyway below, with the help of an old block and tackle he had found in the refuse in a corner of the attic. In that way he avoided the problem of the narrow steep stairs.

However, a new problem arose in the shape of insects attracted to his light and activity. Not that he minded insects; he found them somehow comical, especially the large gangly ones. But inevitably they were bound for his canvases, and he was willing to incorporate only a minimum into the paint. He often wondered what happened to the insects stuck there, encased in acrylic. Did they decay? Become fossils? Or did they remain exactly as they were in life, perfectly preserved for eternity? Eli had hung a Koolatron FT24 Eight-Watt Electronic Bug Zapper just outside the window. It was overkill, admittedly, but it limited the insect infiltrators to a large degree so that he was able to control the texture in his paintings rather than accept whatever happened to fly into them.

Consequently, on this particular occasion, Eli was able to lean out through his unscreened window and look down. Below him, intermittently lit by the light of the Koolatron, a person in a cap that said "Papa's Pizza to Go" on it stood at the door holding a pizza pouch.

"Hey," Eli called down. "That for me?" His own voice sounded rough and unfamiliar. A boy's face peered up from under the cap.

"Yeah, dude. Some woman called for a pizza. Said this address. Yeah, it's for you, dude. Fifteen ninety-five," said the delivery boy.

Eli grabbed some money out of his wallet, enough for the pizza and a tip, and trotted down the steps. Even if he hadn't ordered it, his stomach was telling him it was time to eat. He unlocked the door and pulled it open and faced the teenager with the pouch.

"Hey," he said, and handed the boy the money, twenty-five dollars. "Keep the change."

"Dude! Thanks!" The boy unzipped the pouch and handed the warm box over to Eli.

"Thanks yourself," Eli rasped. *Is that really my voice?* he wondered.

"Yeah, dude. Hey! You made my night. Best tip so far. Enjoy the za!" And with that he took off around the corner of the building to the street in front of Napa where he had undoubtedly parked.

Eli relocked the door and carried his pizza up the stairs. He set it on a card table in the corner near a sink, a small range, a stumpy refrigerator, and a 1950's metal kitchen cabinet, all reclaimed from the town dump. He opened the refrigerator and peered in. There was a crumpled half-eaten package of Velveeta cheese, a few avocados rapidly going south, mayonnaise, five Oreos in an open package, and a whole six-pack of Yoo-hoo plus one more. Eli pulled out a drink and set it next to the pizza. He turned to the sink to scrub his hands, rubbing and shedding delicate plastic layers of paint like a rainbow snakeskin, revealing clean, unblemished olive flesh underneath.

As Eli sat down to the cardboard box, he felt weariness ambush his limbs. He wondered at his rough voice and tried it out again. "How's this for luck: pizza and I didn't even ask for it." Still grating. Still alien. Well, come to think of it, when had he last used his voice? He counted up the days since he had gone out for paint and food and realized with surprise that he had not left the studio, had not spoken to anyone, had not stopped painting, had not slept since Tuesday. He had not even checked his phone messages in three days.

"Eli, old friend, you may be getting a bit obsessive about this painting thing," he croaked. It would take more than a little mumbling to himself for his voice to return to normal, apparently. He gulped down some Yoo-hoo as he looked up at the large canvases hanging from the pulley system he had rigged up. He felt that it was good, the work he had done in those three days. He could roll the paintings backward and forward and shift the piece he chose to work on at any given moment to his work station, which was at the center of a long expanse of brick wall, lit like a grand stage with track lighting.

As he began to chew a bite of pizza, he contemplated the painting of the hour. It was a departure from the usual unfigured abstract. At the center of this latest painting, on an impulse, he had splashed on a large bright white star—no, not a star, more of a supernova—freeing a considerable area of the painting from color. He was beginning to feel the need for shape and structure. He had lately begun to yearn for some relief from the intense ubiquitous color that had become his trademark and, in fact, his payday.

He ate the pizza and swallowed the Yoo-hoo and did not acknowledge his isolation. A rare quiet song played on the stereo. He was just thinking he would try to sleep a bit after he ate when the old bell in the door sounded again and jarred the stillness. Eli figured it was the Papa's guy returning for something, maybe to reclaim the pizza for its rightful owner. He scuffed down the stairs without a glance out the window and opened the door once more. There before him in the dark alley with the electric insect killer buzzing and flashing over her head was a slight middle-aged woman with expensive hair, in an expensive dress—and not much of one at that—holding a wine bottle.

"Hello, Eli." The corners of her mouth drew back to reveal small, pointed, glistening teeth. This smile of sorts recollected to Eli who the visitor was. Of course he knew her. She was his patron.

"Vanessa?" he croaked, standing clueless in the doorway.

"Damn, Eli, you sound like death," she laughed.

"Yeah, well, I've been painting, so..."

"Aren't you going to ask me in?" she smirked. "I brought some wine to go with the pizza."

"Oh, yeah? The pizza... Well, sure, come on in," said Eli, standing back for her to pass up the stairway before he latched the door again. He caught a whiff of something pungent and familiar as she passed. He followed her up the stairs and into the brightly-lit room.

She sauntered around looking at the large open space, taking in the spartan furnishings, the paint-spattered drop cloths, the dozens of stacked and hanging paintings. Her tall, sharp heels grated across the old unfinished floor and snagged the canvas drop cloth askew in places. He noticed her careful blonde waves and perfect tan. She was a thin woman, and taut beneath her silk dress, not unattractive. Eli noticed when women were attractive. She approached him once again, close, and held up the bottle. He took it from her because there was nothing else to be done. He felt wearied and his senses a bit dull, his head cottony. He observed the sharp angle of her collarbones and the depth of her neckline which would have shown cleavage if she'd had any to show.

"Pour us some. Wine and art go so well together," said Vanessa.

Eli moved over to the table and set the bottle down. "So, what brings you over here, late on a Friday night?" He had found his voice at last. He pulled two mismatched glasses out of the cabinet and set them on the table with the pizza and the bottle.

"Do you ever check your phone messages?" she asked in return as she perched herself on his one folding chair. She somehow produced a corkscrew, expertly uncorked the bottle, and splashed wine into the glasses.

"Uh, well, I guess I haven't in a few days." Eli pulled a rusty metal stool over to the table and sat down not quite across from her.

She took a long drink of the dark wine and looked at him steadily. "I'm here to celebrate with my premier artist. You won the Summer 2012 Young Artist to Watch Award. Last Sunday's Atlanta paper covered the show at the May Silva Gallery, and the review was all about *you*, Eli."

"Really?" said Eli, trying to care about a newspaper review. Vaguely, he realized this news might have some effect on his sales.

"And I have never seen your studio," she went on. "Why haven't you asked me over before? I could have helped you with your decorating," she smirked.

Eli did not point out that he had not asked her over *this* time. And even to someone who kept unorthodox hours himself her visit seemed to have unusual timing.

"When I'm here, I'm working. I've been trying to get some commissions done and follow through on a new series for the Denver show too." His voice began to loosen up. He ate pizza steadily, but he could not bring himself to drink the wine in his own glass. The Yoo-hoo and the cheese were too thick in his mouth and would not welcome the acidic bite of the grape. Vanessa poured herself a second glass, fuller than the first, and drew a large wedge of pizza from the box. She began to eat it with startling efficiency in quick, neat bites.

"So this is where you eat, sleep, live, and work, ay?" asked Vanessa, sliding her eyes over to meet his.

"That's right," said Eli.

"And that's all you've got for a bed over there in the corner?" She pointed to the rumpled sheets and misshapen pillows tossed on the low metal frame with its thin twin mattress. "It's no wonder you look tired. Mattress technology has come a long way since that set was manufactured, you know. It's not like you don't make enough."

"Well, I don't spend much time there," Eli said, shifting on his stool. There was a long pause.

"So Vanessa, thanks for coming all the way over here to tell me about the award. I'm glad to know about it. Is there anything else we need to talk about?"

"Yes, Eli. Right." Vanessa stared at him with bottomless dark eyes. She recrossed her legs. "Tell me how the commissions for Buncie Chiswell are coming along. We're nearing the end of her project. It'll be ready soon for the finishing touches. You *did* get those color chips and fabric swatches I sent over? For the *new* colors?"

"Yes, I got those a while back. Her paintings are over there near the corner, the four large ones lined up against the wall. I finished them this week; I just haven't gotten a chance to call you."

"I'll send the truck over to pick them up tomorrow. I'll cut you a check and send it with the guys."

"Great," said Eli between slices. He realized now how hungry he had been. In fact, he couldn't actually remember his last meal.

Vanessa stood, losing interest in the food and drink. She began to roam about. She walked over to the cot and suddenly lowered herself to sit on the edge. She slid her tan legs at a slant. "Umh, these heels are chafing me," she said, and she pulled the strappy things off her feet. She leaned back with her arms propped behind her and looked over at Eli.

"Oh, and Eli, you should get a maid, too," she added, with her eyelids half shut. She laughed a throaty laugh.

He rose and began to shuffle the empty pizza box and glasses, to recork the half-empty bottle. "Yeah, I guess I could do better." There was silence between them as Eli busied himself straightening up and tried to avoid his visitor's persistent gaze.

She leaned forward again. "By the way, I called your little friend, that girl whose card you gave me. For the mural. She's coming over in a week or two to look at the project. I'll need some indication about her artistry before she gets there..." She looked at Eli without blinking. "I'm looking for a sign of which way to proceed..." He looked back into the dark pools that were her eyes and did not want to take their meaning.

"She seems like somebody who needs a break," he said. "I think she'd do a good job for you. I just have a feeling about that."

"We'll see. I can't run my business on feelings, Eli."

Eli nodded.

"I can be influenced, Eli, but not by an appeal to my charity." She looked pointedly at him.

Again, he nodded. He crossed his arms and leaned back against the range, feeling he needed its support somehow. Standing had gotten old, suddenly, after three days and two nights of it.

Vanessa thrust herself back up from the cot and began to range around the room again, swinging the strappy shoes with the killer heels from her black-lacquer-tipped fingers. She stopped in front of his latest painting, the one that was lit from all directions from above, so that every inch of it was bathed in stage-light. So she herself was lit crisply, like a character who had just left the shadowy wings and walked on stage.

Now Eli began finally to really *see* this woman who was his patron, as she liked to call it. He moved a little towards the work area, not too close, but behind her six feet or so. She faced the painting directly and studied it. Eli had a sudden urge to throw a sheet over the surface. He could not see her expression, but her whole attitude was probing and provocative.

She whirled around. Her face seemed a shade purplish beneath the tan. If he touched her she would snap, she was so tightly coiled. Vanessa drew one side of her mouth back in a half-smile without mirth and narrowed her eyes. "*This* is not your gravy, Eli. Remember that. Remember where I've put you and your art. *Don't let me down.*" Her voice was deeper, drier, and quieter.

She turned abruptly. Without another word, she stalked from the room and back down the steps, her bare soles gliding across the wood soundlessly, leaving footprints in the dust no larger than a child's, but otherwise not the same.

Eli heard the door slam below and the bell tinkle once. He moved over to the open window by the stairwell to look down, but Vanessa had vanished. *I'm going to have to take the bell out of that door,* he thought.

He treaded back across the floor in his paint-spattered brogans and stood in the spot where the woman had stood, exactly. He thought he might work some time longer. There in front of him was the painting, untouched in the last thirty or forty minutes, but now the star, the nova at the center of the painting, seemed yellowed with age. It looked all the world to him like a giant stain.

Eli went down and locked the door, then walked slowly back up the steps and flipped the lights and music off. He pulled off his shirt and shoes and lay down on his bed, hoping to sleep, but sleep would not come. His bed smelled like the woman. Eli turned over and over, and over again. It was as if he had forgotten how to sleep.

After an hour or so of twisting in the sheets, Eli leapt out of bed, pulled his shirt back on, slid his feet into his shoes, and headed down the steep stairs and out into the night. He left the alley and turned toward the square. He strode down Main Street past the hulking oak trees that served as sentinels for the old granite Confederate at the very center of the town square. He passed a row of shops—jewelry, antique, barber, optometrist, flower—and Mary Mack's Department Store. In another block he passed the Bank of Liberty, Dismuke's Insurance, Corbie Fried Kitchen, Bubba's Office Supply, Liberty Drugs, Bobbi-Sue's Spa-Licious Nail-n-Tan.

He crossed over to another block and found fewer streetlights here in the residential blocks. He sidestepped a group of teenagers laughing and lurching unpredictably across the sidewalk. "School's out for summer," they shouted the old Alice Cooper rock song. Eli thought this was probably how they would spend their whole summer break—with an endless appetite for each other and nothing else, nothing of consequence, nothing made, nothing accomplished, nothing to show—unwritten stories, unplanted gardens, unread books, untraveled roads, unpainted pictures. He didn't see how kids could be so addicted to social gluttony; he had never had a taste for it, always wanted to be making something. Without that, he was adrift.

He moved on. He passed the long iron fence running around the Methodist church cemetery. He passed many a dark home crouching behind the dense shrubbery of almost-summer, the formidable foliage that was the domain of millions of unseen insects and amphibians, unseen but not unheard in their mixed choruses swelling into the night. Eli walked quickly, destinationless. Ornate wrought iron and low stone walls surrounded impeccably-landscaped yards of homes that were two hundred years old.

He did not know how long or how far he had walked, but at last he came to the antebellum place where he knew the art guild would be having its show in a couple of weeks. The house, set back some way from the road, was very still. In the darkness its white façade was just discernible, its loneliness palpable. He paused, looking up. Reaves Hall was without light and movement, except for a barely luminous mist in the upstairs windows, just a random reflection, or maybe some moonlight seeping through from a hall window at the back of the house.

He heard a cough coming from the grounds and lowered his gaze. Some yards away, between the iron fence and the house itself, sat a figure on a bench to the side of a clump of shrubbery. It was difficult to see, but Eli made out the shape of a girl. He could tell she was young, maybe a teenager, by her posture, by the fluidity of her movement, and by the sheer volume, the mass of fair hair streaming down her back, catching what light there was. As his eyes adjusted, he could see that the girl looked up at the house and then down at something in her lap. She repeated the motion over and over. Eli recognized it; the girl was drawing. And she was alone.

Eli felt alarm for her. He sat down hard on the edge of the stone wall in the inky shade of a maple tree in the already-dark night, resolved to sit vigil until she left. *This is crazy*, he thought. *Why am I doing this?* The insect sound was deafening. After a while in the darkness, as Eli kept still, the whole world seemed to be vibrating and humming, proclaiming life at the top of its lungs through the countless invisible creatures, through the varied mechanisms of the tiny noisemakers.

Half an hour passed, and the same cluster of teenagers he had seen before came careening past in the opposite direction, pushing and joking, totally oblivious to Eli's presence. One of the boys paused for a minute to look into the yard of Reaves Hall, then hurried on to catch up with the others. The night swallowed them whole, their laughter sinking into the insect racket.

Twenty minutes later, a solitary person walked by, his cigar tip glowing in the dark. He paused too, ten or fifteen yards from Eli, looking over at the house for quite a while with his foot propped up on the low wall, the slow burn of his cigar swelling brighter with each deep inbreath of rank smoke. *Does he see her there?* Eli wondered. His muscles tensed. *He must.* But at last the smoker moved on. The girl seemed not to have noticed any of them.

Some time later, maybe an hour after midnight or more, Eli looked into the quiet yard in the now-quiet town and saw that the girl was no longer there. He breathed more evenly, with some mysterious relief. Why had he felt compelled to stand guard for a stranger? He shook his head.

He walked back to his studio, slower than before, locked the door behind him, and stretched himself on the bed, thinking that *now* sleep would come, but it did not. Time and again as he began to drift off, something seemed to seize him, to jolt him back to wakefulness. Finally, he surrendered his longing for sleep and just lay resting, until his limbs could remain still no longer and the studio's windows became pale rectangles with the dawn. He rose, showered in his tiny fiberglass shower stall, put on fresh clothes, and went down to the street to crank his van and drive out to Cordelia's.

He found his aunt already up as he had known she would be. She had eaten her boiled egg at sun-up, undoubtedly, and now she sat in her wheelchair on the front porch of her farmhouse way out in the country. He knew she would sit there, watching and listening, all day. She could still walk some, still take care of the basics, but she seemed so frail now, so vulnerable. A large woman made smaller by gravity, by disease, by time.

"Hello, Aunt," said Eli, climbing up the front steps. He put his hand over hers where it rested in her lap.

"Eli," she greeted him.

He pulled up an old brown wicker chair at an angle to her, not far away, and sat. "How are you feeling today, Cordelia?" he asked, searching her face.

"Oh, I can't complain, son. I'm making out *all right*, I guess."

"Angeline around?"

"Haven't seen her in a few days. Gone camping."

"Well, that figures," said Eli testily, which was not in his nature.

"I can hear in your voice you have some talking to do, son. What's troubling you?"

"I have no worries, Aunt. Just you, out here all by yourself."

"Now, Eli, I have told you not to worry. I like the quiet. Angeline is here when she needs to be." She rocked back and forth slightly. She seemed to be speaking to someone two or three feet to his left.

Startled, he asked, "Cordelia, can you see me all right?"

"Oh, sure, sure I can. I can see everything I need to. Can't quite make out everything in the center of the picture, so to speak, kind of like someone threw a baseball through the mirror and there's that shattered star in the middle, and you can't see anything but black there, but the edges all around it where the mirror's still whole is bright and colorful, clear as day."

"That doesn't sound good," said Eli, catching himself from saying worse and giving way to his alarm.

Cordelia, however, only waved her arm. "It makes no difference, Eli. It happens sometimes. Just part of this old M.S. I have to live with."

"I don't know about that, Aunt. Don't you want me to take you to the doctor?"

"Eli, there is nothing in this wide world a doctor can do for me, and I'm not going anywhere. It's all right, son." The old woman was more talkative than she had been in some time. "Now tell me about you. What's troubling you?" she asked again.

Eli thought for several minutes about what to say. He could tell her about the girl. He could tell her about the award and the pressure to paint someone else's vision. He could tell her about the strange late-night visit from that woman. Was she blackmailing him? Maybe not blackmail, but it felt like she had some leverage over him. He hated that feeling. He could tell Cordelia about the show, about his weariness, about the star and the stain and how his painting seemed to change...

"I can't sleep." The sound of his voice surprised him.

"How so, son?" she said to the Eli just to his left.

"I have trouble sleeping sometimes. I want to sleep. I feel tired. But then I lie down, and it's like I can see myself from above lying in the bed, and I'm afraid at the moment when sleep is about to come that I'll be seeing my own mortality. It will be like seeing myself in death, and I can't let it happen. And then again, sometimes, it's almost as if someone is shaking me awake, not letting me drift off, because there's something I'm supposed to be doing. What is it? What do you think it is, Aunt? Because I just can't figure it out. I thought maybe I did last night, this morning early, but it seems I didn't really." Eli never spoke of himself, only of his art. His speech felt awkward, too raw. Who is afraid of sleep? He felt ridiculous.

Cordelia seemed now to look more in his direction. She leaned forward and said, "Eli, you will see many things which you do not choose to see, things that will disturb you, things that will sadden and grieve you, both in sleep and in waking. You'll see beautiful things too, Eli, more than most, but you'll see both kinds of things because you are a Seer." She looked at him with moist eyes. He could see that they were so, even through the scratched lenses of her old glasses. In a woman with no beauty left in her face and frame, with all her emotion sealed up behind the stony visage of her illness, her enormous eyes were like two forest springs, teeming with life, gazing directly into him with great love and loveliness.

"You can't fix it all, like you can fix whatever goes wrong in one of your paintings. Sometimes, Eli, you just have to lay your head down and let sleep come, come what may. Sometimes you just have to let things go."

"I don't think I can do that, Aunt. I only know how to push straight through until something is done."

"That is commendable, son; that's how you accomplish everything, ever-what-all you get done. But there are things in life, in death, for that matter, that just don't *finish*, and you have to learn when to let them be."

Eli felt better and worse at the same time.

"Tell you what, son," said Cordelia. You just go stretch yourself out on the porch swing over there—see, there's a pillow on it calling your name—and I'll just sit here and carve a little and hum a little and we'll listen to these cicadas just getting cranked up for the day, and I do believe you'll be asleep before you know it."

And Eli obeyed. And it was so.

Lucy's Visit

At first glance, even from a distance, the woman's eyes seemed to angle like a cat's. As Lucy creaked shut the car door and walked toward the home's columned façade, Vanessa Hennessey uncoiled her small, lithe frame from the lush pillows of a wrought iron settee and sauntered toward the visitor with a bowl held casually in one manicured, child-size hand. Vanessa's narrow eyes transfixed Lucy, pinned her down with their unblinking slantwise gaze. She spoke no greeting. Lucy made her way up the herringbone walk, paused, tilted her head to one side and said, "I'm Lucy Bloom. I believe we spoke on the phone?"

Vanessa held her free hand out, limp and curving downward, for Lucy to take. It was bony and cold. The shake, if it could even be called that, was not a friendly one.

Lucy took in the woman, who was perhaps forty or so, but also ageless in a taut, silicone way, so that she may have been, in fact, much older than she admitted even to close personal acquaintances, with the long wavy expensively-dressed tresses of such a woman. Her casually-slung caftan, bare and elegantly-polished feet, and lack of make-up proclaimed her indifference toward the visitor.

"Ah, yes. Ms. Bloom. I find eggs the only satisfying way to begin the day. Two each morning for me," the smaller woman said as she indicated without apology the elegant bowl and spoon in her hand. Lucy quickly covered her discomfort at the forthright carnivorousness of Vanessa Hennessey.

Still the woman did not broach the subject of Lucy's visit. Lucy waited. Vanessa slid the remaining bit of eggs between small, glistening, perfect teeth, surveying the visitor with her narrow eyes.

"I hope I didn't misunderstand the time?" Lucy ventured.

"Oh, no."

"The mural, then? Would you like to show me what you have in mind?"

"Mmmm. Yes. Well. The, hmmm, client's home as you can see is reproduction Old South. I am in the midst of designing touches that bring modern color and flair into the..."

Lucy momentarily lost focus on the design-speak. The scent of eggs with the slight rank edge of the butter they had been cooked in hovered between the two women, the slick residue plainly visible in the bone china bowl held carelessly in mid-air.

"...His clientele expects edgy good taste, not musty tradition, and he entertains often given his line of work."

Lucy wondered at his line of work, as she was meant to. She pulled a small spiral notebook, a pencil, and a tape measure out of her back jeans pocket. Three crumpled Kleenexes tumbled out onto the painted concrete floor and lay there like small white birds who had flung themselves, unknowing, against a picture window. She quickly scooped them up and tucked them back into her pocket, coloring slightly.

Lucy nodded to Vanessa. "What does he do?"

"You *certainly* have heard of the prominent attorney Hunter Brinton? Two grand old local families in one: Hunter and Brinton. It would be quite a feather in your cap to have this client on your resume," purred the designer.

"I guess so, yes," said Lucy. "So the project—what did you have in mind?"

"Mmmm, the portico here calls for, I find, some dramatic updating." Vanessa moved softly around the large portico with no evident destination, her bare feet leaving vague paisley imprints on the cool cement. "Its Southern Living looks are passé now, in the higher end homes of our finer circles. Wouldn't you agree, Ms....?"

"Bloom. Yes. Certainly." Lucy noted "dramatic update" in pencil. The 52-mile drive and the snail's pace of the interview began to work on The Instinctual, far below the workings of her conscious mind, that rhythmic sense that soon her milk would begin to swell uncomfortably. At just that moment the baby would begin to feel again a matching clamor in her belly. The two of them were tethered across space and time through feeding and being fed, a connection that Lucy could never have explained. And surely not to this stranger. The idea, the essence of their bond, was like a tiny uncharted island drifting far from the continents of other peoples' lives.

Vanessa tossed her waves, tilted her head, and squinted at Lucy. "What are your thoughts, Ms. Bloom, on a border to be painted, an aesthetic distance, of course, from the edge of the floor here on the piazza? I am planning for this, ah, *client*, a Greek motif, so perhaps a border like a temple frieze, one that suggests *bacchanalia*. You see my drift, Ms. Bloom?" Vanessa's lips were quite thin, and at present drawn back slightly on one side as in a smile. The eyes, half closed, held no smile, but rather some unfathomable intelligence Lucy did not recognize.

Lucy was taken aback by the sudden realization that the mural was in fact to be a mere decoration on the floor, not a work of art on the wall inside the house. "Uh... yes... well, I believe you are wanting a mural painted directly on the cement floor of the porch, but I see that this same surface continues around the side of the porch into the large carport area. That's a really extensive perimeter in all. So you would like the, uh, frieze to be painted just here on the front porch?"

"Oh, no. Don't you see. The frieze must continue throughout the piazza, so that the motif will pervade the exterior living space. The colonnade here, the *port-a-cochere* there, all unified, all proclaiming the inner vibrance of new plantation living."

Lucy glanced around at the expansive area, all painted slick grey. There must be well over a thousand square feet of it. A border running around the outer and inner edges would require a great deal of time in tedious reproduction of a pattern. Just for people to walk on. Still, it was a job. She felt the gnawing need to produce. Perhaps, if she did the job well enough, it would lead to projects with greater potential. She swallowed her disappointment. She closed her face as best she could to the shock of the request.

"What sort of colors do you envision for this, um, frieze?" Lucy asked.

"Naturally, the colors of the Greek Isles." Vanessa had deposited the bowl and spoon on a wrought iron table at hand and now stretched herself on the settee, her half-smile aimed again at Lucy in bemusement, a little burst of air fleeing the slanted nostrils.

"Rust, turquoise, gold, a hint of umber and sienna and vermilion. *You* are the expert, the *artiste,* Ms.... ah... Bloom. You should know these colors." She yawned, looked out toward the manicured lawn with its impeccable azalea, holly, magnolia, and oak groupings. She curled her legs and arranged the thin, bold silk of her caftan.

Lucy, left standing, suddenly noticed the elegant topiaries to either side of the house's imposing front entrance and felt herself to be absurdly like them, the same height and girth. But she did not, at this moment, feel elegant.

"Do you think you can manage the effect I am looking for, Ms. Bloom?" Vanessa asked, looking sidelong at the visitor.

"Oh yes, definitely. I can draw several sketches for you to preview including the palette you mentioned. You can look them over, and we can go from there."

"And a quote, Ms. Bloom? What fee would you require for the project?"

"Well, it would be based on my time, of course. I charge fifteen dollars an hour for planning and execution. It's difficult to estimate the time necessary to finish the project before we settle on a pattern for the border." Lucy panicked slightly, always unsure in discussions of money, which she encountered very rarely. The panic, at any rate, recurred reliably. She closed her face against it, straightened her spine against it, determined to be professional, and if not that, then at least dignified. She shifted her weight slightly. She was sure that Vanessa Hennessey did not perceive all this in her.

She was, in fact, wrong. Vanessa's slantwise gaze took in all, in every engagement, judged it, and stored it away for future use. Her economy of movement allowed for heightened perception. Her emotional palette lacked certain colors, but she perceived them in others, especially sensing the warmer hues, the weaker ones, all of which amused her.

"A moment, Ms. Bloom." Vanessa swung her legs down from the settee and moved toward the front door. "I want to soak this dish before the egg hardens beyond redemption." She glided through the grand entry and abruptly disappeared into the house.

Minutes passed. Lucy moved to the far side of the portico and surveyed the manicured surroundings. A hummock of ancient magnolia drew her eye, clearly older than the modern-built-to-look-old mansion. Beneath the magnolia, despite the growing warmth of the day, crouched a damp darkness, the darkest area by far in view. How would one balance that strange inkiness in a painting of this spotless landscape? What human dealings had occurred there in the inscrutable shadows in the long-ago time when this place harbored an older, perhaps even grander, dwelling?

Still Vanessa did not reappear. Many more minutes went by as Lucy waited, feeling awkward and conspicuous, her height bearing down on her, her kinship with the strange topiaries mocking her. She waited and marveled at this abandonment in the midst of the interview. As her thoughts idled, she imagined setting up an easel on the portico to paint the grounds, and she thought of where she would place the easel, and how the ancient magnolia with its deep shade would figure in the scene.

And suddenly, the silence made itself known to her. No bird sang or even fluttered. Lucy perceived that while the magnolia advertised itself with great heavy cream blossoms, while the holly and boxwood clustered in lavish mounds, while the azalea snaked across the grounds in perfectly shaped crescents, only the Bradford Pear lining the drive represented the fruit tree, and the Bradford Pear was just for show. No bird sang. No fruit ripened. Yet the effect of the expanse was stunning, intelligently designed, rigorously manicured, and perfectly weedless.

Still Lucy waited. Surely twenty, twenty-five minutes had passed. Like a warm slap, Lucy felt the sudden descent of milk and felt how heavy time lay upon her, and how, in fact, time was not hers at all; it belonged instead to the baby who depended on her for sustenance, to the children who looked to her for care, to the man who sustained them, but above all, to the baby. With certainty Lucy knew that Evie cried at this very instant. With certainty she knew that the sitter would be increasingly unsuccessful at appeasing her, would soon stop trying and just let her cry.

Just as unaccountably as she had left, Vanessa reappeared, with no explanation of her absence, no apology. She just drifted back onto the porch, in a white sheath now, with tiny gold sandals on her tiny feet bejeweled with crimson polished nails. As she sauntered onto the portico, her left clavicle was sharply visible beneath the elegant drape of her thin white dress. She moved close to Lucy who was just turning away from the faultless, appalling grounds. The hand Vanessa held out sideways, with nails to match her polished feet, held a crisp twenty-dollar bill between the second and third fingers.

Lucy looked at the hand thrust toward her and at the now-painted face above it with its thin, uncanny, mouth of crimson encircling small, preternaturally-white teeth. Lucy no longer managed to hide her disconcertment. She had no idea how to interpret this gesture. Her gaze fell back to the hand.

"Reimbursement for gasoline, Ms. Bloom," drawled the interior designer. "Thank you for your *expertise.*"

"You're welcome," stammered Lucy, slowly moving her hand toward the twenty. "I can have your sketches ready by next week."

As the bill slid out from between the manicured fingers, Vanessa raised her head at an odd angle, her sculpted nose lifted as if searching for some elusive scent. She drew back her mouth in her peculiar half-smile grimace and audibly released a small burst of air from her nostrils.

"Oh, I'll be in touch, Ms. Bloom." All the pale beauty of the petite person of Vanessa, the hair, the face, the dress, the graceful limbs, was marred only by the curving ironic slash of the mouth—the mouth, and also the eyes that held Lucy now, slanting almonds, lids half lowered and artfully lashed, harboring within two dark, dank unfathomable ellipses of unknowable color. *She is undeniably striking*, Lucy thought. *But with a beauty more serpentine than feline.*

Vanessa held her look for a long moment, seeing all that Lucy hid. She shook the loose waves on her shoulders and laughed a throaty laugh that bespoke the smoke-filled rooms of untold years past. Still holding Lucy's look, Vanessa strolled off the portico onto the lawn, half-smiling over her bronze shoulder.

"I'll be in touch," she said, and looked away at last.

Lucy felt herself dismissed, and as she walked tentatively to her car, she saw Vanessa Hennessey stroll toward the hummock of towering magnolia where she tore loose a twig with a goblet-shaped blossom. Lucy thought she might tuck the flower in her dress, or carry it back into the house with her and find a porcelain bowl to float it in. Vanessa plucked a petal, then another, and another, then leaf after waxy leaf, until all that remained in her fingers was the cone and its twisted woody stem. Her dark nails shone like blood drops against her white dress; her figure gleamed before the deep shade at the base of the magnolia. She did not look Lucy's way again as the old station wagon rattled down the drive.

It dawned on Lucy that the client was also the lover, and that Lucy was meant to know it. She shuddered.

A hundred yards or so away, where the drive met the main road, the solar-powered iron gate under the large ornate sign for Brinton Plantation swung open just before Lucy reached it. Towards her through the gate throbbed a low black convertible, its top down in homage to the late-morning sun. As the Jaguar accelerated deftly around Lucy and on up the drive, she glimpsed a Ray-Ban-clad, dark-haired, bronze-skinned young man for whom, she was sure, she registered merely as a minor obstacle in his path.

Lucy drove on through the gate and paused before entering the road. She closed her eyes and took a deep breath, then checked her scribbled directions for the 52-mile return trip home. She glanced at the twenty resting on the passenger seat like a brittle stray leaf. She wondered what she had just been paid for; the interview had somehow seemed something different from a consultation.

She still hoped, though, that she might earn some money through painting, even if the job was more prosaic than artistic like this one, even if it was, in fact, soul-sucking. She needed to justify her dream, her urge to make something beautiful, a compulsion as strong and urgent in its way as a labor contraction. She wanted to justify her painting to her husband, for one, and to herself, for another. And she would be proud to contribute to her family's modest living, though it might seem only a gesture compared to Jackson holding down two jobs.

On the way home Lucy thought over the visit to the plantation house and to the strange, silent grounds surrounding it. The place was alien, like a scene painted from the imagination in which all the proportions are a little off-kilter. And the woman was alien as well, her skin too flawless, her teeth too uniform, her face and body too sculpted, her neck a bit too long to seem natural. Lucy longed for and dreaded, all at once, the call from Vanessa Hennessey that was, in fact, never to come.

At length she swung the station wagon into the driveway at home, threw the gear shift into park, and hurried along the walk, through the small yard with its thick mid-June carpet of dandelions and clover, and up the front steps. The sitter met her at the door. Lucy handed the twenty to her and thanked her and took the frantic baby into her arms. Her three-year-old flung himself at her leg and clung there. She waded through scattered toys in the small, sunlit living room and sank into a chair. She laid her hand for a moment on Ian's head and smiled at Jack sitting across the room with his ankles crossed, scrutinizing the funny papers.

As she nestled the baby to her breast, Evie's desperation settled slowly into rhythmic sucking, her tiny fist opening and closing against Lucy's side as her panic faded away. Lucy leaned back and closed her eyes. A powerful wave of relief surged through her as she nursed the baby and gently rocked.

Ian looked up at his mother and wondered why her face was wet. He had never seen her face wet before. Evie's face, yes. It seemed to Ian that she cried all the time. Jack's face, sometimes too. But Mama's face, never. He popped his thumb in his mouth.

All of a sudden Ian knew what he had been missing all day, what had made him feel so empty somewhere around his middle. It was his Mama's tune.

"Whistle, Mama," he said. "Whistle for me." He placed a small blue Matchbox hot rod on her knee and leaned his head against her arm, relieved that his baby sister was no longer crying.

Chesley Fox Chiswell's
Exterior Design

As Buncie Cummings Chiswell's cobalt Viper sped up the circular drive and squealed to a stop, Chesley could see that Buncie was on fire, and he prized passion in women exceedingly. As she erupted from the driver's seat and slammed the door, he admired her fit and sculpted 34-year-old form sheathed in orange and the way that it stood out boldly in front of the Tudor mansion that her forebears had built—when was it? During the Great Depression, it was. As she stalked toward him, he reveled in all the heat that she radiated. She was the fireball of a summer sky, arrived here precisely on time, on the penultimate day of spring. He paused to reconsider his ennui with their marriage of late.

"Chesley! What in the world do you think you're *doing*?" she cried out as her heels clicked across the pavement. Chesley stood with one foot propped up on the side rail of the bumblebee-yellow Bobcat, his hands resting on his thigh, smiling serenely. He knew that this pose showed him off to advantage, and with the machine in the background, well, so much the better.

"Do you *not recall* the conversation we had about this... this... *idiotic* idea of yours?" Buncie was close now, her face inches from his. She seemed not to notice or care that spray struck his face as she spat out the words.

"Well, Chesley? *Well?* How do you explain this?" Her voice grew higher and tighter.

"Buncie, my dear, I have The Vision, and the vision of a visionary cannot be contained," he reasoned.

"But Chesley, this is my ancestral home! This landscaping represents generations of horticultural expertise and cultivation. There are mature plants here that cannot be bought or replaced in their condition. They are heirlooms in their own right! And you're just going to plow over them and disregard all that?" she shrilled.

"Now, my dear, just calm yourself. I have it all in hand. I have a vision, you know, a plan, all in here." He tapped his temple.

"I don't care what's in *there*, Chesley! I care what's out *here*, and this is an outrage! It's unforgiveable what you are doing. I demand that you cease and desist from this work immediately, before the grounds have passed the point of no return!" Buncie held her head back and her eyebrows up and looked at him with her most imperial gaze. Chesley wasn't buying it; he knew Buncie worshipped him and at root treasured his artistic sensibilities. He felt that this dramatic scene was meant to attract his attention, on which she thrived.

"The Garden Club is due to meet here in two weeks, Chesley, *two weeks!* Vanessa has just put the finishing touches on the remodel inside, thank goodness, but this... *this* is just a *disaster!*"

Ah, yes, Vanessa, that sharp little decorator, Chesley mused. Very sleek, very capable, though Chesley's taste ran to younger, fresher women. And less cunning ones. *Good thing I arranged with her to oversee the installation of my sculptures at Reaves Hall tomorrow, first thing. Yes, I've left that in capable hands. Very capable hands.*

"Now, Buncie, baby, think of The Vision," he purred. "You will have the most unique garden and grounds in the historical district."

"But Chesley, they won't be historical anymore!"

"Ah, but you do realize, you can't live in the past. You have to embrace the new. My vision is fresh and contemporary. You know, I did describe the plan to you. You could be more supportive..."

His wife—Wife Number Three, Buncie was—had always basked in the glow of his celebrity, had always supported his showings and whatnot with her stylish, wealthy contacts and, indeed, her chic presence. Her present tantrum was unexpected, but of no real consequence.

"Yes, well. I do *not* support this!" she hissed. "I absolutely do not! I *insist* that you stop at once and move all this dirt back to where it belongs."

Buncie was just arriving back from a stay with her sister at the family place on St. Simons, so she had missed the first few days of initial earth moving. The Bobcat had been delivered only Monday, and Chesley had begun work that same morning. He believed she would come around as the project progressed and be a thoroughly enthusiastic onlooker. At this early stage, he could not expect everyone to perceive the beauty of the outcome he envisioned.

"Chesley! Answer me, Chesley! And wipe that grin off your face! This is disgraceful!" She stomped her heel down on the pavement.

"All right, my dear, please calm yourself. I will take care of everything. You'll see. Trust me to take care of it all," he crooned.

Buncie squealed in exasperation, held up her hands, palms outward, and looked toward heaven. "I *so* do not have time for this now." She fired a ballistic look at her husband and said, her face so close he thought they might kiss, "You are *not* to continue this, do you understand?" She wheeled away on her stylish heels and clicked back to the car where she hauled her oversized Hermès bag out of the passenger seat and stalked up the wide front steps of the mansion. The massive, iron-studded front door with its iron stays spearing across the ancient wood yielded to the fiery Buncy like butter.

Chesley did love fiery women. The trouble was they were

difficult to reason with, to stay married to, in fact. But not difficult to woo, fortunately, and well worth the effort. Chesley chuckled and surveyed the side yard and acreage where he had begun his work. The mud and tread marks were all just temporary. The flat even topography of the staid old place just cried out for molding, for sculpting into something new, something farsighted and creative. The red clay beneath all that green sang out to the potter, and since the hand-wielded wooden rib, metal scraper, steel needle and double loop were far too small for the task, Chesley had purchased for himself a sculpting tool on a grander scale. He had no fears as to mastering the machine. The Vision itself was the crucial thing, and he had dreamt about and visualized and anticipated this project for months now.

He splayed thumb and forefinger of both hands in an L-shape and held them together at arm's length, forming the rectangle of a makeshift viewfinder. He nodded, then climbed over the bucket arm of the Bobcat and folded his graceful limbs back into its cockpit. He pulled the safety bar down into place and cranked the engine. He put the machine into gear and zipped off to carry on the give and take, the push and pull of the clay, contouring the land little by little into the swells and undulations that would comprise his own personal first hole.

The course here would be small, not regulation certainly, for there wasn't enough land here for that, but he would drape in green velvet sensuous mounds and valleys reflecting the curves of the women he so adored, of the untold women he had romanced. Those curves would be enhanced by beautiful shrubberies and accessorized with the jewels of rare flowers. And, of course, the hills and vales and nooks and recesses of his creation would showcase his own stone carvings, all conceived for such a purpose by himself.

The Bobcat bucked over an ancient clump of lilies. No matter.

He would relocate them and give them new life. Chesley bypassed the side yard closest to the circular drive where he had been working earlier and motored over toward the pond in the shady grove not far from the east side of the house. He lowered the bucket, which he had learned to maneuver on Monday through some degree of trial and error, and began to sculpt around the pond. The water had been drained during the winter so that the old recirculation pipes, clogged with decades of sludge and willow roots, could be replaced, but Buncie had been so busy between travel commitments, charity events, and the remodel that she had not gotten around to arranging the work.

Chesley saw that the current state of the pond made this the ideal time to reshape its environs and incorporate it into the design for the small-scale sculpted golf course. The trouble was that there was quite a lot of ivy surrounding the pond, and wisteria too, all somewhat constrictive to the movements of the Bobcat. By gunning the gas, he had found that he could yank the tough, mature vines free. He relished the rhythm of the backward and forward motion, repositioning earth and scraping away vines.

He maneuvered the Bobcat up to the brink of the little pond, picturing a stone pedestal he would have built just here to place a sculpture upon, or perhaps an Italian grotto, as it were, with the sculpture within. Chesley would summon his greatest visionary powers to create a singularly beautiful statue for the extraordinary site. He was imagining now all sorts of possible subjects, and he could feel his mind working like the earthmover, pushing, pulling, discarding, reworking. Perhaps he would even have a small alligator brought in to live in the pond, for drama, for adventure, for dark contrast to the angel he would fashion for the stone pedestal.

After a while, a net of particularly tough long vines caught the bucket, and Chesley gunned the engine in reverse, spinning the treads and inching backwards. The vines refused to give way. He pulled forward and tried again, gunning the engine in reverse. The oversized web of wisteria and ivy and mystery vines as thick as his wrist held him tenaciously. Chesley urged the machine to one last mighty attempt to pull free.

He had never been one for physics, so he really couldn't say what forces caused the Bobcat to suddenly slingshot forward and catapult over the rim of the pond. As if in slow motion, he saw the world outside the tiny cab rotate 90, 120, 150 degrees. He heard brutal clanking and metallic groans. He felt a violent thud on the front armature of the cage surrounding him and felt his head flop like a shaken ragdoll's. He found himself dangling from the safety bar, upside down in the now-dusky cab, facing, just inches away, the sloping wall of the empty pond.

Well, not empty, exactly. The pond side was covered in dense roots and vine tangles of dead water flora. All sorts of centipedes and snails and roaches and salamanders and unnameable creatures of the dark and dank busied themselves in and amongst the tangle just in front of his face. And there was apparently still some amount of water in the lowest spots, which the mosquitoes had discovered long before he had.

He began to shake his head to dispel his disorientation but felt a warning pain in his neck. Absently, instinctively, he managed to brace himself, release the safety bar, and clamber around so that he could crouch on the vineage and mud of the pond floor. Disgusting, but at least he was more or less upright.

Gradually he grasped his present circumstances. He was in a fix. The Bobcat bucket arms were stretched out above the cab, reaching toward the lowest point of the pond floor. The front and only exit to the cage was firmly blocked by the pond floor slammed up against it. Fetid air and questionable light were all he had to breathe and see with. His voice certainly would not carry far, but he called out for help nonetheless. He thought perhaps Buncie would have gone back outside to collect her luggage or to go on some errand. Or perhaps she had even seen the accident, or noticed that the work had ceased. Perhaps she had witnessed the whole unfortunate event from the breakfast table in the bay window of the east side of the house. Yes, Buncie would sound the alarm for him.

This vein of thought branched and meandered for some time, for Chesley was a singularly optimistic person. Several times he thought he heard, faintly, a car motor, but he couldn't be sure from his present insulated situation. He called out all the louder at those moments. Yes, he was in a fix.

The confines of the Bobcat recalled to him a scene from his childhood. He could smell the old unstretched carpet and stale cigarette odor of the storage room. He could feel the windowless, suffocating, still air of the room. He had not thought of this room in many years—why would he? It was a room from the past, and Chesley was all about the present. Ah, yes. The present. Abominable conditions at the bottom of this pond. What was it that made him think of the room? Perhaps the musty smell.

Yes, the room had been decidedly musty, but after a while one grew accustomed to the odor. Because one had to. And one grew accustomed to the silence of the small, windowless, slack-carpeted storage room at the back of Mary Mack's Department Store on the square in Liberty. Even then the building was old.

Chesley remembered the first time his mother had locked him in the room. A gentleman had come round to the store at closing time, the last customer of the day. In weeks to come, the arrival of this gentleman always signaled another visit to the storage room for Chesley. But this particular time, his mother had led him by the elbow, back through the carpeted, mirrored maze of fine clothing and shoes and linens and housewares, to the storage room. She unlocked the door with the key hanging around her wrist. She pulled a chain to turn on the light, smiled her lipstick smile, and squinted her false eyelash squint.

"Chesley, you will stay and play here until Mother comes to get you. It'll be just a little while. You'll see." Already she was slipping a cool thin cigarette from her cool thin metal case. "Now be good and play." She held the cigarette between two straight fingers, the way the Hollywood ladies did, and flexed her hand and arm back and away like a delicate wing. She bent down and twisted her swan-neck to allow him to kiss her cheek, then slid the cigarette between her bright red lips, turned, and disappeared through the door. It shut with a lingering rattle which he soon determined was the turning of the key in the lock.

At first he chafed at being confined. He grabbed the doorknob and jerked it back and forth, more times than reason would allow. To no avail. He listened at the keyhole. He heard a faint tinkling of the bell on the door, then nothing. Not voices, not traffic going past on the square, not even the ring of a telephone.

Chesley, being a cheerful fellow, even at age six, looked around his newfound cell and discovered in it a wonderland. It was musty, yes, and the carpet was slack and speckled with lint and insect legs and long steely pins, but the room contained a treasure: stacks of mannequins, or more accurately, mannequin parts. They looked lifelike in the weak light of the one hanging bulb. He constructed company for himself out of the body pieces and the wigs—mostly ladies, of course. He could never quite make them come out even—a leg here or an arm there left over, short a head for this person, that sort of thing—but he quickly grew comfortable with the nakedness of these companions. He admired their plastic perfection, how they never changed. Their expressions were pleasantly bland, arcane, their make-up always flawless. Chesley came to love them. He noticed how much the women, with their long elegant necks, looked like his mother. But they never scolded.

The department store was exactly like the funeral home down the street. Old carpet, no windows, hushed. But that did not frighten Chesley. Why would it? The funeral home was where he had last seen his father, dressed up in his suit and cowboy boots, looking just like a larger version of himself except with a great fine moustache and a jaunty goatee. And, well, very still.

After that, though, Mother had begun to change. Her voice grew shrill: "Your father squandered the family fortune, Chesley, the inheritance due to me and you. Squandered it!" "Gambling is unseemly in a man if he cannot control it." "It's all left to me to take care of you—stuck in this godforsaken store in this godforsaken town just to pay the light bill and put food on the table. *God-for-say-ken!*" Mother's style got her by, though, got them both by.

As the weeks passed, she would hiss at him when she shut him in, never loud enough for the gentleman to hear: "I don't want to see your face for a while!" "This should keep you out of my hair!" Sometimes even when the gentleman wasn't around: "Always underfoot, aren't you Chesley? We'll take care of that!" But she was a good mother. She always came back. And he had to thank her really. Without the storage room, he might never have discovered his life's calling. He had committed to memory the ideal dimensions of human anatomy, and verisimilitude was a key aspect of his artistry. He loved the graceful ladies with their perfect eyes, never squinting at him, never seeing his flaws. With their perfect lips, never scorning, never shrieking. Their plastic selves were permanent, not fluxing from smile to sneer. He could depend on them.

And so it was natural that one day as an artist he would gravitate to stone. He could impose the visions, the ideals he had in his mind on the stone and it would never change—it would lock people in to the perfect state he envisioned for them. He had many masterpieces within him yet, and they had begun their germination in that small airless room. Yes, she was a good mother.

When had his visits to the room ceased? He could not quite remember. It must have been when Mother left town and he went to live with his Aunt Eunice's family. He could remember nothing about the man she left with except his shiny aqua Ford Falcon Futura convertible and his grey fedora. And of course, Chesley could not go with them. Once they had loaded their luggage, there was no room left in the cramped back seat of the convertible with the red leather interior as red as his mother's lips.

Now, though, here in the Bobcat cage slammed against the base of the pond, there was no doorknob to rattle, no keyhole to peer through, no companions to assemble. Chesley was alone with himself, with only the slimy guts of the pond to contemplate.

It was not until sometime quite late in the afternoon that he heard a siren approaching, and then another, and yet another, and finally footsteps and voices drawing near. He began crying out again, his voice now husky from the pond mold he had been breathing in and from the strain of calling on and off for hours. He heard shouts, heard the rescuers at last calling out to him from the edge of the pond-hole.

"Yes," he croaked, "I'm here in the cab of the Bobcat. Can't seem to free myself."

"It's O.K., Buddy, we'll figure this thing out," shouted a voice vaguely familiar, a voice coming closer. "We're gonna gitcha outa there." Chesley tried to connect a face with that voice. "Are ya injured?" asked the owner of the voice, drawing closer still.

"No... Well, yes... Maybe," Chesley called out wearily, for now that help was close by, he suddenly realized how much the confinement, the damp, the insects, had taken their toll. "My neck seems to be giving me some trouble, some pain."

"All right, boys," the voice hollered, "bring me down the C collar. We're gonna need the back board for this one, too," the familiar voice was saying to his companions. "But first we got t'figure out how to git this machine up and stay-blized to where we can git this guy outa there."

"Yeah, boss, I think we're gonna need a tractor to pull'm on out," said a younger man's voice.

"Reckon so," the boss called back, "but we'll have t'do it real gentle, so as not to scramble'm up in there like that messa eggs we had this mornin'." There was muffled laughter.

"Hey, my brother Henry's gotta old Massey Ferguson Twinny-sebben, sebbenty-five. Do the job, I reckon," said a third voice.

"Yeah, see if you kin get'm on the phone real quick."

"Sure thing, Boss."

Two hours later, after much discussion, after calling for Brother Henry's tractor and waiting for said Henry to show up with it, after much clambering up and down the tangled pond side with ropes and chains and shackles and such, after much camaraderie outside the cab—for the rescuers were clearly enjoying themselves—the boss man directed Chesley to brace himself as much as possible on the sides of the cab and gave the signal to the tractor to begin moving away from the pond, pulling the Bobcat back up the side of the pond, slowly inching it fifteen degrees more upright, then thirty, then forty-five. Eventually Boss Man shouted and waved, signaling Henry to halt. He looked around the cab, pounded and kicked the structure, and seemed to decide that the Bobcat was secure enough for them to go ahead now and get the victim out.

"O.K. Bring that backboard down here now, fellers." Through a gap in the cage Chesley could see two strapping young men making their way down through the tangles with a long narrow board. Boss Man's face appeared before Chesley at long last. He reached in and fastened a collar around Chesley's neck. Then he gripped Chesley's forearm with his hand. Chesley automatically grasped the fireman's forearm back. *A funny way to shake a gentleman's hand*, Chesley thought. But the rescuer did not let go.

"All right, now, Buddy. Time to gitcha outta here. Kin ya walk?"

"Oh certainly." Chesley glimpsed the back board beyond with its two eager carriers. He hesitated.

"Come on, Buddy! We got t'go *now*! This thing could shift on us here on this greasy pond wall," said Boss Man with more authority than before. He pulled insistently on Chesley's arm.

With an instant obedience that took him by surprise, Chesley leaned forward, doubled over, and crept through the small opening on unsteady legs. The feeling was quite gone in them; hours of crouching in the cab had taken their toll. His neck throbbed, and his head reeled, but he was overjoyed to be released from the cramped confines of the Bobcat. He was immediately seized on all sides and muscled onto the narrow board. As the men began strapping him down, he protested, "But really, I'm quite all right. This is not necessary. I can walk on my own, I assure you." He tried to sit up, feeling again sharp pain in his neck.

"Whoa, Buddy!" said the familiar voice. Firm hands flattened him again on the board and fastened straps. Chesley drew in a deep breath and let it out slowly. Unable to direct his eyes anywhere else, he stared upward at the not-quite-night sky.

And then, unexpectedly, a sense of wonder flooded his whole body. The sky confronting him was like a cold, clear, deep pool of water with a few glints of light appearing here and there on its surface. Presently, as the board tilted and rose up the most gently-sloping side of the pond, glints appeared not just in the sky but all around him. The sounds of effort from the carriers slid away, and the jostling as they searched for footing amid the viny slope too, and even the pain in his head and neck. He was borne up into the midst of random blinks of tiny light, miniature lamps signaling on

210

and off. It was as if he were joining them, becoming one of them, as if he were a body being buried at sea, slipping down the plank into the ocean depths, into the welcoming depths where the lights danced, and he felt it to be pleasant.

Suddenly, a face thrust itself between Chesley and the sky. Chesley was good at faces. He finally placed this fellow, the boss, the one who had helped him out of the Bobcat. It was the cabinet maker from Redbud who made the wooden bowls he'd seen once at an artist guild meeting. Diseased wood—spalted, he had called it—turned on a lathe. Inferior materials. Not *real* sculpture, of course, but still—they shared a brotherhood of sorts.

Chesley rasped, "I know you!" A radio or pager or some such thing squawked on the man's hip.

"That right, Buddy? Maybe so, maybe so. Fred Shirley, at your service. You're gonna be all right, now. We're just gonna check you out and gitcha over to the E.R. and let'm work you over. You'll be good as new after that, Buddy." The men strapped his board onto a stretcher and wheeled him across the lawn to the ambulance, where an efficient young female attendant he had not seen before began checking him for injuries and taking his vital signs.

"Are you feeling any pain, sir?"

"When I move my neck, yes. And a little soreness here and there."

"Don't move your neck, sir," she ordered. Well, how could he anyway with the bulky collar all but strangling him? The attendant swiped at his face with a wet cloth, like an overworked mother with just another grubby face to wipe, and he saw the cloth come away covered in mud. She seemed unwilling to smile, resisting his charm. But then he *was* grimy, evidently, and strapped to this infernal board without the use of his limbs, which made charm all the more challenging.

"Sir, what is your name?"

"Why it's Chesley Fox Chiswell," he sputtered, incredulous that she did not know.

"What is your address, Mr. Chiswell?"

"Why, here. I live here, of course."

She asked him endless questions about medical history and such, as if he were an old man, a feeble man.

A female face, though, made him think now of Buncie. He wondered why he wasn't seeing her, why she wasn't here. She must have finally realized he was missing and called for help. She must be aware of all this commotion at the very least.

"Well, Buddy," the cabinet maker interrupted his thoughts, "it's been nice workin' with ya, butcha better leave off from operatin' heavy machinery fer a while." There was a chuckle in the background.

"But, my wife, what about my wife?" asked Chesley.

"I'm sorry, Buddy, whatcha say?"

"My wife, Buncie. Surely you must have seen her? She must have been the one who called?"

"Sorry, Buddy, ain't seen nobody around. Nine-one-one call came in from May-retta Johnson, yer mail lady. You must be the last house in town to getcher mail. Anyways, May-retta, while she was out finishin' her rounds, she done heard a faint call for help in this vicin-ty. Then we just tracked ya down by yer voice and the Bobcat treadmarks leading off inta nowheres." Chesley could hear the tractor again straining to pull the Bobcat back up onto the lawn, still caught in the web of vines. That Henry fellow must be towing the whole mess up into the yard. The tractor would be trampling all his efforts at earth sculpting, must be, in fact, making one heck of a mess.

His rescuer slapped Chesley's thigh and grinned at him as he and the young woman slid him into the ambulance.

"Hey, Henry," Chesley heard Boss Man shout. "You in a hurry

to get the job over 'fore pitch dark settles in?"

"Yes, sir, reckon so," called Henry from farther away in the twilight, over the sound of the idling engine. "Reckon I'll have to leave the tractor here overnight, though. Can't drive her home on the road this late. Y'all don't need to go rescuin' another fool machine operator tonight."

"Yeah, Henry, guess yer right about that. Hey, thanks for yer help. See ya," said Fred the cabinet maker, bowl turner, and volunteer fire chief. And then the doors slammed shut, and Chesley could hear no more. He shuddered, thinking of the deafening clanks the Bobcat had made as it overturned with him inside. The siren cranked up, and the ambulance began to move. The molded metal walls of the vault seemed to bear in on him, closer and closer, separating him from the beautiful lights of the evening that he had only just begun to glimpse.

He started to sweat. Here he was, back in a sort of cell again, though less damp and filthy than the Bobcat cockpit. He yearned to be released from this cell, his second of the day, to be released from the fetters that held him fast. He felt himself young, helpless; he felt tears clawing their way up his throat, struggling to escape. He felt his eyes, the only unbound part of him, sweep wildly around the tiny enclosure. He shouted in his head, "If only I may be released, I will be a new man!"

And then, he thought of Buncie. He thought of Buncie unloading her luggage from the cobalt blue Viper. He thought of Buncie motoring around the arc of the driveway on errands of one sort or another. He thought of Buncie sitting at the breakfast room window glancing out toward the pond. He thought of Buncie, looking down from her window seat in the master bedroom above. Chesley was never to know if Buncie had done any or all of these things that day. He thought it best in the end not to ask.

The Set-up

S ix people arrived at the Corbie County Historical Society headquarters at ten o'clock on an already-hot mid-June Friday. The young mother with the baby on her hip, the two African Americans like bookends, male and female, of unknown connection but always together, and the affluent couple with an unexplained past and an oxygen tank in tow all nodded and spoke to each other a few unavoidable words in the way of incomplete strangers.

They made their way in pairs from the parking area through an immaculate English garden with the hovering aroma of sweet basil and lavender, of fennel and rue, lemon verbena and rosemary. Crammed into the borders along the maze of mossy stone paths were fern and rosa canina, St. John's wort, and laburnum and foxgloves and elder, and even tall mallows with their veined wrinkled flowers like an old woman's mauve crepe dress, covering, echoing, mocking the soft looseness of age.

The visitors' legs brushed against the feast of medicinal and edible and sanctified, unaware of the power in that one garden to heal hearts and souls and flesh. In fact, the gardeners themselves had lost that knowledge, schooled well in the English botanical tradition shown in coffee table books but ignorant of the centuries of Anglo-Saxon lore that had formed it.

And these six, Lucy, Evie, Orvelle, Orilla, Vincent, and Lorraine, were no more witting—they saw the garden for its beauty and nothing deeper. They passed unsuspecting through the quaintness along the path, up the steps, and onto the screened-in back porch of Reaves Hall, an imposing two-story white Greek Revival at the center of the Liberty Historic District. They maneuvered gingerly between the pictures stacked upright in cartons that nearly filled the porch, left there by the other exhibiting artists the previous evening or on their way to work earlier that morning. The art greatly outnumbered the artists who stood now on the porch, evading each other's gazes and hoping in earnest for someone to appear soon to let them in. They shifted their weight, not quite conversing.

Before long, the throb of an approaching engine interrupted the uneasy quiet. A white Cadillac swept into the parking lot. The engine ceased, and a small stout woman grunted her way out of the car. She cruised toward the screen porch like a diminutive battleship steaming toward an enemy encounter. She mounted the steps and tugged open the screen door.

"Morning, all. Magdaline Dismukes, here with the key," announced Magdaline Dismukes, Chamber of Commerce volunteer, Historical Society officer, and calendar art watercolorist.

"Vince, Lorraine," she greeted the older couple. Her body followed her ample chest through the small crowd, key held out before her like a bowsprit, her head raked back with great importance, in undeniable authority and a lifelong effort to appear taller. She fitted the ancient key into place, mastered the lock, and thrust open the door. A strong, unidentifiable odor billowed out, released, like a puff of stale breath that had been held for too long.

"Change in air pressure from inside to out," Vincent explained, as if someone had commented, but no one had.

He and the few others waiting on the porch to help hang the

Midsummer Show filed into the dark gallery just inside the screened-in porch. As their eyes adjusted, they began to make out a long narrow room with clapboards on the interior wall and oriental runners on the floor. This room and the porch itself seemed to have once been part of a wide rear veranda. An antique table-desk stood to one side of a set of French doors with wavy glass set into them, so that what was on the other side, the hulking dark interior of the house, was perceptible and yet a mystery.

The Guild members eyed each other. Vincent interrupted the silence. "This is it? Where is everyone? Where is Eleanor?"

"I think she said something about an appointment in Atlanta," Lucy said.

"Whatever for? It must be something really important for her to miss this. Eleanor never misses," said Lorraine. Lucy just shook her head.

"Well?" Magdaline demanded, looking about at each person in turn. "Who's in charge here?" Under her school-mistress glare the others squirmed a little, thinking they should have an answer for her, but they were, after all, just artists and support personnel, and none cared about In-Charge-ness, let alone wanted to be themselves In Charge. Magdaline pursed her lips, said she thought as much, and sighed in equal parts disappointment and satisfaction.

"All right, we'll make do. We will just have to forge ahead," she said. "Now then, let's see what we have to work with. First let's bring all the artwork inside and set it on the floor along the walls in the gallery here. Then we'll tour the rooms so we can see where the Historical Society has left wall space, hooks and such to hang the artwork. We'll size up the situation and find appropriate places to hang as many pieces as we can. Be careful to keep the artist's card with the piece of artwork and display it visibly."

Magdaline then pinched her brows together and looked severely at the group. "Under *no circumstances*," she went on, "is anyone to

216

put a new nail in the wall! I think I speak for the Historical Society when I say, 'No new nails!' " She pushed the French doors open and bustled through. The doors closed themselves again, and she grunted as she bent to prop them open with black iron doorstops, each one a silhouette of a small boy crouched and leaning forward, frozen for all time holding a lightless lantern high.

"Ah, Magdaline," said the tall gentleman, "clearly this old house has done some settling over the years. Gravity is just pulling these doors back together."

"That's right, Vince. Gravity does a number on all of us as we gather in the years, does it not?"

"That it does," sighed Vincent with a weary nod. He shuffled off, towing the tank behind him, and disappeared through a doorway at the other end of the hall. His wife stood watching him for half a minute. Her large yellow purse moved of its own accord. She scurried after Vincent, only to reappear in the hall several moments later without the purse.

"Bad day for him, Lorraine?" Magdaline asked.

"Yes, Maggie, a little out of breath, a little weak," she answered. "But he'll be all right if he just rests in the front parlor."

"Oh, certainly, let him rest a spell," said Magdaline. "There are enough of us to get the job done if we apply ourselves." The others were already headed to the parking lot to collect more artwork.

Lorraine clicked back across the uneven wooden gallery and porch on bright high-heeled mules with large anemones on the toes, back across the paving stones of the garden, out into the blazing light of the parking area to a silver Escalade where she hefted out a large, heavy painting wrapped in brown paper. She weaved and staggered under the weight of the wood, canvas, and oil that were her husband's cumbersome vision.

Lorraine passed Lucy in the garden as the younger woman ferried her own artwork one-handed from her station wagon, the baby on her other hip. One at a time she brought inside two slender cartons and unpacked them; in each was a new watercolor, one of a magnolia blossom and one of a water lily, both sprawling and uncontained by the paper on which they were painted. They were matted in blush and framed in silver and very heavy from the large expanse of glass protecting their faces.

"Young lady, your job would go faster if you would put the baby down and use both hands," said Magdaline, tending the screen door.

"Well, I don't put her down much," said Lucy.

"Yes, I can see that," Magdaline said, her lips pursed and the corners of her mouth turned down. As if in answer, the baby blinked her long lashes and laid her face against her mother's chest. She held on tightly behind her mother's arm with one little hand while she patted her mother's front rhythmically with the other.

Orvelle, who had been rummaging in the back of an old Chevrolet truck for some minutes, followed the others to the door, carrying a large rectangular shape enfolded by a rumpled coverlet of some sort. The wrapping looked suspect to Magdaline the Sentinel, who still held the door open. She could see only a crazed jumble of loud colors and indefinable shapes, and she took it to be an old worn thing, retrieved from the bottom of a moldy trunk or from some forgotten corner of an attic. Her prominent eyes bulged even more as she fixed them on Orvelle's load. Her mouth puckered; her brows warped; she sniffed in distaste.

"I hope you're not bringing moths inside with that thing!" she called out to the man's broad back. He seemed not to hear. Magdaline was so transfixed by the man's atrocious bundle that she nearly shut the door on the woman following several paces behind him, a human afterthought, huffing up the steps with another carton and a shiny vinyl handbag over her arm.

They all began shifting and unpacking pictures. At last all of the pieces of artwork were lined up shoulder to shoulder along the base of the walls like children in line at school, tall, short, slender, squat, loud, quiet, colorful, and mild.

"Come this way," commanded Magdaline. "Let's survey the rooms and see where to place these paintings." They followed her into the first room on the right, a dark room with a massive mantel at one end and several heavy glass display cases in the center. "And let's not be all day about it," she added, as she eyed the black woman, Orilla, lagging behind.

"Fortunately, you have with you today a docent of this historic house, and as such, I will endeavor to fill you in on the illustrious history of Reaves Hall as we pass through the rooms." Magdaline cleared her throat and continued. "The patriarch of the house during its glorious heyday, when most of these splendid furnishings were introduced, was Doctor Augustus Reaves, grandson of Rich John Reaves, a founding father of Liberty. The Reaves Family's wide connections spared the town from Sherman's wrath during the March to the Sea, so this great family, and indeed the town, sailed largely unscathed through the War of Northern Aggression and the difficulties that followed.

"Dr. Reaves conducted his business in this study; you will note the separate entrance from the side porch and the tiny anteroom along the outer wall where patients could enter and wait for the doctor without disturbing the proceedings of the doctor's own busy household, and vice versa. He was an innovator in medicine and had a keen business and investment sense as well.

"Dr. Reaves had seventeen children with three consecutive wives. He was, as you can see, an excellent provider!" Magdaline beamed. "Not to mention, he helped to populate Liberty with upstanding citizens. Descendants can be found today throughout prominent society not just here in the county but also statewide and nationwide, leaders in the realms of commerce, finance, politics, law, and of course, medicine. There are just a few places to show artwork in the doctor's study since there are so many historical artifacts on permanent display here."

"Now this next room, on the other hand, has quite a few options for exhibiting our *objets d'art*," she said as she led the little knot of people through a connecting doorway into a grand, darkly-paneled parlor at the front of the house. Lorraine was already there ahead of them, in the room where Vincent had been resting. She was swaying under the weight of a large ornately-framed painting, still partially covered. She managed to heft it up onto the mantel.

Magdaline continued: "This is the Grand Parlor, the main public room of the original house, which was built in 1812 as a town dwelling by Rich John Reaves. Such a proud lineage of that stately family!" She preened as if the house and clan had been her own people's legacy. "But we simply do not have time today to go into all its fascinating history."

Indifferent to the tour, Vincent was seated on a velvet sofa facing the fireplace. "To the left, two and a half inches, Lorraine," he said to his wife. They were both absorbed in hanging his painting. Suddenly growls and yips erupted from the yellow hand-bag sprawled across the leather ottoman before the hearth. The whole group turned toward the sound and saw a fierce little face, a snarling black mask with a white ruff and crown, protruding from the bag. The dog seemed to be directing a bewildering amount of wrath at Orvelle, who froze for a moment and then fled the room. The growling subsided.

Lorraine smiled charmingly. "Oh, Muffy does have his issues, like all of us," she sang out. She turned and stepped over to the ottoman. "Don't you, you sweet little thing?" she cooed as she bent down and cupped the flat face in her hands. "Oh, Mama's baby! Sweet thing! Oh, you wouldn't hurt a flea, would you, Mummy's little muffin—anybody with any sense could see that." She turned back to the group and tittered. "He's just not used to... to strangers."

It was hard to make out the animal's features in its midnight face with the flowing white fur fanning out all around it like the corona of a dark, corrupt moon. The dog had shifted from precious to vicious and back again in the span of a few heartbeats. Lorraine kissed his upturned nose and nestled him back in her bag on the ottoman. She turned and tugged the remaining drape off her husband's painting. The others were still staring at her purse.

"Now then," Magdaline said, without acknowledging the scene, "there are a half dozen or so places to hang things in this room, as well as some significant pieces of furniture, some excellent surfaces on which to display three-dimensional work. Let's move on."

Vincent leaned back onto the stiff velvet, breathing in his own special air. He made no move to rise, nor did he glance in their direction as the others followed Magdaline toward the room's large pocket doors. He merely gazed at the woman he had been contemplating for months now, possibly more than months, *his* woman, the woman he had painted, above the mantel. The group moved on, Lorraine included; the dog retreated into his little yellow den; and Vincent was alone once again in his rumination.

"Here on this side of the foy-*yay*," said Magdaline, crossing the broad hall, "we have the North Parlor." Orvelle had mastered his small-dog panic for the moment and rejoined the three women as they trailed after their tour guide, half listening and half lost in their own thoughts. The group traversed the space between a beautiful broad staircase with two graceful turns in it and the front door. They found themselves entering a room that was bright and airy.

To Lucy, in particular, this parlor was a relief after the unrelenting masculinity of the previous rooms. Her imagination flitted about the space with its blush gauze curtains cascading down the length of the tall windows and its wallpaper of floral trails like the festoons of Maypoles. Pale rectangles hovered on the wallpaper, ghosts of old pictures removed to make way for the new art of the Midsummer Show. At the rear of the room, beyond several columns designating a ladies' sitting area, one very large rectangle was just visible over the marble-tiled fireplace. Its void beckoned Lucy to scramble through it, at least in her mind, into a looking glass world long gone stale.

A portrait had hung there of a young woman dressed in acres of pewter satin. In fine European style her small children were arranged around her, holding old-fashioned amusements—a hoop, a toy boat, a child-sized riding crop, a tiny lap dog. The woman's beautiful porcelain face nearly concealed her boredom with posing, her weariness from childbearing, her frustration with the restless children whom she bore but did not herself mother, in most moments, in most matters. She would have others to serve that purpose. The children would speak in other tones, other accents than her own, would seek out other comforts than her own. It would be hard work to look the part of a lady, to act the part of a lady, two hundred years ago. It would take time.

Lucy roused herself as Magdaline and the others in her wake snaked around the columns and ornate furniture and disappeared through double doors to the right of the fireplace. Lucy joined them as they emerged in a grandiose dining room.

"Now *this* spectacular room," lectured Magdaline, "which is so *very* historic, has entertained the likes of governors, U.S. congressmen, war heroes and such, founders and defenders of Liberty and of Georgia itself, you understand." An expansive polished mahogany table dominated the room, and beyond it against the longest wall, directly across from the fireplace, stood a long antique sideboard. Above this hung an enormous gilt mirror with scrolls and flourishes and curlicues. Upon the sideboard stood an awkward, three-quarter-size stone golfer in stone knickers and stone cap, preparing for all eternity to tee off.

"Ah, I see Chesley Fox Chiswell has had his sculptures delivered and installed already," Magdaline observed.

Orilla, who had been silent throughout the tour so far, cut her eyes to Orvelle and muttered, "She serious? That some kind of made-up name, sure 'nuff. Some kind of *white*-folks made-up name." The guide glared at her, and Lorraine frowned. Lucy stifled a laugh. She couldn't agree more.

"And through there," Magdaline went on, pointing out a narrow doorway, "is the butler's pantry leading back past the porch to the old kitchen and all that, the work space. Kitchens in the old days, of course, were built separate from the house because of fire hazards and heat. Those rooms will be the purview of the caterers tomorrow night. You may still hang work in the dining room, naturally. The bulk of the food for the reception will be in a large tent on the grounds at the side of the house."

She pursed her lips and looked earnestly at the group. "And there you have it: the first floor. Let's move on upstairs now. Quickly people! We don't want to be all day about this!" And she bustled back out into the wide central hallway with the entourage trailing behind.

"Oh, yes, here is another of Chesley's sculptures. How did I miss that before? No matter. We are so fortunate to have his work here, quite a touch of class." As they moved toward the stairway, directly before them, in the very heart of the house, stood a massive parlor table of mahogany and marble beneath a huge chandelier partially swallowed up by the two-story gloom above. A few random facets of its hundreds of glass prisms glinted sharply as they twisted with some subtle movement in the old house and clutched at stray sunbeams.

The most singular thing in all the splendor at the center of this celebrated house was the sculpture that stood upon the table. The form was life-size and looking down upon them from its station on the table: a child, a grey ghostly child, with blank stone eyes and a frozen smile. The child held its arms down and forward a bit, palms up, as if about to stretch them out toward someone or something. The clothes, a little suit with round collar and short pants, all stone, were jarring; they sagged and seemed to melt from the child's body. The head was too large, the neck too long, and the spine twisted in a way that was not quite natural.

Lucy saw all these flaws at a glance and yet felt strangely tempted to throw her arms around this boy and gather him to her, to console him, despite his icy smile, despite his stoniness. But then, he would be *so cold...* The baby on her hip echoed her mother's impulse; she reached out her little palm to the boy's hand.

"No!" shouted Lucy as she twisted, jerking the baby away. The other faces in the hall turned toward her sudden outburst in amazement; she amazed herself. Revulsion was surging through her. She knew absolutely that she could not let Evie touch that cold hand.

Without another word, she turned with flaming face to climb the staircase, one burnished tread at a time, attentive—as was her practice when carrying a child on the stairs—to the grave necessity that her step be sure. Especially now, when she was feeling a bit light-headed, a bit nauseated, probably from the smell, that oddly pervasive smell, that grew more noticeable with every step closer to the upper floor.

* * *

Fires had not burned in the upstairs fireplaces in generations, and perhaps The Smell emanated from the chimney. In any case, the odor demanded as much notice as a strong personality. The Guild members reacted in their own peculiar ways. Lucy tried to put a name to it but failed; she felt it as an unwelcome presence forcing itself on her. Lorraine thought of how a house needed to be lived in in order to be adequately clean. Magdaline's nose was small and not given to oversensitivity at any rate. Orvelle noted The Smell and dismissed it; he was used to odd smells at the plant—heated wood, sawdust waiting to spark, day-old sweat, and on occasion, singed hair. But Orilla, now, Orilla *knew* that smell, knew it for what it was. It had been human once, but not for a long, long time. *This house done had a lot of livin' in it*, she thought to herself, *a lot of livin'—dyin' too. Still gots the mala-vicious residue.*

The artists stood in the large open landing at the top of the stairs as Magdaline bustled about indicating the four sizable bedrooms and the attic access beyond them. "Now there are places all through these bedrooms where you can hang pictures. If we run out of available wall hooks, we've got some table easels for the smaller pieces. And, oh yes, there are some three-dimensional pieces, some wood bowls and whatnot, I understand, in those boxes down on the desk on the back porch. So! Let's get to work!"

Orilla turned to Orvelle as the group was milling around rubbernecking a bit and getting set to go back downstairs. "I ain't doin' this up-and-down business, Orvelle. My ankles won't hold up. I'll just wait here and help hang the stuff when you-alls gets it back up here."

"Oh, sure nuff, Oh-rilla," Orvelle said, his hand on her shoulder. "You got no call to be going up and down these stairs. Shouldn't a'come up the first time," he said.

"Well, now, I had to see it, didn't I?"

"Sure, sure. That right. Let me get to it then," he said to her over his shoulder. "You know I gots to finish and get you on home before second shift start."

"That right," she said, "and I gots t'get over to the McAdamses' before the children get home from school."

Orvelle followed the white woman with the puffy beauty-shop hair and the flowers on her toes—the one who kept the vicious dog in her bag—back down the big old stairway. He was careful not to overtake her, though her steps were small and ridiculous. Orilla leaned half her bulk on the uppermost banister. She smiled inwardly as she watched them go—inwardly, because Orilla had learned long ago to veil her face. Her eyes pulled over toward the door to one of the back bedrooms, what the bossy woman who looked like a tugboat had said was the children's room way back when.

The others had gone downstairs to start moving pictures around. All but the young lady with the long hair and the baby on her hip. She just started to go into the room and then backed out in a hurry. She saw Orilla looking at her and said, "Something's not right in there."

"That so?" said Orilla. She decided to see for herself and shuffled around one side of the landing, past the girl with her baby, and into the room. Though it was nearly as large as the others, it was dim, the darkest, least-windowed room upstairs. The only daylight was from a single window at the far end of the room, and though the electric lights were on, they were high and weak, helpless to dispel the gloom. The ceiling sloped steeply on one side, and the air was mighty close. Three cannonball beds—flat, low and lumpy as could be—were lined up in a row with dainty, fragile bedspreads that would do nobody any good. You probably couldn't even sit on them without them giving way.

In the shadowy corner farthest from the hall was a small plain door with a simple iron latch. Orilla knew without opening it that behind the door was a steep, narrow flight of stairs leading down to the back of the house, steps that had been worn smooth by generations of hardworking unpaid feet, steps polished shiny by the oils of the skin of countless human soles, with a more costly,

226

precious luster than any modern-day power machinery or refinishing goop could come up with. Maybe the steps were broken now, rotted, in disrepair. No one remembered *them* or cared for *them*, only the fancy rich-folks' grand staircase.

Beyond the beds, toward the window, stood a dressmaker's dummy of wire and wicker, nothing but an old stuffed corset on a stand, it seemed to Orilla, a headless, legless mockery of a woman.

Orilla moved further into the room and turned to face the fireplace. She held her shiny purse before her, dangling over one of her wrists which were crossed, resting upon each other and upon her ample middle. She cocked her head. A rocking chair sat to one side with a tattered wicker sewing basket beside it.

On the other side was a convoluted wooden cradle, scuffed on the rocker where a foot, or generations of them, had rocked it over time while the owner of the foot mended by firelight or spun wool or sang a low song. So much wood had gone into the making of that cradle that it might have floated in the flood like Noah's ark. More likely, it was made that way for showing off, not for being watertight. After all, what else did you really need for a baby but a dresser drawer? Some bright scraps sewn together for warmth? Or for that matter, the soft, strong crook of a mama's arm?

The fireplace was laid for a fire, just for show. On either end of the mantel stood two candlesticks with little glass teardrops dangling down on little blackened silver chains. An old brass snuffer lay in between. The walls in the room were covered in faded, worn-out wallpaper with large yellow roses the color of the skin of an old white woman with liver problems. And on the wall next to the fireplace, the one tall wall in this room with the sloping ceiling, was an enormous stain of some sort, and here Orilla's eyes rested for some time.

She took a deep breath and stepped back abruptly. "Lord, ha' mercy," she muttered in a low voice. She wheeled toward the door and marched out of the room. She trod back over to where the young mother was standing, pale and serious, just outside.

"Uh, huh, you right about that room. It be a little off-color. Been a lot of comin' here, and a lot of goin'. Been love in that nursery; been other things too. This here's nothin' but a old house with all the things a old house collects. Don't you worry none." Orilla gazed over at the baby girl whose cheek rested against her mother's chest, her eyes taking in Orilla solemnly but without fear. A thinking child.

"You best stay out of that one room with your baby, though," Orilla added, "and know you be blessed yo'self with that little one. She mighty sweet. Little angel. Gonna grow to be real humble, like her mama, with a sweet, sweet spirit. She a treasure, no way around it."

The young woman smoothed the baby's bare arm absently. "Yes," she said, with a sober faraway look. "Thank you."

After a long moment Orilla's intent stare roused her. She started and said, "Oh! Your name is what, now? I don't believe I've heard it, but I remember seeing you several times. I feel I should know you."

Orilla softened. "Name's Oh-rilla. It from the Spanish tongue—Oh-rilla like the seashore, though I never seen it. Not once." She chuckled. "And do I *look* Spanish to you?"

"No, I guess not. But I think it's a beautiful name," said Lucy.

"And I knows you. You be Lucy, Lucy of the Light."

"Uh, yes... Yes, I'm Lucy," the young woman answered. "And you're right, my name does mean light, in French, I think. But how did you...? Well anyway, I'm pleased to meet you, Orilla," she said. She had edged away from the door to the yellow rose room and, Orilla noted, did not go back in.

"Guess I'd better help hang some of this artwork," she said, taking leave of Orilla, "even if I am only one-handed." She waved the free hand not holding her daughter and laughed as she started down the stairs.

Now Orilla was alone with the room, alone with all the rooms upstairs where the real living had happened. She settled herself onto the window seat at the back of the broad, open landing with her back to the windows that looked down over the fancy garden. She nestled her purse on the seat close by her side as if it were a bashful child. She could feel the house breathing, shuddering with people's movements here and there downstairs, unaccustomed to the tread of feet passing along its wide worn floorboards, settling still and forever into the Georgia red clay beneath. She cut her eyes toward all the corners, keeping a watch on the shadows. She sat still, a dark monolith silhouetted before the bright wavy glass, immovable by scent or shadow or nudge. She hummed an old church tune. The shadows stayed at bay.

As she waited, Orilla decided to work out the names of the other folks there hanging the pictures. "Those names got to be in my head somewhere, after all those meetings I been to," she muttered to herself, "though I never thought I be needin' to know 'em." *Old Uncle Sam, his name be... Vinson. Wife name Lorena. And Miss Bossypants, what her name be? Magpie, or some such. That fit her just right— all that quare-less squawkin' she keep up. And what her last name be? Dis Somethin'... Disputes.* Just as she had about got them figured out, the distant voices and scrapings and footsteps downstairs grew louder, and the artists creaked their way up the long staircase, toting along what could not be hung downstairs.

First came Orvelle, carrying a pile of paintings effortlessly. He had light, sure footsteps for such a big man. He smiled at Orilla as his head rose above the top step like the sun coming up in the morning. The three women came behind him, one at a time, carrying smaller pictures. And slow grating footfalls trailed after them, the steps of the grey-faced man, who was disconnected from

229

his tubing now. He was breathing like a cross-cut saw, rough in and rough out, though he carried nothing but his own personal burdens. He collapsed into a high-backed, hard-stuffed chair in the wide hall.

The others set the paintings down on the floor around the hallway, and the bossy woman, the Disputes woman, began directing them to hang the artwork in this room or that, wherever it seemed to fit on a nail or a hook left naked for the purpose. With all the activity, the upstairs seemed almost normal now. Orilla heaved herself up and joined in. She noticed they all avoided the old nursery. Finally, there were four small-ish paintings left and no place for them but the walls of the yellow rose room.

At that moment a voice called out from below, "Hello!" A new voice. "Hello?" All seven of them upstairs froze at once, ears pricked up, too surprised to call out. Quick young steps mounted the ancient stairs two at a time, and a young man with curly brown hair, and lots of it, appeared in their midst carrying a large painting.

"Morning, everyone!" he said.

"Eli?" said Lucy.

"Oh, hello," he said, grinning at her.

"And who are you, young man?" demanded Magdaline, who had found her voice again. *And Hallelujah for that*, thought Orilla. *World would just fall apart without that woman talking.*

"Eli Cooper," he said. "I just joined the Guild. Paid my dues the other day. Eleanor Wood told me you'd be hanging the show today, and I brought one of my paintings along. Anything I can help with?" he asked. With a hammer and fishing line protruding from a ragged jeans pocket, he did, in fact, look very handy.

"A little late for that," said Magdaline. "We could have used you an hour or two ago. We're just now coming to the last room. Everything *seemed* like it would come out exactly right." She eyed his large canvas. "I don't know what we can rearrange to accommodate you."

They all moved together into the old nursery, Magdaline, Lorraine, Vincent, Orvelle, Orilla, and Eli. Lucy stood in the doorway. The baby kicked her toes toward the doorjamb, but Lucy held back, watching.

"Kind of funky in here," observed Eli. "Does it smell weird, or is it just me?"

"Yeah, it funky all right," muttered Orilla, under her breath.

Magdaline looked put out. "Oh, nonsense. It has *character*," she said. "Let's put the landscape over here on this wall, the two still lifes there, and the portrait of the little dog will be charming here over the cradle. Then we're done."

"Eli still has the painting out here in the hall," Lucy pointed out from the doorway.

"Ah, yes," said Magdaline. "Well, that will just have to go out there or somewhere else, wherever it will fit. Downstairs in the hall—outside the powder room, maybe."

Orvelle took the paintings from Lorraine and Magdaline one at a time and hung them.

"Wait a minute. What about that wall there? What are we going to do about *that*?" said Eli, pointing to the giant stain beside the fireplace, the stain that no one wanted to acknowledge. There was a long uncomfortable silence.

"Why not hang something over it?" asked Lorraine. "This young man's painting is large, isn't it? Perhaps it could cover the bad spot?" It sounded like she had experience hiding stains and putting the best face on things.

Lucy dragged Eli's painting over and propped it against the upper landing railing out in the hall, opposite the door, where they could all see it. There was a pause while everyone looked at the canvas. It was large, unframed, and covered front-and-edges with heavy layers of acrylic color, scraped and built up and carved and

231

eroded. In the center was a hot white starburst, pulsating against the color.

"Oh, no. Can't put that kinda energy in a room like this!" said Orilla. "And besides, it might soak up that whatever-it-be that been bleedin' through that wall for a hundred fifty-somethin' years."

All the faces in the room turned to her, stunned. The Guild had forgotten Orilla was there. They had always disregarded the ordinary, middle-aged, heavyset black woman who before had never mumbled more than a word or two in their midst. She wasn't an artist, after all, just someone along for the ride.

"Well? You don't want this young man carryin' that extra baggage 'round with him every art show and museum and what-all he go to, do you?"

"Do you have a better idea?" demanded Vincent.

"I don't think we need to cover it at all," said Magdaline with her old authority. "It's part of the *ambience*, the character of the home. It adds to its historical feel, and I think that I speak for the Historical Society when I say that people will not want to see that history glossed over."

"Oh, you gots om-bee-ants all right. You gots character. You gots historical. And you gots plenty of gloss!" said Orilla.

Magdaline, unused to spirit, was mute.

Lorraine cleared her throat and spoke up. "I think we should cover it somehow. That stain kind of leaves a... a pall on the whole thing here." The others nodded. "And, plus, it just isn't very *pretty*."

"Maybe some kind of drape?" suggested Eli. "I've got extra drapes for my show booth out in the van, some long lengths of raw linen that might fit right in with the historical theme of the place."

"Flimsy old linen, that thin loose-wove stuff, ain't 'nuff to do the job," said Orilla. "Need somethin' more substantial. Somethin' with a hand. Somethin' with a history of it own self."

232

They all stood looking at the wall for a long, long minute.

"I knows the thing for it," said Orilla at last. She looked at Orvelle and nodded.

"I'll go get it," he said. He sidestepped Lucy and the baby in the doorway and strode around the landing to the staircase. They could follow his progress by the creaks and groans of the wide wooden stairs and the floor below. The others stood around, shuffled a bit, anxious to be out of the room, to be done with this business and on about their lives. Orvelle returned moments later holding the bright wrapper that had covered his largest painting.

Magdaline gasped. "You must be joking," she said.

"On the contrary," said Vincent. "A quilt is just the thing, I think."

Magdaline did not contradict her old acquaintance, and a charter member of the Historical Society to boot. She squirmed in silence.

"Here, let me help you with that," Eli said to Orvelle, and the two men held the top edge of the quilt up as high as they could reach against the wall. It tumbled free in thick, rich waves to the floor. Lorraine settled the folds so that the quilt hung straight and the design was unhindered.

"How we gon' fasten it here?" asked Orvelle.

No one responded.

"Well, it was a good idea," said Lorraine, stepping back to take in the bright colors, "but I guess if there's no way to—"

"Nail it," said Orilla.

"Perhaps you did not hear me say earlier: There are to be *no new nails in the walls*," said Magdaline emphatically, slowly, as if speaking to a deaf person, an old person, a slow person.

"Nail it," repeated Orilla.

"Now, Oh-rilla," said Orvelle, looking distressed. "You don't want no hole in your quilt! You knows you don't!"

"Don't matter," said Orilla. "I can mend over any-*thing* put a hole in my quilt. Gots patches all over it already. What's a few more gonna mean? Just make it better. *Um*-hmmm."

"But how 'bout that stain? What if it get on your quilt, make it stink, turn it brown, somethin' like that?"

"Can I *wash*, Orvelle?" She wagged her head at him in disbelief. "Really? Does I *know* how to get any livin' stain on this *earth* outa stuff? You knows I does."

Not a person in the room could find it in himself or herself to contradict Orilla now. It was clear she would win this battle.

Eli pulled five black nails out of his pocket, put them between his lips, and drew out the hammer. He let his corner drop, and reached up to Orvelle's corner to nail it fast. Loose plaster or masonry or mice or bats or some such matter scuttled down inside the wall as the hammer struck the first nail.

Magdaline began one last attempt at order. "But the Historical Society will—"

"—deal with it," said Orilla, slamming the door on the discussion.

The men continued straight across the top of the quilt, working together without a word. Finally, they all stood back near the foot of the beds, Lucy and the baby beyond the doorway, to look at Orilla's quilt covering the stained yellow rose wallpaper. Their faces showed amazement, satisfaction, resignation, befuddlement, pride, relief, and awe. This last belonged to Eli.

Orilla noticed the young man's brown curly hair almost reached his shoulders. It was nearly as curly and long as Orvelle's.

"That is one fine piece of art," Eli said. He turned and looked directly at her, green eyes to her grey. "I go to art shows all over the southeast and I've never seen anything that can compare with your quilt." Orilla just nodded.

"Well, the stain is covered, I'll give you that," said Magdaline, and she turned to go. "I don't know how I'll manage the fallout over those holes in the plaster, though." She scowled at Orilla on her way out.

The others were leaving the room now, too, collecting wrappers and trash from around the upper floor, the detritus of picture-hanging. Lucy walked into the room and she stood beside Orilla and Eli to get a better look at the quilt. Evie bounced on her mama's hip and waved her arms. The child leaned toward Eli suddenly and grabbed a fistful of his curls. Lucy laughed and pried her little hand open. He flashed his beautiful teeth at them both, then turned back to the quilt. But in that moment, Orilla had gotten a look at them in profile. *Those two*, she said to herself, *Eli and Lucy, they like two peas in a pod, somehow.*

"I love how the colors work together," Eli said. "I'd never think to use them in the same painting, but they are so striking. It's all that black that makes them hum." Turning to Orilla, he asked, "What was your inspiration? What gave you the idea to put these shapes and colors and little scenes together?"

She cocked her head, deliberating. "I got to say, it just life. *Um*-hmmm. I just looks in my bag. I gots stuff from my whole life in there—all these scraps, some I just like, some gots meanin', bit from a friend, bit from the store, piece of my daddy's shirt, grandmama's apron, piece of Orvelle's coverall, old napkin from crazy old neighbor lady, lots of stuff in my bag, *um*-hmmm. I just pulls out the pieces, lays 'em flat in my lap, cuts 'em up a bit, moves the pieces around, and around some more, till it seem like they sing, you know, and then I knows I gots it. Sew 'em together into a square. Sometime it be a scene, somethin' I remember, somethin' I sees in my mind. Sometime it just be shapes, colors. Then I lays all those squares out, moves 'em all round, sews 'em together, stuffs 'em and quilts 'em, and that's it."

She went on. "You know, some of them fancy quilters, they say it all gots t'be cotton. But it don't matter to me what it made of. It just matter what it *is*. It all depend on how it fit together, not how it be by itself."

All the other voices were muffled now, downstairs and far off, and though the quilt looked fine on the wall, though the odor was a bit lessened, still the unsettling presence remained, a presence like that of an angry genie in a bottle, only different, as though the genie with all its malice was on the outside and they themselves were in the bottle.

The three all turned to leave the room. Orilla looked back over her shoulder at her quilt and paused. "That just fine, then," she said. She flicked the light off on the way out, and joined the others on the landing. The young people stepped back to let Orilla pass, and she led the way down the staircase. With her pocketbook looped over one elbow and her other hand on the banister, she looked engrossed in the act of descending, but her slow, heavy progress did not prevent her from seeing the scene behind her in her mind's eye.

The mother with the silky black hair resettled the baby in her arms. The young man touched her elbow briefly as she and the baby moved around the upper railing to the top of the long flight of steps. He waited for the women to reach the bottom of the staircase. Then he picked up his own painting, held it high over his head like a trophy, and trotted back down the grand, wide, groaning, twisting steps, nimble as a whitetail. The perfect place for his star waited below.

* * *

When they had finished the final details of hanging the show, the artists gathered up the empty boxes and wrappings that had held the artwork and filed through the grand hallway where Magdaline stood waiting with her key of authority to lock up. She told them each in turn, "Tomorrow night at six o'clock—in our formal wear, now, mind you." Her composure was completely intact once more.

Eli had hung his painting in the hallway, opposite the foot of the stairs, and Lucy could see that he was already outside, halfway to the parking lot, as she passed through the French doors into the long gallery. Magdaline bent to move the iron doorstops behind her, grunting. The glass doors swung back together with a smack like a portcullis dropping down at the castle gates. Lucy jumped.

She crossed the gallery and stepped out onto the porch where warm, sweet air greeted her. She breathed easier. Her bare arms were cool from the old house, but her cheeks burned thinking of Eli. She had seen him twice now, and could not account for the strange connection she'd felt to him both times. What if it were somehow romantic? The thought alarmed her, and she pushed it away.

She was so ready to take Evie home and leave this stale, shadow-filled place behind. The others had already left the house before her, all except Magdaline, who was locking the door with the air of a person behind schedule. Orilla was at the far side of the garden just climbing into the truck where Orvelle had pulled up as near as possible to collect her. Eli waved to them as he strode past. The older couple's silver Escalade was accelerating up the side street toward Main. Lucy paused on the porch, looking at the two remaining cartons that had contained her paintings propped against the wall and at the baby in her arms.

"Can I help you, young lady?" asked Magdaline, though it was clear that she had more important matters pressing. She was settling sunglasses onto her nose.

Lucy said, "No... I guess I can... Well... I'll just put the baby in her carseat and come back for the cartons."

"Fine. Have a good day!" Magdaline pocketed the key and

bustled out the screen door and away through the garden.

Lucy, however, was stopped short by the midday, near-solstice sun, blinding after the dusky house. The baby sneezed twice. Lucy squinted and picked her way carefully along the path as Magdaline sped off in her white Cadillac. She began to settle Evie into her carseat. Then she thought better of it and decided to nurse her since they were alone now in the empty parking lot. She slid into the back beside the baby seat.

Hours had passed since she had last nursed. She was a little uncomfortable, though the baby had not yet clamored for a feeding. Lucy untucked her shirt from her jeans and nestled the baby into place. The day was hot, especially in the back seat of the station wagon, so she left the rear door ajar, hoping for a breeze. As she held Evie close, the baby's belly and her own clung together from perspiration. A cooling rivulet slipped out of Lucy's hairline, over her temple and down to her jaw, but Evie's cheek was rosy, rhythmic, and content. She did not seem bothered by the heat. One hand was tucked behind her mother's back, and the other slapped lightly against Lucy's chest, an outer heartbeat to mirror the inner one. Her tiny toes with a mind of their own sought out the seat back, the armrest, anything within reach, while the rest of Evie was occupied otherwise.

Soon she sat up and gurgled. Lucy leaned forward and patted the baby's moist back, peeling her own damp back off the vinyl seat. She arranged her clothing and smoothed Evie's, then settled her back into her carseat. She strapped her in and exited the car, shutting the door absently behind her. The windows were left cracked just a bit from when she'd parked the car earlier, but Lucy hurried toward the house to retrieve the cartons before the noontime sun could have time to intensify the heat in the car. She navigated the maze of garden, climbed the porch steps, and grabbed the two large cartons. Together they were unwieldy, but she managed to wrestle them back to the parking area and around to the rear of the station wagon. She set them down, and found to her surprise that the latch for the rear door of the car would not open. She reached into her pocket for the key.

Panic seized her as she felt the empty pocket. She checked her other pockets. She scanned the gravel at her feet. She circled the station wagon, tugging at each door in turn. Already sticky from nursing in the warm car and from the exertion with the boxes, Lucy felt a trickle of sweat finger its way between her shoulder blades. She peered in through the window and saw her keys dangling from the ignition.

She looked back to the baby who beamed at her with shattering trust, content with her belly full. She kicked her bare feet vigorously. Lucy forced herself to smile and wave. If she showed her panic, Evie would get worked up and cry, hard and then harder, and then she would become overheated all the sooner. Lucy had to do something, fast. Her mind flashed her husband to her side. She saw the condemnation in his face, off on this harebrained quest, dragging Evie around where she need not be, and to what purpose?

Lucy cast her eyes around at her surroundings for the first time. There were some historic residences, but they seemed perfectly uninhabited, their occupants at work at this time on a Friday. They looked forbidding at any rate with their impeccable lawns and perfectly preserved facades. She did not want to walk several blocks to the town square for help and leave Evie alone here in the car. *If I only had a cell phone right now!* she thought. But then, you couldn't get reception here in town or anywhere in the whole county, and who would she have called anyway?

The most promising building close by was the rambling, white, turn-of-the-century funeral home she had passed on Main Street just before turning in the side street around behind Reaves Hall.

She hesitated. She looked back at the smiling baby, now with her foot in her mouth. Evie must have pushed the automatic locks with her toes while she was nursing, and they had only been activated as the car door swung shut. To look at the car, one would not think it new enough to have power anything. She waved again, trying to inspire the baby and herself with confidence, and tore herself from the car.

She flew diagonally through the garden in the direction of the white clapboard she glimpsed through the gnarled fruit trees and towering camellias in the side yard of the Reaves Hall property. As she approached the funeral home, she glanced back and could just make out a glint of chrome where her baby sat blissfully playing, growing hotter by the minute.

The building looked entirely vacant but for the black Cadillac hearse parked in the carport. The front door looked somehow unapproachable, so she darted in through the carport to the screen door at the side of the building. She rang the bell. Not waiting for an answer, she knocked loudly. She paused and strained to hear sounds within. She knocked again, and eventually the door opened. A sixty-ish welcoming face wearing too much makeup and a well-practiced smile greeted her.

"Hello, honey. How can we help you?" she said.

Lucy felt absurdly guilty, like she was disturbing some hallowed process, the secret continuous grieving that must be carried on indefinitely in such places and which must take the undivided professional attention of people like this woman to manage.

"I... I... well, I'm sorry to bother you..."

"Oh, do come in!" said the large smiling mouth.

Lucy reluctantly moved in through the screen door, just, and found herself in a narrow room with avocado carpeting.

"Yes, well, I was moving some artwork into the Historical Society house over there, next door, with a group of people, other artists, and I was the last to come out, and it seems that I... well, I somehow locked my baby in the car, with my keys in the ignition, and with it so bright and warm and all, I've got to get her out *really fast.*" Her voice broke at the last.

"Oh, honey. Who hasn't done something like that? I declare." She turned her head over one shoulder and bellowed, "Clyde? Clyde! Come on out here a minute."

She turned back to Lucy. "What's your baby's name, sugar?"

"Evie. She's Evie." Lucy was seeing spots. She tried to slow her breathing down.

"Awww, so sweet. *And* Biblical."

Not one but three men of different ages and sizes and dress, but all with versions of the same face, appeared in the little side office where the women were standing. The men looked expectant, like they had missed a triple play in a Braves game on T.V. and had hurried in for the instant replay.

The oldest gentleman, the one wearing the formal black suit, said, "What's all the ruckus about, Gladys?"

"Now, hun, this girl's gone and locked her baby-girl and her keys in her car over there behind the Hall, and we've got to help her break in."

"Gladys, honey, they don't call it breaking in if it's her own car." He turned to the girl who didn't look old enough to have a driver's license, let alone a baby, and said, "It *is* your car, isn't it?"

"Oh, yes. Yes, it is!" she answered. Lucy felt sick again.

"Gladys," said the man in the suit, "call Dee-Ann over at the nine one one and tell her to get a message to Norris—Norris is the deputy 'round here—and tell Norris to put on the flashers and get on over here. Listen, we don't bother with the city police; they take too long. I wager Norris'll be here in one minute, two minutes tops," he assured Lucy. "He's probably right over yonder at the Corbie Fried Kitchen eating a pork chop. Always looking for an

241

opportunity to cut on the blue light, Norris is."

"Oh, thank you so much!" said Lucy.

"Honey, I'll go on back over there with you and stay with you till Norris shows up," said the ever-smiling woman.

"That would be wonderful. You are so, so kind!" said Lucy, and they retraced her path out the screen door, through the old orchard, and into the English garden.

"Oh, I feel so bad! I can't believe I let this happen!" wailed Lucy, twisting her hands together.

"Now, just calm yourself, Honey. Norris'll be right here as soon as he finishes chewing his mouthful, wipes the grease off his chin, and tips Tara a five," Gladys reassured her.

Moments later, they approached the station wagon, sagging and worn, but undisturbed. Lucy broke into a run and rushed over to the window behind the driver's seat. She peered in while the funeral home lady came along more slowly. There sat Evie, rosy with heat but still content, making squawking sounds like a backfiring car, mesmerizing herself with toes that moved independently of each other, like a row of little wiggly worms. Lucy gazed at her daughter's face and struggled to bury her panic. Her throat ached.

"Is anyone left in the house, dear?" asked Gladys, nearing the car.

"No... no, we're all out," Lucy said, only half paying attention.

"Oh, all right, if you're sure..." Gladys paused, then went on. "It just seemed like someone was looking down at us from up there," she said, matter-of-factly.

"No, that can't be," Lucy responded. "I was the last one to leave." As the woman's words slowly registered, Lucy looked up to the second floor bank of windows across the back of Reaves Hall. She saw nothing but clouds reflected in the uneven glass.

"Oh, I'm just being silly, as usual, making shapes where there aren't any," Gladys went on. "But then folks *do say*... Oh well. Trust me, Honey, in this business I'm in I would *know* if there was anything to see of that sort—the supernatural, don't you know, anything left behind after death—and there's not!" She chuckled. "Oh, land! I can't tell you the number of times I've had to spend the night in the funeral home babysitting, so to speak, a cadaver. It's state law, you understand. Can't leave them unattended, unsecured. Now, I don't know what in the world they think would happen if you just locked 'em up alone in there, what kind of mayhem *that* would bring on." She checked her flow of conversation as she noticed the strain in Lucy's face. The girl was a peculiar shade of green.

"Now Honey, just don't you worry. Norris will be here fast, real fast, and your little girl is going to be fine!" She peered in next to Lucy. "Ooooh, she is such a doll!"

"Oh, thank you. Eight months and already giving me grey hairs." Lucy tried to laugh.

"Get used to it; you've got a lot more of *that* ahead of you! Years and years of grey hairs. Just wait till she's a *teenager*," said the woman, who seemed to know what she was talking about.

At that moment a siren cranked up not too far off and grew louder and louder until a gleaming cruiser wheeled into the parking area and pulled up next to the women. A deputy eased himself out of the driver's seat and strutted around his car to where they were standing. He pulled out the ample cloth napkin that was tucked in his ample shirt and tossed it through the open window onto his front seat. Inside, a Styrofoam cup coated in black drippings squatted on his front dashboard.

"Afternoon, ma'am," the deputy said to Lucy. He pressed his chin to his chest, suppressing a burp. "Miss Gladys," he nodded to the older woman. "What we got here?"

"Norris honey, we have a baby-girl locked in this-here station wagon, along with the keys, and this young lady would like you to open up the car for her." Norris looked at Lucy.

"Yes, sir. Please hurry if you can," she pleaded. "I think it's getting really hot in there."

"Shoot, yeah, I can take care of that for ya, no problem," said the deputy. He strolled around to the trunk of his cruiser and opened it. Lucy doubted the man would show any more urgency for a case of cardiac arrest, bank robbery, or train wreck. She tried to picture him chasing down a purse-snatcher, but failed. He pulled out a long, narrow, flat piece of metal with a hook cut into one end. In thirty seconds Lucy's door was unlocked.

She whipped the car door wide and unhooked Evie, who laughed from her belly at the suddenness of it all. Lucy lifted her out in her damp little sundress and smoothed back the few wet curls on Evie's almost-bald head. She held her close and breathed in the child's sweet smell. Then she looked over Evie at the deputy and the ever-smiling woman and thanked them for their help and for their kindness. They took leave of her and of each other and went their separate directions, on their way to forgetting a fairly unremarkable incident in their remarkably unremarkable days.

Lucy walked with Evie for a little while to console herself and to cool the child down. The fragrant garden quivered now with photosynthesis and pollination and all sorts of insect activity in the prime of the day, but Lucy noticed none of it. She saw only her feet moving around and around the maze of the garden paving stones. She discovered herself to be trembling.

She carried the baby back to the car and fastened her in, and they began the trip home with the tired old air conditioner turned on full blast, the remnants of a mouse's nest rattling around in the fan housing. Lucy's face was alternately burning and chilled, and she wept. She decided not to tell her husband, with whom she shared everything, about the details of her day.

The Midsummer Show

Georgia had long since forgotten the traditions of the Old World in which, for centuries upon centuries, the summer solstice, St. John's Eve, or Midsummer as the day was misnamed, was celebrated with bonfires and feasts and lovers' trysts and both holy prayers and devilish mischief of all sorts. The day was just as long now as it had ever been. It was still by definition the longest day, and as such was laden with boons and misfortunes more than perhaps any other day of the year, not that folks attributed their luck to any spirits, whether good or malevolent, in this modern day. The members of the Guild had many daylight hours to prepare for the high "holy" evening of their cultural year, and they spent those hours in every way imaginable.

The golf threesome did not meet that Saturday, June 23. Chesley Chiswell had been advised by his doctor to avoid strenuous upper body activity until his neck healed, some six weeks, perhaps. He chipped away fretfully, ineffectively, at a small block of stone in his workshop until six o'clock when he put on his blazer, shirt, and slacks. He tied an alizarin silk cravat over his neck brace and smiled in satisfaction into the mirror.

Bob Short sweated the day away in shirt sleeves and a tie at the school board office that Saturday, helping to interview teachers for the coming year. At six o'clock he changed into a suit with a crisp white shirt fresh from the Laundromat.

Vincent DiAngelo lay upon his bed in a darkened room most of the day, resting, filling his lungs with oxygen as well as he was able, storing up strength for the coming evening. At six o'clock he changed into a semi-retired tuxedo, which he had worn to convention banquets and the like in years gone by.

Lorraine, however, did not miss the Saturday bridge game with the girls at the club, and Muffy accompanied her as usual. Her salon hair and nails sufficed for both her engagements that day, and she was home early enough from the club to freshen her make-up and slip into the sequined dress she had bought for their last cruise. She selected a large purse to match and transferred her necessities into it, leaving plenty of room for Muffy.

Eli Cooper went to check on Cordelia. He found her quietly sitting in her wheelchair on her front porch, impervious to the heat. He asked her to be his date to the reception.

"No, Eli," she said. Her voice sounded faint and faraway. "I'll just sit here and admire God's handiwork. I don't believe my wheelchair could navigate that big old house in town, the crowd and all, and my legs want to carry me less and less these days."

"I'll help you, Cordelia. I really think you should display your carvings. I wish I'd thought of it sooner, but I'm sure we could still find a place for them."

"No, son. I'll ask you only to take this with you," she said as she pulled something from her apron pocket. "Find a place for it in a room with a quilt. It will be just right in a room with a quilt," said Cordelia. Had he ever told her about hanging the quilt in the yellow rose room upstairs? Eli didn't think so. She held out her waxen, ropy hand and placed in his a carved bird.

"All right, Aunt, I'll do it, but I wish you were coming with me." He did not question her strange request. Over his shoulder he flung back a look of concern which she could not see with her

246

fading eyes.

He returned to his studio and threw on a black t-shirt, rumpled khakis, and an old tweed jacket with patches on the elbows. The outfit, which he wore to every one of his openings, had worked for him without exception, and he saw no reason to vary it. He slipped back into his paint-spattered brogans, ran his fingers through his hair, and was ready to go.

James the Organic Farmer debated whether to drive the truck into town for the show or to ride the mule. Sadie had been quite ornery all day, and the extra energy required for the trip might help work out some of her attitude. At any rate, he was always looking for a way to decrease his carbon footprint. However, he had thought of stopping at Wal-Mart on the way to town to replace his work boots. He had put it off for a couple of weeks, thinking they might just turn up somehow, sometime, but they had not, and his tennis shoes were looking worse for the wear. That's it; he could not park Sadie in the Wal-Mart parking lot, so he would take the truck and just hope that no one would ask him for a ride home. He showered outside, toweled off, and put on a suit, the one he had worn to his sister's wedding and his grandfather's funeral, with his best red bow-tie.

Lucy Bloom hustled about the kitchen, fixing an early supper, washing a sinkful of dishes, and wiping up Gerber sweet potatoes spewed from Evie's rosebud mouth. The baby was sleeping through the night regularly now and sometimes forgot to nurse before bedtime. Maybe Lucy would not be missed too much for the next few hours. She set out the carved figures for the children to play with after they ate and stole away to the bedroom to change into her one nice dress, the loose-fitting blue one which she wore to weddings. It was only slightly out of date. She swept a brush through her hair and slipped into her shoes.

"Are you sure you're all right with me being gone this evening?"

she asked her husband as she kissed the children goodbye.

"I told you already, Lucy Girl, I want you to go and have a good time with your artist friends. I would go with you on your big night, but somebody's got to stay with these guys," he said. She tried to picture him there, at the show. Who would he talk to? James the new-age farmer? Aylin, the gypsy? *That* could be dangerous. Eli?

"Hey." He grabbed her and put his arms around her and his face in her neck. "You look beautiful. Just be sure you don't go home with anyone else!" he teased.

Yes, Jackson would definitely be out of his element, Lucy thought, and he was sparing her the awkwardness of his presence. It wasn't his world. The bigger question was, was it hers? She was like a plant with two stems: On one side she was the lone blossom opening to the sunshine; on the other she was the stem itself, bearing the new green leaves and the buds. She felt off-balance. But her face flushed with the prospect of seeing her paintings hung with the rest. She did not know how beautiful that blush made her in her simple blue dress to the man before her.

"Oh, I'll be back," she said. "You can count on it." She turned her face to his and kissed him. "It'll be late, though, eleven thirty or twelve." He would be sound asleep by that time, if the baby cooperated. Saturdays he was especially exhausted.

"I'll save a place for you right next to me," Jackson said, and he smiled and kissed her back.

Lucy left the house and headed out to her first stop, the Whitetail Cove Golf Course. She felt naked, incomplete, like she was forgetting something. It was strange to be alone.

Aylin Borden, meanwhile, had freshly reddened hair thanks to a visit to the pink bathroom in the basement apartment of Mrs. Law. She wore a tight off-the-shoulder top that covered her loose upper arms but still showed plenty of flesh, her long, full gypsy skirt, two armfuls of silver bangles, and huge silver hoop earrings that brushed her shoulders as they weighed down her ears. She had applied extra make-up so as to look more dramatic than usual. As she peered into the mirror, she saw with satisfaction that the new discoloration on her shoulder did not show beneath the thick layer of concealer. She took a last fortifying swig from the wineglass by the bed.

Her carpet bag sat at the ready just inside the door. But for now, she took nothing in her hands. She swept out of the cottage past the pale grey cat on the stoop licking its paws. She sashayed along the path through the woods to the gravel access road and strolled down to the gates. She waited there for some time before the old station wagon appeared in the golden glow of late afternoon.

Eleanor Wood had spent the day preparing sketches for a new series of portraits. At five, weary and warm from the upstairs studio that could never really be cooled in summer with sunlight streaming in, she stopped for the day and began dressing. She eased a simple black dress on over the surgical tape and the incision, about which she had had good news. She fixed her hair simply, in a bun at the base of her neck. It was difficult to reach up with her arms, and her preparation took a bit longer than usual. It would be a busy evening with all her presidential duties, but she would not be distracted from the most important thing tonight.

At about six o'clock Eleanor pulled into the driveway across the street, cut the engine off, and made her way up the driveway through an obstacle course of plastic toys. She approached the door and pressed the button for the doorbell. She heard a stampede of feet running to and fro, but no one answered the door. She knocked. Eventually, the door opened and her neighbor, Mr. Sampson, looked out questioningly.

"Hello, Mr. Sampson. I'm Eleanor Wood from across the street? We met at the neighborhood barbecue?" said Eleanor.

"Oh, yes," said Mr. Sampson. "You're here for Morgan."

He turned to a somber little girl beside him. "Sudy, go call Morgan to the door, please." Two or three small faces of various shades peered around him. The man stood studying Eleanor as if she were a strange mushroom that had just sprung up in the yard.

"So you're the artist, huh?" He did not invite her in, nor did this omission disappoint Eleanor.

"That I am," she replied. "I'm grateful that you have allowed Morgan to go to the meetings and the show with me. She has considerable talent, I believe."

"I don't know the first thing about talent, Helen, but I do know about promise, and I don't see much in that girl, I gotta tell you. I don't know where she's headed, I'll be honest. Maybe just back to the old cycle we see, kids, babies, drugs, foster care, more kids, more drugs... you know the story."

"Well, I do believe being with other artists is encouraging to her. She seems to be coming out of her shell a bit."

"If you say so. Anyway, thanks for taking an interest in her. It's nice, I'm sure," said the man as he scooped up a little boy crawling through his legs.

Morgan appeared in a church dress and sandals. Eleanor smiled at her and told Mr. Sampson, "I'll have her home by eleven. Is that all right?"

"Oh, sure," he said. "Just please keep an eye on her around all those other artists."

"I certainly will," said Eleanor. She and Morgan picked their way through the toys in the yard, climbed in the car, and were off. Reaves Hall was not far, only a mile or so, at the other edge of the historic district, so Eleanor had little time to beat around the bush.

"Morgan," she said glancing over at the girl beside her biting her fingernails, "there's something I wanted to talk to you about, to... to ask you. The fact is... I just rattle around in a big old empty house, and I couldn't help but notice how full the Sampsons' is. I realize you'll be eighteen before another year is up, and well..." She could feel that Morgan was looking intently at her. She could tell without looking that Morgan had stopped biting her nails.

They reached a red light. She turned to the girl, her hands squarely on the wheel. "The thing is, Morgan, I would like to adopt you." Morgan's mouth fell open in spite of her long years of experience controlling her face.

"I've looked into it, and I've learned that it might take nine or ten months to complete the legal process, and by that time you'd almost be an adult in the eyes of the courts, but still, I'd like to adopt you, and you would have a home as long as you wanted one, and if you'd like to stay on, to finish out high school, if you'd like to work as my apprentice, I'd be happy not to be alone in that big old house."

Morgan sat staring, not speaking. Eleanor feared she had alarmed the girl. She had no wish to set her back, to be a stumbling block to her progress.

"It's all up to you, of course. I wish I could say that you could think about it as long as you like, but if the process is not complete by your birthday, then adoption is no longer possible." She realized the light had turned green so she turned her face back to the road and started off again. Still, Morgan had not spoken.

Eleanor drove in silence, worrying that perhaps she had overstepped her bounds. She had to concentrate on driving as the road grew more congested. She passed the house and grounds and the enormous tent where the reception would begin soon and turned down the neighboring side street and into the parking area. Only a few cars and the catering vans were there before them.

She swept the car into a parking place and cut off the engine before turning once again to look at the girl beside her, who seemed smaller and younger in her second-hand Sunday school dress. The girl sat looking straight ahead, her hands gripping each other in her lap.

"You don't have to decide right away," said Eleanor. Morgan turned toward her, and Eleanor was moved to see a tear rolling down her otherwise impassive face. She could have no way of knowing how rare that occurrence was for the girl.

"No," said Morgan quietly, "I don't have to think about it. It would be lovely, just lovely." She almost smiled.

"There's just one thing."

"What is that?" asked Eleanor, her own eyes watering.

"If I were your apprentice," the girl said, "which I'd like very, very much—there is no way I could be anything but an artist; there's nothing else for me—but if I were your apprentice, then would I still have time to paint my houses? I feel like I have to paint the houses, all the houses, I see in my mind, until there aren't any more. They won't go on forever; I'm pretty sure about that. But I'm not finished with them yet."

Eleanor's heart brimmed. "Of course. You're free to paint houses, to paint anything. And when you're ready to move on, that's entirely your decision." She pulled a Kleenex from her pocket and dabbed at her eyes. She was overjoyed. She would have a new purpose, a new young person to care for and teach and help along. And this girl would have a future. She *deserved* a future.

"We'll talk to your foster parents tomorrow and start the wheels turning." They sat for a moment in easy silence before Eleanor roused herself.

"Now I guess we'd better get inside and get this show on the road." They climbed out of the car and walked through the garden, making their way through the flock of caterers and musicians setting up, toward the waiting Hall.

All over Corbie County, people were showering and dressing and otherwise gearing up for the evening ahead: artists and Historical Society members and executives retired to horse country life and curious locals and a myriad of other interested persons. After all, it was the only show in town.

* * *

The ride for Lucy and her passenger was strangely companionable, at least to begin with. The two women, one young and the other of advanced middle age, had found common ground in their creative impulses, if not in their other inclinations. Now they hovered in the shady territory between acquaintance and friendship which men accept easily but which women find awkward. Lucy was surprised to find that she was actually happy to see the flamboyant Aylin, but then, she did not have much time to spend with adults. By now she was somewhat used to the woman's mysterious nature and explained her away as a flower child from the sixties.

As Aylin swept her skirts into the passenger seat, her essence drifted in with her, eclipsing the old car smell. Her eyes were bright and black. She seemed more eager, more exotic, and years younger than Lucy remembered her. Lucy herself felt just the opposite: a little dumpy, a little ill, a little off-kilter.

"I'm sorry I'm late," Lucy said as they drove away from the golf course gates. "I had to run to the store for diapers when I realized we didn't have enough to make it through the night. Then I had to feed everyone and get the children ready for bed."

Aylin made no comment.

"I figured the store would be closed by the time we're finished at the reception."

"Yeah, I guess so," murmured Aylin, clearly on another planet from diapers. "Yeah... it'll be a long night," she added, almost to herself.

Lucy guided the car at a safe twenty miles per hour through the winding streets of Whitetail Cove.

"Hey, the show looks great," she said. "It didn't take long to hang it yesterday since the hooks were already in the walls. There was just about the right number of spots for the artwork we had."

"I can't wait to see it, and in that rich old place, too," Aylin replied.

"The house definitely has character—spirit, I guess you could say." Lucy concentrated on her driving for a minute while she avoided a couple of potholes. "Your pastels look fantastic where we hung them, all together in the big, formal parlor, side by side. They look like they were meant to be there."

"Thanks. I feel good about them, myself," said Aylin.

"The framing is beautiful. Who did it for you?"

"Oh, I took them to a little place up in Athens."

Lucy paused. "Well, I find it pretty hard to pay for frames. They're so expensive now, and I don't really have the extra money to spend on that, especially not knowing if I can sell them and get my money back."

"Yeah, I know what you mean. But I just traded for these."

Lucy wondered what Aylin had traded, feeling certain that she did not have much for tradable resources. She felt reluctant to ask, though. It seemed intrusive, and she wasn't sure she wanted to know the answer anyway.

She wheeled the old wagon past the oversized Whitetail entrance sign. As she pulled out onto the state highway, she narrowly missed an early possum, lugging its ugly bulk across the road on some stealthy mission. She gripped the steering wheel and accelerated gradually to a top speed of fifty miles per hour. A wrong choice, a sudden movement, even at a moderate speed, could end in disaster. She had lost control once, and almost a second time back in April before the Guild meeting, and she was determined to keep her vehicle on the right path. Visibility was the thing, though—late-afternoon glare struck as she navigated a curve—sometimes it was hard to see the best path.

Aylin coughed, and Lucy recollected the woman beside her. "Well, the frames really set off your pictures," Lucy said. "They are... I don't know... mystical."

"Huh, go figure. Guess it was worth it then," Aylin said. "So how many of you were there to hang the stuff?"

"Let's see. There was Vincent, the older man with the oxygen tank, and his wife. Then there was Madeline or Magdaline or something? A little lady? And there were those other two, the man and woman that are related somehow. He's tall and paints and she sews. Her name is Orilla?"

"Oh, yeah, I know who you're talking about. That it?"

"Yes, pretty much. But then at the end the artist with the big fancy booth at Box Hollow came by, Eli Cooper."

"Oh, I *definitely* know *that* one! Now *there* is an attractive man," said Aylin. "Is *he* going to be at the show tonight?" she said with a suggestive cackle.

"I think so." Lucy cracked the window for fresh air. Her face felt hot.

"You don't *know*? You didn't *ask* him? I would have gotten that information out of him for sure."

"We didn't get around to that subject. But I think he'll be there. He just joined the Guild, and he has a large painting hung in the show."

"Huh, a large painting." She shot Lucy a sidelong glance and chuckled under her breath.

They rode along together more relaxed now than when the children had been with them on the way to Box Hollow a month or two ago. Aylin did not ask about them.

After a pause she said, "So what about you? How many watercolors do you have in the show?"

"Um, I only got two done in time to frame them, and I couldn't really afford the money I spent on *them*, anyway," Lucy said.

"Just *two*? Lucy, this is your big chance! And you only got two done?"

"Honestly, I worked every free moment I could, and some that weren't so free, but there just weren't enough of them." She paused, and then said, "My time isn't really my own."

"You just do it, girlfriend. You just pick up the brush and do it. You owe it to yourself."

Lucy readjusted herself in her seat and sat up straighter at the steering wheel.

"My hands are full—they are really, really full—and I don't have a place set aside for painting, you know, a place where I can leave it and come back to it. My space is not exactly my own either."

"Space, time, hands, whatever. It's all excuses."

"Well, if I try to work when the children are awake, which is most of the time, it's noisy and distracting; they're always needing something, crying, shouting, singing, interrupting." She felt guilty confessing this. She felt it was some sort of betrayal.

Aylin looked over at her and leaned closer. Lucy glanced at her. Aylin was nodding in sympathy. Her eyes were very, very bright, oddly so. "I know *just* what you mean. It's exactly like that with the elderly woman I sit for. You just want to make it stop. You'll do anything to make it stop. It's like you just want to put a pillow down over their face and make all the noise *stop*."

Lucy felt her jaw fall open. She closed her mouth deliberately and swallowed. Her eyes tore themselves from the road—they could not help it—and took in the woman beside her. She realized that she had been seriously mistaken about this person, this companion, so to speak, whom she really did not know in the least. Aylin was still leaning toward her with her knowing smile and her gleaming eyes and her thick, awful makeup. Her whole demeanor said that she had just discovered a profound commonality with Lucy which, in fact, was not remotely there. Quite the opposite, actually. Lucy felt a wave of nausea sweep over her. When she remembered Aylin's persistent offer to babysit, she shuddered.

And then, strangely, in the midst of her horror she felt an overwhelming sadness for this woman who dwelt so far outside the sphere of human warmth. Lucy wanted to protect Aylin from her revulsion.

"Your pastels will do well tonight," she heard herself saying in a small voice. "People will recognize the beauty and the invention you put into them."

Aylin withdrew into the passenger seat, sighed, and after a pointed look at the speedometer, looked straight ahead into the golden ripe afternoon. "I certainly hope so," she said. "It's about time."

With relief Lucy spotted Reaves Hall up ahead and said, "Looks like we're here, and definitely not the first to arrive." The parking lot was full, and cars were beginning to fill in the sides of the lane. Maybe, hopefully, the crowd would dilute the essence of Aylin, which had settled on Lucy like a miasma.

"Fine with me," said Aylin. "I always like to arrive at these things when the party is in full swing."

Lucy prodded the station wagon onto the green shoulder alongside a spiked iron fence that marked the edge of a stately yard not far from Reaves Hall. She and Aylin left the car and began walking toward the house. Violin strains drifted through the slanting daylight along with the sound of voices and a small dog barking querulously. They made their way through the parking lot overflowing with all kinds of vehicles from new, low, and sleek to faded, banged-up, and obsolete.

They entered the paved pathways of the English garden where a few sparkling people were holding drinks and laughing excessively, already. Weaving through them, Aylin and Lucy passed by the string trio positioned in the garden where its sound could travel around the beautiful, manicured space, into the house, and through the side orchard where an enormous white tent gleamed in the late afternoon. Aylin slowed when she spotted the tent and the caterers hustling back and forth between it and the kitchen.

"That looks like a good place to start," she said.

"Okay. I'll just go on in and find a bathroom," Lucy said as she kept moving toward the house, thankful for an excuse to be parted from Aylin.

Just outside the back porch she nearly collided with a short, red-faced man in plaid careening toward the screen door from the direction of the tent with a sloshing liquor glass in his hand. She stepped back to let him pass and opened her eyes wider in surprise: He was the man who had made a show of quitting the Guild at the first meeting she had been to, Boone Somebody. She hadn't noticed any paintings by him when they had set up the show yesterday, but she might not have recognized his signature, certainly not his style, and perhaps she had just missed them. Maybe he was only here to see someone else's work, but that didn't seem likely.

She passed through the door after him onto the narrow porch and into the dark gallery, where a glittering docent was accepting donations to the Historical Society at the door. Lucy asked about a bathroom and was directed through the wavy glass doors into the central hallway where a small door, second on the right, opened into a tiny powder room fashioned from a closet beneath the main staircase. Here Lucy stayed for some time, feeling more ill than before. The words Aylin had spoken and the sympathetic attitude with which she had said them, the assumption she had made of Lucy's complicity in her thinking, the supposition of their sisterhood, were playing in endless loops in her mind.

Some minutes later, the docent welcomed the next to enter, a young man with a neat beard and a bow tie. He carried a plate of grilled vegetables and a drink. He held his head at an inquisitive angle. He wanted to search for his picture, and for Lucy's, which he believed he would easily recognize. The central hallway was jammed with people in evening attire and Sunday best. Shy of so many people in such close quarters, he veered into the first doorway at hand, to his right, and entered into a darkly paneled room with numerous lamps that incompletely dispelled the dimness. There were few windows to help the lamps in their mission.

Two or three people, no more, were milling about here, and James could see why. This was clearly a men's-only room, aggressively masculine with antique weaponry hung on the walls and an undeniable staleness, the ghost of decades of cigar smoke, tainting the air. Spread across a huge broad table at the center of the room was a collection of tools ranging from tiny and sharp to large and blunt. An engraved sign read, "Hennessey Collection of Antique Medical Instruments."

James generally enjoyed the perusal and, in fact, the use of antique tools, but he shuddered as he looked down at the mallets, the pliers, the saws and all the cutting tools of various sizes, many showing signs of heavy use—notches, nicks, worn places. Arranged in several glass cases around the table were smaller instruments—scalpels, needles, picks, and other strange, unidentifiable implements. There were numerous bottles and vials with antique labels: Pinkham's Tablets, Root Tonic, Syrup Ipecac, Dixon's Aromatic Carminative Compound, Paregoric, Dismal Swamp Chill & Fever Tonic, Dr. Whateley's Energy Elixir, Uncle Rex's Fast/Sure Cure for Shop & Kitchen Wounds & Punctures.

James shifted his gaze to the artwork on the walls of the room. His eyes rested first on a work hung over the carved tobacco-colored mantel: a large oil painting, painted in great detail, of an angel greeting a young robed woman—the Annunciation. It looked like an exact replica of a painting he had seen somewhere, one of those old famous ones. But at closer view, he could see that from the angel's outstretched arm dangled a yo-yo at the lowest point of its round-trip flight path. The angel painting was flanked by two similarly-painted oils showing dogs playing golf, and dogs drinking and playing poker. These seemed vaguely familiar to James as well.

Before the fireplace stood two men in animated conversation. One James recognized as the crusty old gentleman who had dissed the Guild at the first meeting he had attended. The second was unfamiliar, a handsome young-ish guy in clerical collar, who seemed fascinated with the angel painting. James had no desire to enter into religious debate, if that was what they were up to; he had not been to church since he was a child except when it could not be avoided, for a wedding or a funeral. He did, however, feel oddly disturbed by the obvious satire in the painting. He stored away this puzzling reaction for further analysis and turned to the adjoining wall.

There before him hung three unsettling works, nearly identical, each one an oversized, oddly-colored, distorted depiction of a man with lank hair and dark heavy-framed glasses. The man looked straight out of the cheap canvas board with poster-paint eyes that should have been nearly obscured by the glasses, and yet they were piercing, able to maintain eye contact with the viewer. The paintings were untitled, but they could have been called *Insanity: Three Views*. Somehow they seemed appropriate in this room with its medical instruments. James wondered if the doctor whose office this had once been had practiced psychiatry as well. Probably not.

People probably just locked up anyone who was really different in those days. Still, there was something a little "off" about the old doctor's study.

A moving shadow in the corner of the room caught his eye, and he looked suddenly toward it, noticing then that the shadow was in fact the unspeaking man from the three paintings, in the flesh. He seemed to be sequestering himself from the light. James was ready to move on to another room.

* * *

Vincent sat on the velvet sofa with his wife flitting about him in her sequins and resplendent hair, chatting with first one and then another of the glitterati of Liberty. "Since he came to us two months ago, we have *never* been separated," she was saying in a high voice, motioning to her purse and its inhabitant. Lorraine had placed her large shiny red crocodile bag on the sofa next to Vincent. Muffy's dark gargoyle face peered out of his stylish cave, alert to any oncoming threats, prepared to protect his mistress and master if need be.

A young bearded fellow in a bow-tie passed through the door from the adjoining room, the doctor's study. Vincent nodded to him in acknowledgement. The young man nodded in return but moved on past Vincent into the room without exchanging words. Just as well. The young fellow had something of the socialist about him.

The rhythmic hiss of Vincent's oxygen lay hidden under the tangle of prattling voices, but he sensed it, much as he would have sensed the in-breath and out-breath of an actual person at his elbow. He appreciated the social scene, but he was content to remain in his velvet-and-oxygen cocoon until such time as someone should want to come and admire his painting over the mantelpiece. He gazed up at his *demoiselle* there in satisfaction. All of his best effort and a great deal of time had gone into this final version, and he felt he had captured her essence at last. Now perhaps he would feel at peace; she had haunted him for so long.

Vincent felt he had truly arrived in the art world now, with the completion of this nude in oil. He shifted in his seat so that he could better see the room. Lorraine was chatting close at hand with the mayor and her husband. Perhaps *they* were admiring his painting. Farther off in the room he saw several people sitting on a pair of sofas near the windows engaged with each other but not with any of the artwork.

He spotted the country fellow with the wooden bowls, leaning back, arms crossed, against the table where his work was arranged. The young socialist with the bow tie seemed to be peppering him with questions and looked over his shoulder furtively at one point. Vincent followed his gaze to the red-haired hippie woman who was looking—and here he surprised himself—good tonight, better than usual anyway, even if she was in another of her outlandish hippie outfits. She seemed high on life, or high on *something*, with her frizzy hair grazing her shoulders and her eyes wide open and her lips painted dark red. She had a wine goblet in one hand and a small plate loaded with cheeses, pâté, and crackers in the other. She was gesturing with the cheese plate toward several pastel paintings nearby, most likely her own, in the midst of an animated conversation with none other than Vincent's golf companion, Bob Short, who seemed oddly interested in the pastels.

Vincent saw nothing remarkable in the paintings, just chunks of Greek architecture drifting around in the sky. At least the details were painted in a realistic way; perhaps that is what attracted Bob. Vincent watched the ebb and flow of people in the room. The little bow-tie fellow left the parlor. The redhead spotted him and departed abruptly from Bob, in hot pursuit.

Vincent's legs grew restless. He stood up and moved stiffly toward the hall, trailing his oxygen tank along. He glanced back over his shoulder; he *was* reluctant to leave his lady behind. The little dog yipped sharply, twice. Vincent paid it no heed and moved out into the wide front hallway on his way to find refreshments.

* * *

The grand front door of Reaves Hall was open to the rosy evening and to the guests still arriving in clusters up the broad walk and across the veranda. Magdaline Dismukes had deployed herself there as mistress of the evening and protector of the house and grounds, to greet newcomers. Orilla, Orvelle, and their guest stepped up the imposing front steps, three abreast.

Um-hmmm, here that Magpie woman again. Orilla could see beyond the woman standing in the doorway into the fancy, brightly-lit hall and thought, *Lord, Lord, what a light bill these people gon' have.* As Orilla's group approached the open entryway, the Disputes woman stationed there turned away and spoke to the old Uncle Sam with the oxygen tank, crossing the hallway behind her. They carried on some little conversation while the three newcomers waited just outside; the hostess was blocking the entrance. Before too long, Magdaline turned back to greet them with a wide smile, *loaded with everything but real*, thought Orilla.

"Good evening!" said the wide mouth. "So glad you could come to the combined Corbie County Historical Society and Artists Guild Reception. You may choose to start here to the left in the Grand Parlor. Refreshments are in the tent in the orchard at the side of the house."

Orilla nodded and stepped boldly through the doorway into the huge fancy place with the huge fancy history. Orvelle took the arm of the other woman, all decked out, with her Sunday hat and all, and escorted her into the house. They moved as a phalanx into the first room to the left.

* * *

Lucy emerged from the powder room and headed up the long hall toward the front of the house just as Orilla and Orvelle and a woman in an enormous hat appeared in the open entry. The thought struck Lucy that she would rather talk with them than with the highly-polished strangers that jammed the place, swirling their drinks and smiling at each other's over-white teeth. Wandering in their direction, she came upon the huge starburst that Eli had painted and felt herself sucked out of the room, out of the crowd, out of the moldy history of the house, into the cosmos with other bright things where she felt dizzy with altitude, color, and warmth. After a few minutes, she tore her eyes away, steered around the table with the appalling ghost-child statue, and trailed behind Orilla and her companions into the Grand Parlor.

Upon entering the room, though, Lucy lost all thought as to why she had come. Her face flamed at the sight of the nude over the mantelpiece. *Well,* she thought, *I guess you have to prepare yourself for nudes at an art show. Somebody in a group of artists is bound to think they have to do it; it's just inevitable.* But this is the reason Lucy shied away from ever taking a figure-drawing class: She never could be sure if a model would show up clothed or unclothed, and she was too embarrassed to ask ahead of time. It would be thought juvenile and uncultured, prudish at the very least. She told herself that tonight the other artists and guests would find a nude in this place unremarkable.

She turned her back on the fireplace and drifted toward the center of the room where she spied wooden bowls arranged on a table. While she stood there admiring them, she could feel the mournful larger-than-life woman over the mantel staring at her, demanding her attention. She concentrated on one bowl in particular, thinking it would make a nice gift for her husband. *Yes, Jackson would like this. Simple and solid and strong, just like him.* But when she turned the bowl over, Lucy saw that the asking price was a hundred thirty-five dollars, beyond her reach. Unless, of course, she actually sold a painting, and then...

A boisterous voice drew her attention to the small group standing near Aylin's pastels. Orilla and Orvelle and the woman with them were in deep discussion over Aylin's Greek sky paintings.

"I'm gonna say this lady—what's her name?" The stranger leaned forward to inspect the card. "Ay-lynn, done painted a replication of God's Good Heaven." The woman's hat plume bowed and dipped, dancing with her ebullient speech.

"Yes, ma'am, you could see it that way, for sure," murmured Orvelle.

"Look to me like a stage waitin' for somethin' to happen," said Orilla.

A clamor suddenly arose off the velvet sofa, a fierce growling and yipping that cut through the civilized symphony of voices in the house. Lorraine hustled on tiny shiny shoes over to the sofa where she collected her huge red purse, and minced her way toward the door. The face of Muffy, wrath incarnate, protruded from the top of the bag, directing all his fury at Orvelle and the ladies. The dog seemed ready to catapult himself from his red lair through the air like a diminutive, furry, snarling dragon. Orvelle froze as though he had looked Medusa in the eye.

Lorraine hurried past, giggling helplessly, with the seething, lunging bagful over her shoulder. "I guess I'll go look for my Vince," she tittered to the room on her way out, as if that covered the whole occurrence.

Lucy looked over again at the three people standing in a tight knot before Aylin's paintings. They formed a noble silhouette before the luminous paintings of "God's Good Heaven."

"Creature of the Tormentor!" the woman in the hat cried after the dog. "Lord Jesus in Heaven preserve us from that Evil Seed!"

"It just a dog," said Orilla.

"Gots teeth though," said Orvelle, who relaxed only when the dog's angry clamor faded down the hallway. He had sweated through his pristine white shirt. Orilla turned to face the room and noticed its dozen other occupants, silent and gawking. She glared back until they looked away and resumed their conversations.

She spotted Lucy and moved toward her, over to the table with the wooden bowls. "Quite an evenin' in this fancy old place, Lucy of the Light," Orilla greeted her.

"Yes, Orilla," Lucy smiled, "*quite* an evening. What a crowd!" She paused, unsure what to say after the commotion. "I really don't understand why someone would bring a dog to something like this."

"People do what they please. Gots to be prepared for that. No way that dog gon' get through me to take a chunk out of Orvelle, anyhow," she chuckled. She held her shiny black pocketbook in front of her, dangling over her crossed wrists. Lucy and Orvelle exchanged familiar nods.

"This here our 'quaintance Overseer Crutchfield," Orilla said, introducing the woman in the hat. "And this here our artist 'quaintance Lucy."

"Nice to meet you," Lucy said with all the enthusiasm she could muster in order to make up for the dog. "How are you this evening?"

"I am *blessed!*" exclaimed Overseer Crutchfield. "Now tell me, young lady, did you make these pretty bowls here?"

"Oh, no. I can't make anything like this. I paint flowers. But

266

these things here, they're just wood—it's not like they're alive or anything—but they seem warm, don't they? Almost human, somehow." Orvelle nodded doubtfully, and Orilla's eyebrow inched up.

The lady in the hat said, "Well, I don't know about that. I'm no art expert type person, but these are nice, yes indeed. All these bowls and pictures and what-all here are nice—well mostly nice." She cut her eyes toward the nude over the mantel and flinched. Lucy suddenly saw that it was not only she herself who was trying to ignore the somber naked presence over the mantel, but also every other person in the room. Certainly the four of them standing here beside the bowls, anyway. The artist, Vincent, had certainly succeeded in creating a presence.

Overseer Crutchfield continued. "But you should see the picture Brother Orvelle here did for this lady in our church, this poor, sweet, bereaved elderly lady who just lost her husband, Lester Farrow? He passed? Praise Jesus, Brother Orvelle painted the nicest picture of the Dear Departed, alive and well and full of the spirit. He just looked at Mr. Lester in the coffin and went home and painted him bright as day. It's a *miracle!* It's such a *blessing* to that lady! She got her husband's smile to keep her going in the lonely times now that death done hath them parted, but only for a little while, yes, just a little while, *thank* you, *Jesus!*"

Lucy could not be sure, but she thought she saw Orilla roll her eyes at Orvelle.

She looked with new interest at the tall, powerfully-built, quiet man with the long ringlets and the bright white shirt. She took in his intelligent grey eyes and gentle nature. He must have read an inquiry in her look which she really did not want to put into words.

"It wadn't hard. I looks at Mr. Farrow in his sleek silver coffin and at that tiny little lady, his wife, all broke up with sorrow and the arthritis, and I knows that painting just gon' come out fine. I

267

only paint something I have a feeling for."

"I know exactly what you mean," said Lucy. Still, she felt appalled at the idea of painting a dead person. Then again, maybe it wasn't so different from a cut flower.

"So, did you... take pictures...?" Lucy asked.

"Yes, pictures," answered Orvelle, "with my flash camera."

"That's just remarkable. I imagine you gave that lady a lot of comfort."

Orvelle nodded. "With the help of the Good Lord of Heaven and Earth I believe I give her some little bit."

Lucy was distracted then by a handsome young man in a clerical collar who walked through the connecting doorway from the old doctor's office, ice tinkling in the glass he carried. A thin, expensive young woman followed with a glass comfortably settled in her hand as well. They moved with marked social ease; they could have been at just another fraternity party, if they had been five or ten years younger. They were navigating toward the imposing fireplace when the painting over it caught their attention.

The rector stepped back a step and gazed unabashedly at the woman pictured above him, draped in murkiness and nothing else, cramped and contorted in the box of the ornate frame, drab and anonymous. He swung his glass in his hand. The ice clinked. He drank deeply from his glass while his glittering eyes probed the painted figure. Then the young rector threw his head back and his chest out, and exploded in a huge tenor laugh. He laughed long. He laughed hard. Every face in the room turned to him and then to the mournful painting above the mantel.

"Sweet Lord Jesus, preserve our souls," said Overseer Crutchfield under her breath, her plume bobbing and swaying. "And he a man of God, too!"

Neither Orvelle nor Orilla nor Overseer Crutchfield nor Lucy nor anyone else could avoid any longer looking at the painting that represented Vincent's entry into the serious art world. The nude drew their eyes as if it were a freeway accident or a house engulfed in flames.

"I think we be leavin' this room *now*," said Orilla in a low, commanding voice.

"Lord'a'mercy," agreed Overseer Crutchfield.

All four, Lucy too, headed for the doorway and out into the brilliant hall, the rector's laughter fading behind them. Orvelle, Orilla and their guest turned down the main hall.

"Saints preserve us, is *every* room going to be that way?" The hat plume quaked.

Lucy, trailing behind, came across Magdaline still self-stationed in the front doorway.

"What was all that uproar about in the Grand Parlor?" she asked, frowning slightly.

"Oh, that was just a man who had a, well, an unusual reaction to a painting," Lucy replied.

"What painting?"

"Vincent's."

"*Vincent's?*"

"Yes, Vincent's."

"How inappropriate." Magdaline pursed her lips severely. "I saw Vince come out a few minutes before that. I'm glad he wasn't in the room for such a rude outburst."

"I know. It would be hard not to take it personally. Your art feels like a piece of yourself, with all the nerves attached."

"And he's so fragile since the accident."

"Tell me," said Lucy, unable to resist. "What happened to Vincent?"

"You don't *know?*" Magdaline frowned. "He was on a plane that went down several years back, off the coast of Venezuela, in the ocean. American Airlines Flight Twelve Fifty. It was all over the

269

news." She looked at Lucy expectantly, but Lucy did not recall; maybe she was occupied by a new baby at the time.

"Only three people survived," Magdaline went on. "Vincent's lungs collapsed and never entirely recovered. Changed him forever."

"Oh, I see," Lucy said, shocked at the scale of the man's trauma. "What a dreadful thing."

"It certainly was," said Magdaline, before turning away to greet some latecomers clattering in high heels across the broad front porch.

Lucy went back in the parlor again, for just a short look. Now she perceived far more than awkwardness in the painting over the mantel. She could see the embodiment of fear and pain and entrapment and exposure and vulnerability that she never would have recognized without knowing the artist's story. The longer she looked, the more trapped and breathless she felt herself.

The young minister and his wife stood with their backs to the painting now, jingling ice in their glasses, laughing and chatting, a charming picture in and of themselves.

* * *

Aylin felt vaguely disappointed that she had somehow missed the little farmer with the truck. She was ever on the alert for an interesting ride home, and she did not mind a bit the rough, earthy nature of the old farm truck. She had followed him out of the parlor and wandered around looking for him, but he seemed to have disappeared.

She saw Lucy come out of the large masculine front parlor and pause a moment with the Dismukes woman. Aylin made her way toward them.

"Lucy, have you seen this sculpture in the front hallway? No one seems to be noticing how hideous it is!"

"Oh, really?" Lucy replied. Madam Dismukes, however, was not amused by her comment.

Aylin pulled Lucy by the arm away from the scowling woman and pointed. "I guess that's the sculptor over there beside it, the guy with the bleached hair and the neck brace, coming on to that little yellow-headed girl."

They moved a bit closer to the grand focal point of the hallway, the piteous stone child under the chandelier. Aylin noticed that Lucy shuddered, unaccountably. The sculptor was leaning toward the girl and looking wolf-like with his grin and his manicured van dyke beard. His voice, raspy, over-cultured, and California-foreign, carried across the din of the crowd, having a high time.

"You should certainly visit my studio sometime, my dear," he was saying, "It is quite fabulous. I have numerous works at different stages of completion, commissions and inspired works, and whatnot."

The girl did not speak, only nodded. Her eyes darted sideways and took in the nearby women. *Pleading for a lifeline*, Aylin thought.

"Yes, I have many masterpieces in me, many great works yet to be realized, dozens of them already envisioned... right... here." He tapped his bronze advancing forehead and smiled—more like leered, Aylin thought, like he was about to eat something tasty.

"The magnificent thing about working in stone is that it is so permanent, compared with other media. When one creates a work in stone, one can be sure it will last for the ages. True immortality for the artist."

The girl nodded politely. She began to sidle away from the sculptor, but he persisted. He talked and grinned and inched himself closer until she was backed up against the massive round table. His breath would be on the girl's face. Aylin walked up to the table and fingered the gallery card with the artist's name on it.

The sculptor seemed oblivious to her and Lucy, so focused was he on the youngest, blondest female in the vicinity.

"Will you look at this?" she murmured to Lucy pointing to the gallery card. "Chesley Fox Chiswell. What kind of convoluted name is that? He had to have made it up!"

Lucy glanced toward the artist around on the other side of the table.

"Oh, quit worrying!" Aylin said. "He didn't hear. He doesn't even know we're in the room. Come to think of it, he *is* a good looking guy, in a con-artist sort of way."

Aylin walked directly around the table and up to the girl and her admirer. "Hello, I can't help but *marvel* over your *fabulous* sculpture," she said to Chesley. Then she looked at the girl and said, "Don't forget, you promised earlier to show me where your paintings are hung. I've been just dying to seeing them." The girl looked like a small, fragile animal caught in the headlights. She nodded and Aylin took her by the arm, steering her away from the table.

They took only a few steps before they paused in front of a large acrylic painting hung over the sideboard that was pushed up against one long wall in the hall. Like much of the furniture of Reaves Hall, the sideboard was so heavily lacquered that it had ceased to look like wood anymore. But the painting over it was compelling. Lucy also came up to gaze at it, and Aylin sensed Chesley the Wolf-man nearing them from behind.

"An eager young painter, this fellow Cooper," opined the bearded sculptor. "Not without potential."

"Oh, you know him, do you?" asked Aylin.

"Yes, he was here only minutes ago. A shame about the eye; he would have been a good-looking fellow otherwise. Seems to have affected his vision, too, his art, as it were. Doesn't seem to be able to make anything look like it's supposed to."

"Yes, but it's dramatic, you must admit, energetic, and the texture is remarkable," countered Aylin.

"Ah, but verisimilitude is the thing, my dear," Chesley Fox Chiswell told Aylin with patience. "This other business, this abstract nonsense, is just child's play."

"Uh-huh," Aylin said. She turned to the yellow-haired girl, her arm still looped through the girl's. "We were about to see your paintings. Did you say they were this way, in the..."

The girl still had not said a word. Aylin didn't have a clue who she was, but she did *know* her; she could spot an innocent a mile away, especially if one were wearing a Sunday school dress, and she knew when a woman, especially a young one, could use a helping hand. Lucy, for instance, was nice enough, but she needed a little backbone, needed to learn to stick up for herself. And this girl, well, she couldn't even *speak* up for herself. But she would learn, and hopefully not have to endure too much pain in the process. Aylin could not even remember when she had been that girl, but she knew that she had been, just the same, and she looked at her with equal parts contempt, sympathy, and longing.

They had turned their backs to Chesley Fox Chiswell and left him to his sculpture and the thicket of people flooding down the hallway. Aylin heard a voice calling above the din as they walked away, "Mr. Chiswell!" It was the little woodworker fellow with his unmistakable accent. "Hey, Buddy, how ya makin' out since yer little mishap the other day?" *Mishap*, she thought to herself. *A sculptor might have any manner of mishap. Working with stones and sharp tools was undoubtedly risky. Wouldn't want to try that in the nude. But the horse collar? His neck? How had he managed that?*

"I'm going in the powder room over there," Lucy was saying. "I'll see you later." She veered suddenly away from Aylin and the tongue-tied girl toward a small door under the stairs. Lucy's sudden departure ignited a flicker of curiosity in Aylin, but she dropped it like a short match as she saw Eli Cooper step through the French doors just ahead.

She stopped in his path. "Eli Cooper?" she said, cocking her head youthfully. "We have just been admiring your painting!"

"Have you?" he replied. "Uh, thanks." He looked at the girl with a curious expression and smiled. "Hello," he said.

"Hello," she replied, and Aylin looked sharply over at the girl with her newly-discovered voice. She wondered if they knew each other. She hadn't seen Eli at the Guild meeting, so she didn't see how they could have met. But then, you never could tell about people's connections.

Aylin shifted her gaze back to the young man. "Oh, yes. We have. It's such a fine, big painting with so much conviction and power," she went on. "It's really quite startling, and hung in the perfect place, too, right in the center of the house, near that *very attractive* staircase." She looked at him and lowered her lashes a little. "Perfect," she added. *His* lashes were so dark. And curly. And Chesley clearly was an idiot about women and what they admired in a man, because the eyelid that drooped slightly lower on the one eye just drew a woman's attention to the thick lashes and the green eyes and the otherwise flawless symmetry of the olive face framed by brown curls.

She wondered fleetingly what kind of car he drove. She would try to find him again later. And if not him, then that little guy with the farm truck. His shyness wouldn't last.

"Thank you," Eli replied, looking past Aylin now toward the center of the hall. "Oh, please excuse me. I see some folks standing by my painting over there; they seem to be looking around for the artist." Eli Cooper strode over to the starburst above the ponderous sideboard doing its ridiculously baroque best to drag the star down, but not succeeding.

Aylin looked after him for a moment and sighed. Then she

ushered the girl, whose name she still did not know, through a doorway into the ornate dining room. She carried on a one-sided conversation as they moved through the crowd that swelled around the enormous table.

Aylin suddenly jumped back. "Oh, good God!" she said. "There's another one!" Near them along the rear wall of the room was a huge buffet with a stone golfer on it. For a moment, Aylin thought she had heard the silent yellow-haired girl laugh, but the din of voices was so loud, she decided she had imagined it. She did in fact want to see the girl's paintings. She remembered them now from the last Guild meeting. They had been fresh and striking, and Aylin lived to be struck.

She weaved her way through the dining room with the girl in tow, anxious to leave behind the room with the awful golfer and the plastic golf course landscapes that accompanied him. The only decent thing in here, she thought, was a curious still life over the mantel. She hustled the girl toward the door to the next room in their quest for the little house paintings. They crossed the threshold into the ladies' sitting area, which was set off from the larger North Parlor beyond by several elegant white columns. Here they came across a cluster of people gazing up over the fireplace.

The young girl stepped around them, spotting her pictures hung across the room, but Aylin stopped short and gaped. A good-looking, well-appointed man stood with an older fake-blonde stick of a woman wrapped halfway around him. His glance slid over Aylin with no sign of recognition as she entered the room. But *she* would know *him* anytime, anywhere, for the rest of her earthly days. It was Mr. Brinton, the rich, tanned driver of the sleek black Jag, although he looked oddly pale, blanched actually, at this particular moment. The arrogance she remembered was peeled back to show a disconcerted man. And he really had shown no flicker of recognition for her. Aylin's attention shifted to the woman, dressed in body-hugging gold, looking for all the world like a statuette at the Oscars. *Why did that Brinton man look so pale*, she wondered, *as if he had seen a ghost?*

"The girl has no depth, no allure, clearly, no experience of the world. Same with the artist," the thin woman was saying through carmine lips. "It's the sort of painting I call 'Grandmother Art.'" Her eyes were like slits as she smirked at the portrait over the mantel.

"Oh, come now," the old man with the oxygen tank said to her. "Surely you must recognize Margaret Apple, the eldest daughter of *The* Apples." He frowned at the outspoken woman. "She would be quite a catch for any man: beautiful, young, spirited, cultured, the eldest of very wealthy parents, just a lovely girl. *Quite* a catch."

The woman narrowed her eyes again and laughed a dry throaty laugh broadcasting to the room her worldliness and depth. Aylin felt safe in her anonymity. She would not wish to be known by the rich young man or his party anyway.

Now she turned her gaze to the object of discussion over the mantelpiece. She was shocked to see there a face she knew so well, the amber-eyed, auburn-haired young woman she herself had painted at this very man's request. How was it possible? The throaty laugh echoed in her mind. The woman was proclaiming her triumph—*that* was it. Aylin judged the man, Mr. Brinton, to be under her power. But he must have been in love with the girl. Why else would he have commissioned her picture? And then rejected it? Aylin's humiliation at the Marathon Gas Plaza came back to her like a punch in the gut. Well, it didn't matter. These people meant nothing. Art was everything.

She noticed then a second portrait beside this one, that of a younger child. She knew it to be the portrait that the Guild president—what was her name? Eleanor—had shown them at one of the meetings. Clearly, by their masterful portrayal, the personality they revealed, the light in their eyes, the movement captured just for a stolen instant, the two paintings were by the same artist, an artist skilled beyond measure. They were plainly meant to be a set. The parents had commissioned them, she supposed. Very wealthy people who could afford the finest portrait artist for miles around. And there she stood—the artist in question—over by the window with her back turned, in quiet, calm grace, with her unassuming brilliance. Had she earned it by struggle? By deprivation and pain?

An overwhelming sense of betrayal slammed Aylin like a storm-swollen river breaking against a dam. But betrayal by whom? By what? A fire ignited in her breast, and the flames licked upward toward her neck and then to her face. The room fell away for her, and she stood alone, naked, exposed, a fraud, a victim, a soul compelled to create but thwarted at every turn. She could not even express to herself the name of the pain in her chest. And Aylin, wrapped in her shroud of un-nameable suffering, fled the place in anonymous ignominy.

* * *

Lucy came out of the powder room feeling slightly refreshed by the cool water she had splashed on her face. She had not yet looked in on her own paintings, but she thought a little sip of water and some crackers might help steady her, so she headed through the French doors, across the narrow gallery, and out onto the back porch. As she opened the screen door and started down the steps, she heard the string trio abruptly stop. She sensed a change in the weather. The air felt heavy, free, and wild. A tent flap slapped against itself. She heard a familiar jangling off to her left in the twilight and calculated that Aylin must have walked outside shortly before her, and was probably just now turning the corner of the

277

house, headed once again for the flapping refreshment tent. At her pace, she must be familiar with the path.

A ruckus—raised voices, animal sounds, scuffling—sounded upon Lucy before she could make out what was happening in the now-dusky garden before her. She recognized the voice of Magdaline Dismukes, clearly worked up into a state. "This is *disgraceful,* Lorraine, just *disgraceful!* This animal cannot be allowed to stay in the garden! To whom does it belong?" A loud braying halfway between laughter and choking answered her.

"Oh, my word! This thing should be locked away somewhere! *Disgraceful!* And tonight of all nights, with all these elegant people here!"

"Goodness gracious, yes, it *is* something of a disaster," said Lorraine, her dress twinkling in the fading light. "We certainly do *not* want a scene."

Lucy's eyes adjusted, and she could make out a dark, stiff-legged hulk beyond the two women, right in the center of the garden, with its long ears splayed out like the arms of a windmill.

"Sadie?"

As she stepped down onto the path, Magdaline whirled to face her. "What do *you* know about this... this... *creature?*" she demanded.

"Actually," said Lucy, surprised at her own knowledge, "I believe the mule may belong to James the Organic Farmer, the one who does the pencil drawings of the farm? He had his mule with him at the Box Hollow Festival, and I think maybe this is the same one. But what it's doing here, I don't have a clue."

Magdaline glowered at this news.

"I haven't even seen James yet tonight," Lucy added. "Is he here?"

"Well, I really cannot recall this person," said Lorraine, her large red shiny bag slung over her shoulder. It gleamed saucily in the garden, not yet robbed of its color by the advancing evening.

"Since you seem to know this man, do go find him immediately!" Magdaline told Lucy. "It's only a question of time before—"

At just that moment, the mule lifted its tail menacingly. All three women had lived in a county filled with cow pastures long enough to know what was about to ensue.

"I'll go," Lucy said, and she spun around and flew back up the steps, only to run full-speed into the young man in question, coming out the screen door.

"Oh! I was just looking for you," she said.

"Oh, really?" said the young man. "I've been looking for you all evening. I can't quite find where my picture is hung."

"You!" Magdaline jabbed a stubby twisted forefinger at him. James straightened abruptly like a hapless schoolboy caught in the back of the class reading comic books. His cheerful countenance froze into a caricature of itself.

"This is *your* animal, *is it not?*" she said.

"Uh... uh... uh... well, yes." He looked at the mule and said, "Sadie? What are you *doing* here?"

He turned back toward the fireplug of a woman, stumpy, red-faced, and ready to burst. "I don't understand how she could possibly be here. I left her at home in her stall, miles and miles away from town."

"I don't care how she *came to be* here, young man. I only care that she *is* here. Indeed, I care very much that she *is* here in this garden on this night of nights. You will remove her from the premises! Immediately!" she ordered.

Sadie threw her neck down with her head up and her nostrils out. She bellowed so long and so loudly that all human conversation had to cease until she'd had her say.

"Oh, certainly..." James's voice cracked as if he were thirteen again. He cleared his throat. "Yes, I will take her away—well, that

279

is, just as soon as I have seen my painting." He glanced at Lucy. The wind whipped her long black hair against his face. She retrieved it hastily and held on, lest it should fly away from her again. "I'll take her—Sadie that is—and, well, uh... my truck, hmm, well..." The logistics escaped him.

"This is an historically accurate garden, young man, and quite valuable too!" Magdaline snapped. "A reproduction piece done with great tastefulness and expertise, and at considerable expense. What if that animal were to run amok? Trample these heirloom plants underfoot? Knock down the tent? Interfere with the caterers? Terrorize the guests in who knows what atrocious manner? The donkey must go—*now!*"

"Actually, she is a mule, not a donkey, which you can see in her horse-like size and in her—"

"I have no time for a lecture, young man. Just get rid of it."

"I could tether her here in the garden for a few minutes; I have a rope in my truck," James offered weakly. Still, Lucy had to give him credit for not backing down too easily. And she could see his disappointment in not getting to see his own picture displayed here at the show.

"There will *be no tethering!* Anyone can see a little rope isn't enough to hold that beast!" Almost on cue, Sadie flared her nostrils and snorted explosively. Magdaline jumped back.

"Under *no circumstances* will this animal be tied up here!" she hissed, struggling to control her volume. "This is the most enchanting part of the grounds. It needs to be kept pristine. Until this... this... *disruption*, which you have allowed by your carelessness and lack of responsibility for your livestock, people were strolling here, listening to the chamber music, enjoying the evening, the culture, the aroma of the garden. As you can see, the string trio has already been interrupted." Her face purpled in the twilight, and drops of sweat glistened on her upper lip, where a quiver was setting in.

"And what is that smell, for goodness's sake? Oh, Lord, this thing, donkey, mule, *whatever*, is dropping MANURE!"

Lucy felt James the Organic Farmer bristle beside her. He drew in a deep breath and straightened himself to his full height, which was not much higher than his adversary's. "Yes, ma'am, well, you know, ma'am, with all due respect, manure *is* what makes things grow." Magdaline's eyes were bulbous with ire, even in the gloom.

And then a voice spoke through the near darkness, out of the deepest shadow of three tall yews, a voice brittle and overwatered at the same time, a voice weary with civilization, accompanied by Aylin's trademark jangling bracelets: "Oh, *please*. Just call shit, 'shit', and be done with it."

The four other Guild members in the garden and the musicians off to one side attempting to act nonchalant were utterly silent now, so that the hive-hum of a manor-ful of carousing voices and the warring drone of insects saturated the air between them all.

At that moment, Lorraine stumbled a bit on her high heels as her purse lurched. Muffy ejected himself into space, landed, and threw himself in fury at the beast in his path. Sadie was quicker than she appeared. Her legs flew out sideways, first one, then another. She snorted and cast huge hooves at the darting Pekingese, who seemed unaware that he was smaller than the mule.

"Oh!" Lorraine shrieked. "My Muffy will be killed!" She dashed in to retrieve the dog, dodging the murderous mule. Lorraine was remarkably nimble for a sixty-ish woman on teetering heels. James jumped into the fray, but Sadie eluded his grasp. Her lips drew back in a jeering grimace.

"Remove that thing! *Now!*" Magdaline ordered.

James finally caught hold of Sadie's bristly mane and smoothed her neck, shielding her eyes with his body from the white frenzy of the dog so that Lorraine managed to scoop up her precious armful before he suffered any severe blows. She backed away, cradling the dog in one arm as she cupped his flat face in the other. He wheezed and snorted as his owner cooed, "Ooooh, sweet baby Muffy! Oh, how could that big beastie attack you so? Mummy's sweet little muffin." In the midst of the dog's shadowed face, his bared teeth glistened in the twilight—unacknowledged evidence of a savage heart.

Several paces away, James stroked the mule and spoke her name over and over. She began to relax. Then he looked directly over at Lucy, disregarding the other women in the garden, and said, "I would like to have seen *your* paintings above everything else. I'm sorry to have to go."

Lucy was at a loss for words and held her palm up weakly in an awkward wave.

James turned, his shoulders drooping, his bow tie askew, and led Sadie toward the parking area, clucking and scolding like a mother hen. The mule shook her head and neck fretfully, huffing, grumbling, stepping haltingly forward. The wind whipped her tail haphazardly. James and Sadie disappeared into the dusk, Disappointment and Disgruntlement, the pair of them.

The garden grew peaceful again as the warriors dispersed. The string trio wordlessly resumed its Beethoven sonata, gentle and reliable as crickets. Lucy entered the tent for a glass of water and a few crackers. Through clumps of strangers talking and laughing loudly she wended her way, invisible to the revelers except for a few older men whose alcohol consumption had loosened their eyes in their sockets. She bypassed mountains of shrimp, meatballs, pâté, cheeses, fruit, petit fours, and long tables loaded with liquor and wine. She found Perrier and crackers and headed back inside without lingering.

She meandered through the house, perusing the artwork. She had not seen Aylin in the tent, nor passed her on the walk, nor seen her in the porch or hall or dining room. She thought she heard a faint jangling again at some point. Maybe Aylin had found someone new to corner after the skirmish in the garden. Maybe she was working on another ride out to Whitetail Cove. *She's talented or lucky or both,* Lucy thought to herself. *She always seems to be able to find her own way...* And anyway, Lucy had no desire to drive her home, no desire at all. In fact, she would be relieved never to see Aylin again. She shivered at the violence of her thought. Odd to shiver, on such a warm night.

Lucy passed the awkward petrified golfer, the neon golf-scape paintings, and a curious still life over the dining room fireplace. She set down her half-empty plate and glass on a tray on the enormous glossy table. She passed through the connecting doorway to the North Parlor and, alone in the crowd, admired for some minutes Eleanor's remarkable portraits of the two sisters. She noted the three small still lifes of Magdaline's arranged together over a settee: a covered bridge, a spray of daffodils, a fern frond with mushrooms. She saw Eleanor the Gentle, and Morgan the Yellow-haired, smiling with their heads not far apart like mother and daughter, deep in conversation about the bold little house paintings on the square canvases in front of them. Lucy wandered on through the airy North Parlor.

Then she stopped short with a nudge of recognition, as if her own child had shown up here unexpectedly at the show. She gazed up at her twin watercolors of the flowers. She could lose herself in looking at them as surely as she did in painting them, feeling herself surrounded in color, soft planes, and hard lines. She knew and loved every curve the same as she did the sweet miraculous curves of Evie's cheek and neck and arm.

Suddenly, she felt a touch on her elbow. Before she could tear her eyes away, a familiar voice said, "Are you all right?" Lucy looked over at the brown-curly-haired young man with the beautiful eyes. Eli.

"Oh, yes. I'm all right," she said, and she realized that actually she was. She felt much better than she had earlier. *It must have been a fluke*, she thought. *Not a virus at all.*

"Your paintings," he nodded toward them, "they look perfect here, and especially in those silver frames. They are really elegant. You should be proud of them."

She nodded in response, but her face flamed. "Um, thank you."

After a pause she said, "But *your* painting is really amazing. I could just stand and look and look. It's simple and complicated at the same time."

"I would say the same about yours," Eli said.

Lucy shrugged, not knowing how to answer.

"Cordelia—how is she doing?"

"Oh, she's not too strong, here lately. But stubborn!" He shook his head. "She doesn't want anyone fussing over her. Still, I can't help but worry."

"She's a beautiful person, your aunt, beautiful and generous, and if she is a little stubborn, I guess she should be allowed that."

"She seems to know what she wants, anyway, which is more than a lot of us can say."

"That's true," Lucy agreed.

They looked at her flowers without speaking. The din of voices had grown ever louder in the house as the evening had progressed.

Eli turned suddenly to Lucy and said, "Would you like to help me with something?" He reached into his pocket and pulled out a carved bird, a crow perhaps, but small for a crow, maybe only half-size. The grain of the wood was plain to see, though something had been rubbed over the surface to stain it a little dark and a little glossy. The eyes had been crudely painted black.

"That's Cordelia, all right," said Lucy reaching out to feel the feathers. "I mean, it's so simple, just like the little animals she gave my children. It's like she can distill a thing down to its essential shape."

"It's a calling for Cordelia," Eli said. "Carving is as much a part of her as her heartbeat. She does it with her hands and with her soul—it sounds sappy, but I swear she does. She really doesn't even use her eyes anymore."

"My children love playing with those little figures and the boat. They tell her story about them over and over."

"Oh, she's one for stories, that's for sure." Eli smiled. "So, would you like to help me find a place for this? Cordelia told me to put it in the room with the quilt. She said it would be just right there. I don't know where she got that idea from, but she doesn't ask much of me, so I figure I should humor her."

"Oh, yes, I think you should definitely humor her. And of course, I'm glad to help. I guess it'll have to go in the nursery upstairs. That's the only place there's a quilt, right?"

Lucy shuddered as she pictured the room. But she would not mind entering it so much with Eli. She noticed he was eye to eye with her, or not much taller anyway. He seemed so familiar, almost as if she had known him in her childhood, though she had only met him twice before tonight.

"Yeah, I guess so," said Eli, "It'll have to go up there. Maybe it's not as crowded upstairs anyhow. It would be nice to have a little breathing room for a bit. It's really jammed with people down here." They turned and squeezed through the crowd toward the hall.

As they made their way through the throng, Lucy glimpsed a face near Chesley's ghostly child sculpture that she had hoped never to see again. The face belonged to a woman in a tight gold dress with elegant gold hair and blood-red mouth and nails, and she was following Eli with an unblinking, unfathomable gaze, laced with something that Lucy could not name. It was not innocent, whatever it was. She did not appear to have wasted half a glance at Lucy's face, but Lucy imagined she could feel the woman's razor stare on their backs all the way up the staircase. Eli never wavered, never looked aside from his own path, not toward the woman, not even toward his own painting as they passed it, and—Lucy observed—if this night was any indication, it was a rare thing for an artist to enter a room his creation is in and not look at it.

As they reached the turn at the landing half-way up, she felt the crowd slip away behind her—the high society scene, the din, and the woman's stare all fading away. Lucy clutched the smooth banister, feeling light-headed as they neared the top of the impressive staircase that creaked and moaned like a thing alive beneath their matched footsteps.

Long, long ago, when those boards were alive in the usual sense, they had grown upright as part of an infinitely more impressive old-growth forest. The wood had creaked and moaned all those centuries ago as well, but then it had been in delight for the play of the Georgia wind through their whole trunks and boughs and through their sisters and brothers all around, flexing the full lengths of their grain in a dance no man could imitate, a dance beyond compare. They had moaned too at The Cutting, when they had been sacrificed to make way for cotton, still much longer ago than anyone living could remember. They had moaned then in agony and alarm to their neighbor trees, with the silent shrieks of their pungent pine resin. Now all that remained of the voice of the forest was the staircase and the groans trapped inside.

As the two artists stepped up into the open sitting area at the top of the stairs, Lucy caught a whiff of a haunting smell she remembered from the day before. She could hear lilting strains of the string trio from the garden below. *How could such gentle measures reach so far and drift their way through so much commotion?* Lucy wondered. *Bright sound, dark odor, doing battle.*

They strolled from room to room upstairs, delaying their mission with the bird in unspoken accord. In the first bedroom they saw several more of Magdaline's watercolors and some horse portraits. In the second, they saw a few garden sketches, a fine watercolor of quail, and a detailed colored pencil drawing of a black bear. In the third, they found lined up on the mantel the lively crayon drawings by the two men who, Lucy remembered, drew together during their lunch breaks at the plant. The men stood there, colorful and vital, in that dried-out bedroom with its brittle old furniture. A group of family or friends surrounded them, joking and laughing about nothing in particular. Their ease and cheer seemed out of place, like new wine in the old wineskin of the somber room.

Finally, Lucy and Eli entered the nursery with the yellow rose wallpaper. Orilla's quilt wafted with some errant draft as they crossed the threshold. Eli strode to the window and screeched the resistant sash upward. "It's so stale in here," he said. Then he moved back toward where Lucy was, facing the fireplace. Eli stood still, looking for a moment, shaking his head a little.

"Lucy," he said to her, and she realized he had not said her name since the day they had met when he'd read it off her card, "this piece here should be in a museum, maybe one for African-American art. I'm going to ask around, do a little research to find just the right place, and then I'm going to talk to Orilla about it. People need to see what this woman does!"

Lucy nodded. She agreed wholeheartedly, but she felt ill at ease here again, where The Smell was stronger, but not so strong as it had been before the quilt was hung yesterday. The hair on her bare arms stood on end. Her scalp prickled. She backed away from the fireplace and looked around the room. Though several lamps were lit, the light in the room had a strange quality, as if mere electricity could not penetrate the gloom, and yet the air itself seemed electric.

She spotted the little landscape painting that James had done, hanging there in the nursery where he had not gotten the chance to see it. Somehow she found it touching that he had felt his drawings were not serious enough for the show, and he had painted instead, although he was neither confident nor proficient at it. Even so, his rolling field with dark pines edging it and a portion planted in shocking neon sunflowers was charming purely because of its uncalculated nature, its simplicity, like the young man himself with his unrepentant mule, his first real beard, and his forlorn farewell.

She turned back toward Eli, who was gazing at the quilt with his back to her. His brown hair curled over his threadbare tweed collar. He seemed just now to realize how warm it was upstairs, warm and damp and oppressive even, swamp-like. Without taking his eyes from Orilla's quilt, he pulled off his jacket and tucked it over his arm. Eli in all his health and vigor stood between Lucy and the stunning quilt; the quilt hung between the two of them and the awful yellow-rose stain.

He appeared to have forgotten the bird he still held in his left hand; he was caught up in studying the intricate play of color and shape and symbol in the quilt. Lucy stepped closer and took the bird gently. She perched it on the right end of the mantel nearest the quilt, near the candlesticks which threatened to rain crystal down upon the bird's head. Eli looked up, stirred from his reverie, and they both moved back a little to look.

In the low light the bird's eyes gleamed, black as shot. Its feathers were glossy. Its head was cocked, its beak slightly parted as if about to speak, and it looked for all the world like a living crow there in the room with them. What had seemed a crude carving in the brilliantly lit North Parlor here in the dim light seemed real.

Now they stood, side by side, and Eli took Lucy's hand. The

gesture felt oddly familiar and comfortable, like a long, low echo from childhood. She looked into the tiny shining eyes of the crow, and the shining eyes of the crow gazed into her grey ones, and there was a moment when Lucy understood. She heard words as clearly as if they had been spoken aloud in the room: "Lucy, dear, where is your treasure?"

And strangely, she knew everything. She knew her kinship with the man beside her, like two smooth river stones that had lain one next to the other in a sweet-flowing riverbed since before time, gazing up at the sky through the crystal waters, creating and recreating pictures in the clouds above, pictures in the stars above. She knew that everything that called her was part of one whole. She knew that one love must be put aside for another in order to grow what must be grown. She knew what she must do, and peace enveloped her.

Lucy felt pressure on her hand where Eli was squeezing it gently. He was looking with some curiosity into her face. She smiled. *If I'd had a twin, it would have been you.*

"What was that song you were whistling? It was soft—I couldn't quite make it out, but it seemed familiar, somehow," he said.

"Oh—was I whistling?"

He nodded. "You were. Something simple—old, maybe." Then he paused, looking a little worried. "Are you all right?"

"Oh, yes. Yes, I am," she said. "Quite all right." She turned to him and he dropped her hand, looking a little embarrassed.

"Eli, you will keep painting, won't you? Painting from your heart, I mean? You won't let anybody sidetrack you from that?"

"I can see where to go from here, for the first time in a long time," he said, and Lucy wondered if the bird had spoken to him too, and what it might have said.

"How about you?" he asked, as if it really mattered to him, as if it were important.

"Yes, I can see my way too. I'll paint again, when the time comes." Then Lucy inclined her head toward the mantel. "Cordelia was right. The bird looks perfect there, don't you think?"

"I think so," he agreed. "I don't know how she knows these things."

* * *

The house stiffened its timbers, bracing itself against the tremor of social intercourse succussing inside its skeleton. Within the very gut of the old house the dim room on the upper floor crouched waiting, just waiting, for that vitality to abandon the house again to the Hall's own devices, to slow decay and the residue of centuries of lives left behind, with only bats and mice to disturb its slumber. The summer sun-warmed air that wafted through the open windows was repugnant to The Room. It was used to stale, unruffled memories in private gloom. There was nothing to do but wait. In the meantime, it *was* amusing to see the interplay between the intruders and the traces of the past that had left scars and stains and odors and scraps of energy behind.

The handsome young couple that came together with the bird, for instance. They walked into the room like lovers, to all indications, and The Room stirred with interest, craving some indiscretion, some betrayal, but all that was received was revelation, and The Room cared nothing for recognition, truth, conviction, renewal, love, all the bright white things. The pair stared at the abominable wall covering a long time, and The Room froze, breathless, longing to be free of the smothering blanket. But all they had done in the end was place the bird on the mantel, turn, and leave, free of the burden of the past that The Room emitted. *They* had received the past as a gift. It gave them wings. The Room smoldered in fury for it knew the past as an iron fist, an iron chain, an iron lock. Its fury crackled through the air and blew a light bulb—too late, for the couple had already left the room.

They had not found out its secrets, The Room smirked. Others would come this night; they had been passing in and out all evening. And perhaps one of them, or more, would know something of the secrets, would appreciate them, but not yet. The Room rested back on its haunches, ruminating. A strong puff of wind hammered the window sash against its casing. A storm was coming.

The young maid had been brought during a storm, wet and worn, long ago. She arrived without shoes, and without shoes she remained. She had been installed in the nursery where many a nurse had come and gone before her, sometimes in rapid succession. The children of the house triumphed over them as surely as did their father, if not in the same ways. Her background was sketchy; the lady of the house had said something about a swamp up Virginia way where a band of riders had rounded up stragglers. They transported them, dispersed them to places where labor was in demand. These riders—*southern* patriots—were paid something for their trouble, their hands shaken heartily for the service they rendered the struggling new society following the war.

They called her Lily, after the swamp lily flower, although she was dark-skinned and although, or maybe just because, they could tell by the proud angle of her face when they said it that it was not a name she had ever before been called. When she arrived, her own apron had had a letter B embroidered on it in blue. The cook was made to remove the letter when Lily's old, filthy clothing was boiled.

Lily was an excellent nursemaid, and she was sly at dodging the master's attentions, sleeping in the rocking chair in the children's room instead of the pallet she was provided in the little borning room off the kitchen. The lady of the house tolerated this deviation, though she would not acknowledge the reason behind it.

It soon became evident that Lily was with child, and must have been so when she arrived, but her footsteps up and down the narrow back stairs to the kitchen bringing the children their evening tea grew no heavier and no slower, and she never grew very round. The Lady abided her because of Lily's talents and lasting power. In time, a few months after she had arrived, Lily became suddenly slight again, and The Room overheard that her child, a robust boy, had been taken to be raised by a shriveled-up old woman in the Glades.

This woman had worked her childhood, youth, and prime away in the fields for other Reaves Family relations back in the time before wages. Now she was freed, and she was old, no longer desirable as a worker. She lived far back in the Glades, the marshy area in the last remnants of old-growth forest hereabouts. Far out in the county, it was, where most white folks were afraid to go for the malaria, for the wild panthers, and, it was rumored, for the lawless marauders who dwelt there away from decent society. But the woman was known to keep babies who were inconvenient or ill-conceived. No one knew how she survived or how she cared for the children in her old age. But then, it didn't much matter.

As for the children of the grand house, Lily kept them occupied and cared for their needs as was her lot, but gravity seemed to have its way with her, making her smaller, bent, and unsmiling. Still, she was a fine-featured young woman, which the master of the house, the doctor, could not ignore. He caught her one day on the back staircase, and in time Lily bore another child; she had no choice in the matter. This new baby too was taken to the old woman to rear.

The lady of the house spoke of it one day to the tutor in the nursery while the children were at their studies or otherwise distracted. "She's a hussy," said the lady. "She seems to have gotten herself a string of men; Lord only knows who they are and where she comes up with them. I would not keep her but for her reliable work with the children. She is able beyond compare to keep them fed, clean, and occupied, and she never troubles me over any matter, large or small."

Lily did her job. She cared for the children and made them mind. They did not dominate her, a mystery to The Room, as they had all their other nurses.

And then one day, Lily was simply gone, a new pretty young nurse in her place. That was about the time that the closet next to the fireplace began weeping, The Room recalled. The doctor had it sealed over, but still dampness would bleed through the new wall. Perhaps a stray leak in the roof that allowed rain to travel down the side of the chimney was to blame, the doctor said. Plaster was added, then wallpaper ordered especially from France, then a tapestry, but the wall remained permeable. The Room felt it must bleed through in that place or be stifled, and no human could prevent it from being so.

In all the time that Lily had worked in the nursery, the room had never heard her voice, for the lady said she never spoke; never once did she utter a word. The Room never knew what became of her babies. The lady never spoke of them again. But The Room knew by watching that babies grow into children and then into adults who echo the patterns of their sires and their dams throughout their lives. But who would *her* children echo? The anonymous far-away father, the masterful doctor father, the silent enduring mother? What strain would win out in the battle for their souls? One thing was certain, if those children should one day meet the others that Lily raised, there would be no kinship between them.

The Room knew all these things from watching and listening

and from drinking in the jealousy and fear and anger and confinement and deprivation and sorrow of the incalculable hours lived within its walls. These human emanations must be released! Still, all these long years later, The Room must exhale.

As Midsummer crept toward night over the unheeding revelry below, light, smart steps clipped across the upper landing and into The Room. An exquisite golden creature entered, sheathed in refinement, unblinking. She tossed the cultured waves of her gilt hair over her sharp shoulders as she swept into the nursery. Her calculating glance quickly took in the features of the room, the paintings, the carving, the quilt.

A succulent, richly-suited man trailed behind her. As he sauntered to the center of the room, looking around carelessly with his hands in his pockets, the woman slinked up to him, grabbed him by the shirt, and thrust a hungry, bright red kiss on his mouth. "Baby I want it," she purred.

"And what is that?" he responded coolly.

"That quilt right there."

"You want that ragged old thing? Why? It smells funny to me."

"The smell of money, Brinton. This quilt here is the finest thing in the show. The artist won't have any idea what it's worth. I can get it for a song. Same thing with those crayon pictures in the other room and the crazy guy's portraits downstairs."

"The crazy guy pictures? They're just so weird. The colors are so random."

"Obviously he's color blind. You forget: I come from a long line of doctors. I can diagnose all kinds of things."

"Yeah, but Baby, those pictures—they're just amateurish stuff."

"Outsider art. It's hot. Trust me. I know what I'm doing."

She grabbed him and pulled him close again. He kept his hands in his pockets. "I can't argue with that," he said, lowering his eyelids.

"These people are untrained," she drawled. "It's what the art world craves right now. The sicker and the poorer the story, the better the clients like it. And the artists are too naïve to know what they've got. I can buy all these for a song, and sell them at the gallery up in Buckhead and make five figures, easily, especially with this quilt. Money, Brinton, I'm talking about money and lots of it. It's a great system. It makes the artist happy, flattered. It makes the patron happy, helping out the underprivileged. It makes me happy cashing the checks—everybody wins!"

"Baby, if you want it, get it," said the man, looking bored. The woman twined herself around him and ran her blood-red nails down the side of his face and neck.

Vibrations from the stair treads shivered The Room ever so slightly. Only a heavy body could shake the room in such a way. It held its breath to see who would come. A short, dark form filled the doorway as the dumpy woman from the day before, the woman who had made the cursed wall covering, entered the room with slow shuffling steps. "Weak!" The Room yearned to shriek at her. "Feeble!" But all it could do was flicker another light bulb. The newcomer looked up sharply at the faltering lamp, undeceived. She paid no heed to the other people in the room but stood before the quilt with its pictures of creatures and scenes, a satisfied look creeping across her face. She knew the quilt had power.

In a darting side glance, the golden creature took in the shapeless dark woman in the shapeless drab dress with the ridiculous shiny dollar-store pocketbook, and immediately knew her to be the maker of the quilt. She gauged her to be none too intelligent, judging by her dogged and slightly belligerent expression. She uncoiled herself from her companion and turned toward the frump.

"Honey, it's your lucky day," the blonde said, her eyes half closed and her mouth half drawn back in a semblance of a smile.

"I want to buy your quilt, but I don't see a price."

"That because it not for sale," the large woman said flatly.

"Nonsense," said the Golden One, "I'll write you out a check right now." She gestured to the man, who drew a checkbook out of his pocket. "Everyone's got her price."

"Not me," said the black woman.

The Golden One took the checkbook and drew a slender silver pen out from the fold. "Say, one fifty? That would come in handy. Surely you'd rather have the money in place of the blanket here. You can't spend a blanket, you know." She smiled knowingly.

"Not for sale," the black woman repeated.

The Room wished the two women would forego haggling and come to an agreement so that the quilt could be stripped away and the wall could be free once more. Just the nails that held the quilt in place, in and of themselves, were an abomination. Clearly the smaller woman was used to getting what she wanted. No one could look like her and not be skilled at knowing her way, at getting her way. But the large woman stood immovable before her quilt like a chiseled boulder. The shiny purse was looped over a wrist that was folded over the other wrist resting upon her ample middle.

"I will go as high as two hundred," the Golden One said. "That's quite a lot for an unknown, untrained quilter such as yourself." The quiltmaker did not acknowledge the offer with a reply, or even a look.

"And then there are, of course, the nail holes to consider... Two hundred is generous for damaged goods."

The large woman just stood, still looking at the quilt, as if she had not heard a word. Instead, silence settled in.

"I am prepared to offer three hundred dollars, and that is my final offer. You will regret not taking this money."

"Not for sale," said the quiltmaker once again.

"Listen honey, you have tonight and only tonight to seize this opportunity. Do you think someone would ever come to your house to purchase your little handmade items? I don't suppose so. You clearly have no gallery, no agent to represent you. I would consider, however, acting as such for you; here is my card." She reached into Brinton's pocket, pulled out a business card, and held it out to the artist between two slender, elegant fingers with nails smooth, red, and shiny as fresh blood.

At last the large woman turned, her eyes widening at the sight of the card. She left her wrists resting one upon the other and pursed her lips as if tasting something sour. "I don't *think* so," she said. Her eyes were a startling grey over her close-up glasses. The pupils dilated fleetingly.

"I knows what you is," the quiltmaker said. "Ain't gonna be no buying of quilts this evenin', so you just take yo' checkbook and yo' skinny white butt somewhere else and leave me and my little handmade eye-tem be."

Brinton brought his hand to his mouth; in shock or in admiration, The Room could not tell.

"Ain't gonna be no usin' of Orilla tonight. You want to use those other folks, that their bidness." The black woman was generating her own electricity. The air fairly snapped. The Golden One's eyes flashed, onyx catching the light. The women faced each other like two magnets repelling.

"You are making a mistake," the Golden One hissed. "I am positioned to make you a star in the art world. You would pass that up?"

"I makes my picture quilts for somethin' 'side riches and fame. Got no call for those things. I makes my quilts to match what I see, to show my mind, to work through all the foolishness this worl' dish out." She jutted her head at the thin woman.

The Golden One shook her glamorous curls in disbelief. Her open mouth revealed two rows of tiny teeth, small and pearly and sharp. She slapped the checkbook shut, grabbed Brinton by the hand, and pulled him from the room. Her heels sounded like gunshots on the hapless wooden steps, though she was not heavy enough to make them creak; she was as light as a fiendish spirit and no more.

All the way to the bottom the shots rang out, cutting through the muffled voices congealing into bedlam in the house below. The Room could hear the thin woman recover her voice. She was trying to disguise her wrath with confident, honey tones, but the avalanche of words gave her away.

"Brinton, baby, let's get those crayon drawings and the crazy guy's pictures to resell. I'll get a tidy sum from flipping those things. We'll get the Greek pastels for your house. You can send one of those little girls from your office over in the Range Rover to pick them up since they won't let us take them tonight. All those pieces wouldn't fit in the Jag anyway. Write the check and let's go before they start announcing the ribbons."

"Whatever you want, babe, just get it."

"It's fabulous that we found those Greek pictures. They'll be perfect at your place, Brinton, baby; I know just the spot for them in the boudoir. What a steal—five matching pieces for only..." The voice joined the swell of all the others as it neared the bottom of the stairs.

Back in The Room, the heavy black woman stood unmoving, her gaze on the quilt. She stood a long time. The Room huffed in frustration, and a corner of the quilt lifted away from the wall. "Um-hmmm," grunted the woman in satisfaction, "that just fine, then." And she turned on her heel without a backward glance and trod back down the suffering staircase.

A sudden, violent gust from the darkening sky clattered the shutters outside the nursery window. The silk shawl draped around the dressmaker's dummy fluttered like the wing of a bird caught in a snare. The Room sat back on its haunches and curled its shadows around itself to wait once more.

* * *

On the main floor, a change in the rhythm of voices and the pattern of mingling signaled a coming climax in the course of the evening. The thumping bass from the DJ's sound system outside under the rollicking tent rattled the wavy old windows in their age-loosened frames; the string trio had been sent on its way, and the party outside had reached its full intensity. Still there was a fair-sized crowd left inside, drinking in the rich history of the Hall and savoring the fine art, the wine, and the cheese. Members of the Historical Society, including Lorraine and Vincent, Mr. and Mrs. Apple, and Magdaline Dismukes, dispersed among the rooms to direct guests into the main hall for the presentation of awards—for some, the culmination of the evening and the months of preparation, for others, a chance to personally prevail, for still others, a mere curiosity.

For Eleanor, awards were like high tides in the ebbing and flowing of art events over the years, noteworthy but not climactic. But then Eleanor was steady as the ocean tides herself, not given to drama even when drama was perhaps due. She knew that often the undeserving got the spoils, and the deserving collected only the crumbs from the table, in art shows as in life, so she did not attach too much consequence to winning.

She stood beside the antique desk in the foyer where the awards waited in a neat pile of rich ecru envelopes. Morgan had followed her and stood not far back in the crowd, to one side of the hallway. She had seemed unwilling to stray far from Eleanor's side during the last part of the reception, and that was just fine with Eleanor. Morgan's shyness seemed a rational approach to an unruly world.

Magdaline bustled up to Eleanor through the crowd from the back gallery where the cashier had been stationed. With a flourish she presented to Eleanor a list of sales for the evening and the preliminary totals of percentages going to both organizations. It had been a good night. Magdaline remained at her elbow.

Pennington Apple strode handsomely to Eleanor's side wearing a sharp suit, a Baptist haircut, and a politician's smile. He announced to the crowd, "Welcome! Welcome, everyone! May I have your attention, please." The crowd quietened, and he went on. "The Corbie County Historical Society is so very pleased and honored to have the Liberty Artists Guild join us this year for our Midsummer celebration. I think we can all agree that this has been a night to remember." There was spirited applause. He turned to Eleanor.

"We've brought a little culture to Liberty—good music, fine art, great food, and plenty of spirits. We've raised money to preserve the past and support the arts. Everybody wins! Why not make this a combined annual event, then?" There was more applause and cheering.

Eleanor mustered what she hoped was a gracious smile. She disliked being on stage, but artists must always appreciate their patrons, and the Apples were a rare local family: wealthy, discerning, generous, everything this community needed to nurture its budding cultural life. She was aware of the multiple purchases the designer Vanessa Hennessey and her escort had made this evening as well, according to Magdaline's list—some surprising purchases, indeed, but a boon to those four artists, nevertheless.

"I will now, without further ado, turn the presentation of awards over to Ms. Eleanor Wood," announced Mr. Apple. "I know that you are all waiting with bated breath to hear the winners of the evening. Eleanor?" More applause.

Eleanor cleared her throat. "Yes, good evening." She looked

around at the sea of faces and felt slightly off balance. "First, I'd like to say thank you to the Historical Society for such a lovely venue and for all the Society's efforts toward this splendid reception. Our friends outside under the tent would no doubt agree." The crowd laughed. The bass throb carried on like a menacing jungle beat in an old B movie, oblivious to the genteel ceremonial moment inside.

"Second, I'd like to say that I am most impressed with the artwork here this evening, and I feel that it's quite a shame to have only a few awards to give out. Please don't feel discouraged, artists, if you don't receive an award. The breadth and depth of the work in this show is far greater than the sum of its parts: You have together drawn a portrait of our community in a singular way. There is some fine, very fine work here this evening. Thank you, artists, for sharing it." More applause.

"We've had quite a few purchases from the show, and as you know, the Historical Society and the Artists Guild will split the thirty percent commission, so your purchases go to a good cause. We haven't quite finalized the totals yet, but it's a considerable amount. The money is earmarked for preserving this beautiful old building and its history and establishing a scholarship fund for a deserving graduating high school art student.

"I'll share with you a few of the purchases tonight. Please thank these patrons for supporting the arts in Liberty: Aylin Borden's series of pastels was bought by Mr. J. Hunter Brinton; Boone Carmichael's *Angel with Yoyo* has been bought by the Reverend Tufts Allen, our new Episcopal priest in town—reportedly to be hung in his study at the church; Vanessa Hennessey has bought the crayon paintings of Charlie Blue and Solomon Tingle and also the three self-portraits of Mr. E.G. Thanks to Ms. Hennessey for her support of the arts and especially emerging artists—her encouragement and investment are invaluable. Mr. and Mrs.

Pennington Apple have purchased the two portraits of their daughters. The little landscape painting by James Caldwell has been purchased by Ms. Lucy Bloom, and the painting *Evie's Magnolia* by Ms. Bloom has been purchased by... let's see, it's not marked here... by an unidentified party.

"And we have several more sales which I will not read at the moment, because I know you're eager to hear about the prizes. But purchasers, thank you, and you may retrieve your paintings on July thirty-first, when the exhibit is over. All of this amounts to several thousand dollars for the Liberty Artists Guild and the same for the Corbie County Historical Society, all in all an extremely successful and enjoyable night." She paused and smiled out at the crowd.

"Now, I'd like to thank our two judges for the show: Vera Crabtree from Athens, who unfortunately could not be with us tonight, and Mr. Pennington Apple." More applause. Mr. Apple held up his hand and smiled broadly.

"The judges both mentioned to me how difficult the choices were... And here we have them." She picked up the smooth, thick envelopes. She handed the stack to Magdaline to hold and opened the first envelope. "The purchase award by the Corbie County Historical Society to keep in its permanent collection here in its headquarters goes to Mrs. Magdaline Dismukes for *Mushroom and Fern.*" Magdaline made her mouth into a small o as the applause sounded. Her color deepened three shades in pleasure. She took her envelope and handed the rest to Eleanor to manage before returning to the crowd to gather in her congratulations.

The president slipped a thick folded paper out of the next envelope in the stack and announced, "Honorable mention goes to Fred Shirley for his spalted maple turned-wood bowls." The audience clapped enthusiastically.

"Fred?" said Eleanor. "Fred? Is he still here? Has anyone seen him?"

A voice called out. "Fred had to leave. His pager went off. Something about a house fire at Whitetail Cove."

"Oh, thank you," said Eleanor. "I'm sorry he missed the awards. Will you take his ribbon and certificate to him?" she asked the owner of the voice.

"Sure thing." A plain-dressed man came forward to take the envelope. Eleanor thought how amazing it was that Fred could take diseased wood laden with rot and fungus and make such a gorgeous thing from it. The transformation seemed almost holy to her.

She suddenly remembered the awards remaining in her hand. "Oh, yes. Next we have Third Place." She shuffled the envelopes and opened one. "Third Place goes to Ms. Lucy Bloom for her watercolor *Evie's Magnolia*." The crowd clapped loudly. The drum beat from outside could barely be heard for a moment.

"Lucy... Is she here? Oh, there you are. Congratulations, Lucy!" she said as the young woman with the waterfall of silky black hair moved toward her from the doorway to the North Parlor. The girl looked stunned as she took the thick envelope. *She never imagined she'd win anything*, Eleanor thought. *As good as she is, it never entered her mind.*

"And Second Place is a tie," she went on. "We have two winners. Second Place goes to Chesley Fox Chiswell for his sculpture *Champion Swing* and to Bob Short for his acrylic *Eighteenth Hole, Whitetail Cove*." Bob looked pleased and surprised. Chesley, who had been standing quite close to the front, looked like he held a sugarplum in his mouth; he was not surprised in the least. As the two men came forward, Eleanor saw Bob shoot a look of concern over at Vincent, standing soberly with Lorraine and his ever-present oxygen tank. Vincent looked deflated. As if he had put all his remaining life force into his *demoiselle* painting and now even the oxygen tank could not respire him. She felt a pang of compassion; he would feel the lack of a ribbon acutely.

Chesley and Bob collected their envelopes and returned to their places in the crowd. *Ah*, Eleanor thought, *but golfers do stick together*. Pennington Apple's enthusiasm for the game was legendary. That was the only explanation for the second place choices. And Vera Crabtree, bless her heart, would not have had the wherewithal to contradict someone like Mr. Apple at his most adamant.

"And now, First Place goes to... well it goes to... Eleanor Wood for the two portraits of Audrey and Margaret Apple." Eleanor colored as she read her own name aloud; she could feel the heat in her face. She fervently wished her prize could have gone to someone else. She could barely hear the applause for the sound of her heart beating in her head.

"All right, friends, now we come to the high point of our evening: Best of Show." Eleanor could think of several works deserving of this award. Lucy's were wonderful, but she had already won a prize. She thought of the large abstract painting in the front hallway, the starburst. She scanned the crowd for the face of the young man with the olive skin and curly hair. When she had first seen him, she had felt a twinge in her womb; he so reminded her of her oldest son. But now she could not locate his face. Several other paintings were fine as well. That still life with the bird, for instance...

But no, Eleanor thought, *I would have to give the top prize to the quilt upstairs*. It was not an official entry in the show. Even so, its images were engraved into her mental vision: mostly creatures of some sort, but people and trees, too. All seemed of equal weight. They were natural, free, innately innocent, instinctively composed. And the use of black—it was so masterful. The use of color to counteract the darkness was so skillful.

She did not see the quiltmaker's face. Oh yes, there it was, next to the tall muscular fellow who did the little landscapes, the one who looked just like her. And his name was just like hers too. Eleanor always tended to mix them up. She had been tempted to name her own twins similar names, but thought better of it in the end.

The crowd had quietened, waiting for the news. She opened the last envelope and pulled out the sheet of paper inside. "Best of Show goes to... Orvelle Armstrong for his oil painting *Crow Song*." *That was the one with the bird,* Eleanor thought, *the fascinating still life over the mantel in the dining room.*

Orvelle shone head and shoulders above the crowd, beaming like a lighthouse. Beside him Orilla glowed even brighter, clutching her purse to her middle. The crowd clapped, but many started to turn away before Orvelle could pass through the throng from the back of the hallway to collect his envelope. The crowd murmur rose so that Pennington Apple had to shout his closing words: "Thank you, Liberty, for coming tonight! Stay and enjoy yourselves as long as you like, and see you all at Midsummer next year!"

As Orvelle approached, Eleanor held her hand out to him. "Such a fine painting, Orvelle," she said. "I'm so intrigued by the objects you put together in the still life. The pitcher, a bundle of wildflowers and cattails laid out, the old book—*Robinson Crusoe*, I think it was?—an old fashioned child's shoe, and the black bird overlooking it all. And that starburst of light glinting off the old hammered pewter of the pitcher. How did you decide to put those particular things together?"

"Well, Ms. Wood, it just what I sees. I just paint what I sees, what I have a feeling for," he said.

"Your painting is absolutely remarkable, and you deserve this ribbon." She shook Orvelle's big hand that held her own with hardly any pressure at all. She looked him deep in his grey eyes and smiled. "Congratulations."

"Thank you so much, Ms. Wood," he said.

"God bless you," added the short round woman beside Orvelle who shared his face. Eleanor was startled. She had never heard the woman say a word before, though she had of course seen her at several Guild meetings. *And what did I do to deserve this blessing?* Eleanor wondered.

"You a good woman. The best," said Orilla. She nodded once and turned to go.

Eleanor was so taken aback that she did not think to say to Orilla what she wanted to about the quilt. But then she was quite sure her words would mean nothing to the woman; *her* reward, Eleanor somehow knew, was in the pure joy of making of things, not in how they were received.

The crowd had thinned. People had moved outside, whether toward their cars or to join the other revelers in the huge white tent that sprawled like a many-legged spider hunched over its teeming egg-sac. The night was dark and close. Fickle gusts slapped the tent with increasing energy. The fitful wind had extinguished all of the little lanterns illuminating the garden, so that the area behind Reaves Hall was lit only halfheartedly by the weak reproduction porch lights.

Eleanor tied up some loose ends inside, gathered up her things, and collected Morgan, whose eleven-o-clock curfew was rapidly approaching. As they crossed the porch, they felt the sounds of revelry vibrating the floorboards, and if the insects of Midsummer were still singing, no one could have heard their song. Some of the carousers would be at it well into the night, but Eleanor's part in the evening was over, and she was not sorry to leave—she was all of a sudden quite weary. She and Morgan stepped down into the garden and headed along the path toward the parking area.

Suddenly, a gust slammed a loose upstairs shutter against the house, and they looked up automatically. The windows of Reaves Hall shone with a steady light, all except for the one lone rectangle where the loose shutter hung. The light inside this one seemed to flicker, as if flames darted and licked about the room. But a fire there was impossible, Eleanor knew. The alarm system had been installed and tested thoroughly only a few weeks before, and it was not sounding now. And besides, the sash was up a little and no smoke billowed out. The wavy old panes seemed to distort the light within into an almost-human form. It looked as if someone were peering down at them. Well, perhaps someone was. Or perhaps it was just a trick of the glass.

At that moment a deep groan overtook the sound of the party music. The wind blew harder from one side, then from the other. Eleanor grabbed Morgan's arm and pulled her close. They crouched instinctively as the sound of shredding canvas ripped through the air. The music faltered and then ceased, and the lights went off all at once in the house. The garden was in utter blackness, except for a few struggling tiki torches stationed beyond the tent for mosquito control. And except for the one upstairs window that still flickered faintly.

Eleanor looked up into the sky, her heart galloping. A slender grey column of swirling mist and dust that flashed like ghostly confetti was just discernible in the inkiness. The wraith bobbed and danced and dodged closer and closer to the ground, resolving itself into separate flickers of paper that spiraled toward them and fluttered piece by piece to the earth, not just where she and Morgan crouched in the garden, but all around the grounds of the old place. Morgan reached out and caught one. She held it up close before them, but neither one could make out what was written on the brittle paper, if anything.

Soft thuds and rustlings could be heard here and there around them—what was that, hail? But no, it wasn't hail. Eleanor's heart lurched as she looked down and saw a crumpled dark form in the moss between the stones of the path not far away. Maybe a stricken bird? She reached out without thinking to pick it up and felt smooth wood in her hand. She rubbed her fingers over the figure and said out loud, "It *is* a bird, a carving." She shook her head in bewilderment. She held it out for Morgan to see, but it was only a smudge against Eleanor's barely visible palm.

The wind left as suddenly as it arrived. Excited voices erupted over toward the tent, but they were not voices of pain. Eleanor thought she would let the very capable Corbie County Historical Society take care of any liquor-enhanced hysteria that might arise in the wake of the odd weather phenomenon. She tucked the bird in her pocket and turned to the silent girl beside her. "Well that was strange. I've never seen anything like it. Have you?" Morgan shook her head, her eyes huge.

"I think it's high time we went home," Eleanor said. The girl nodded. As they passed through the garden, they noticed pale litter strewn here and there, papers bent and twisted but all of one size and shape, not bright enough to be read. On Eleanor's car they found another of the papers, caught in the windshield wipers as neatly as if it were an advertising flyer someone had deliberately tucked there. Eleanor pulled it off, folded it twice, and put it in her pocket.

It was not until they were in the car that a strong odor registered with her. "What is that *smell?*" she asked, but she knew before she finished the question what it was. Some animal, a large one by the look of things, had relieved itself in the garden, and now she had another souvenir of the evening, firmly pressed into the bottom of her shoe. There was nothing left to do but laugh, and laugh she did, and Morgan joined in with her, and their laughter tendriled out into the damp night air, rich and sweet and free.

Later, after Morgan had been delivered safely home and Eleanor, weary and sore, began to undress for the night, she thought to empty her dress pockets. In them were the paper from the windshield, weathered to antique parchment, and the wooden bird she had picked up from the garden walk. Tomorrow she would work on finding the carving's rightful owner. But for now she studied it, holding it upright in her palm.

The carver had rubbed something into the grain of the wood to darken it. The bird appeared to be a crow, though smaller than its real-life counterpart. Its round, black inquisitive eyes gleamed. *If it were real,* Eleanor thought, *this bird would surely not sing the most beautiful song of the forest. But it would see storms and fire from way afar off and not shrink from them. It would see the lay of the land from above. It would notice small things. It would seek out shiny things.* The painted eyes seemed to look into her soul. She had heard once that crows could distinguish between human faces, that they could sense which human was friend and which was foe, that their memories were keen, that they grieved their lost. No telling what else they were capable of. Yet people feared them, maligned them, or simply overlooked them. They rarely listened for the music in their rough crow voices.

Eleanor finished preparing for bed and turned off all the lights but the lamp on her bedside table. As she eased beneath her covers, she thought about the fullness of the evening and knew that sleep would not come soon, if at all. Thunder growled in the distance. She tucked the bird under her pillow; she would see what dreams it brought her. She unfolded the paper which had come down from the sky, smoothed it with her palm against the bedcovers, and began to read.

* * *

On the sparsely-travelled road out to his part of the county, moving at a mule's pace, James had had plenty of time to think. He could not have dreamed up a more awkward situation. He deeply rued the fact that Sadie had chosen the moment she had to leave a deposit in the fancy English garden. He understood that some folks just didn't live in a world where manure was a part of things. The fact that she had made her way there in the first place was astounding, an amazing animal feat in the tradition of *The Incredible Journey*. O.K., maybe not that remarkable, but still. She was one smart mule, and in spite of the scene she had caused, he was rather proud of her. But he had not been willing to let her walk home unburdened after what she had put him through, so he had led her to a low stone wall by the parking lot, hitched up his tailored suit, and climbed on. He had ridden her bareback several times before, just not fifteen miles in the dark on a Saturday night with this crazy wind whipping around. Sadie carried him sweetly, reliably, like this excursion was the most natural thing in the world, like they were off on a lark.

Not more than a few miles from town, atop the mule trudging alongside the state highway, he thought he saw his own truck drive past. He must be seeing things! He was not used to hard liquor, not that he'd had time to have much of it. There must be dozens of ancient beat-up trucks in the county, and maybe they all looked the same at this hour on a Saturday night. He felt the rhythm of the animal beneath him. Sadie knew to stay on the tall grassy verge rather than the road. It was much easier on her hooves. *That truck better not be stolen,* he thought to himself. *My new boots are in it, too.*

He pictured Lucy with her long, smooth hair and grey eyes, projected her onto the screen of darkness before him as he rode along holding on to nothing but Sadie's bristly mane. He admitted to himself that he liked looking at Lucy's face, especially when she talked. She wore no makeup. That seemed rare these days. And so what you saw there in her face was nakedly honest, and very, *very* nice to look at. She was such a good painter, too, and he was disappointed at not seeing her paintings at the show and talking to her about them. Granted, he would have liked to see his own picture hung there, too, even though he knew it wasn't exactly a masterpiece. But he *had* made a special effort for the show, the show which ended for him pretty much in disaster. Well, his truck just *better* not be stolen. Who but he would want it? No, it could not possibly be stolen. He was just jumpy and paranoid after the scene at the reception. Sadie tossed her head and snorted, as if she could read his thoughts and was agreeing with him in order to get back into his good graces. It would definitely be a while before that happened.

The insects had hushed their grating racket, probably hunkered down away from the gusty winds. And rain? Was there rain coming? He hoped not. The only sounds in the oppressive darkness were the thudding of Sadie's hooves—though maybe he felt more than heard that—an occasional low growl of thunder, the sporadic gossip of restless leaves, and loudest of all, his own breathing, quickened by the exertion of remaining on Sadie's undulating back. His truck was a more comfortable ride; that was certain.

Quite a few miles later, just before he turned off onto the patchwork road with the ragged shoulders that led past his farm, James heard a sound pierce the thick night, building slowly from a faraway whine, growing steadily louder. Looking back over his shoulder he saw a pulsing red light and a sharp vector of headlights sweeping across the rolling hills, now visible, now invisible. The road before him began to glow fitfully, and he saw a shadowy herd of deer in the pasture to the right, just off the road, milling about and staring, agitated. Suddenly they turned and bolted, and all that he could see was their luminescent white tails, ever-diminishing flames hovering and flitting as the deer zigged and zagged toward safety. He wondered what it would feel like to follow them, how free he would feel if Sadie took off after them, if Sadie were one of them, carrying him along however far to whatever place deer go when the spooking fades away. *What a crazy idea*, he thought. He was not one given to flights of fancy.

Over the top of the nearest hill a vehicle appeared with undiluted light and sound. The white SUV flew past, an official-looking vehicle with writing he could not make out and the red siren on top toiling away to alert car, deer, and mule alike of some anonymous crisis. James felt a sense of impotent alarm. The siren stirred up feelings of concern, of warning, but how could he do anything about the unknown calamity? His path was brightly lit for a few moments as the SUV rushed ahead, but the emergency vehicle quickly abandoned him to the darkness, alone again except for the mule. How in the world would he get his truck back again, assuming it wasn't stolen? He would have to find someone to give him a ride into town, maybe tomorrow afternoon.

Sadie turned down the dirt and gravel drive to his place even before James realized they were there. She trotted down the gentle slope toward the cabin and slowed to a walk following the track around it to the barn. James could see a warm glow on the horizon off to the southwest. Perhaps it was lightning, but it seemed too steady for that. Perhaps it was light from a distant town dispersed farther than usual by the tropical atmosphere. Perhaps it was a fire.

All was snug on his place, as it should be, just as he had left it, save for a large piece of trash blowing across the paddock, swirling and tumbling in a little eddy of wind. James slid off the mule's back, feeling relief in his own backside after the two-hour ride. He stretched and twisted, loosening his cramped muscles, as the mule bent down to tug at a dandelion. Sadie was demure and obedient, a model mule, as he brushed her and watered her and led her into her stall. Of course, that could be just because she was weary—he could feel her flank trembling a bit—from making the long walk twice in one day.

"Good night, old Sadie Girl," he said, and slapped her

affectionately, though she didn't deserve it in the least.

Rounding the door of the barn, his eye fell upon the trash, arrested in its wanton dance by the side of the barn. He stopped short, backtracked, and reached down to pick up the paper, one corner flapping like the injured wing of a fallen bird. It was a large paper with surprising heft—not just some old newspaper or advertisement blowing in the wind. In fact, it was a singular piece of paper, heavier than any he had come across before, dark, and rough on one side. He could not quite make out the image on it.

He looked up at the sky and waited for the clouds to shift. The moon had risen, but it shone only erratically through the troubled vapors. Soon, however, an opening in the clouds revealed it; the moon shone bluish and fully round, and a ring gradually appeared around it, glowing faintly against the turbulence. Weary as he was, James looked and looked, unable to take his eyes off the natural phenomenon above the far-off stand of trees beyond the pasture.

James recalled that this night with its full moon and unsettled air was in fact Midsummer, and he remembered from his comparative religions class that many ancient peoples, and some not so ancient, had celebrated this night, the summer solstice, as a high and holy time. Just as often they had celebrated the night with mischief and bacchanalia. Whatever their approach, they were all, to a person, desperate for good fortune, good harvest, good favor—whether of God or of Love or of Nature—for the coming twelve cycles of the moon.

Finally, clouds crept across and obscured the light. James looked down at the paper in his hands and realized he had missed his chance to make out what was on it. He would take it inside with him.

He walked back to the house, unlocked the door and swung it open. He smelled the earthiness of leather and wool and newly dug potatoes and good books, the smell of home, a far cry from the staleness of the stuffy historic place in town that seemed worlds away now. He lit a kerosene lantern and stretched the wayward paper out on the table, anchoring the four corners with his compass, a canning jar, a sea-salt shaker, and a leather-bound copy of *Walden* his mother had given him.

Now in the lantern light he could see on the weathered paper a picture done in artist pastels, blurred but still rich in color: a partial image of a strong auburn-haired woman, her arms held high—in triumph or defiance or supplication, it was hard to say which—draped in some gauzy stuff, standing on a pedestal lifted high into the sky, with ominous, heavy clouds behind her. He could just make out the shape of pale transparent wings, huge wings, but delicate, more like dragonfly wings than angel wings.

He touched the surface of a stormy corner with a tentative finger. It came away grey. The picture looked old, very old, maybe not even from this century. There was no signature. But then that could have been lost over time; the picture had surely been beaten against fence posts and trees, flayed against rocks, trampled by feet or hooves, ground beneath tires, hammered by rain and hail. Where had it blown in from? There was no telling, given the agitation of the sky tonight. And yet the image was still there, fuzzy but recognizable.

He liked it. He tacked it to the wall over his cot. He thought of the winged woman as a survivor. She would be his muse.

He stripped off his clothes and dropped them on the floor. He was bone-weary, and the suit would need to go to the dry cleaners anyway. He hated the chemicals in those places, but there was nothing else for it after all the suit had been through tonight. He gazed at the picture, wondering again at its journey. He turned out the lantern and climbed under his sheet. And just before sleep came, James the Organic Farmer had a thought: *Look at the bright side of things, James. The evening may not have been ideal—it may have been disappointing and downright uncomfortable, in fact—but at least you didn't have to give someone a ride home.*

* * *

Aylin swung her legs down from the cab of the truck and stretched out an espadrille until it found firm ground on the rough gravel of the track that dead-ended behind the golf course. *Lucky that little fellow with the bow-tie left the keys under the floor mat.* She had known before she reached the parking lot that she would find them there. Not the smartest idea on his part, but then who would want to steal a truck like this one? She heaved the door closed with a low laugh. He wouldn't be needing it tonight anyway.

Aylin turned down the trail to the cabin, invisible in the deep shadow of the night woods. Her eyes adjusted slowly as she padded over the pinestraw-cushioned path, as silent and sure as a panther. Sharp points of light showed in the woods where a few foolhardy fireflies braved the menacing atmosphere. Surely it would storm soon and release all the pent-up energy she could feel in the air. She picked up her pace. It was odd to be here in the woods without the undergrowth sounds that usually filled them.

Suddenly a small misty shape darted out of nowhere, nudged her leg hard once, twice, and then disappeared down the path to the fire circle with its tail high, a crook in the top. A few yards further, by the cabin door, as she felt her shoes scrape on the old flagstone under the overhanging roof, she felt something else underfoot, something alien, soft and lumpy. She groped for the switch and flicked on the weak yellow bulb beside the door. There at her feet lay a tiny creature that had been a chipmunk perhaps, a vole, a baby squirrel, some little fuzzy denizen of the forest, yet it lay now on its back stripped of its fur, with its tiny feet raised in a gesture of entreaty. Its predator had peeled back the outer trappings and left bare, exposed, the helpless tender meat inside. He had left it for her. Very unexpected.

Aylin stepped around the carcass and thrust the door open. On a chair just inside slouched her tapestry bag. She slung the boots she had grabbed from the truck, their laces tied together, around a strap and hefted the bag on her shoulder. Everything she would need most was in it, she knew—good thing she'd been able to collect her pay from the kitchen table at the Laws' today. She had stuffed the cash deep in the inner pocket. The bag was heavy, but manageable. She took a long slaking drink from the wine bottle on the table. She stared at the bottle in her hand a minute, corked it, stuffed it in her bag and swept out the door.

She took a few steps, then stopped short and turned around. She stepped back just over the threshold and breathed in deeply. She inhaled decades of maleness, of fish oil and cigar smoke, of hard liquor and poker games and big talk. In spite of all that, the cabin had served her well. It had been oddly satisfying to impose her woman-self upon it and draw what she needed from it. *Good bye, old place,* she thought. *Rest in peace.*

Aylin pulled the door closed behind her, flicked off the switch for the yellow bulb, and weaved in utter blackness down the path toward the clearing. Scufflings in the leaf litter let her know she was not alone. The birds and insects were silent, awaiting the weather, but small creeping things were still on the move. As she entered the clearing, she shrugged her bag off her shoulder and onto the ground. The little comma carved out of the woods long ago gleamed softly as the moon peered through a small hole in the tumultuous sky. A single moonbeam stretched down like the paw of an animal reaching out through a hole in its cage to grope around unseeing, to feel for some escape.

Yes, Aylin could see the clearing well enough. There stood the stone altar at the rear of the fire circle, now just a pillar of charcoal in the dim light, all its subtle colors hidden by the gloom. But there it stood, just the same, as tall as a man, as still as a mountain, as old as sin. Older, much older, she thought, than the fishing cabin. But she must be about her business quickly, since the threatening weather threatened to undo her.

She moved over to the old stump where the rusty coffee can guarded her matches. The pale grey cat was curled around the can, licking its paws with ardor. The cat rose to meet her and arched its back. As it jumped down, the can scraped across the rough stump and fell, casting the matchbox into the scrub. The matches spewed all around. But it was no matter. Aylin only needed one. She leaned down, poked around in the woody trash, and brought her hand up in triumph. She slipped the match into her pocket.

She continued rummaging at the edge of the clearing for some other odds and ends: partial delicate skeletons, former victims of the cat, possibly; rubbish caught at the edge of the woods where it had blown and snagged on trunks and roots, perhaps cast off by golfers or by the old men that had used the cabin in forgotten times; an old wig that had seen better days, once her faithful friend, which she had tossed months ago onto the trash heap; dry branches. She piled all of this skillfully in the fire circle. If there was one thing Aylin was truly good at, it was building a fire. She had learned it in Girl Scouts about a hundred years ago, it seemed. She laughed a short laugh, without mirth, appreciating the irony.

Aylin reached into her bag now and pulled out several garments, balled up together. She set them where she could add them to the fire once the branches were fully engaged and she could be sure of their obliteration. She drew out of the bag some old paintings as well. She would not be taking them with her, only the pastel sticks themselves in their shifting nest of dry rice. She laid the paintings out prone on top of the twigs and branches and trash, like a body on top of a funeral pyre.

She retrieved the match from her pocket and lit it. She held it to the kindling at the base of the fire, then touched the flame to the corner of one of the paintings and watched the flames stretch high and bright. The match dwindled to its stub, burning her fingers. She dropped it. She stood very close to the fire, her creation, very close. It was not her first fire of the evening, but she had not had the luxury of watching the other increase.

The wind gusted, and Aylin jumped back. The growing flames writhed and stretched dangerously. Perhaps the fire would not be contained. But that was none of her concern, she told herself. And anyway, the gust left as quickly as it arrived; the pictures were consumed, just a flash in the pan, so to speak; and the flames settled back down to the adolescent fire stage.

On an impulse, Aylin moved backward several paces. She gathered her skirts, took a running start, and leaped over the top of the modest blaze, singing her skirt just a little. Now she laughed outright. She had a vision of herself, cat-like, fleeing the burning hem of her skirt, trailing out behind her in the night like a flaming tail, while the locals chased her with makeshift weapons—garden implements, golf clubs, maybe even shotguns, through the crazy twisting roads of Whitetail Cove. But no, the skirt was not flaming now, just smoking a bit. And no one was chasing her. Not yet.

More gusts took the flames higher quickly, and Aylin decided she would not risk another leap, as exhilarating as that might be. She stood back and gazed for some time into the bonfire, forgetting all about the moon, which was hidden behind the clouds again. The wind carried the flames toward the glowing stone altar, blackening a few of the nearer stones. Now was the time. She added the garments from the pile beside the stone circle, one at a time to be sure they caught: a tank top, a skirt, an old-fashioned pair of long, slim, ladies' black dress gloves. She waited. She watched them curl and shrink away into unrecognizable shapes.

On a whim, she reached down to her ankles and unwound the cords that were biting into her flesh; she pulled off her espadrilles, and threw them one at a time into the blaze. She had the boots now, after all. What a stroke of luck that they had been there in the truck waiting for her, in mint condition and the perfect size, too. They would serve her well for now; she had a long way to go.

The fire was glorious with long slender dancers' arms that beckoned, vanished, beckoned again. Aylin stood holding the last piece of the clothing from the pile. She rubbed the wool between her fingers, back and forth with a vengeance, as if to grind the yarn to shreds. Her jaw clenched, and her brows forced their way down forming deep pitch shadows that hid her eyes in the firelight. She stepped up to the blaze again and tossed the hat onto the fire. She glowered as a face stared back at her for a moment. The wool caught and twisted worm-like, alive with the burning, the lips jeering as much as ever until at last they were just gone. Aylin took a deep breath and let it out slowly.

She dragged over a few more branches from the verge of the woods and heaved them onto the fire so that it would burn long after she left, so that her mark would remain here. The wind gusted hard. Aylin's hair and skirt stood out straight to the side of her. A stray leaf stuck her cheek, and sparks snapped and tumbled across the fire circle. A few pieces of trash blew into the clearing. They seemed to come from the sky, but that wasn't possible; most likely they had blown down from the golf course. A paper caught against Aylin's leg and she reached down automatically to retrieve it. On the old, shriveled paper was a crude drawing of a small stone structure, just visible in the firelight.

She looked up sharply at the stone altar before her and back at the sketch. No, this was not the same, though it did look strikingly similar. But the drawing's stone altar was really a fountain, maybe a spring even, with water flowing out and vines and flowers

319

growing over it. Aylin looked once more at the charred stone altar in the clearing where she stood.

And suddenly she saw what she had failed to see before: The stone configuration here was nothing more than a place for old men to cook fish and tell lies, painting their own pictures with words and inventing their own lives to impress the others. It was no altar, after all. She crumpled up the paper and threw it into the fire.

Aylin pulled the boots from her bag and shoved her feet into them. That would lighten the load. She settled her tapestry bag onto her shoulder and turned her sooty face from the fire. She followed an old obscure path down toward the lake, her knees jolting into the steep slope. Her mind, though, was weightless now, airborne, like a stone jostled loose, tumbling, skipping, flying down a hillside. The firelight that chased her lagged further and further behind until all was dark. Soon the slope leveled out and the lake was close at hand; she could hear it sloshing as little gust-stirred waves nudged the shore.

Aylin knew well how to disappear. First, she would tramp through this untouched stretch of lakeshore. Thanks to the wetlands, Aylin had a few swampy miles to herself. She could see two, three bonfires lit on beaches far across the lake. She could make out tiny figures moving around them, tending the fires and the figments of their own lives.

She trudged along the cove in night now blacker than coal, leaves rattling high up as the wind bedeviled the treetops. But her business was down here, in the darkness. Ahead she caught a glimpse of a blue light. She stopped, startled, wary. She studied it as it wavered and swayed, then vanished, only to materialize some yards away, hovering and swaying and repeating its weird dance, sometimes drifting over its twin reflection in the still water of the cove, sometimes drifting amid the trees and scrubby water-edge growth. *Ah, well, not human,* she breathed in relief. *Only swamp fire.* And somewhere in her dark, dark mind she recalled hearing once that swamp fire was good for travelers to follow. And so she did.

She would call herself Aella next time. The muck sucked at her boots, but she resisted; she slogged along. Aella. Not too different, but different enough. She liked it. Aella. Aella Black. She formed it with her tongue, practicing, so that when the time came to catch a ride, when she reached the highway that led to Alabama, she would roll it out smoothly. Aella Black. She didn't know the script or the scene, couldn't see that far ahead yet, but it would come to her. It would arrive complete in her mind's eye like the images of her paintings did, the temples floating in pure, unadulterated blue. And she was like her temples; she floated, not rooted to the earth—free from the encumbrances of society that held other people back. She was free to merely create. Oh, it had cost her; she would give you that. She well knew the cost.

Aylin rested a moment and bent down close to the inky water. The moon angled through a break in the sky and sent just enough light filtering down through the trees for her to see her pale arms and the pale oval of her face quivering on the surface of the water. She smoothed the cool liquid over her arms, lavished it over her face. Her damp hair splayed around her head and shoulders, she knew, she felt.

As she straightened, she saw reflected in the water not her own pale visage but something else that was near her, to the side and behind, something she had not noticed as she had kept her gaze ahead on the dancing flame: a pale grey ghost of a cat who had woven his paw-steps into her footprints all this way. His reflected green eyes locked with hers. While the cat stood motionless, his phantom-self shimmied and swayed and shifted shape in the dark mirror of the lake: an ancient, secretive, cunning Narcissus.

Smoke wafted through the air, from one fire, from another, who could say? Aylin watched for the blue flame, the smokeless one, and when it came, she set out for it again.

* * *

Cordelia sat on her front porch, more still than life knows how to be. She was too weary to move inside, but she really didn't mind the night. She peered out into it, distinguishing nothing, not even fireflies. How many hours had the darkness lain about her? *Eli will come soon*, she thought, *dear Eli*.

It was heavy, this night, and silent, for the start of summer. She felt that her work was done, and she sighed. She had indeed done good work this day.

No, that was absurd! She was forgetting herself. She had never left her post here on the porch. Her body seemed to have given up all its demands for food, for drink, for movement, for any form of relief. It was almost as if her body had gently ceased to be, leaving her mind at liberty.

The silence was dense, like silence is when it ought to be full of sound. Close at hand, in the old-growth hardwoods just behind the house, a lone bird called. "*Ah*-liv-a-ree-*ell*... *Ah*-liv-a-ree-*ell*," it sounded like. *What kind of bird makes that call?* she wondered. It was familiar somehow, like a voice from back home, but she could not quite put her finger on it. She thought she knew all the bird calls in the south, savored them in her ear—their sweetness, their quarrelsomeness, their piercing screams, their soft coos—but this was one she had not heard in a long, long time. It was unusual, rare, almost human. *What kind of bird...?* she asked herself.

Cordelia peered through glasses that no longer served her, no longer helped her see. They were more of a separation, a partition from the world than a connection to it now, for most of her seeing was internal. Maybe she could no longer see outward at all, she thought, for she could see nothing of the yard quivering with life just beyond the porch. She could feel it there, crouching, waiting, till it could sing again unencumbered by the oppressive stillness.

Perhaps it would rain. Perhaps it would storm. She thought now that she could just distinguish a glow on the horizon, a distant fire—perhaps a bonfire on a hill like the ones her Cornish grandmother had told her about from the ancient days of her girlhood across the ocean, or perhaps it was her grandmother's grandmother, or a granny farther back from some other far-off land, who had passed down the stories.

At any rate, everything was dark now. Her vision, even the vision of the far-off glow, was extinguished. Cordelia's eyes closed, and she was back in the swamp, her beloved swamp, and the scorching from the fire was a distant memory, and she drifted in the little wooden boat laden with the most beautiful twisted swamp roots waiting to be carved and polished. She trailed her hand behind in the coffee-colored water. It was not deep. She pretended to trace the maze of patterns left by the playful ripples of the broad lake on the rich lake bed just inches below her fingertips.

Cordelia smiled, truly smiled—surely just the relaxing of her spasms in sleep, deep delicious sleep. She was free, free from the contractions, the spasms, the strange darting lights, the heavy limbs, the obscured vision, free from the limitations of this world. She had prematurely moved into the freedom of the next, but now all was as it should be. The bird sang close at hand, perhaps just behind her on the porch railing, "You are free... You are free." She sighed once more, long and slow.

* * *

It was a beautiful thing at the end of the Midsummer Show when the papers came swirling down in the garden, curtseying and dancing, looking the way paper does when repeatedly wetted and dried, like old newspaper caught in a woodpile and left there, forgotten, fragile as last year's fallen leaves. Lucy bent down to pick up the feathery, grave thing that settled soundlessly at her feet. She strained in the dwindling light to see what was printed there on the pale, crinkled face of the paper and caught her breath: It was a crude sketch of a stone fountain she had seen before. How was it possible that this, one of Cordelia's tracts blown skyward at Box Hollow all those weeks ago, should drift down here, now, in this place? If only Eli were here to see this! But no, she knew he had already left. He had felt an impulse to go check on Cordelia. Lucy's path and his had already diverged; it was enough for her to know him.

Lucy caught a scent. The wind had kicked up a heavenly fragrance when it rioted through the herbs in the garden. Standing at the verge of the parking lot, Lucy leaned down again and broke off a sprig of sweet basil. She put it in the pocket of her one good blue dress. Lucy saw other guests a ways off under the tent, and Eleanor and the girl closer, looking at the falling papers. She wondered if the message was the same for everyone.

Aylin was nowhere to be seen when Lucy left, and she was immensely relieved. She drove home alone. The winds continued to gust, blowing bits of leaves and debris across her headlight beams. *Strange*, thought Lucy, *I always feel so nervous in a storm, and that fishtailing episode on the way to the Guild meeting back in April didn't help. But not tonight.* Tonight she felt calm, as if a hand was steadying her in the middle of her back. She felt somehow that *this* storm, when it came, would set some things right.

Then she shook her head. *What a crazy thought*, she told herself. She thought of James and hoped his mule had gotten him home by now, before whatever violence the storm would bring. She hoped that Eli had reached Cordelia, and that she would be safely tucked in for the night. She hoped that her family was well, content, and asleep. She hoped many things.

The roads were nearly empty. That was odd, on a Saturday night, but then most folks were probably either distracted by their revelries or hunkered down from the storm for the night. The deer were out in droves, however, so she had had to slow her speed.

At last she swung the station wagon into her driveway and suddenly slammed on the breaks. Blocking her way was an enormous mound of foliage. The huge magnolia from next door had blown down across her path, clear across the driveway, which was already wet, though she had seen no raindrops yet herself. The tree had been loaded with blossoms for weeks, but now it lay prone, torn from its glory by a capricious wind, perishing. Blossoms lay strewn about, pummeled and bruised and limp, like mournful gale-beaten doves.

Lucy put the car in park and cut the engine. She screeched open the car door and stepped out. She approached the fallen tree and searched among its limbs until she found a perfect unblemished blossom under a sheltering branch. She plucked it and cupped it in her hands. A little rainwater shimmered at the bottom of the cup, reflecting the moon, which had broken through the thick, swift clouds for just a moment. Some yards ahead, at the house, all the lights but the kitchen-table lamp were out. She stood a bit longer, cupping the blossom, thicker and stronger and older than any other flower she knew of.

When she entered the kitchen from the front porch, she went directly to the cabinet and pulled out from up high a simple glass bowl, the one with the glass beads around the rim, a remembrance of her grandmother. She filled the bowl with water and set the blossom, with its rainwater pool still inside, adrift on the water, to sail or to rest as it felt inclined to do, sheltered inside the gently curving glass. She set the bowl with the blossom on the table and hoped for the best. How long would it last? The water gently rocked the flower back and forth, back and forth, until at length it stilled.

Arranged in clusters all around on the table were the carvings, Cordelia's creatures and the little boat. Jack and Ian and Evie must have been playing with them again this evening. She thought of her husband looking on, leaning over them and finding wonder alongside the children, finding wonder inside himself like she knew he would have, speaking in that low gentle voice he often used with them that said, whatever the actual words he spoke, love.

Lucy moved through the house, her new knowledge like a budding blossom in her breast, layer upon layer of promise just beginning to unfurl. Mothering was like that: heavy, many-layered, and delicate, easily bruised if dropped unheeded and stepped on or forgotten. But at its heart was a secret knot of power. Place it in a vessel with water and sunshine and cool fresh air, and then just try to *keep* it from blooming. Great spirit and vigor flow into the petals, every moment a changing silhouette, altogether a greater creative act than the most eloquent Old Master's painting, and not to be disparaged.

Lucy checked on Jack. His mouth was open, his head thrown back, his eyes darting back and forth beneath well-lashed lids, his hand twitching in his dreams. *Jack's dreams*, she thought, and shook her head slowly, remembering.

She checked on Ian. His knees were drawn up beneath him; his bottom was in the air, his head turned sideways with his mop of hay-colored hair splayed out in every direction and a wet spot next to his mouth on the pillow. A stick lay just beside his half-open hand. *Only a father would put a boy to bed with a stick*, thought Lucy, smiling.

She checked on Evie. She was fast asleep in her crib, looking as pure and pale and round as the blossom in her great grandmother's bowl. And nearby in the old iron double bed Lucy could hear her husband's slow regular breaths, deep and unburdened.

She went in the bathroom and picked up her toothbrush. She squeezed the toothpaste out and began to brush. Immediately she felt such revulsion at the taste that she threw up once, twice in the toilet. The nausea of earlier in the evening returned with a vengeance. She braced herself on the counter and leaned over the sink to let it fade a little. She looked then at herself in the mirror and saw that the bird had told her right. It was certain now. She slipped out of her blue dress and draped it over a chair by the bed. She eased off her shoes and pushed them under the bed with her toe. She slipped into her nightgown, simple, cotton, white, with slender straps over the shoulders. Her hair hung like a curtain over her bare shoulders and down her back.

She padded off to find her best scissors, the knife-edge scissors in her sewing box, and carried them back to the bathroom. She smoothed a portion of her hair between two fingers and held it there as she began to cut, just below her ear. She measured out portion by portion all the way around, and then evened it out a bit. She gathered the dark mass of hair and smoothed it together. Then she took it with her to the kitchen.

There she reached down the battered tin box of watercolor paints from the cabinet over the refrigerator. She opened the lid and fingered the thin tubes inside: Alizarin Crimson, Cadmium Yellow Light, Sap Green, Ultramarine, Umber, Ochre, Cerulean Blue. She stroked the silky hair of the brushes, not so different from her own. Lucy nestled the paints and brushes together. She picked up the long sweep of her hair from the counter and coiled it on top of the paint. It lay there, curling around itself, like a living thing, like a small animal snugged in for the winter. Then she shut the metal lid and latched it, carried it out onto the porch and into the yard and around to the rear of the house where she found a shovel leaning.

She made her way to the back corner of the yard where the weeping willow stood. Her children did not play here because of the gnats that congregated on warm afternoons, which was a shame, because the willow's fronds curved over almost to the ground, making the most excellent of caves. Here Lucy began to dig, a tricky proposition with bare feet, but the soil was moist and loose in this particular spot. She did not have to dig very deep; the box was small. She buried it and patted down the dirt. She would plant some shade-loving flowers here as guardians of the box. They would deter her from the temptation to dig it up too soon.

She parted the trailing branches and left the little willow-womb, stepping back out into the yard. No light was visible except occasional distant flashes from a storm that seemed to take its own sweet time in coming. She caught a trace of smoke in the air, then thought, *No, I'm just imagining that. On a dark night like this a fire could be seen from miles around, and I don't see one anywhere.* She headed back to the house to replace the shovel. But she could not bring herself to leave the open air and return inside just yet.

The night air exhilarated Lucy, alone in her simple nightgown with the silent summer darkness breathing on her skin like a lover. Her bare feet whispered through the damp grass. The recent sprinkling of rain had nestled quickly into the roots of the long grass stalks and left beads of water behind, dewy pearls that glistened when the distant lightning flashed. Lucy squatted down and rubbed her hands in the grass, her fingers spread wide. Then she wiped them, dew and all, on her hot face and all along the length of her arms. She stood, refreshed.

Just then the heavens let loose a sudden deluge, and she ran for the house, soaked and a little dizzy when she reached the porch. She felt clean, entirely clean. Thunder rumbled long, low, and close. She looked out into the storm and thought how the lavish, drenching rain must be washing away her footfalls from the grass, must in fact be heavy enough to wipe away the deepest footprints anyone might make this night. She shivered.

Lucy eased open the door and slipped back into the house. She padded down the hall to her room and pulled off her wet gown. She remembered then the sweet basil in her dress pocket and drew it out. She sat with great care on the bed and eased the sprig gently beneath the pillow of the sleeping man beside her while the rain, already slackening, tapped out its music on the roof.

She slipped under the covers and soon began to drift. *The baby will be a girl... Her name will be Cordelia... We will teach her all about dreams and carved creatures and blossoms that last only a short time and palaces built of scraps of paper and marks in the earth and living water and buried treasure and the beauty of stones.* And as Lucy faded slowly into sleep, she thought she heard a softly whistled tune like a sweet birdcall drifting behind.

Epilogue

The June 28 edition of the *Corbie County Chronicle* contains a few articles of interest to the reader.

* * *

"Home and Elderly Resident Lost to Fire: The *Chronicle* reports that stations 2, 3, 7, and 8 in the county responded to a house fire belonging to the person of Q.E. Law, Jr. on Hedgewood Drive in Whitetail Cove. Despite four engines being fully engaged in fighting the fire, the house was a total loss. Only a sudden downpour prevented the fire from spreading to nearby structures and properties.

There was one fatality, Mrs. Q. E. Law, Sr., who was residing in the lower floor apartment of the house. (Please see obituary section in this paper.) The rest of the family was not at home at the time. It is not yet known whether Mrs. Law perished in the blaze or died of natural or other causes prior to it. A full report is expected from the county coroner by the next publication of the *Chronicle*.

The Fire Department in conjunction with the Corbie County Sheriff's Office is currently conducting an investigation into the cause of the fire. A person of interest in the case has been named, a Mr. James Caldwell of Apt-to-Miss Road, whose truck was found

330

abandoned Sunday on a maintenance trail behind the eighteenth hole of the Whitetail Cove Golf Course."

* * *

"Obituary: Eunice Ludmilla Claxton Law, 91, of Whitetail Cove, died at home on June 23, 2012. Mrs. Law was born June 24, 1920 to the late Mr. and Mrs. Wilfred Fox Claxton. In addition to her parents, she was preceded in death by her sister, Blanche Claxton Chiswell, as well as by her husband, Mr. Q. E. Law, whom she assisted for many years in the operating of Law's General Merchandise on the square in Liberty. She was well-known for her keen business sense. She was a seven-decade member of the First Baptist Church Young Married Ladies' Sunday School Class. She is survived by her son and daughter-in-law, Mr. and Mrs. Q. E. Law, Jr., and by two grandchildren, Ludmilla L. Sherman and Wilfred E. Law. Also by a nephew, Chesley F. Chiswell. The family will hold a private graveside service at Liberty First Baptist Cemetery at some date yet to be determined.

* * *

"Obituary: Cordelia Wise, 74, of Liberty, died at home of natural causes on Saturday, June 23 after a prolonged illness. She was a woman of faith. She loved nature, art, and children. She is survived by her sisters, Elizabeth Cooper, of Smithfield, Virginia, and Bertie Mason of Suffolk, Virginia; and seven nieces and nephews, including Eli Cooper of Liberty and Angeline Mason, also of Liberty. Her ashes will be scattered on the shores of Lake Drummond in Virginia at a memorial service to be held in September."

"Local Artist Makes Good: Mr. Eli Cooper of Liberty has been named Young Artist to Watch for 2012 by the Atlanta Journal/Constitution. The AJC article cited Mr. Cooper's 'original and prolific use of natural colors and textures to unite the plastic medium of acrylic painting with the new Green sensibility.' Mr. Cooper will be represented by nationally renowned art dealer May Silva of Atlanta, says the AJC."

* * *

"Historical Society Links with Artists Guild for Unforgettable First Annual Gala: The Corbie County Historical Society hosted its yearly Midsummer Fundraising Gala last Saturday evening, June 23, at the Historical Society Headquarters at Reaves Hall on Main Street. Half of the funds raised at the gala will go to support the upkeep and promotion of the Hall and its rich history. The other half will go to the Liberty Artists Guild in its promotion of the arts in Corbie County, including the establishment of a scholarship fund for a deserving high school senior art student.

According to Historical Society spokesperson Magdaline Dismukes, 'A glorious time was had by all.' Said Mrs. Dismukes, 'There was nothing to blemish the occasion, nothing at all.' When asked by this reporter if the gala was affected in any way by the unusual weather system which swept across the county late Saturday night, the Historical Society representative described a 'freak wind that tore the reception tent, spewed rubbish around the grounds, and caused an electrical short in an upstairs bedroom.' Mrs. Dismukes assures this reporter, however, that all has been put back to rights."

READER'S GUIDE

Questions for Discussion

1. In "Eli's Encounter," compare the encounters Eli has with Vanessa, the anonymous girl on the bench, and Cordelia. What does each encounter show about Eli's nature? Which encounter do you think is most significant to him?

2. Eleanor Wood offers to adopt a child. What are her motivations? Are they wholly unselfish? Does it matter? What are some other examples in the novel of characters who mother children that are not "their own"? With what forces does nurture collide in the story?

3. Lucy has a "passion for painting...unfurling in her." What impediments to this impulse does she face? What is your reaction to how Lucy resolves her dilemma in the end? In what other ways could she have responded to her conflict?

4. How does Cordelia's swamp tale fit in with the rest of the novel? Where does the theme of twins reappear?

5. The will-o-the-wisp appears in three crucial scenes of the novel. What does the phenomenon represent to the characters who experience it? What will happen if they follow the strange blue flame? In what other scenes does a light/blaze/star appear?

6. Trace the theme of travelling throughout the novel. How is travelling a metaphor for Lucy's personal journey? Whose true nature is revealed during a car/truck/mule ride? Share an

experience you have had of a revelation or discovery on a ride of your own. What unique opportunities does travelling, even on just an ordinary errand, afford in relating to other people?

7. Discuss the section of "The Midsummer Show" that is told from the point of view of the yellow rose room. How does the supernatural aspect of this section give voice to the traumatic history of the place? When is history truly a "thing of the past"?

8. How does surprise figure into the plot? What event(s) surprised you? What character surprised you?

9. Who is freed, literally or metaphorically, in the novel? Describe how Lucy, Aylin, Vincent or others are seeking liberty. From or for what do they want to be free? How do they find the freedom they seek?

10. What is the significance of each of the items in Orvelle's prize-winning still-life?

11. Near the end of the novel, Aylin observes people on a beach across the lake "tending the fires and figments of their own lives." In what way are our lives "figments"? In what ways is Aylin's life a figment? What do you know or imagine of the character's life before the novel's time frame? What do you imagine is to come afterward?

12. Who is your favorite character? Why?

To see artwork by Eli, Lucy, Aylin,
and other fictional artists of the Liberty Artists Guild,
visit *The Liberty Guild*'s companion illustrations
ongoing at
https://libertyguildunbound.wordpress.com

and follow author-artist Linda Hulburt Aldridge
on Facebook and Instagram
@thelibertyguild

Made in the USA
San Bernardino, CA
05 December 2016